Finding Father

Susan Correll Foy

No part of this publication may be reproduced, stored in or introduced into a retrieval system, or transmitted, in any form, or by any means (electronic, mechanical, photocopying, recording, or otherwise) without the prior written permission of Susan Correll Foy.

This book is a work of fiction and all characters exist solely in the author's imagination. Any resemblance to persons, living or dead, is purely coincidental. Any references to places, events, or locales are used in a fictitious manner.

Scripture is taken from the Holy Bible, New International Version, copyright 1973, 1978, 1984 by International Bible Society. Used by permission of Zondervan. All rights reserved worldwide.

Copyright © 2014 Susan Correll Foy
All rights reserved.
Printed in the United States of America

To Sharon
My first reader, fan, and faithful critic

ℬ *Chapter One* ℰ

As Kendra's fingers touched the keys, the beautiful, haunting melody of "Moonlight Sonata" flowed out of the baby grand piano as if the two were one, created together as one organism. What tragedy or grief had inspired such genius in Beethoven? The terrible loss of his hearing, or unrequited love? If she had Beethoven's genius, perhaps she could take the tragedies in her own young life and produce beauty like this. With her own mediocre talent, all she could do was return to this sonata at every crisis she faced, allowing it to express her heartbreak or despondency. Now it seemed fitting to play it this one last time, when she was on the verge of losing her music forever.

At the end of the first movement she stopped and turned to the woman sitting nearby on the living room couch, judging the lovely tone of the hammers on strings to decide if the instrument were worthy of purchase. She had never mastered the third movement and decided it would be unwise to attempt more than the first, especially as tears were beginning to well up in her eyes.

"Well, you play so well, and it's really lovely." The woman rose and lifted her hand to touch the fine mahogany. "Probably too good for my girls, but I don't want to buy a cheap piano. My husband said to get something nice. How much are you asking?"

Kendra swallowed. Start high, not low, her mother had advised. "I'd like to get seventy-five hundred for it."

"Hmm." The woman touched one of the keys with a light frown. "I saw one in a store for five thousand. I was hoping to not spend more than that."

"I think this is worth more than five." She didn't like to haggle, it seemed indecent somehow, but she didn't want to give away her treasure for nothing. "What about six and a half?"

The woman pursed her lips. "Well, I'll give you six. I think it's worth that much. I'll give you five hundred now and the rest when we come to pick it up. We're going to need movers for this. I'll have to let you know when we get it scheduled." All business, she opened her purse, took out a wad of bills and began to count them.

Feeling bereft, Kendra nodded and took the bills as the woman counted them out. "We have to be out of the house by the middle of June. That's the only reason I'm selling the piano, because I'm moving, and won't have room for it in my apartment."

"Okay, I'll certainly get it before then. Thanks so much. Nice to meet you...?"

"Kendra."

"Nice to meet you, Kendra. It's a lovely piano. I hope my girls play as well as you do someday."

Kendra stuffed the money into her jeans pocket and pasted a smile on her face again. Waiting until the woman had disappeared inside her car, she returned to the piano stool and dropped onto it. Tears blurred her vision, spilling on the black and white keys.

It was silly to be crying over a piano, she knew. Of all the things she had lost in her life, the piano was really nothing, a piece of wood and ivory and string that could easily be replaced someday. Not like losing a father, a brother, a mother, a home, a career, a future. But maybe that was why this hit so hard today. It wasn't losing the piano itself, but all that it represented, everything from her past that had disappeared, her present that was changing so rapidly, and her future that would never be.

She heard the rattling of the doorknob, the opening of the front door, and quickly dried her tears just as her mother, arms full of shopping bags, glanced through the living room doorway and saw her sitting there.

"Kendra? Who was in that car pulling out as I pulled in? Was it someone looking at the piano?"

"Yes." Kendra dried her hands on the side of her jeans. "She decided to buy it. She agreed to six thousand and put five hundred down. I have it here."

"Six thousand! Well, that's not bad, is it? That will make a nice down payment for your car after you give Patsy her rent money. I really don't want you and Elizabeth riding around in that piece of junk you're driving now."

"Yes, I was happy she offered that much."

"I'm so relieved that it sold. Now all the big pieces are gone, except for your bedroom set that you're taking with you, and a few other things that your brother wants. I hope Gregg gets them out soon. Have you decided if you're taking the little kitchen table and chairs?"

"No, Patsy says that she doesn't need it." Kendra's future roommate had a two-bedroom apartment already and most of the rooms were furnished. No room for the piano – just a bedroom for Kendra and her daughter Elizabeth to share. It was all Kendra could afford on her bank teller's salary.

"Okay, I'll tell Gregg he can have it." Her mother set her bags on the couch and opened one, taking out a rectangular jewelry box. "Look what I got for you for the wedding. Isn't this pretty?"

Kendra opened the box to reveal a silver necklace with rose-colored stones. "It's nice."

"I thought it would go well with your gown. I found earrings to go with it too. Let me put it on you."

Bonnie came close to her, unclasping the necklace, then peered at her face. "Kendra, what's wrong? Have you been crying?"

Kendra stared down at the piano keys. "A little."

"Oh, goodness, child! You weren't crying over the piano, were you? You don't even play it that much anymore."

"Yes, I do. I play as much as I have time. And – and I was hoping that Elizabeth could use it when she gets older."

Bonnie put the necklace back in its box and dropped down into the rocking chair. "Elizabeth can have her own piano someday. A smaller one, not a baby grand. Really, honey, of all things to get upset about." Bonnie snapped the box shut. "I'm just relieved that it sold."

"You don't understand," Kendra began, and then her throat closed up and she couldn't go on.

Bonnie sighed. "You mean because it belonged to Daddy. Is that it?"

Kendra turned to run a finger over one smooth white key. "It belonged to Daddy, and it was part of everything that we planned for when I was young. You know how hard I worked on my audition music – I had that dream of being a concert pianist. Or maybe just a music teacher, if that didn't work out. And then when Elizabeth was born, I didn't have time for my lessons anymore, and I couldn't go to college, and had to get a job. But at least I had my piano. Now I don't even have that."

Bonnie frowned down at the floor, as if searching for a comforting response. "I wish we could have kept it for you somehow. But it would be ridiculous to transport it all the way out to Gordon's house in Chicago, when we wouldn't even use it. And you need a safer car, so it just seems sensible to sell it."

"I know." Very sensible from her mother's point of view. Bonnie was moving on to a new life with a new husband in a new city. She didn't need or particularly want reminders from the past, even the happy marriage that had ended in death five years ago. Her life had taken a wonderful turn for the better when she decided to marry a man she had met through her work and move with him to Hong Kong for a year. And during the recent months of her mother's sudden bliss, Kendra had tried to hide the grief she felt in losing the last vestiges of her childhood. Her anxiety bordered on panic as she pictured herself all alone in the world with a small child and no one she could depend on. She felt tears well up in her eyes again and bit her lip to try to suppress them.

"Oh, Kendra." Kendra couldn't tell if her mother were more sympathetic or annoyed. Bonnie reached out and patted her back. "Listen, honey, I'm so sorry you're feeling this way. I know it's a big change, but I thought you might be excited about moving in with Patsy. If it doesn't work out, maybe you can come out and stay with us when we get back from Hong Kong. But it just wouldn't work to take you and Elizabeth over there. We'll only be gone for a year at the most, and then you can come see us in Chicago. Maybe you can move in with us – if Gordon thinks it's okay –"

Kendra glanced sideways at her mother's conflicted expression.

It was the first time her mother had tacitly acknowledged what Kendra suspected: Bonnie's fiance really didn't care for the idea of Kendra and Elizabeth moving in with them. She forced herself to voice the question that she had kept to herself ever since her mother had unexpectedly announced these wedding plans. "Why can't you just wait till Gordon gets back from Hong Kong to get married? Why the big rush?"

Bonnie frowned and twisted the new ring on her finger as if groping for words. "I know it's hard for you to understand, Kendra. I know I seem old to you, but I'm only forty-eight, and I don't want to be alone for the rest of my life. In a few years you'll be married and gone, and I'll be all alone. I've dated a few men since your dad died, but no one that I really clicked with. No one that I could imagine settling down with, until I met Gordon. I know I'll never meet anyone else like him again. If I don't take this chance now, I might never have another one. And – and – a year is a long time, especially for people at our age. If I wait till Gordon comes home next year, things might be totally different. Do you understand?" She studied her daughter's face, clearly seeking reassurance.

If you don't snatch Gordon up now, someone else will before he comes home again, Kendra thought with a sense of irony. *He wants you to come with him and you don't want to take the chance of losing him. Even if it means selling my home and uprooting me and Elizabeth.*

She felt a stab of compunction. She did want her mother to be happy. Her mother had been a great support to her during the last three and a half years – first during her traumatic pregnancy and then in the early days of trying to raise a child with no husband. The midnight feedings, sleepless nights, trying to finish high school while caring for an infant – she couldn't have managed without her mother. Bonnie had grieved after Kendra's father's death, and now she had found someone new. Kendra should be happy for her. And in one way her mother was right. If Kendra were given the opportunity to begin a new life with a new husband, would she refuse it to stay home and be a companion to her mother? She knew she wouldn't.

Aloud she said, "I do understand why you want to marry him.

But I feel so alone. You've always been there for me, and now I don't have anybody."

Bonnie ran her hand across her daughter's shoulders, back and forth in a scratching motion, the way she often had when Kendra was a child. "Well, you have Kyle. You seem happy with him. You wouldn't want to move away and leave him, would you?"

"No." Should she confess her other disappointment to her mother? What reaction would she get to that? "You know, I was really hoping that when I told Kyle I had to get my own place, he would suggest we could move in together. But he didn't. When I made a comment about it, he said that he couldn't afford to move out of his parents' house yet."

"Oh, gracious, I didn't know you were even thinking about that." Bonnie fell silent for a moment; her hand fell to her side. "I don't know if that's a good idea, Kendra. You're both pretty young for a serious relationship like that. Now I know you've had to grow up early, but Kyle hasn't, and he's probably not ready for that kind of commitment. And you don't want to start a long string of live-in boyfriends, do you? That's not the way to raise your daughter."

Kendra shook her hair back from her face. "Of course not! You know I'm not like that. But – but I was hoping in a little while Kyle and I would get married. Don't you think that could happen? You know, Sarah Pruitt had a baby in high school and got married just last month."

Her mother gave a light shrug. "Sarah married the baby's father. Kyle doesn't have that same feeling of responsibility. For your sake I hope he does decide to settle down soon, but he's only twenty-one. I wouldn't count on it, Kendra. I don't want you to get hurt."

Kendra fell silent. Kyle was very loving and kind to Elizabeth, but he wasn't her father. As her mother had said, he could choose how much responsibility he wanted to assume, and at the moment it wasn't very much. She and Kyle had been together for five months now and he was her first serious boyfriend, her first love. One of the happiest moments of her life was when he said he loved her too. But what did that actually mean to him? If he wasn't willing to be committed to her, to be available to her in her hour of need, what did he mean by love? That he had warm and fuzzy feelings for her, that he was physically attracted to her? She didn't like these thoughts, but they had been recurring more and more.

"Listen, honey, I'm sure it will all work out in time." Her mother spoke in a half-brisk, half-comforting tone that said she was ready to move on to happier subjects. "I'm sure you're just nervous about this big move, and that's understandable. But you're such a brave, strong girl, with all that you've gone through at your age." Bonnie rose, pulled Kendra to her feet and drew her into an embrace. "You're such a good mother to Elizabeth, you work so hard, you're so reliable and dependable, and I'm proud of you. And you're beautiful, too. I know that once you get settled in with Patsy, you'll develop a new life and a new set of friends, and everything will work out. You'll see. As for Kyle, just take things one day at a time."

"I'm sure you're right." Kendra wiped her eyes against her mother's shoulder, trying to take comfort in her mother's praise. Of course her mother thought she was beautiful; all mothers said things like that. Pretty enough in spite of her straight, plain brown hair and glasses, with a nice figure, but not someone who really turned heads. But the other compliments were probably true, anyway. She was dependable and she tried hard to be a good mother. She pushed her dejection to the back of her mind to be faced later, alone. "Oh, I meant to tell you that when you were gone, the restaurant called. Something about the choice of desserts."

"Oh, thank goodness, I was waiting for her to get back to me. I'll go return that call now."

"And you're getting married at St. Michael's? You talked to the priest about that?"

"Yes, we're meeting with him the next time Gordon comes out from Chicago. It seems like a waste of time – I mean, we've both been married before and should know what we're doing – but that's his policy. I guess we have to follow his rules if we want to get married in the Church."

Kendra rose from the piano stool and helped her mother gather up the bags littering the couch. "Remember how when I was little we used to go to church all the time? Now we only go at Christmas and Easter, or for weddings and funerals. You know, I miss that sometimes." Looking back, her childhood aroused an aching sense of nostalgia. Compared to the turbulent years afterward, it seemed so happy and secure, with God in heaven and her father on earth, protecting his family as he should. Now her father was far away and God seemed nowhere to be found.

"That priest!" Her mother almost spat the word. "All the money we gave to that church over the years, and where was he when your father was sick?"

"He came sometimes –"

"A very few times. Well, he can find someone else to hit up for money from now on."

Kendra wondered if her mother was angrier at the priest or at God, who had seemed deaf to her prayers during that terrible time and during the years since. "Sometimes I worry about Elizabeth. I feel she's growing up without any religion at all. Do you think that's bad for her?"

Her mother shrugged. "Well, you can take her to church if you want to, Kendra. I did my duty when you kids were little. Although sometimes I wonder how much good it did."

Kendra had no answer for that. She had always believed in God, mostly because it seemed easier than not believing, but where was he really during the hard moments of life? Had he cared at all about her father's tragic battle with brain cancer, or the struggles that had engulfed the family since then? Did going to church make a real difference, or did she simply want to provide for her daughter the illusion of peaceful security that she herself had known as a child? Elizabeth would never know a father's love and care. Kendra hoped she would eventually have a stepfather, but at the moment even that possibility seemed far away, if her mother was right about Kyle. She wasn't sure, but maybe knowing something about God could give her daughter a bit of the security that was missing in their lives.

She was starting toward the kitchen when from the floor above she heard a small voice call out in a high-pitched sing-song, "Mommy! Mom-meeee!"

Bonnie turned around, glancing toward the ceiling. "Isn't that child asleep yet?"

"I put her to bed a half hour ago," Kendra whispered. "Maybe we were talking too loudly."

They both stood silent for a moment, listening, and then heard the scampering of little feet across the floor above and down the stairs. The child's tousled dark head peered at them over the bannister.

"You naughty little girl," Kendra laughed, but in her present emotional state she didn't have the heart to be stern. She set down the bags as Elizabeth ran to her. Kendra picked her up and nestled her against her shoulder.

"I couldn't sleep," Elizabeth complained against her ear. "I heard you playing piano. I want to play piano."

"Oh, just for a minute, but then you need to get back to bed." Kendra kissed the top of her head and stroked the tangled dark curls, so different from her own straight, lank hair. Elizabeth was her consolation for everything she had missed out on: college, her piano career, her carefree youth. Surely if she had waited twenty years, she couldn't have produced a more beautiful child. Even strangers stopped to admire Elizabeth. She knew that her daughter looked nothing like herself or her own relatives, and was secretly grateful no one but herself knew where Elizabeth's beauty had come from. It was the only thing Elizabeth had received, or would ever receive, from her father.

She carried her daughter to the baby grand, sat on the stool and perched Elizabeth on her lap. The child banged on the keys for a few minutes while her mother bounced her on her knees. They had played this way together so many times, but soon the piano would be gone.

She felt tears come to her eyes and quickly she tried to think about something else. She had to be strong, for Elizabeth's sake if not her own. She couldn't indulge her grief and anxiety this way. What could she find to look forward to?

"Elizabeth is having a birthday this month!" She shook the hair back from her face and forced a bright note into her voice. "How old are you going to be, honey?"

Elizabeth turned from her concerto and held three fingers up to her mother.

"You're growing up so fast!" Kendra bent down and kissed the warm little neck. "It seems like you were a baby just yesterday!"

"I'm not a baby!" Elizabeth pounded louder on the keys.

"No, you're a big girl. Did Mommy tell you that we're going to the zoo on Saturday? Kyle is taking us. We'll see zebras, tigers, giraffes – it will be fun."

Elizabeth stopped her banging and again turned inquisitive blue eyes up to her mother. Kendra could see the wheels turning in the little head. "Is he my daddy?"

Kendra smiled. She had wondered when Elizabeth might ask something like that. "No, he isn't. Not yet. He's just – well, Mommy's friend."

The child thought for a moment, concentration in her eyes. "Where is my daddy?"

Kendra's heart fell. That was another question she had anticipated and dreaded. She chose her words carefully. "I don't know where your real daddy is, honey. That's why you never see him." She kissed the child's dark curls. "But you know, if he knew what a beautiful little girl he has, I'm sure he would want to see you."

It was a lie, of course, but a necessary one. Elizabeth's father was a scumbag, and Kendra prayed that she would never cross paths with him again. If he knew Elizabeth existed – which Kendra had done her best to prevent – he would never acknowledge her or want anything to do with her. But that was a painful truth she could never tell her daughter.

Chapter Two

Steve slid into the booth of a favorite restaurant he often frequented near the college campus. The Formica table was still damp from the busboy's wiping, and now the waitress slapped a packet of silverware, wrapped in a napkin, in front him.

Cassie slid into the booth across from him. She wore a dejected expression, and Steve knew that something was bothering her. They had been seeing each other for three months, more or less, but the relationship wasn't going anywhere fast. In a month he would graduate and they would go their separate ways if he moved back home, as he planned to. Maybe that's what was bothering Cassie. Maybe she was going to ask him for more of a commitment tonight, to ask him how he felt about her. He hated conversations like that but had the feeling Cassie was working up to one.

How could he let her down easily? He didn't want to hurt her, but girls made it almost impossible sometimes. They expected so much from a guy who was just looking for a good time. He bit his lip and stared down at the menu, as if he didn't know it by heart.

The waitress came to take their orders.

"I'll have a cheese steak," Steve told her. "Ketchup, fried onions, lettuce, and tomato." He closed the menu and glanced at Cassie.

She shrugged. "I'll just have an order of French fries."

"Is that all?" He wanted to put her in a better mood, to maybe delay the dreaded discussion. "What about a sandwich?"

"That's all I'm hungry for." She gave the menu to the waitress.

Steve shrugged mentally. "How'd you do on your mid-term

yesterday? The one you were studying for all weekend. That was yesterday, wasn't it?"

Cassie took a sip of her water. "It was hard, but I think I passed. They had a few questions that I know the professor didn't go over in class. He said he would go over everything on the test, but I know he didn't."

"Maybe it was in the reading."

"Maybe. I hate the reading."

Steve grinned. "I'd rather do the reading than sit through those boring lectures. I fell asleep in class Monday. Rich had to poke me and wake me up at the end of class. Too much partying over the weekend, I guess. And Dr. Simpson rambles on in that quiet monotone that puts you to sleep."

"I guess." He could tell Cassie wasn't thinking about class or the weekend parties. "Steve, I need to talk to you."

He sighed inwardly, but forced a smile. "Sure. What is it?"

"I'm pregnant."

Steve felt the blood drain from his face. It was the last thing he had expected. Cassie met his eyes and there was no hint of a smile on her face.

"You're sure?"

"Yes. I got a test on Monday."

"So – so how far along, do you think?"

"Almost two months. I'm three weeks late. No, four tomorrow. I kept hoping it was just a fluke, but it wasn't."

Tears filled her eyes and she wiped them with her napkin. He knew he should try to comfort her, but he had nothing to offer. Finally he had been caught. He had dodged a bullet that other time, when he'd heard a rumor during his sophomore year that another girl was pregnant. This time he wouldn't be so lucky. He could only stare at Cassie as she wiped her eyes. Fear made him go hot, then cold.

You can do this. The words seemed to come from outside his shock and fear, in the rational part of his brain that was still thinking. In a few weeks he would graduate from college. By the time the baby was born, he could be settled in an apartment with a teaching job, able to take care of his family. Cassie could finish

Finding Father

school part-time, perhaps, while he worked. They could get married, or maybe just live together for a while, until they saw whether it would work out. His mother would have a heart attack at the idea of him having a child out of wedlock, but people did it all the time these days. It could work.

But even as the thought crossed his mind, he knew he wasn't going to make the offer. He didn't love Cassie. He had never lied and said he loved her. They were just supposed to be having a good time. He didn't want to get married yet, and he wasn't ready to be a father. He would be lying if he pretended otherwise.

"What do you want to do about it?" He tried to speak evenly, to hide his fear.

"I don't know." Cassie looked down at the tabletop. "I was hoping you could help me decide that."

"I don't know, Cassie." He took a sip of his water to avoid her eyes. "It's a big responsibility. I don't know if I'm ready for that."

Her face fell and he saw her bite her lip as if to keep from crying again. He hated to see girls cry, but what was he supposed to do? Marry her just to make her feel better? That was so unfair.

"My parents will flip out if I tell them about this," she said. "I have another two years of college, and then grad school. A baby would ruin everything. If you don't want it, I can't do it by myself."

"I guess neither of us is really ready for this." What was he actually saying? He wanted her to make the decision, so he didn't have to put it into words, so that he didn't have to feel responsible. It was a woman's choice anyway, wasn't it? That's what everyone said when they talked about the issue.

૪૦ ૦૩

The clinic had the cold sterile feel of a hospital or doctor's office, with bright lights and stacks of old magazines on the tables next to the rows of chairs. Cassie sat beside him and filled out reams of paperwork on a clipboard, and then they waited. Other girls sat in nearby chairs, some alone, some with female friends. The room was mostly silent and the girls seemed to avoid making eye contact with each other. Steve saw only one man other than himself.

At least I came with her. He tried to feel noble and failed in the attempt. A sick feeling in his stomach got worse and worse as they waited. He wanted to run out of the building and vomit, but he knew that would be unfair when all this was his fault as much as hers.

The waiting room was cold. He found himself shivering as time dragged on. Didn't they have heat in this building? Usually medical buildings were hot, not cold. He couldn't seem to get warm in this place.

They waited and waited. An older lady who looked a bit like Steve's grandmother passed through the room and behind a door, out of sight. Did that woman actually work in a place like this? He remembered all the books his grandmother had read to him as a small child, and then the times his grandfather had pitched to him so he could practice hitting a ball. The family vacations at the beach, the singing at Christmas and Easter, which he had hated as a teenager. What would his grandparents say if they knew where Steve was right now? He could picture the expression on his grandmother's face, the look in her eyes. No, he couldn't think about them right now. They were old and didn't understand his life. Besides, they would never know.

A nurse opened the door and called Cassie's name. She rose and went to the door. Before she disappeared she threw Steve one final glance of helpless anxiety.

The door closed. Steve strained his ears for any sound from the examining room, but he heard nothing.

That was his child in there who was being sucked out of her body. His son or daughter would never grow up now. He wanted to run into the room, to tell the doctor to stop, to tell Cassie that he would do whatever he had to do to help her, to take care of his child. But he didn't. He just sat with his face in his hands, biting his lower lip to keep the unmanly tears from spilling out of his eyes.

ಬ ಛ

"Well, Steve, have you had any luck finding a job?" His cousin Heather took a bite of the chicken cordon bleu which formed the main course of the wedding menu.

"Not yet." Steve shrugged and wiped his fingers on his wadded napkin. "Howard found me a summer job working for someone from your church, and now I'm filling out applications. No interviews yet."

Scott, on his other side, grinned sympathetically. "That's never fun. Good luck with that."

Joyce and Kate began to clink their knives against their glasses to make the bride and groom kiss, and others at the table took it up. Steve glanced up at the bridal party table in time to see his cousin Tom lean over to kiss his new bride. Everyone clapped.

"So what are you doing this summer?" Steve asked Heather, although he really had little curiosity.

"I'm going on the mission trip that the church is sponsoring. We're going to Bulgaria to run a Bible school for two weeks, and then we're going to Romania to work in an orphanage for a week. I've never been overseas before; I'm so excited." Her eyes sparkled as she spoke.

"That's nice." Steve had heard his stepfather Howard say something about the mission trip but had paid little attention. His family was all so religious – all except him – so he wasn't surprised that Heather planned to participate. He had rather dreaded coming to this wedding and having all his cousins ask when he planned to come back to church, but so far no one had bothered. Maybe they considered him a hopeless case by now. Maybe they were right.

He was young and bright and talented and attractive; he had a college degree to his name and the whole world before him, but for the last two months he had been clutched by a bewildering sense of depression and apathy that he couldn't shake or explain. He'd had a hell of a good time in college, but when he looked back, it seemed so empty. Where had the fun gone? He needed to start his real life, his adult life, but as he went through the motions of working and job-hunting, nothing seemed worthwhile anymore. What was the point of it all?

"Now he's really kicking hard!" Meredith laughed, and Kate leaned over and put her hand on her cousin's stomach to feel the kicks. Meredith was pregnant with her second child and kept patting her stomach and talking fondly about "him," as if the baby were a real person. She had just found out the sex by ultrasound and the other girls asked her a ream of questions about the pregnancy. The sight made Steve think of Cassie and he hated looking at her and listening to her. He would never be a father now – and he was glad – but he didn't like being reminded of it, either.

"So what did you think of that old-fashioned ceremony they had?" Meredith asked the table in general. "I'm glad I didn't have to promise to obey Scott! That would be a hard vow to keep."

Scott gave his wife a playful nudge. "We'll see if Renee actually keeps that vow after the ceremony. I know where I'd put my money."

"What was that bit about 'plighting their troth?'" Joyce asked. "Does anyone say that anymore?"

"Troth? Isn't that what animals eat out of?"

The rest of the table hooted with laughter. "That's trough," someone explained.

"I just finished a class in Chaucer," Steve told them. "He talked a lot about troth in his stories. It means – it means your personal honor, your sacred honor. When you plight your troth you're pledging your personal honor that you're going to do everything you promised."

Scott grinned. "I like the vows better when I understand what I'm saying."

"Be quiet, everybody. They're getting ready to cut the cake."

The bride and groom laughed and kissed and fed each other cake, eyes sparkling with anticipation. Steve guessed that they were probably both virgins, a suspicion that never would have entered his mind if he didn't know his family so well. A year, even six months ago, the knowledge would have filled him with incredulous contempt, but now he just felt sad and jaded in their presence. Looking at Tom, he found it strange that his cousin was actually three years older than himself. Why did he feel so old? How had his youth somehow slipped away?

Maybe he just needed to get back on the dating circuit. He hadn't really dated anyone since Cassie, probably a record length of time in his life. Maybe that was his whole problem. If he had made mistakes with her or with other girls in his past, it was too bad, and he needed to move on.

The next Friday night he went to a bar and managed to chat up an attractive girl named Miranda who appeared slightly older than him. He knew he couldn't take her back to his house, not with his mother home, and so was pleased when she invited him home with her.

She lived in a small, messy apartment which she tried to quickly straighten when they arrived. Steve pushed some magazines aside to find a seat on the couch and she brought them each a beer. For a few minutes they made desultory conversation as they drank. He could tell that the alcohol had taken effect as she became more and more talkative, telling him about her life, slurring her words as she spoke. Okay, go for it, he told himself, time to move on with your life.

He put his arm around her and kissed her. She responded warmly.

"You're such a nice guy," she said, and he was astonished to see tears fill her eyes. She must be pretty drunk. Well, so much the better. "It's hard to meet really nice guys, you know? I've had some real losers in my day."

"Yeah, I'm sure that's hard." He tried to sound sympathetic as he pulled her close and kissed her again. He hoped she wouldn't begin a long litany of all the rotten guys she had known. That would certainly kill the mood.

She allowed another kiss before she spoke again. "I've had a pretty hard year this year. It's been really bad. You know, last fall I went to a party and I was raped."

He drew back and his mouth fell open. He could only stare at her, frozen in place on the couch.

She was crying harder now. "I guess I was kind of drunk. I wasn't really drunk – not blacked out or anything. But this guy got me alone and he just wouldn't stop. I kept telling him no, no, but he wouldn't leave me alone."

Steve knew he should say something, but he heard a strange roaring in his ears along with a rising sense of panic.

"Oh, man." He knew it sounded idiotic. "That's – that's terrible."

"After that I got really depressed. I was going to school full-time, but I flunked out that semester. I decided not to go back in the spring, because I didn't know if I could handle it. For a while I was even suicidal. But I've gotten over that now, and I'm doing better. I've found a job I like and it's going pretty well. It's just hard dating, you know? It's hard to know how to trust someone."

"Yeah, I can see that." The words came out of his mouth automatically while a drum-beat throbbed in his head. *Let me out of here. I've got to get out of here. Let me out. Let me out. Let me out.*

"Maybe I shouldn't have told you about that." She managed a weak laugh, her speech thick. "I guess I shouldn't have. I just wanted you to know where I'm coming from."

"I see." He didn't really see, or care, why she had told him any of that. He just wanted to get away as fast as he could. His mind was spinning as he looked toward the door. He couldn't just run out, could he? That would be too weird.

She leaned toward him, and when he made no move to hold her, she put her head against his shoulder. Steve felt like a mannequin posed on the couch, unable to move.

"Do you want to stay here tonight?" she whispered against his neck.

"Uh – I don't know." How could he get out of this? "You know – I really don't think that would be a good idea. I live at home, and I – I have some things I have to do tomorrow. Before I left, my mother told me not to be out late tonight, because we have to go somewhere in the morning." He couldn't believe he was actually using his mother as an excuse to get away from a girl. He knew it sounded ridiculous, but it was the only idea to come to his mind.

Miranda drew back and watched him with a puzzled expression. "You don't want to stay?"

"I – no, I think I'd really better not. You know, I appreciate the offer – it's been really nice meeting you – you seem like a really nice person –" He was actually sweating and babbling. "But I think I'd better leave now." He stood up, knowing that anything else he could add would only make the situation worse. "Thanks for the beer – and – and everything. It's been great. Maybe I'll see you next Friday." He ran for the door.

He jumped behind the wheel of his car and gunned the engine as he pulled out into traffic. He hoped he wasn't too drunk to drive, but he couldn't worry about that now. Why did he feel that a million demons were chasing him all the way home, shouting in his ears? *You are the scum of the earth. You are a rapist and a murderer. You've committed the worst crimes of all. You killed your own baby. You belong to us – to evil – and you will never get away.*

The house was quiet when he got home from Miranda's. It was the first time he had been out drinking since he'd moved back home last month. He didn't want to wake his mother or sister – he didn't want anyone to see him in this state. He stumbled to his bedroom and undressed, then climbed under the covers and pulled them over his head. He wanted to hide in his closet or under the bed. But nothing could block out the jeering voices of the million demons in his head.

Chapter Three

From the stairwell landing Kendra could hear music and voices emanating from the apartment she had been sharing with Patsy for the last seven months. Instinctively she paused and flinched. Patsy had told her about the party tonight, so Kendra had deliberately taken Elizabeth to a children's movie to keep her out of the house. Now it was past ten o'clock – long past Elizabeth's bedtime – and she had to get her daughter in bed. But she guessed that the party was far from over.

Elizabeth dragged at her mother's hand as they climbed the stairs. She had fallen asleep in the car on the way home but had woken when Kendra took her out of her car seat. She was getting heavier to carry so Kendra let her walk, but now she lifted the child in her arms to shield her.

She turned the key and opened the door as the pungent odor of burning marijuana assaulted her. She had never smoked it herself, but would never forget that distinctive smell from her high school days. Fortunately the room was dimly lit, but she could see enough to recognize signs of chaos. Two people lay passed out on the floor. A couple were making out on the couch. Glasses and dirty dishes littered the coffee table. The whole room vibrated from the rhythm of the stereo. Patsy was nowhere to be seen.

Feeling her stomach muscles clench, she pushed passed the guests and started toward the hallway and the small bedroom she shared with Elizabeth, but stopped at the sight on the kitchen table. The light illuminated the table and a circle of young men in the chairs. One of them was smoking a joint, and one leaned over a pile of white powder in the middle of the table.

A cold fear fell over her. Turning her head, she clutched Elizabeth to her and hurried to the bedroom door, flipping the light switch. But the room wasn't empty. A half-naked couple gyrated on Elizabeth's bed, only pausing to look up when the light turned on. For just a second the four of them stared at each other in horror.

"Please *get out of my room!*" Kendra didn't know if she actually screamed the words or if they came out as a whisper. She grabbed Elizabeth and turned her head away from the sight as the couple grabbed their clothes and pushed past her out the door. Kendra slammed the door behind her and locked it, falling against it as she gasped for air.

Elizabeth tugged at her mother's shirt, her eyes heavy with sleep. "Why were they in my bed, Mommy? What were they doing?"

"Nothing, honey. They are Patsy's friends and they didn't have any business being in our room." She heard her voice shaking and knew she had to control herself in front of her daughter. She couldn't have a panic attack now. She pulled her coat off, then her daughter's, and found the child's pajamas. Tonight they would skip brushing teeth. It wasn't worth taking Elizabeth back into that mayhem.

She tucked Elizabeth into bed and kissed her on the forehead, hoping the child could fall asleep with the music blaring from the living room. Perhaps she should go out there and insist that Patsy's friends turn it down. The thought made her freeze. Instead she turned off the bureau light and turned on the small, dim light that she used when Elizabeth was sleeping and she needed to be in the bedroom. She found a pair of sweat pants and a tee shirt for herself that would make her feel less exposed than pajamas if she had to go back to the living room.

She hated parties like this. She was probably one of the few students in her high school who had managed to graduate without attending any parties. No, that wasn't true. She *had* attended one party with her brother Gregg – the summer after her father died. That one was the first and last.

She pulled down the covers of her own bed and climbed in, sitting up against the headboard with the covers pulled up to her chin. The percale sheets were cold against her arms and she shivered. How stupid she had been back then! Only sixteen, and actually excited to attend a real party when her brother invited his college friends over. Wearing her most sophisticated dress with heels and more makeup than usual, hoping she could pass for eighteen so that she wouldn't seem out of place. Hoping some college boy might actually notice her.

And then one had. She would never forget the first time she saw him, just inside the front door. He stood out from the other boys with his good looks and dark hair and the lean, compact build of a swimmer or wrestler, even though he was slightly shorter than the others. He turned and smiled at her, and Kendra was lost.

He sauntered up to her, smiling his dazzling smile. With her heels she was almost as tall as he was, and she looked into his vivid blue eyes. Kendra felt the heat rise to her face.

"Hi," he said. "I'm Steve."

"I'm Kendra."

"Kendra. I don't think I've ever met a Kendra before."

"I guess it's an unusual name. My dad's name was Ken."

"I haven't seen you at any of these parties before."

"No, I guess not." She hadn't planned an answer for that one. "I haven't been to many parties this summer. I – I've been busy."

"Busy?" He smiled again, an amused smile, she thought. "So what have you been doing to keep yourself too busy to party?"

She shifted her weight from one high heel to the other. "I've been – I've been working, trying to save money for college. I just graduated in June." It was a lie; she was only sixteen, but she saw no sign of disbelief on his face.

"Well, I'm glad you made it to this one. I have to leave for college next weekend, so this is my last big fling before I have to hit the books again."

She felt relieved that the conversation had moved to the safe ground of his life instead of her own; she wasn't an experienced liar. "Really? What college is that?"

"I go the University of Virginia, down in Charlottesville. It's a big school; I like it there. I'm a sophomore this year."

Kendra nodded, blushing again as he met her gaze. "Oh, you're my brother's age. He's going to be a sophomore too. What's your major?"

"Right now I'm undeclared. My father wants me to major in business, but I took a business class last year and thought it was so boring. I don't know if I could stand it for four years. I like English and history, but I know they don't pay well."

"You could be a teacher," Kendra suggested.

"Yeah, I've thought of that, but I don't know if I'd like to teach. I remember what I was like in high school. I was too rowdy." He grinned, a mischievous twinkle in his eye.

"I've thought about teaching," Kendra confided a bit shyly. "I want to major in music, and I'll probably end up teaching."

His eyes lit up. "Do you like music? Back at college, I play the drums in a little band. We're not professional or anything, but we play at parties sometimes."

Kendra decided not to mention that she usually played classical music on the piano. "That sounds cool."

He talked about his band and his parties and his cool college friends as he took her to the kitchen and poured them each a drink. Kendra had been completely dazzled.

What a fool she had been! Had she actually thought a guy like Steve had any kind of interest in her beyond sex? She knew better now.

She shivered now under the covers and tears filled her eyes as a new song began on the stereo and filtered in to her room through the door. Was that one of the songs Gregg's friends had played that night? Over four years ago now, but she recognized it – the very same song. The same song that she played in her recurring nightmare. And like that night, she was trapped in her bedroom, afraid to leave, feeling vulnerable and violated. She felt the sense of panic begin to rise in her again.

She couldn't just sit here reliving that awful night over and over. She had to think about something else or she would go crazy. She pushed back the covers, climbed out and dragged her cedar chest in front of the bedroom door so that no one could break in. She went to her bookshelf and scanned the titles, searching for one that would take her far, far away from this terrible feeling. Her gaze fell on *Gone With the Wind*, one of her favorite books. Scarlett's troubles were different from her own, but reading about tragedies in a book was somehow more bearable than reliving her own.

※ ※

She awakened the next morning to the jangling of her cell phone. Glancing at the clock by the bed, she realized that she hadn't set the alarm. It had been so late when she finally fell asleep, and she had forgotten that she would need to wake Elizabeth for church.

She fumbled in her purse and found the phone. "Hello?"

"Kendra? It's Amy. I was just calling to see if Elizabeth is going to church today."

Amy babysat for Elizabeth during the week when Kendra worked at the bank. She was married with three young children of her own, including one that was close to Elizabeth's age. For the last couple of months Elizabeth had been attending Sunday school with Amy's children.

When Amy first invited Elizabeth, Kendra had been hesitant to let her go, for they were supposed to be Catholic, even though they rarely attended anymore. But in the end she decided that it would be profitable for Elizabeth to learn something about God, and that at age three it probably wouldn't be much different than what she would learn at the Catholic Church anyway.

"Amy, I'm really sorry – I overslept today. But listen – maybe – maybe I could just bring her to church myself so I don't make you late." It would be a good excuse to get out of the apartment. She could hear stirring without and knew that some of Patsy's friends were still there.

"That's great, Kendra. And we have a class for adults too, if you want to try it. I think our teacher is really good. We're starting the book of Esther."

The name meant nothing to Kendra, but she got directions to the church and then woke Elizabeth. After dressing both of them and brushing their teeth, she glanced in the mirror as she ran a comb through her hair. Her dark eyes looked tired, and her straight brown hair limper than ever. She should use a curling iron, but that would take too much time.

She took Elizabeth's hand and grabbed a couple of granola bars to eat in the car in place of breakfast. The apartment was still a mess, and hung over guests were beginning to stumble around. She certainly hoped that Patsy would clean up the mess while she was gone. She knew she would need to have words with Patsy when she returned, but she wanted to wait till everyone else had cleared out. She wasn't sure how she felt about attending Amy's church, but right now anything seemed preferable to staying in the apartment.

The church was a small modern building just a few miles away, with no stained glass windows and only a cross above the door to show the building's function. She stepped inside the door with trepidation, wondering how she would know where to go. To her relief Amy appeared and led them both to Elizabeth's classroom. Kendra greeted Elizabeth's teacher, a girl not much older than Kendra herself.

"Our class is upstairs," Amy said.

It would be too awkward now to refuse, and in any event she had nowhere else to go but home. She followed Amy to the classroom, hoping to be inconspicuous. The room was bright and clean and carpeted, and contained a few rows of folding chairs, a whiteboard in the front, and a stand for the teacher. About twenty adults filled the chairs, most of them couples in their twenties and thirties, although a few were older couples. Kendra was sure she was the youngest person there, and maybe the only single woman.

"This is my friend Kendra," Amy announced to the room. Kendra felt herself blush with surprise. "She's visiting today." Amy leaned closer and whispered to Kendra, gesturing to a stocky man of about thirty-five. "That's Todd, the teacher.

Todd greeted Kendra and began the lesson. Kendra noticed that everyone else seemed have a Bible. Amy opened her own Bible and held it for Kendra to follow as one of the men read the first chapter.

"Let's get a little background on the book of Esther, first of all," Todd began. "We know that Mordecai and Esther were descendants of the Jews that were carried off during the Babylonian Captivity. So the Jews at this time were worshipers of God who were living in a heathen culture, under a very heathen king.

Finding Father

"Now when I was a child and learned this story in Sunday school, I was always told that it was a romantic love story, and that the position that Esther won was a cross between a Miss America crown and a happily-ever-after Cinderella ending. In reality, this was not much of a love story, and there was nothing very romantic about it.

"The king in the story was Xerxes the First, who was a despotic, decadent, debauched king. The first chapter of Esther tells us that he would have drinking orgies for his noblemen that would last for days. At one of these orgies, Xerxes got so drunk that he demanded that his beautiful queen come and display herself for all his inebriated noblemen. This would be the equivalent of a modern man asking his wife to do a strip-tease dance for his drunken friends. The queen, of course, refused to obey."

Kendra listened in fascination. She hadn't known that the Bible contained stories like these. Who would have imagined it? Who would have guessed that people had wild parties back in Bible days too? She had always thought the Bible was full of old rules that didn't relate to modern life.

"So how did Xerxes respond? First of all, he retaliated by stripping the queen's title from her. And secondly, he decided to console himself with sex. Xerxes wanted to have sex with every beautiful girl he could find, and the way he did that was by taking them all into his harem. Chapter Two tells us that he took so many girls into his harem that he would spend one night with each one, and then he never had to see her again afterward.

"So how do you think Esther felt about being one of these girls? We know that family was important to devout Jews, and a devout Jewish man wanted his daughter to marry another devout Jewish man and raise devout Jewish children. When Esther became part of the king's harem, it meant that she would probably see very little of her new husband, would probably never have children, and would live in seclusion from her community of observant Jews. But she surely had no choice in the matter."

One of the students read the next chapter of the Bible aloud, and a discussion ensued. When Sunday school ended Kendra was surprised that the hour had passed so quickly. She had become so engrossed in the story of the beautiful girl married to the debauched heathen king that she had nearly forgotten about the situation waiting for her at home.

Amy invited her to stay for the church service, but Kendra made her excuses, collected Elizabeth, and headed for home. She and Patsy had been sharing an apartment for months now, but their lifestyles were completely at odds with each other. Patsy often went out to bars with her friends. Kendra was under the legal drinking age and couldn't have taken Elizabeth to a bar anyway. Most evenings she stayed at home, doing laundry, reading stories to Elizabeth, watching television or reading novels after putting her daughter to bed. The loneliness ate at her soul. But where else could she go? She couldn't afford her own apartment on her small salary – her mother still had to help her with the expense of Elizabeth's daycare. She knew of no other friends who were looking for a roommate. And even Kyle, her first love, had deserted her.

She opened the door to the apartment with trepidation. To her relief the living room was mostly straightened and empty. Patsy was sitting at the dining room table, eating a slice of buttered toast.

"So your friends are gone?" Kendra didn't try to keep the acerbity out of her voice.

"Yeah, finally. I had a hard time waking up Travis. I was ready to dump a glass of water in his face, but that might not have done it, either." Patsy looked up at Kendra with a grin, which faded when she saw her friend's expression.

Kendra set her purse on the floor, found a couple of puzzles for Elizabeth and settled her with them in the living room, finally returning to the table. She sat across from Patsy, lowering her voice as she spoke. "You told me you were having a party. You didn't tell me there would be drugs here."

Patsy shrugged. "You mean the pot? Come on, Kendra, everybody smokes pot. It's safer than alcohol – you know that."

"But it's not legal. And it wasn't just pot. There was some other drug on the table, right here. Cocaine or heroin or –" Kendra really didn't know enough about drugs to recognize them by sight. "Or something. What about that?"

"I didn't see that. I was back in my room with Ethan. I can't watch what every single person does here. Come on, Kendra, you're making a big deal about nothing."

"It's a big deal to me!" Kendra heard her voice rising and made an attempt to lower it so that Elizabeth wouldn't hear. "And then, on top of everything else, a couple was having sex in our bedroom! Right when we walked in."

"Well, sorry. You should have locked your door before you left. I didn't know anyone would go in there. They didn't take anything, did they?"

"I hope not. I didn't see anything missing, but that's not the point. Elizabeth saw it, and she probably saw all the drugs too. Patsy, I don't want my daughter growing up this way. It's not good for her. Don't you see?"

Patsy glared at her, jumped up from the table and stalked to the kitchen, dropping her plate in the sink with a clatter. "Well, she's your daughter, Kendra, not mine. And why are you so upset about the sex? I know that Kyle spent the night here a few times, and you can't tell me you were just holding hands. I'm sure Elizabeth knew about it too."

Kendra felt her face burn and she bit her lip hard. Her relationship with Kyle was not something she wanted to remember or talk about, especially with Patsy. He had pushed for sex within the first few months and she had given in, even though she wasn't completely ready, knowing it was something that all guys would expect sooner or later – most of them sooner. She had tried to please him, to make him happy, but in the end she had lost him anyway. He hadn't loved her the way she loved him, and at the first difficulty had bailed out. Since then, the thought of dating anyone new made her freeze.

But at least she wasn't like Patsy, who had a different boyfriend every month.

"I guess I was stupid," she said in a thick voice. "But I didn't let Elizabeth see that. She was always in another room. And Kyle didn't use drugs, and didn't get drunk – well, not often, anyway. And not in front of Elizabeth. And he was the only one – the only guy I slept with. It really bothers me the way you're bringing home a different guy every week, and she's going to think that kind of life is normal."

She could tell by the expression on Patsy's face that she had finally hit a nerve.

"Well, aren't you so perfect! Why don't you just come out and call me a slut?"

"I didn't say that –"

"That's what you meant, anyway. For your information, Ethan and I are talking about moving in together. We're getting serious!"

Kendra looked down at the table and shrugged. "Oh. That's nice."

"And I told Ethan that I didn't want to put you out on the street, especially with your daughter, but he wants to move in at the end of the month when his lease is up. And I'm going to tell him he can do that. You'll have to move out then."

Kendra raised a shocked face to Patsy. "You want me to move out?"

Patsy shrugged. "Look, Kendra, you're the one who's not happy here. You have a daughter and you're always worrying about what she's seeing or thinking. That's just not my life. I don't want to live that way. I think we just need to face it and move on."

"But – but that only gives me two weeks! You should give me at least a month to find somewhere else! Where will I go?"

"Get the want ads. There are always people looking for roommates. But it isn't going to work to have all of us living here together – I'm sure of that. And Ethan's moving in at the end of the month."

Kendra stared after her as Patsy marched back to the shower. She really shouldn't be shocked by this development. She had seen as well as anyone that this living situation wasn't ideal for any of them. But for some reason she had thought that she was the one more inconvenienced by it than Patsy – that she would be the one to decide when it was unbearable. Perhaps having a child in the house was more annoying than her friend had let on. It certainly cramped Patsy's style. And this quarrel was the final straw.

ஐ ௸

Kendra glanced around the seedy neighborhood nervously

before climbing out of the car. Some of the neighbors' yards were overgrown, with trash lying around. Since it was winter, no one was out of doors, but she wondered what it would look like in the summer. She was glad she had decided to stop on her way home from her bank job before picking up Elizabeth from Amy's.

Of the want ads she had checked out, this was the only promising possibility. When she had called, some of the women had seemed friendly until Kendra mentioned that she had a three-year-old daughter, and then the tone changed. One woman said that she was a nurse and slept during the day, and couldn't have a child making noise. Another said that her house wasn't set up to accommodate a child. Kendra came to the conclusion that very few people would be willing to live with a child who wasn't related to them.

She knocked at the front door and a young woman with black hair and a tattoo around her neck opened the door. As she stepped into the house, the smell of cigarettes greeted her. At least it wasn't pot, she thought with irony. But since it was only five o'clock, the pot might appear later.

"Let me show you around the house," the girl said. "There are three of us living here – no, now it's four, because Eric's girlfriend just moved in. The rent is four hundred a month, but it would be five hundred for you if you're bringing your daughter. That's what we told Eric too. There are four bedrooms and two bathrooms, so you and I would share a bath. And of course, we all share the kitchen and living room. We've never had a child living here before, so I guess the main thing is that she'd need to keep her toys and things back in the bedroom."

It was even worse than Patsy's requirements. Poor Elizabeth would practically be a prisoner in her bedroom. The house was dirtier than Patsy's as well. And from the look of things outside, Kendra wasn't sure she would want her daughter to play outdoors.

"Well, that was the living room, and here's the kitchen. Sorry, I guess we haven't cleaned here in a while."

Kendra looked around, her heart falling. Dirty dishes everywhere. Ashtrays and papers piled on the kitchen table. And it smelled like – like cats or rotten food, she wasn't sure which. She could stand dirt and clutter in every other part of the house, but she needed a clean kitchen. If she moved in here, she knew she would be the maid.

She glanced into the empty bedroom, which at least was reasonably clean except for some stains on the carpet. The bathroom was old and small, and she would have to share it with someone, but she could manage if she had to.

"Thanks for showing me." She forced a smile as she opened the door to depart. "I'll give you a call and let you know what I decide."

She climbed behind the wheel and started toward Amy's house, her growing despair turning to panic. If she didn't move in here – what were the other options? A homeless shelter? Surely that would be worse. But at least it might give her a little more time to look and find a better home.

She had never in a million years thought about having to take her daughter to a shelter. If only her mother hadn't moved so far away. If only her father hadn't died and left her alone. If only she had one other relative who cared about her and would help her. Unlike her brother, who didn't care at all.

She knocked on Amy's door and stepped inside when her friend opened it.

"Thanks for keeping her longer today. Come on, honey, we've got to get going."

"So how was the house?" Amy asked in a bright tone, handing Kendra the stuffed animal that Elizabeth liked to carry. "Do you think it might work out?"

"I don't know." Without warning, Kendra burst into tears.

"Oh, dear, that doesn't sound good!" Amy leaned toward her and patted her shoulder in an attempt at comfort. "What happened?"

So Kendra spilled out the whole story of Patsy and the party and their quarrel and her fruitless attempt to find another place to live, and her fear of being homeless. When she had finished, she did feel a bit of relief in having shared the burden with someone, although she had no idea if Amy would be able to help.

"I'm so sorry this is happening to you." Amy shook her head, a thoughtful pucker between her brows. "But Kendra, I'm sure there's a solution here somewhere. I'm going to pray about it. Is it okay if I pray with you now?"

Taken aback, Kendra nodded. She had never thought about praying about a problem like this. Since the day her father had died of a brain tumor and all the family's fervent prayers had gone unanswered, prayer had seemed like a waste of time. But what could it hurt? Maybe Amy knew more than she did.

Amy took Kendra's hands in her own. "Heavenly Father, you see this situation that Kendra is in, and her need of a new home. And Father, you promise that you will provide for our needs, and so we ask that you will provide for Kendra in this situation. Please lead her to the right place that will be safe for her and Elizabeth too. And that through this Kendra will see your great power and how much you love both of them."

"Thanks." Kendra dried her eyes with the back of her hand. She wasn't sure the prayer would do any good, but she was touched that Amy cared enough to offer it. She took Elizabeth's hand and turned toward the door.

"I'll ask around and let you know if I hear of any possibilities," Amy added. "Don't worry, Kendra. I'm sure something will turn up."

She drove home and prepared dinner for herself and Elizabeth. Oddly enough, she felt more peaceful since her conversation with Amy. Perhaps it would help if she prayed herself about the situation. It might show God that she was serious. Of course, if God hadn't cared enough to spare her father when he was dying, maybe it was foolish to think that he would care anything about Kendra's living situation. But if he did care, she would have to take the chance of feeling foolish in order to see what he would do.

Chapter Four

"I know you've all probably heard that terrible story over at Faith Baptist, or I wouldn't mention it," one of the women in Kendra's Sunday school class said. "But I just don't understand how a minister, someone who studies the Bible and prays and preaches sermons every Sunday, could get involved with a call girl. Maybe men are different, but I just can't imagine becoming so hardhearted that I could do something like that and not feel guilty at all."

Kendra had decided to attend the class for the second week. She was curious to learn the fate of the beautiful Jewish girl who became queen, but more importantly, she wanted to impress God with her seriousness and desire to do right. Maybe he would be more likely to answer her prayer if she did. Now the conversation in class had strayed from Esther's sudden elevation to queen, to the sexual scandal that appeared to be rocking the Christian community in town.

"We don't know that he doesn't feel guilty," one of the men inserted. "I'm sure he does."

"But it wasn't enough to stop him, so it couldn't have bothered him too much. If it were me, I just couldn't live with myself."

"Why are we so shocked when something like this happens?" Todd asked the class. "It's because we like to think of ourselves as pretty nice people who occasionally do a few wrong things. But if we really believed what the Bible says about us, that our hearts are desperately wicked, we wouldn't be so shocked. Saddened, of course, but not very surprised. The truth is that any of us are capable of falling, and when we pretend that isn't true, we are in the greatest danger."

Kendra pondered his words. She had always thought of herself as a pretty nice person who occasionally did a few wrong things. Not a bad person. Really bad people were ones who went to jail, or deserved to go to jail. Not someone like herself, who never tried to hurt anyone.

She suddenly remembered that morning, when she had yelled at Elizabeth and smacked her in anger as they were getting ready for church. Other unpleasant memories emerged to nag at her conscience. Anger and bitterness towards people in her life who hurt her, like Gregg and Patsy and – others. Spiteful comments directed at some of her coworkers. She knew she was good at covering her private faults and appearing pretty clean on the outside, but she wouldn't want anyone to see what really lurked in the recesses of her heart.

Was it possible that she was a sinner as well, who needed to be saved? Of course she was – she had learned that as a child. "Forgive us our trespasses, as we forgive those who trespass against us." She remembered that prayer well. It meant that she, Kendra, had a heart that was full of evil. It was a new, and very uncomfortable, thought.

She collected her purse and, as she was leaving the classroom, a middle-aged woman with reddish hair and a pleasant face approached her. "Are you Kendra?"

Kendra nodded.

"Hi, I'm Betsy Reese. I was talking to Amy Templeton this week and she asked me to pray about your living situation. Have you found anything yet?"

"No," Kendra said.

"Well, the person I thought of is my niece. She recently bought a townhouse, and has talked about finding a roommate to share living expenses."

After all her failed attempts, Kendra didn't want to get excited too quickly. "The problem is my daughter. She's only three, and most people don't want a child living with them."

"Well, I mentioned that to my niece, and she said for you to give her a call. I wrote her name and number down for you."

"Thanks." Kendra took the piece of paper the woman handed her, with "Allison Andrews" and a phone number written after it.

She allowed a tiny flicker of hope to rise in her as she drove home. As soon as she had changed her clothes and fed Elizabeth lunch, she dialed the number. A woman answered.

"Yes, my Aunt Betsy told me about you. If you'd like to come over and see the house, this afternoon would be a good time. Maybe you should bring your daughter so I can meet her too."

Kendra had no choice but to bring Elizabeth, and prayed that her daughter would be especially well-behaved as they visited. She followed the directions Allison had given her and found the neighborhood. It was a new development, with rows of neat, pretty townhouses and well-kept lawns.

The door opened to reveal a tall, blonde young woman, her hair pulled back in a ponytail, wearing jeans and a sweatshirt. She smiled at Kendra.

"Hi, come in. I'm Allison. You must be Kendra. And this is your daughter? She's adorable."

The living room was small but neat. Kendra was relieved to see that it was clean, but displayed few breakable knickknacks. She and Allison sat on the plaid couch and chatted for a few minutes while Elizabeth sat beside her mother and sucked her thumb. Kendra had not been able to break her of the habit.

"I've been here about six months now," Allison told her. "It's a nice neighborhood, and I'm glad I bought it. But I'd like a roommate to help with expenses, and I'd like the company too. I don't really enjoy spending all my evenings alone."

Kendra explained a bit about her living situation, and that Patsy had only given her two weeks to move out now that her boyfriend was moving in.

"Well, you don't have to worry about that with me," Allison laughed. "No boyfriend, no husband, no prospects either. I had some problems with a roommate in the fall who was always getting drunk and coming home all hours of the morning. Maybe it was none of my business, but I worried about her, and it bothered me."

Thinking of Patsy, Kendra wanted to laugh. "I couldn't do that anyway. I have my daughter to worry about."

"I don't think a child would have slowed Candy down much. And I do have one other rule." Allison hesitated a moment as she eyed Kendra. "No men sleeping over. That's something I feel strongly about."

Kendra's only sensation was relief. "You don't have to worry about that either. I haven't had a boyfriend in over six months."

"Well, you never know when you'll find one, and I just wanted to be up-front about that. Do you want to see the house?" Allison jumped up. "Let me show you around."

The kitchen was light and roomy and, more importantly, clean, with a back door leading to a wooden deck in the small backyard. Looking out the back window, Kendra saw a paved path running between the backyards, and, in the distance, a playground. Elizabeth could ride her tricycle and play there in the warmer weather.

"I only have two bedrooms," Allison explained as she led the way upstairs. "I had the choice between two large bedrooms or three small ones, and I thought I'd rather have large ones since I don't have children. So you'd have to share with your daughter, but you'd have your own bathroom right next door."

The bedroom was a comfortable size, with a large closet. "Elizabeth and I could share this. We share a room now."

"Do you have furniture you'd want to bring?"

"I only have a bedroom set, and a little table that I have in the living room now. Would you have room for that?"

Allison pursed her lips. "We could probably find space somewhere. I also have a basement. It isn't finished, but it's clean and dry. We could put an extra couch and TV down there too. Your daughter could keep her large toys there."

Allison led the way to the basement, Kendra and Elizabeth following. As Kendra descended the steps, she stopped at the vision against the basement wall.

"You have a piano!" she exclaimed.

"Oh, that! My aunt wanted it out of her house, and I said I could take it. I don't really play; I took lessons as a kid, but I haven't kept up with it. So I don't use the piano much."

Kendra ran her fingers over the keys and began the first notes of "Moonlight Sonata." It had been months since she had played, but the music returned to her fingers automatically. The piano was a bit out of tune, but had a nice tone. Perhaps she could save money to get it tuned. It would be a small price to pay to actually have a piano to use again. It almost seemed like a sign, a special gift from God, or her father who was looking out for her in heaven.

Kendra found herself getting more excited as she explored this lovely house. Allison Andrews seemed so friendly and easy-going, so accepting of Elizabeth. She told Kendra that she was a second-grade teacher and mentioned two young nephews who were close to Elizabeth's age.

"Your daughter's so pretty." Allison touched the child's curls. "She looks Irish, with that dark hair and fair complexion. Is your family Irish?"

Kendra shook her head.

"I have some cousins who are half Irish, and they have that unusual coloring. And look at her blue eyes, with those long lashes! She'll knock the boys dead when she gets older." Allison laughed. "You and I will probably still be living in this house, and she'll get a man before either of us."

"I hope not," Kendra said.

"Believe me, I hope not too. I've told God many times that I'm ready for Mr. Right, whenever he wants to send him along. But he doesn't seem to be in any hurry."

"God, or Mr. Right?"

"Either one," Allison laughed. "I'm almost twenty-seven, and my biological clock is ticking away. But I'm still waiting."

Allison said that Kendra could move in the next weekend, and they agreed to a trial period to decide if it was working out. As she drove home, Kendra found herself buoyant with hope and relief. Of course, it was too soon to count her chickens; she might have problems with Allison just as she had with Patsy. But Allison didn't seem anything like Patsy. Kendra felt so comfortable with her, even in the first meeting. Was it possible that she was a Christian too, like Amy and Betsy and Todd and the others she had met in church? Either way, this new home seemed like a most extraordinary answer to her prayer. She could hardly believe that God had provided for her so quickly and extravagantly, and her heart filled with gratitude.

☼ ☼

Kendra inserted her new key into the lock and pushed open the door. From the kitchen the smell of baking fish drifted out to meet her and Elizabeth. Allison stepped into the living room to greet her.

"Do you want some dinner? I got home a little early today and decided to be ambitious and actually cook for a change. I made enough for three of us."

"Wow, that's really nice." After working in the bank all day she was tired, and it *was* nice to come home to dinner. "Maybe I can cook for you tomorrow."

Allison bustled around the kitchen, taking a tray of tater tots out of the oven and scooping them into a bowl. "It's no fun to cook for one person so I usually buy take-out, or eat frozen dinners. But every now and then I want a real meal. I bought some salmon on the way home. It's pretty quick and easy."

Kendra hung up her own coat and Elizabeth's. She lifted Elizabeth into her booster seat and tied a bib around her neck as Allison set out the food. Allison prayed over the food and Kendra scooped some tater tots onto Elizabeth's plate.

"I know you don't go to your aunt's church," Kendra began after she had swallowed a few bites. "Do you attend somewhere else?"

"I go to Bethel Bible Church, not far from here. My grandparents have been at that church forever; they were some of the original members, and my dad is an elder. My mom's parents – the Kirks – they are still really involved in the church, even though they're in their eighties. My grandfather visits people in the hospital, and my grandmother leads a Bible study. They have five children and fifteen grandchildren," Allison explained, "and we're all Christians." She looked quite proud as she said this.

Kendra knew little about large families, Christian or otherwise. "Is that unusual?"

"I think so. I don't know many families like ours. Uncle Jack moved to New York, but everyone else lives nearby. I've always been close to my cousins too. Do you have a large family?"

Kendra shook her head. "Only my mother, but she's in Hong Kong with her new husband. I just spent Christmas with her there. I have one brother, but I only see him once or twice a year. My parents moved here from the West coast, so I don't have relatives in the area. Really, it's just me and Elizabeth."

Allison gave her a look of something that resembled pity. "Oh, that must be strange. I see my sisters and cousins all the time. I'm going shopping on Saturday with Heather and Anne. We have to buy baby presents for Renee's baby shower. You know my Aunt Betsy – Tom is her son. This is her first grandchild, and she is so excited she can hardly contain herself."

"I need to congratulate her." Kendra couldn't help but feel a twinge of envy for Allison. What would it be like, to be part of such a large, close, loving family, to have aunts and uncles and cousins making a fuss over her daughter? She could hardly imagine it, but the contrast made her more aware of her aloneness.

Elizabeth said, "Can I have more tater tots?"

Kendra picked up the bowl. "I think there's enough. Why don't you ask Miss –" she paused and looked at Allison. "What do you want Elizabeth to call you?"

"Maybe you could call me Aunt Allie," Allison suggested. "That's what my nephews call me. Would you like that?"

"Elizabeth doesn't have any aunts. That's a nice idea." Kendra felt pleased that Allison would make the suggestion, grateful that Allison was so accepting of Elizabeth.

Allison passed the potatoes to Elizabeth and scraped the last of the salmon onto her own plate. "This Friday I have the Timothy group, so I'll be out for the evening. It's a singles group," she explained, seeing Kendra's puzzled expression. "So many activities in the church center around married couples and children, so this is a way for the single people to get together."

"Why do you call it the Timothy group?" Kendra asked.

"Oh, I think Heidi came up with that name. You know, Timothy was a young pastor in the Bible, a protégé of Paul. I guess Heidi thought he would be a good role model for all of us. Why don't you come with me sometime, Kendra?"

Kendra hesitated. "I guess I couldn't bring Elizabeth."

"Not to the Bible studies – she would be bored. But you could bring her to some of the activities."

"Does anyone else in the group have children?" Kendra had heard of groups designed for single parents.

"Not among the core group. But we've had children come to a few activities and no one ever seems to mind."

Kendra was less worried about the group liking Elizabeth and more worried that they might look down on Kendra for being an unwed mother. She had attended the Sunday school class at Grace Fellowship for about a month now and had even begun attending the worship service, but she kept to herself and really didn't know anyone except Amy. At the Timothy group that would probably be impossible. But maybe she should try it, if she could save money for a babysitter.

☼ ☪

Steve locked his bedroom door so that he wouldn't run the danger of interruptions. He felt an uneasy, queasy feeling in his stomach as he picked up his cell phone. It was late Sunday morning, the time of week that he remembered being most likely to find Cassie alone and sober. Perhaps she had changed her number in the nine months since he had seen her. In that case, he wouldn't know how to contact her unless – he probably had the phone number of some mutual friend that he could call. Anyway, he knew it was time to stop procrastinating and bite the bullet.

He looked for her name in his contact list and dialed. After three rings he heard Cassie's voice. "Hello?"

"Cassie?" He had to swallow quickly. "Hi. This is Steve."

"Yeah, I saw your name come up." She sounded cool, which didn't surprise him.

"How are you doing? What's going on?"

"Fine. I'm still here in Charlottesville. I have one more year till graduation."

"Right, that's what I thought. And then grad school?"

"I think so. Are you working?"

"Yeah, I was lucky. I found a job in a high school. It's going pretty well, but I have long hours, since it's my first year."

"I guess that's the way it goes."

Silence. Steve groped for his next words. He had known this call would be awkward, and he was right.

"Listen, I haven't seen you since graduation, and I was wondering how you were doing after – you know, everything that happened."

"I'm fine," Cassie said. "It's all water under the bridge. I never think about it anymore."

"Really? I think about it a lot."

"Well, it's a little late for that." He could hear the cool irony in her voice.

"Yes, I know it is." He paused and took a deep breath. "And that's why I'm calling. I want to apologize for how I acted in that whole situation. I was really wrong, and I'm sorry. I should have been there for you and the baby. I should have been more supportive, and I'm sorry."

A long pause ensued. For a moment he wondered if she had hung up, and then he heard her breathe. "Well, there's no point in that. It's over and done with. I think we made the right decision, after all."

"I know we made the wrong decision," Steve said, "and I'm sorry for my part in it."

"Well, it's too late now," Cassie said. "I've moved on with my life. I don't waste time thinking about it. You should probably do the same thing."

Steve fell silent a moment. "I'm glad you're doing okay," he managed finally. At least this was easier than bitter recriminations on her part. "I wanted to say – if there's anything I can do to make up for it – but I guess it's too late for that."

"I guess so." Another silence. "Well, anyway, I'm glad to know things are going so well for you. Thanks for calling." Was it his imagination, or did he hear a slight softening in her tone?

The phone went dead and he sat down on his bed, wiping his sweaty palms on his pants. Well, that was done. It could have gone better, but it could have been worse. At least he had tried. Of the apologies he had offered in the last six months, this one was the hardest. He could only think of one that would be more painful, but he might never be called upon to make it.

He bit his lip and winced. Why did he keep remembering that one girl? The night he had met her was one experience from his life he would rather wipe out of his memory. He hadn't seen her in over four years now – almost five – since that summer just before his sophomore year of college. But he had no idea where she was now, and no idea how to contact her. He might be able to figure something out – through the internet or mutual acquaintances – her brother was a friend of a friend. But would that be the right thing to do? Maybe it would be more cruel than kind. Maybe it would make everything worse.

For the time being he would just wait until he knew clearly what he should do. He wasn't sure if that was wisdom, or cowardice.

Chapter Five

A group of about ten young people, mostly in their twenties, were gathered in the living room of the house Kendra entered with Allison, and several more arrived after them. Allison dropped onto the couch next to another young woman and pushed her playfully.

"Hey, make room for Kendra. I finally talked her into coming. Hey, everybody, this is Kendra, my new roommate. This is Leanne, Ruth, Serena, Vince, Randy, Dan, Ben, Heidi, Penny, Mark, and Eddie."

"Do you remember all that?" A young man with a shock of wild blond hair grinned at Kendra. "We'll test you on it by the end of the night."

The girl with honey-colored hair and a buxom figure, sitting next to Kendra on the couch, gave her a squeeze. "Oh, I'm so glad you came! Allison told us about you. I'm Leanne, by the way. I guess you don't go to our church, do you? I've never seen you there."

"I go to a church called Grace Fellowship." Did that matter? Everyone at the group seemed to go to Allison's church.

"Oh, I know that church. I have some friends who go there. By the way, this is my roommate, Ruth." She gestured to another girl sitting close by, a slim, black-haired, oriental girl who seemed to lack Leanne's exuberant personality.

"It's nice to have you, Kendra." A tall, weedy young man who reminded Kendra of a scarecrow nodded and smiled at her.

"And that's Randy, our illustrious leader," Allison added.

"Don't listen to anything she says about me." Randy grinned.

"Illustrious is going a bit far. I prefer 'brilliant.' Now, since we have someone new tonight, I suggest we go around the room, say your name, and choose one adjective to describe yourself. I've already given a word for myself."

A round of laughter greeted this statement. Kendra listened carefully to the names and descriptions, although she knew she would never remember them all.

"I'm Serena and I'm outspoken!" The young woman tossed her long dark hair as she spoke, and the room laughed. "This is Vince and he's uptight."

Several of the others laughed, but the guy next to Serena only frowned. "I'm only uptight around you, Serena."

"All right, you two, put your daggers away." Randy was clearly in charge. "And here we have Dan, and what word could possibly describe him? What word could do him justice?"

The dark, saturnine young man smiled sardonically. "Mysterious."

"I'm Heidi," began a very pretty girl with soft brown hair and a sweet face, "and I'm –" She broke into giggles.

"Heidi's sweet," Allison said. "There's just no other word for her." From her tone, Kendra wasn't sure if the statement was a compliment or not.

When the introductions were finished, they spent some time singing while the guy named Mark played the guitar, and then they began the Bible study. Randy's style was a bit different from Todd's in the Sunday school class; he acted as a discussion leader as they read the passage and talked about what it meant and how they could apply it their lives. Everyone joined in, and Kendra listened with wonder. This group was much like her class at Grace Fellowship, except that the members were all young and single, and they seemed to be good friends with each other. As she listened to the discussion flowing around her, she was struck by their spiritual vibrancy. They were all so alive; no one seemed bored or indifferent. She had never met a group of young people quite like these. Where had they been all her life? Could she actually become part of a group like this?

She began attending every Bible study and soon realized that it was the highlight of her week. The studies filled a new spiritual hunger she had never been aware of before, just as the friendship of the other young people met her social needs. Everyone was warm and welcoming, although she got to know several of the girls more quickly than others.

Leanne, the girl who sat beside her the first night, was especially friendly and Kendra felt drawn to her. Leanne had a habit of hugging everyone she met, male or female, and Kendra soon realized that it was part of her affectionate, enthusiastic personality. Her roommate Ruth was also friendly to Kendra but in a quieter way. Ruth seemed shy and spoke less than the others in the group discussions, while Leanne, Allison, and Serena always had an opinion to voice.

Serena was one of the older women in the Timothy group and Allison's close friend. Already married and divorced at a young age, she had been living with another man when she became a Christian; she often talked about her former boyfriend and prayed for him. She had a habit of speaking in a forceful and sometimes loud voice when she wanted to make a point. Kendra thought her brassy personality an odd contrast to her long hair and feminine looks. At first Kendra felt uncomfortable around Serena and mentioned to Allison that she often felt Serena was making fun of her. Allison assured her that Serena treated everyone like that; it was her way, and she didn't mean any harm by it.

Kendra was surprised to find that Serena and Heidi were friends, because it seemed at first glance that no two women could have been more opposite. Everything about Heidi was soft and gentle, from her large blue eyes to her sweet voice. She took an organizational role in the group and helped plan the activities, and always went out of her way to greet any visitors. Kendra found her very kind, very spiritual, but very serious, someone who did not pick up on humor too quickly.

"Let me tell you about Heidi," Allison began one evening when Kendra remarked on the impression she had made. "Every guy who comes into the group goes out with Heidi first. I think there's some kind of rule about it. She's had more boyfriends than everyone else in the group put together. Randy dated her for a while, and then Eddie did, and Jesse a few times, and she even went out with Vince,

God bless her. I don't get it. How does she attract so many men? Do you think she's prettier than anyone else? Than Serena or Leanne?"

"Not exactly." Kendra pondered a moment. "She *is* very pretty, and she has such a sweet personality. It must be some combination of her looks and personality that men find attractive."

"I guess so," Allison sighed.

Kendra was already well aware that Allison was frustrated by her own dating life and probably resented the fact that Heidi seemed to draw men so easily. In spite of that, the women in the group all seemed to be friends. "Everybody gets along really well here. I haven't noticed any problems between people."

"Yes, I think we do get along real well. The only two who seem to grate on each other are Serena and Vince. Serena used to be something of a feminist, and Vince comes from a very conservative church where they almost think women are evil. As if we have nothing to do but seduce men and lead them astray." Allison giggled. "I don't think any of us want to seduce Vince!"

Kendra laughed. "Really!"

"Anyway, Vince tends to make these disparaging comments about women. The rest of us just ignore him, but Serena gets pretty mad sometimes."

"I can see that." Kendra had noticed a few of those comments herself.

"And I'll tell you about the men, just so you know. Mark has a girlfriend in another state. Yeah, that's too bad; I know he's good-looking and nice. Jesse dates every girl about three times and then moves on. Dan never dates at all. Ben's really shy. If you like him, you'll probably have to ask him out yourself."

Kendra digested this information. All the guys seemed nice, but so far she hadn't met anyone who really grabbed her attention. Mark was the handsomest, Randy was very nice and spiritual, but homely, and Jesse with the wild blond hair seemed the friendliest. But at the moment she wasn't sure if she really was ready to date again at all.

৪০ ৫৪

"Do you have plans tomorrow night, Kendra?" The Bible study at Randy's house had just ended and the young people were helping themselves to the snacks in the kitchen. Randy poured himself a glass of root beer from the bottles on the kitchen table; he smiled at Kendra. "There's a Christian band playing at a church nearby, and I was wondering if you would want to go with me."

Kendra was completely surprised. She had gotten no hint before now that Randy was interested in dating her. For a moment she just stood in silence, wondering how to respond, when a lucky memory came to her.

"Thanks, Randy, that sounds nice. I already have plans with Allison for tomorrow night. But thanks for asking."

"I know it's late notice. That's what I get for asking at the last minute, huh?"

Kendra managed a laugh in return, wondering if he was looking for encouragement and whether she should offer any. When she told Allison later in the evening, her friend scolded her.

"For heaven's sake, Kendra, we can go shopping any time. You shouldn't have used that excuse. I would have understood if you wanted to go out with Randy."

"I wasn't completely sure I wanted to go," Kendra admitted.

"Why not? He's an awfully nice guy. I'd go if he asked me."

Why did she feel uncomfortable at the thought of dating Randy? He was certainly very nice, as Allison said. But she wasn't especially attracted to him in a romantic way, and she didn't want to get paired up with someone so quickly. Besides, why did Randy, who seemed so spiritual and was the leader of the group, want to date someone he barely knew, a single mother who had only been attending church for a few months? The whole situation made her feel awkward, and she was rather relieved that she'd thought of an excuse.

Later that week she met Leanne for lunch and wondered how Leanne would have reacted to the situation.

"Are you dating anybody?" Kendra asked. She took a sip from her iced tea.

"Not right now." Leanne frowned with an expression of regret as she picked at her salad with her fork. "I dated Randy last year for about six months, but we broke up right around Christmas."

"I didn't know that." Kendra tried to picture Randy and Leanne as a pair.

"Yeah, I really liked him." Leanne hesitated a moment, as if deciding whether or not to confide in Kendra. "I think if I've ever been in love, it was with Randy. It was really hard for a while when we broke up."

With a pang, Kendra remembered Kyle and her broken heart when that relationship ended. She knew she would never want to attend a singles group with Kyle after an experience like that. "Why do you still come to the Timothy group now?"

Leanne looked up, obviously surprised. "These are all my friends," she said simply. "I don't want to lose them all. Randy and I are still friends, even though we're not dating anymore."

Kendra wondered if Leanne and Randy had been sleeping together, and blushed at the thought. Somehow she wouldn't respect Randy as much if she believed that were true.

"He hasn't started dating anyone else," Leanne added, "so that makes it easier, at least for right now."

Kendra decided that she was glad she had turned Randy down for the concert. Perhaps it was better to be friends with everyone and not date. She didn't want to ruin her new friendship with Leanne, or one of the other girls either, over some guy she didn't particularly care about. In time, when she knew everyone well and felt secure of her place in the group, perhaps she would meet someone special. For now, it could wait.

ಬ ೃ

As the months passed, Kendra had the odd sensation that she was already involved in a new relationship. It wasn't romantic, and certainly not sexual, but her new friends and her relationship with God consumed her mind in much the same way a new boyfriend would have. It was the first thing on her mind when she awoke in the morning and the one thing she looked forward to throughout the week. To study the Bible, to pray and sing together, to spend time talking and laughing satisfied her in a way that nothing else in her life ever had.

I don't think I really was a Christian before, she reflected during one of these meetings. *I always believed in God, but I never really had a relationship with him. I always knew that Jesus died on the cross, but I didn't understand that he died for me, that I was a sinner who needed a savior. And I had no idea what it meant to live the Christian life and that it involved more than just going to church on Sunday morning. I'm so glad I met these friends who can point me in the right direction and help me understand what it's all about.*

The one difficulty was what to do with Elizabeth during these events. She was able to take her to the social activities, to movie nights or game nights, volleyball or bowling, but she knew her daughter would become bored and disruptive at a Bible study. The costs of babysitting on Friday nights added up.

"My mother babysits for my nephews sometimes on Fridays, so Meredith and Scott can go out together," Allison remarked one Friday night when Kendra couldn't find a babysitter at all. "Maybe she wouldn't mind watching Elizabeth too."

Kendra hesitated to ask for such a favor. Elizabeth wasn't Mrs. Andrews' grandchild, after all. But Allison called her mother, who agreed that Elizabeth could come that night. When Kendra returned afterward to pick her up, she was glad to hear what a sweet, well-behaved child Elizabeth was, and that she played nicely with Ryan.

"I miss having little girls," Judy Andrews added, patting Elizabeth's curls. "I love Ryan, of course, but he can be so rough."

"Ryan can be really bad," Allison agreed. "Sometimes he has my sister in tears. Elizabeth is an angel in comparison."

Kendra knew that Elizabeth could be very unangelic, and couldn't help feeling lucky that Allison had such a nephew that made Elizabeth look good in comparison. Mrs. Andrews was so nice in being willing to babysit for her sometimes. It would be awfully nice if Elizabeth had a real aunt like her.

☯ ☪

The next Friday Randy led a Bible study on the fatherhood of God. The main text he used was the verse in Romans: "For you did not receive a spirit that makes you a slave again to fear, but you received the Spirit of sonship. And by him we cry, 'Abba, Father.'"

"Remember, in the Old Testament the Jews never spoke of God as their father. They called him their Creator, their Lord, their Savior, their Provider, their Deliverer, but not their father. Only Jesus called God his Father, and as God's adopted sons, we also have the right to go to him and call him Father."

They looked up many other verses that spoke of the fatherhood of God, and the discussion flowed around the room until Heidi spoke up.

"You know, I really appreciate this study, and it's especially timely for me. This week I got a call from my father. He told me that his new wife is having a baby. I guess he expected me to be happy or something, but I didn't know what to say or how to feel. Some of you know we've always had a pretty strained relationship, and it's hard for me to know how to handle it. I've always felt so rejected by him. He was never cruel or abusive, he just never seemed to care much, and he left my mother and sister and me when I was ten. Whenever we do talk, it's so difficult to feel connected to him or to feel that he cares." She stopped and bit her lip.

Kendra was sitting close enough to see that she had tears in her eyes. "I've always heard in church that God is our father, and it's hard for me to understand what that means. I love Jesus, and I love God, but it's hard for me to see him as my father. This is something that I've always struggled with, so I'm glad you decided to teach on this topic, Randy."

A brief silence greeted Heidi's words. Then Randy rose and moved his chair to the middle of the room. "I think we need to pray for Heidi tonight. Who wants to join me?"

He gestured, and Heidi rose and moved to sit in the chair. Dan and Leanne also rose and came to stand around Heidi and put their hands on her. Dan began the prayer, asking that Heidi would find healing in her relationship with her father, and the other two followed.

As Kendra listened to the prayers being offered, a new realization struck her.

God really is my Heavenly Father. I've heard that term all my life, but I never really understood it till now. Ever since – ever since January, when I went to church for the first time, he has been guiding and providing for me, just the way a father would. First in bringing me to Grace Fellowship, and then giving me a new home with Allison, and now this wonderful group of friends. Oh, Lord, you are so good to me, and I can really trust you to take care of me, just as my own father would if he were alive. Thank you for allowing me to be one of your children.

Tears of gratitude and joy pricked at her eyes as the prayer ended. She noticed some of the other girls wiping their eyes as well. For a few minutes the room seemed especially quiet, but as Randy closed the meeting the normal chatter gradually resumed. From the kitchen she heard Allison and Penny clattering dishes and laughing as they set out the snacks.

Kendra fetched a plate of snacks from the kitchen and joined Leanne and Serena, who were in the middle of a conversation.

"Did you hear what Randy said about the retreat earlier?" Leanne's expression displayed her disappointment. "There was a scheduling mix-up, so we don't get the camp for Memorial Day and after that it is rented out for the whole summer. I am so bummed. That was so much fun last year." She laughed as her eyes lit up with memories. "Do you remember how the guys threw all the girls in the swimming pool?"

Serena tossed her hair. "Jean didn't like it."

"No, poor Jean." Leanne glanced at Kendra and picked a potato chip off her plate. "Jean doesn't know how to swim, and she begged the guys not to throw her in the pool. Most of them left her alone, but one guy was determined that every girl was going in, and he dragged poor Jean, kicking and screaming, and threw her in."

"And she sank just like a stone," Serena waved a carrot stick in the air. "That was so obnoxious. Was Vince the one who did that?"

"No, not Vince, it was the new guy. I think he had a crush on Jean."

"Oh, Vince paired up with that wild-looking girl that weekend, the one with the skimpy clothes and the pierced belly-button and the tattoo." Serena laughed loudly, then lowered her voice to prevent Vince from hearing. "And Vince is the most uptight, conservative guy in the world, and nobody could figure out what they saw in each other."

Leanne giggled. "After the retreat, Steve asked Vince, 'Whatever happened with you and what's-her-name?' Vince answered in a solemn voice, 'We broke up. It was God's will.'" Leanne mimicked Vince's deep, somber voice. "Then Steve whispered to me, 'Well, I could have told him that!'"

Kendra laughed along with the others.

Serena added, "You and Steve starred in *Gone with the Breeze*. That will go down in film-making history as the worst acting ever." She rolled her eyes at Kendra, who had a question on her face. "Eddie's an amateur film buff, and sometimes he gets us to act in his productions. Last year he made a parody of *Gone with the Wind*, with these characters named Brett and Charlotte, and he got Steve and Leanne to act for him. But they were so bad that it was hilarious to watch."

"I didn't think we were that bad –"

"Oh, please, you were pathetic. You kept botching your lines, and Steve couldn't keep a straight face."

"I thought Steve was pretty funny, especially when he said, 'Frankly, Charlotte, I don't give a hoot.'"

"But he was laughing the whole time. You two were hopeless. I just hope neither of you tries for a career on Broadway."

"Who's Steve?" Kendra asked. She had heard the name several times.

"Oh, he goes to our church," Leanne said. "He's Allison's cousin."

Kendra nodded. "Allison has so many cousins; I can't keep them all straight."

"Dan's girlfriend," Serena smirked. "I always call him that because they hang around together all the time and neither of them ever dates anyone."

Leanne's eyes widened in amusement and alarm. "Do you say that to Dan and Steve?"

"Oh, all the time. Dan just glares at me with that surly expression he has. Steve always laughs."

"A lot of guys would get mad if you said something like that."

"Oh, those two guys can take it. Neither of them are girlie men."

The name Steve always created a negative sensation in Kendra, even though she knew many men with the same name. But this Steve sounded very different from the one she remembered from Gregg's party. She couldn't imagine that Steve fraternizing with her new Bible-reading, hymn-singing friends. The thought gave her a certain degree of comfort.

ಏ *Chapter Six* ಟ

"Allison, when I saw this card, I immediately thought of you." Serena added her card to the pile of birthday cards next to Allison's plate. Allison picked it up and slit it open with her finger.

The card showed a picture of a handsome man with a caption that read, "I tried to buy this for your birthday, but he escaped in the gift-wrapping department."

"The story of my life," Allison sighed. "They all manage to get away somehow. You know the song that goes, 'Good-looking guys come a dime a dozen'? I'm still looking for that department!"

"We'd all like that department," Leanne chimed in, "and it definitely isn't our singles group!"

The table of women broke into laughter.

"I think there are a lot of nice guys in our group," Kendra said.

"Oh, sure, but try getting a date out of one. They're all women-haters, or afraid of commitment."

"And now Allison's twenty-seven and never been kissed," Emma added.

The group chuckled again.

"Well, I can't say that," Allison giggled, and lowered her voice to a stage whisper, "but I'm probably the oldest virgin in Pennsylvania!"

"And doesn't want to be!" Serena laughed without bothering to lower hers. "Poor Allison's praying for deliverance!"

Another wave of laughter circled the table as Allison clasped her hands together and looked to heaven in a gesture of supplication. But her words lingered in Kendra's mind, and later that evening when they had returned from the restaurant, put Elizabeth to bed, and were having a snack in the kitchen, Allison mentioned the topic again.

"I keep wondering if I should be doing something to meet new men. I've tried visiting other churches, but that didn't work, and this is where my friends are. Unfortunately, most of the teachers in my school are women, and the only male teachers are married."

"Yeah, I can see that makes it hard to meet people." Kendra hesitated and lowered her voice, although there was no one around but the two of them. "Did you mean it when you said you're still a virgin?"

Allison set her glass of iced tea on the kitchen table and looked at Kendra. "Well, yeah. Does that surprise you?"

Kendra toyed with her half-eaten cookie as she thought of Steve and Kyle. "How did you manage that?" she blurted out.

Allison knit her brow, looking puzzled. "Manage it? What do you mean?"

Kendra felt her cheeks grow hot, but she was into the subject now. Allison certainly realized that she wasn't a virgin, anyway. "The guys I've dated seemed like they cared about sex more than anything else. Maybe I've had bad luck, but I don't think they're so unusual, from what I hear."

Allison hesitated, and Kendra sensed that she was choosing her words with care. "I try to make my standards clear up front, and I only date guys who have the same beliefs that I have. I realize, of course, that I won't date as much as some women, but that's the decision I've made, and I'm not sorry for it. I believe God will bring the right man to me eventually – although sometimes I get a little impatient," she ended with a laugh.

Kendra studied her cookie carefully. "And you actually meet men with the same standards as you?"

"Yes. I'm not saying Christian men are perfect, and some of them don't behave as well as you might wish. But the ones I've dated have always respected my position – or they didn't stick around."

"It's not like I've been with very many guys." She didn't want Allison thinking that she had been promiscuous or anything. "Only two, really. And – and I didn't really want to, either time."

Allison hesitated. "So – why did you?"

Kendra bit her lip. Should she tell Allison the whole story of Steve Dixon and the party when she was sixteen? Part of her wanted to, but when she thought of Elizabeth she stopped. She didn't want anyone to know how Elizabeth had been conceived, especially now that the child was old enough to talk and understand adult conversation. Kendra didn't want her to be stigmatized. Allison was kind and well-meaning, but it would be too easy for her to whisper the story to Serena or someone else in the group, and soon everyone would know. "Well, the first time I was only sixteen. I met this guy at a party, there was some drinking, and he – we got carried away. That's how I got pregnant with Elizabeth."

Allison was silent a moment. "Elizabeth never sees her father, does she?"

"No, he doesn't even know about her. I don't want her to see him. He was a jerk. And the second time I was dating a guy, and we said we loved each other and the whole nine yards. And then – he started pressuring me for sex. I had mixed feelings about it after everything I had been through before, but I really thought we loved each other. It seemed to me that everybody has sex. So I went along with it, and then we broke up afterward anyway."

She had tears in her eyes as she finished and bit her lip to try to hold them back. In some ways Kyle's betrayal was worse than Steve's. Steve had never pretended to care about her, and Kyle had.

For a moment Allison sat in silence, regarding Kendra with a sad, somber expression.

"I guess I've had rotten luck with men, haven't I?" Kendra forced a shaky laugh.

"You know, Kendra," Allison spoke in a decided tone, "you just need to make up your mind that you're going to wait for the right man and not let yourself be pressured into anything. These relationships clearly haven't done you any good. Decide what your own standards are and don't let yourself be talked into compromising."

Kendra smiled ruefully. "You make it sound so easy."

"Oh, it isn't easy, believe me. I've certainly had my share of temptations, and I haven't always been perfect. But I'm glad I've waited, even though I don't have men knocking down my door."

"I just hope I'll meet a guy who feels the same way," Kendra sighed.

"They're out there; you just have to look hard sometimes. The guys in our group are pretty solid, from what I've seen. Randy, Eddie, Dan, Vince – I don't think you'd go wrong with one of them." She brightened with a sudden idea. "Hey, maybe I should introduce you to one of my cousins."

Kendra nodded, wiping the last of the tears from her eyes. "You have a lot of cousins. How many of them are guys?"

"Six, but some of them are too young for you. Matt and Josh and Derek are still in high school. And Tom's married. But Joe and Steve are the right age for you. They're both nice and cute."

"That would be great." She liked what she knew of Allison's family. She giggled. "Just think, if I married one of your cousins, we would be related."

"Yeah, that would be cool. I'll have to introduce you sometime."

Kendra frowned as she took another cookie. "Do you think Elizabeth would be a problem for them?"

"I don't know. Probably not for Steve. I'm not sure about Joe. Anyway, you know Joe's mother. She's my Aunt Betsy."

"Oh, she's his mother too." It was hard to keep all Allison's relatives straight. "Maybe I've seen Joe at church sometime."

"Maybe, but he doesn't go to Grace Fellowship anymore. He's joined some big Presbyterian church."

The comment reminded Kendra of another topic she wanted to discuss with Allison. "You know, I've wondered if I should switch churches and go to yours instead. I like my church, but there aren't many single people my age. Everyone is older and married, or they're still in high school."

"Well, Grace is smaller than Bethel. Aunt Betsy's kids complained about that too. Why don't you visit Bethel sometime and see if you like it? You certainly have lots of friends there now."

"My mother keeps telling me I should be going to a Catholic church," Kendra sighed. "But I've learned so much at Grace Fellowship and the Timothy group, and I've made so many friends.

It's funny, because she never attends herself, and doesn't say anything to Gregg about going to church either, so why does she care? I guess she thinks it's better to go nowhere than to one like ours."

A thoughtful expression crossed Allison's face. "You know, Kendra, I've always wondered about your brother. He doesn't live very far away, but you never seem to spend time with each other. Don't you get along?"

"Oh." Kendra shrugged, picking up a cookie and studying it with no desire to eat it. "We sort of had a big falling out when I was in high school, and now we just see each other for holidays and things like that. We both went to Hong Kong to visit my mother at Christmas, but I haven't seen him since."

"What was the falling out about?"

Allison was not shy about asking personal questions – Kendra had already learned that. It had been a long time since she had talked to anyone about Gregg, but she was feeling particularly close to Allison tonight. Perhaps she should try to explain.

"When I was sixteen, my mother was away for the weekend, and my brother decided to have a party with his college friends." She wet her lips, groping for the right words to explain what had happened. "That was where I met the guy I told you about – Elizabeth's father – and we started making out on the couch. And – and afterward, when I found out I was pregnant, Gregg told me the whole thing was my fault, because I led the guy on. Gregg made me feel like some kind of a slut, even though he had invited the guys over and they were all drunk and using drugs."

She stopped and glanced at Allison. Her friend wore a compassionate, but puzzled, expression.

"That wasn't very nice of him." Allison frowned. "But – well, you could have told the guy no, couldn't you?"

Why had she even bothered? No one would understand, and Kendra couldn't bring herself to reveal more of the story. If Gregg, her own brother, had blamed Kendra even after understanding everything, she couldn't expect more compassion from Allison. She turned her face away so that Allison wouldn't see the sudden tears start in her eyes.

"It's hard to explain." She shrugged and rose from her chair. "Gregg and I just don't have much in common now, and it's hard to be part of each other's lives."

☯ ☪

Steve took a bulletin from the usher at the door and headed down the aisle toward his customary section of the sanctuary. He saw Eddie sitting near the end of a pew and slid in next to him. While the pianist played quietly, he opened his bulletin and scanned it. The Timothy group was playing miniature golf next weekend, and having a pool party at Heidi's house on Labor Day. He had attended the group for a few months last fall – almost a year ago now – but then decided it wasn't the right place for him – too many girls hunting for boyfriends. He wasn't ready to date again yet, and would rather not have to deal with all that. Although he did enjoy the other young people in the group. Dan and Eddie were his best friends, and he liked Heidi and Leanne a lot. If he were to date anyone, he would probably pick Leanne.

He looked up as Allison walked down the aisle beside him, followed by another young woman and a little girl around four years old. He hadn't seen either of them here before. They must be friends of Allie. He glanced at the young woman's profile as she passed him, and then stopped. She looked so familiar – he was sure he had seen her somewhere before. Medium tall, shoulder-length hair, passably cute, but with a great figure – in his old days he would have given her a seven out of ten.

Allie and her friends slid into a pew a few rows ahead of him. Steve leaned to the left so he could see around the person ahead of him, waiting for the girl to turn to the right so he could get a better view of her face, feeling oddly nervous. He knew her from somewhere. He had an uncomfortable feeling that she was some girl that he had slept with at some point in his life, but he didn't remember her name. It couldn't have been a long-term relationship. And not someone he had met in college, or what would she be doing here, two hundred miles away in Pennsylvania? That would be a bizarre coincidence. Maybe some girl he had met during one of his

Finding Father

summers at home, during the more promiscuous stage of his life.

And then he remembered. A chill fell over him and he broke out in a sweat. The girl from that party. Her name was – Kendra. The one he had remembered, and hoped he would never see again, and feared he would.

He had prayed that if God wanted him to speak to her, that he would bring her across his path. In his heart he hadn't believed it would ever happen – he had thought he was safe. But now he knew he was wrong, and that God wasn't going to let him off that easily.

ಌ ಃ

Kendra enjoyed her first service at Bethel Bible Church. She saw right away that the church was bigger than Grace Fellowship, with people of all ages. The service contained more contemporary music, with a worship team that played guitars and drums. When the pastor got up to preach, Kendra noticed that he was a bit younger than the pastor at Grace, with an energetic style.

Overall, she liked the church very much. It would be hard in some ways to leave Grace, but she had so many friends now at Allison's church. As she left the sanctuary, she waved to Ruth and Leanne and Dan on the other side of the church. She spotted Randy talking to Heidi. Allison stopped to speak to another woman in the lobby, and Elizabeth wandered off to explore.

Kendra waited by Allison's side, listening with half her attention to the story of someone's new baby. The church members milled around the large open room, chatting in small clusters. Kendra glanced around for someone else she knew.

And then she saw him. Steve Dixon.

He was standing not ten feet away from her in the lobby. For a moment she felt as if her mind must be playing tricks on her, that the person must be someone who looked like Steve Dixon, just as sometimes in the bank she might notice a man who resembled him. But there was no mistake. Steve was looking directly at Kendra with recognition in his face, wearing an uncertain expression, as if he were trying to decide whether or not to speak to her.

Quickly she looked away.

She felt her heart begin to race and the blood drain from her face, and for a moment feared that she would get sick or faint right in the church. Oh, if only Allison would hurry, so they could leave this horrible place. Of all the places she had feared meeting Steve, she had never once thought of a church!

She glanced back at him. Now he was speaking to an older man in a gray suit, who might have been one of the ushers. Steve himself was wearing a pair of khaki pants and a blue polo shirt. He looked perfectly at home, as if he attended this church every week. He looked exactly as she remembered him from the party five years before, just slightly older. The man in the gray suit appeared to be relating an anecdote, and Steve nodded and smiled as he listened.

He glanced back at Kendra, and she looked away.

Thank heaven, Allison was finished talking and they could leave! But Allison glanced around the lobby and must have caught Steve's eye, for she gestured to him. To Kendra's horror, he actually approached.

"Steve, have you met my roommate? This is Kendra."

"Hi," Steve said. He looked at Kendra, then at the ground, to the right, left, and finally back at Allison. He swallowed and wiped one palm against his slacks. Kendra opened her mouth, but no sound came out.

"Your mother tells me you're taking some graduate courses this summer," Allison said.

"Yes, I'm taking a class in Russian literature. We're reading *War and Peace* and *Crime and Punishment.*"

"Yuck." Allison wrinkled her nose. "Better you than me. But it's good that you're starting on your master's degree. I'll probably never get there."

"Well, I figure now's the time to do it, when I'm living at home and don't have many expenses." He glanced again at Kendra, who stood listening to this exchange in frozen silence.

Allison followed his gaze. "Are you ready to go? Where's Elizabeth?"

Kendra glanced around the lobby and saw Elizabeth examining a table a few yards away. "Elizabeth, honey!" Her voice sounded strange to her ears. "Come on, we're leaving!"

Elizabeth ran to her mother. Would Steve recognize her too? Of course not; he didn't know the child existed.

Kendra took her daughter's hand and almost ran from the church. She strapped Elizabeth into her car seat and waited for Allison to join them in the front. Her heart was racing as if she had run a mile and she felt on the verge of hyperventilating. As Allison climbed into the car and started the engine, Kendra took several deep breaths and tried to calm herself, hoping her friend would notice nothing unusual in her demeanor. How well did Allison know Steve, anyway?

Allison pulled into the line of cars waiting to leave the parking lot and glanced at Kendra with a bright smile. "Well, what did you think?"

Kendra's mind drew a complete blank. "About what?"

"My cousin Steve. Do you think he's cute?"

Kendra felt as if all the air had been sucked out of her lungs. "He's your cousin?" she gasped.

"Yeah, my Aunt Marilyn's son. Joyce's brother." She glanced again at Kendra, clearly puzzled by her tone. "Why? Do you know him?"

How could she possibly answer such a question? "I – I think I met him once, a long time ago."

Should she tell Allison the whole truth? She would have to think hard about that.

"Oh, that's funny. It's a small world." Allison shrugged off the coincidence as she pulled onto the highway. "But I've found that in the Christian community in this town, everybody knows everybody. So I guess it's not so surprising that you've met Steve."

"Is he a Christian?" She couldn't keep the incredulity out of her voice.

Allison glanced at her in perplexity, then laughed. "He is now. He probably wasn't when you met him. He went through a pretty wild stage back in college." Kendra thought that was the understatement of the year. "Then he started going to church again, and we heard that Pastor Mike was discipling him, and the next thing we knew, he was going around witnessing and quoting Scripture at everybody."

Kendra digested this astonishing information in silence.

The light turned green and Allison laughed as she accelerated. "I remember last Thanksgiving. My grandfather asked him to pray before we ate, and Steve prayed this long, beautiful prayer, complete with Scripture quotes and everything. The whole family just stood there in stunned disbelief. Meredith whispered to me, 'Do you believe what's happened to Steve? It's a miracle!'"

Kendra could make no reply to this. Could it be possible that Steve had really become a Christian? The idea was incredible to her, but he had certainly convinced his family. The only thing clear to her in this whole bizarre situation was that she could never set foot in Bethel Bible Church again. The thought of seeing Steve Dixon every week was unbearable.

But when she talked to her mother on the phone later that day, she found that her mother's ideas on the subject were even more drastic than her own.

"Kendra, you need to move out of that house right away."

"Move?" Kendra had already considered the idea and rejected it. "Mother, I don't want to move. This is the perfect place for Elizabeth and me."

"But now that guy knows where you live. What if he tries to find you?"

Kendra had already thought of that. "He knew where I lived for four years and he never once showed any interest. Besides, he doesn't want to see me any more than I want to see him. He doesn't want his family to know what happened."

"Kendra, guys like that have no shame. He doesn't care what his family thinks."

Kendra remembered what she knew of the Kirk family, and what Allison had told her today about Steve. She thought that he would, indeed, care. "Where could I move, anyway? It was hard enough to find this home."

"You can come out here and live with me and Gordon."

"Oh, Mother!" Living with Allison for six months had made her more reluctant than ever to move to Chicago, now that her mother had returned there from Hong Kong. "You know Gordon doesn't want us there!"

"I know, but this is an emergency. I'll explain the situation to him and he'll understand."

"I don't want to move yet. If Steve were stalking me or something, that would be different, but I don't think he wants anything to do with me either. I'll just stay away from that church."

Bonnie was silent for a moment on the other end of the phone. "You know you could get a restraining order against him."

"I know. But he hasn't done anything yet." It was strange that she found herself being more rational in the situation than her mother. "I can't get a restraining order against him for going to the church he's attended all his life. I was the visitor there, not him."

"Oh, I wish I weren't so far away! I feel so terrible that you have to deal with this all alone. I wish I were there to protect you."

Kendra bit back a tart reply, that it was a tad late for her mother to think of that. "Really, Mother, I'll be okay. It was upsetting to see him today, but I'll just stay away from him in the future. Don't worry." She paused. "The one thing I'm not sure about is what I should tell Allison. Should I tell her what happened with him?"

Her mother was silent for another moment; Kendra heard her sigh. "I don't know, Kendra. He's her cousin, after all. If you insist on staying at that house, it seems you'd only be asking for trouble. But I wish you'd think about moving."

"I know, Mother. I'll think about it."

"Please call me right away if anything happens. Please."

"I will. I promise."

She had no desire to move out of Allison's house at the moment, but on one point she had to agree with her mother. As she considered the question over and over during the next week, she felt certain that no good would come of telling Allison her history with Steve. She didn't know exactly how close Steve and Allison were, but it was only natural to assume that in such a tight-knit family Allison would feel a certain loyalty to her cousin. Moreover, she knew that it would be almost impossible for Allison to keep such a family secret to herself. Allison would whisper the story to her mother, who would tell the aunts, and soon everyone would know. They were all thrilled by Steve's supposed conversion; the last thing they wanted to hear was a tale from his sordid past.

Besides, what good would come of telling? Steve would be embarrassed, but Kendra might be even more humiliated when all was said and done. If he felt backed into a corner, he would probably respond by either denying the whole story, or trying to blame Kendra for what had happened at the party that night. And if Gregg, her own brother, had defended Steve and blamed Kendra, she could hardly expect a different reaction from Steve's own family. The whole situation would be unbearably awkward, and Kendra might feel compelled to move out of Allison's house whether she wanted to or not.

The more she considered all possible outcomes, the more convinced she felt that any benefit was so unlikely, and the possibility of shame and embarrassment too great, for her to confide in anyone. If Steve began to stalk or threaten her, of course, that would be a different story. But for now, she would rather lie low and stay out of his way, and hope that none of her new friends would ever need to know the truth.

ꙮ *Chapter Seven* ꙮ

As much as she tried, it was impossible for Kendra to keep thoughts of Steve's startling reappearance in her life out of her mind for long. How had such an incredible coincidence occurred? She relived the moment repeatedly during the following week, recalling her sensations of shock and horror. Had Steve been as shocked as she was? He had certainly seemed nervous and uncomfortable, but not to the extent that he tried to avoid her. He had clearly seen her before she saw him and could have ducked back into the sanctuary before she had a chance to notice him.

Why had God allowed such a terrible coincidence to happen? She had been so sure she had seen his hand at work in her life during the last eight months. This beautiful home with Allison, her new circle of friends – both of these had seemed like direct answers to her prayers. Had she been mistaken? Why would God use these dramatic provisions to lead her into the path of the one person she despised and feared more than anyone? It seemed like such a strange, baffling, even cruel thing to do. Could she still trust God, in spite of such an incomprehensible chain of events?

That week she had the nightmare that had come to her repeatedly since the night almost five years ago when she had first met Steve Dixon. She was on a stage at her high school, playing her favorite "Moonlight Sonata" for a big assembly, but as she played the piece she realized it didn't sound right at all. She kept hitting wrong notes and instead of the sonata she heard a loud rap song with vulgar words. Laughter spread from the back of the auditorium, becoming louder and louder. Then she looked up, and a group of boys from the school came onto the stage and began pulling her piano to pieces as she played. Panicking, she yelled at them to stop, but they ignored her and laughed as they pulled pieces from the piano. Then one of them took a piece of wire from the inside of the piano and came toward her, extending it in his hands with a vicious smile. Terrified, she opened her mouth to scream, but no sound came out.

She awoke in the dark bedroom, her heart racing. She reached for the bedside lamp, hoping that it wouldn't waken Elizabeth in the other bed.

She hadn't had this nightmare in a long time. Before Elizabeth's birth it had occurred regularly – along with another dream in which she heard a stranger moving through the house and knew that sooner or later he would find her in her room. In that dream she tried to run or scream, but her legs were frozen and no sound emerged from her throat.

When she was in high school and had these dreams, she would often get out of bed and climb in bed with her mother. Being close to her mother always made her feel safer and stronger. The only thing that would have been better was to have her father nearby. If only her father had lived, everything surely would have been different in her life. Now both her parents were so far away that she had no one she could really lean on. Only God – and he hadn't protected her that night, any more than her parents or Gregg, who had thrown the party in the first place. That stupid, awful party.

That night she had been so shocked by the sight of drugs on her kitchen table, and Steve using cocaine, that she had escaped to her bedroom, determined to stay there the rest of the night. But the party had gotten louder and louder and she was worried a neighbor might call the cops. And she had thought of Steve and how cute he was, how it had felt when he kissed her, how he had really seemed to like her, and how he might go back to college the next weekend and she would never see him again. And so in the most fateful decision of her life, she had decided to go downstairs and find her brother, to tell him he needed to get his friends under control so that they didn't get in trouble.

She had padded down the stairs barefoot, her awkward high heels abandoned, and at the foot of the stairs she turned to start down the hall to the kitchen. She saw Steve at the end of the hall, next to the kitchen doorway, talking to another girl. She was leaning against him as he was smiling at her.

Blushing hotly, Kendra ducked into the dining room before he could spot her. That room also led to the kitchen and was dark and shadowy from the light of the hallway. She started around the cherry dining table, only to stop dead at the sight of a couple on the dining room floor. The girl was sitting on top of the boy and they were –

Startled, hot with embarrassment, she beat a hasty retreat. She had seen sex scenes in movies before, but it wasn't the same. The cameras never showed everything on film. Who on earth would have sex in the middle of the dining room floor, where anyone could walk in and see? Someone too drunk or stoned to care, of course.

She backed out of the dining room. Steve was still blocking her path to the kitchen, so she ducked into the living room. The music playing on the stereo seemed louder than ever and the music had a heavy rap beat. The room vibrated with a male presence, with male bodies and loud male voices. Nervously lowering her gaze, she saw that someone had spilled his drink, leaving a purplish stain on the green carpet. Her mother would have a fit! Would that stain ever come out?

"Hey, baby." A tall blondish guy with a straggly goatee approached her. He put his arm around her shoulders. "Are you alone? Come keep me company."

Kendra tried to duck away from him. "I'm – I'm looking for my brother. Do you know where Gregg Walton is?"

The boy laughed and pulled her toward him again. He squeezed her hip. "What do you want your brother for? That doesn't sound like much fun. Stay with me, I'll show you a good time."

"No, I really need to find him – " She pulled away from him again and as she turned around, she realized that she was surrounded by boys, blocking her way to the door and the stairs.

"Hey, Pete, what do you have there?"

"This little slut isn't being very friendly."

"That's too bad. We need to help her out."

"Yeah, we need to teach her some manners."

"Come on baby, don't be so shy. We're really fun guys."

Kendra looked from one to the other, her heart beginning to pound. They were all drunk or high and she knew she couldn't reason with them. "Let me go," she begged, and knew she sounded pathetically weak and scared and feeble.

One of them grabbed her arm, another put his hand on her backside. They were all touching her, laughing all the while, and frantically she tried to push them away. She wasn't strong enough and there were too many of them. "Leave me alone," she begged. "I just want to go upstairs to my room."

One of the guys pushed her backwards and she stumbled onto the sofa. She looked up at the circle of laughing, terrifying faces above her. A picture flew into her mind of a pack of snarling dogs who smelled fear.

"Let me go upstairs! Please let me go!"

"No, you're going to give it to us right here." Pete looked around at the circle of faces. "Who wants to go first? Ray?"

Kendra's heart stopped. They were serious. They weren't joking. They weren't just playing, trying to scare her. They were serious. She tried to think what she should say, what she should do, but her mind was blank with cold fear. She had never, never imagined herself in such a situation. She began to shake.

The guys were all looking at each other as if each were waiting for someone else to make the first move. "Let's get Steve," someone suggested. "He was with her earlier tonight."

Pete grinned and glanced behind him to the living room doorway. "Hey, Steve," he yelled. "Get in here! You're gonna get lucky!"

A sense of unreality, of pure disbelief, settled over Kendra, turning her numb. Someone pushed Steve on top of Kendra. He smiled down at her.

"This girl's hot for you," Pete said. "She wants to see your moves."

Gregg! Where was Gregg? Why didn't he come help her?

"Where's my brother?" she cried in a panic. "Gregg! Gregg!"

Finding Father

The blaring music drowned out her frantic cry. The boys laughed. "Gregg can't come now, he's busy," someone said, and Pete added, "Yeah, he's doing that blonde girl out back."

Frantically Kendra searched the circle of faces for an expression of relenting. They all seemed to consider her predicament a huge joke. There were five of them and only one of her. Gregg wasn't going to come to her rescue. She could never fight them all, never.

"Don't hurt me," she whimpered as she felt herself pushed backwards onto the couch.

ಬ ಲ

During the next few days Kendra tried to block this terrible memory from her mind as she once again attempted to put the whole experience behind her. It had been a dreadful shock seeing Steve at church, but there was no reason she would ever see him again. She couldn't let herself be completely freaked out about it, or sink back into the black hole of depression that had sucked her down immediately after the party. She was glad that she was busy at the bank during the day, and in the evening she found a good book on Allison's bookshelf to fill her mind. She often used books as an escape from a racing mind and obsessive thoughts. On Sunday she returned to Grace Fellowship and Todd's Sunday school class. This church was better anyway.

On Tuesday of the next week she fetched the mail from its box as usual. As she flipped through the bills and advertisements, she saw a letter addressed to herself in an unfamiliar hand. The return address was a post office box; only the initials "SKD" in the top left-hand corner gave her a clue to the sender's identity.

Her stomach dropped and her heart began to race as the familiar sensations of anxiety, verging on panic, swept over her. She carried the pile of mail into the house where Elizabeth was playing with her blocks in the living room, dropped it on the kitchen counter, and took her letter up her bedroom, where she locked the door behind her.

She slit open the envelope with her finger and drew out a piece of lined white paper, covered in a small, neat script. She could feel her heart thumping in her chest and she had to pause to wipe her damp palms on the bedspread. She took a deep breath as she unfolded the paper.

Dear Kendra,

I was very surprised to see you at church last week, as you also seemed surprised to see me. I didn't know that you were Allison's roommate, and you probably didn't realize that I was her cousin. But as soon as I saw you, I knew why you were there and that I needed to write this letter.

I want to tell you how very sorry I am for the way I behaved the first time we met. I didn't mean to hurt you, but I know that I did. I was using alcohol and cocaine that night and was not completely in my right mind. I have thought of that night many times and have felt very terrible about everything that happened.

I want you to know that I am a Christian now, and I am trying to live a life worthy of the Lord. I don't use drugs or have sex anymore. I have asked God to forgive me for everything and I hope that you will be able to as well.

I would appreciate it if you could write back and let me know that you received this. I would also like to know what you have told Allie about us. I want to make sure we are saying the same thing. I am willing to tell my family whatever you think is appropriate.

Once again, I am sorry for any pain I have caused. I pray for God's blessings on your life.

Sincerely,
Steve Dixon

After his name he had written his e-mail address.

Kendra read the letter through twice, and then began to cry. She buried her face in the bedspread and cried deep, wrenching sobs until she was exhausted.

So Steve Dixon had a conscience after all. He felt bad about that night. He wanted to apologize, after all these years.

How could he think that saying "I'm sorry" would erase all the pain he had caused? The nightmare of the party, the fear and humiliation of her pregnancy, her mother's tears, the quarrel with

Gregg, her ruined career plans – and Elizabeth growing up without a father. How could any apology make up for all that?

She picked up the letter again and read it a third time, and a fourth. As she read, a fierce anger began to burn in her gut. He wanted to ease his conscience so he could move on with his life. He wanted her to pat his head and say, "That's all right, don't feel bad about anything." Well, she wouldn't do it. He would certainly move on with his life, but not before she let him know exactly how much suffering he had caused. He didn't even know that he had a daughter – or anything that Kendra had suffered during those nine months of fear and anguish. Just once, she wanted him to feel a tiny fraction of the pain she had endured.

She dried her eyes and washed her face and went downstairs. Allison always had an exercise class on Tuesday nights. She waited until Allison had left for the evening, opened her old laptop, and found her e-mail. Her fingers created a furious clacking on the keys as she typed.

Dear Steve,

I received your letter. I want you to understand exactly what you did to me.

The night I met you at that party, I was only sixteen years old. I had never used drugs or had sex in my life. That night, you and your friends ganged up on me and told me I had to have sex with you whether I wanted to or not. It was the most terrifying experience of my life, something I will never forget. Afterward I had nightmares for many months. Then when I realized I was pregnant, I prayed that God would let me die. Fortunately that didn't happen, and I have been able to build a new life with God's help. But it has been very difficult, and my life will never be the same as it was.

I know that as a Christian I'm supposed to forgive you, but I don't know how to do that. Maybe you could pray for me about that.

She stopped and looked at the sentence she had just written. Why had she written that? She meant it facetiously, but would Steve take it that way? She decided to leave it in.

As for Allison, I just told her that I had met you once a long time ago. I don't see any reason to reveal all the sordid details.
Kendra Walton

She read the letter through one more time and hit the Send icon. Finally, after all these years she was able to speak her mind to Steve, and the accomplishment gave her a flash of bitter satisfaction. But had she said the right thing? Maybe she should have waited and not written back right away. Maybe she should have thought it over for a while first. Either way, it was too late now.

෨ ෬

She heard nothing more from Steve Dixon for several days and began to wonder if her angry response had cowed him into keeping his distance. If he had expected a reassuring note of forgiveness, he was certainly disappointed, perhaps angry or embarrassed, and probably would avoid any communication in the future. But on Friday evening she received an e-mail in reply.

Kendra,
Thank you for your note. I'm glad you wrote back, although it was a hard letter to read.
I wish there was something I could say or do to erase all the pain that I caused you. I guess that is impossible now. I can only tell you again how very sorry I am. I wish I could go back in time and change the past, but I can't.
You seem to imply that I am responsible for your daughter. If that is the case, I hope you will let me know what I can do to provide for her. I want to take responsibility for my actions.
Allie seems happy that you are living with her. I hope you are happy there as well. She is a great girl.
Once again, I hope you will let me know if there is anything I can do for you.
Steve

Kendra read the terse little note several times. Should she

respond to this letter, or simply ignore it? It seemed to contain a dismissive tone, as if Steve were tired of apologizing and wanted to put the whole episode behind him. Or was she misreading him? It was so hard to tell in a letter.

But he had guessed that Elizabeth was his daughter. She hadn't intended to tell him that, but clearly she had. In her first flush of anger she had wanted him to be aware of the life-changing consequences of his actions. But how should she respond now? She didn't want Steve Dixon involved in Elizabeth's life, and she guessed that he didn't want to play a father's role, either. "I want to take responsibility for my actions," he'd said. What he really meant was that he hoped he wouldn't have to, that Elizabeth was someone else's problem. He didn't care about his child, and he didn't deserve her.

She was too shaken by the whole confusing mess to respond to Steve immediately. What can of worms had she opened with her hasty, ill-judged e-mail? She needed to talk to someone, to seek counsel, so the next day she called her mother and tearfully spilled the whole story into her ear. Her mother was the one person on earth who knew everything and had stood by her.

"Kendra, Kendra, Kendra!" Her mother's alarm traveled clearly through the phone lines. "Why on earth would you tell him about Elizabeth? What were you thinking, honey?"

"I wanted him to know that he had a daughter." Kendra's voice broke as she brushed her tears away with the back of her hand. "I wanted him to care about her – to care about all the damage he did."

"Oh, honey." Bonnie sounded like she wanted to cry as well. "Don't you get it? Now that he knows about Elizabeth, you might never get rid of him. He could make your life hell. He could – he could go to court and try to take her away from you."

Kendra felt a cold fear fall over her body. "He couldn't do that, could he?"

"He might not be able to get custody, but he could certainly try. You could spend thousands of dollars trying to fight him in court. He could get your friend Allison to say you're an unfit mother. Believe me, if you've heard some of the stories of custody battles I've heard, you wouldn't take any chances."

"But – but he doesn't want Elizabeth! He's never cared anything about her!"

"He might do it out of spite. Or – or to make himself look good to his family. You never know what a guy like that will do."

Kendra stared unseeing at the carpet at her feet, horrified by the possibilities her mother had suggested. "So – what should I do now?"

Her mother's voice was urgent. "Write back to him and tell him it was all a mistake. Tell him he misunderstood. Tell him – tell him that you had a boyfriend in high school and he was Elizabeth's real father. Tell him whatever you have to say to make him go away."

Kendra bit her lip and swallowed hard. "It just seems like I'm letting him off the hook too easily. He should pay for what he did."

"Of course, in a perfect world he should. He should have gone to jail, but he never will now. You don't want this guy in your life or Elizabeth's life. If you don't get rid of him now, you never know what might happen. Trust me on this one, Kendra."

The sensible part of her knew that her mother was right. She didn't want Steve Dixon hanging around, making her life miserable. After hanging up, she opened her laptop and began to compose a response.

Steve,

Thanks for getting back to me. I think you misunderstood what I meant in my last message. I actually had a boyfriend at the time that I met you and he was Elizabeth's real father. I shouldn't have blamed you for that, but it felt like your fault because the two things happened around the same time and –

She stopped, swallowed, and reread what she had just written. It really made no sense. In spite of her mother's warning, her pride revolted at the thought of telling such a ridiculous story. Steve might believe it because he wanted to believe it and she was giving him an easy out. But was it right to lie? And what about Elizabeth and her needs? She couldn't imagine that Steve would, or could, actually be a real father to the child in any way, but someday Elizabeth might need something from him – like a kidney maybe –

and if Kendra lied now, he would never believe her later.

What he really wanted was a balm for his conscience, an excuse to walk away without feeling guilty. She could give him that without resorting to a lie. She deleted everything she had written and began again.

Steve,

Thanks for your concern. You don't need to worry about me or Elizabeth. We are fine and don't need anything from you. We're happy living here with Allison. You are right: Allison is a nice girl and a good friend. I think it would be best for us both to go our separate ways. I hope that God will continue to work in your life as he has so far.

Kendra

She read the letter over several times before she sent it. She felt rather proud of the last line. It sounded very spiritual and even a bit patronizing. Surely this would give Steve the closure that he needed to move on with his life and stay out of hers for good. For herself, she could not imagine any such closure.

Chapter Eight

"Do you want to swim a little, honey?" Kendra held out her arms. Elizabeth jumped to her and Kendra managed to catch her before she went under the water. She bounced the child in the water a few times, making Elizabeth giggle. "Here, you hold onto my shoulders and swim after me, okay?"

She paddled in the shallow end of Heidi's pool, pulling Elizabeth along behind her. Even the shallow end was over Elizabeth's head, and she still couldn't swim. By next summer the little girl would be five, so maybe then Kendra should find a place for her to take swimming lessons. From the grill in Heidi's backyard where Randy and Jesse were working, the scent of hot dogs and hamburgers drifted over to them. The guys had brought the meat to the Labor Day party, and the girls had brought salads and drinks.

"Mommy, can I have a hot dog?"

"Sure, honey, just ask Randy for one. You might have to wait a minute until they're done."

She lifted Elizabeth to the edge of the pool and watched her run off, then swam the length of the pool several times, her mind drifting back to the e-mails she had exchanged with Steve in August. To Kendra's relief, she had heard nothing more from him in several weeks by e-mail or letter. Clearly he had gotten the message that she wanted him out of her life as well as Elizabeth's. Probably he was equally relieved to be allowed to walk away from such a messy, uncomfortable situation.

But he had asked for her forgiveness and Kendra felt confused whenever she remembered the request. What did forgiveness mean in a situation like this? Did God expect her to erase the past from her mind, to blot out the memory of the night of the party and all her suffering afterward? Did he expect her to conjure up some sort of benevolent emotion toward Steve Dixon? At the moment she felt nothing positive at all, nothing but residual anger and the intense desire to never see him again. Perhaps that was the best sort of forgiveness she could manage – for the two of them to go their separate ways, to put the past behind them, and agree not to interfere in each other's lives. She believed she could manage that level of forgiveness. As for anything more, she felt completely inadequate.

After several laps she climbed out of the pool and sat on the edge next to Heidi and Serena, letting her feet dangle in the pool as the water ran down her body in trickles. She could hear that the two friends were involved in an intense conversation.

"Why would Jesse invite him?" Serena was saying. "He doesn't have any business here. That really upsets me. I'm going to talk to Randy about it."

"What are you talking about?" Kendra asked. "Who did Jesse invite?"

Heidi sighed. "There's a couple in our church who are separated, but not divorced. The elders are trying to work out a reconciliation. Anyway, the husband said something to Eddie and Jesse about coming to the pool party today. Eddie wasn't sure how to respond, but Jesse said, 'Oh, sure, you should come. That would be great.'"

"He's married!" Serena spoke in the loud tones she used when she wanted to make a point. "He doesn't have any business coming to a singles group!"

"Well, it's always difficult with people who are separated but not divorced. On the one hand, we want to encourage people to reconcile with their spouses and not act like they're single when they're still married. On the other hand, when someone's been abandoned by their spouse, they need the support of a group like this. They feel so alone."

"Al wasn't abandoned by his spouse!" Serena swung her long

wet hair back from her face. "He was beating her."

Heidi winced. "How do you know that?"

"Well, that's what Allison told me and her father is an elder. He should know. And his wife has been living with the Weldins. They told me that Al calls the house all hours of the night and screams at whoever answers the phone. He's a nut case."

"That's awful," Kendra shuddered. It was equally clear to her that the church was like a huge family and nothing could be kept secret among its members.

"I didn't know that." Heidi swung her feet in the water, frowning. "I know he still sees his kids. I ran into them at McDonald's a few weeks ago."

"Oh, it takes a lot for a man to lose his parental rights. Usually it doesn't matter what he does to the mother, as long as he doesn't hurt the children. But I don't understand why Jesse would invite him today. If he shows up, all the men should get together and throw him out. I'd do it myself if I could."

"Well, Serena, Jesse didn't know all this. He was just trying to be friendly, I'm sure."

From the corner of her eye Kendra saw someone open the gate to the back yard and cross the grass to the tables under the trees. She turned to see Steve Dixon.

Her stomach dropped with the now-familiar feeling of sickness and dread, and her heart began to race. Not Steve again! What was he doing here?

Heidi saw her startled movement and turned in the direction of her gaze. "Oh, there's Steve. I invited him, but I wasn't sure he would come." She raised her hand to wave to him, but Steve was looking in the opposite direction.

So Heidi knew Steve as well. Did everyone in the church know him? Kendra tried to keep the tremble out of her voice as she spoke. "I've never seen him at this group before."

"He came for a little while, but he dropped out last fall, I think." Heidi stopped as if unsure how much to say.

Serena grinned. "That was after what's-her-name."

"Kim."

"Right." Serena laughed loudly. "Every time Steve walked into the room, she was over by his side with her tongue hanging down to the ground."

Heidi shook her head with a regretful expression. "That was too bad. Steve thinks all the girls in this group are looking for boyfriends. That's why he never comes anymore."

"That's a stupid reason. I'm not looking for a boyfriend."

"I know."

The conversation moved on, but Kendra didn't hear it. Her attention was fixed on Steve and every muscle in her body tensed to escape if he came near her. But he seemed to show no interest in the pool or awareness of Kendra's presence. She saw Leanne go over and hug him, and then he turned to talk to Ben and Dan. After a few minutes he wandered over to the food table and helped himself to a plate of food.

Kendra suddenly wished that she were wearing her clothes. Her bathing suit was as modest as any of the others, but she felt naked and exposed. She reached for her towel to cover herself if he approached.

Instead of coming to the pool, when Steve finished his food he walked over to where Elizabeth was kicking a ball around the grass. Kendra froze and her heart raced as she saw him speak to the child. Elizabeth smiled and answered him. They began to kick the ball to each other, Steve shortening his kicks to match Elizabeth's shorter strokes.

Kendra gripped her hands together until they hurt. She couldn't stop Steve from talking to Elizabeth or playing with her – not without making a scene that no one would understand. She could only watch and make sure he did nothing to hurt her daughter.

After a few minutes, Elizabeth ran to a tire swing hanging from one of the trees. Steve lifted her into the tire and gave her several pushes before returning to his friends. Kendra felt the muscles in her shoulders and arms slowly relax.

Finally Elizabeth climbed out of the swing and ran to her mother's side. "Can I swim again, Mommy?"

"Sure, honey." Kendra slid into the pool and took her daughter in her arms. Kendra held her under her arms and pulled her through the water.

She swallowed and hoped that her voice was normal. "What was that man saying to you, honey?"

"He asked me my name. He asked if I lived with Aunt Allie. He asked how old I am, and when my birthday is, but I couldn't remember."

Kendra felt a flash of alarm. Steve had asked about Elizabeth's birthday, and he was certainly clever enough to count nine months off on his fingers. Well, the date was no secret; Steve could find out somehow if he really wanted to.

She glanced back to the group under the trees. Steve and Eddie headed toward the house and disappeared inside. A few moments later they reappeared wearing swimming trunks, with towels slung over their shoulders. Kendra scrambled out of the pool and lifted Elizabeth out with her.

"Can I have a cookie, Mommy?"

"Sure, honey. Get a cookie, and then we're leaving." With shaking fingers she wrapped her towel around herself as she saw the two men, along with Randy, move toward the pool. "Run over to the table with the food and look for one. I'm going into the house to change."

Elizabeth ran off. Kendra headed toward the house, glancing once at Steve as she passed him. He met her eyes and nodded in a brief acknowledgment. He was just as handsome as he had been five years ago at the party, and the realization filled her with helpless anger.

It wasn't right, it wasn't fair that he could treat women like dirt and just walk away. It wasn't fair that he could ruin her life while his was so perfect!

She collected her clothes inside the house and went to the bathroom to change, furious thoughts bubbling up in her mind. She would love, absolutely love, to tell all Steve's nice Christian friends what she knew about him. She would love to humiliate him the way he had once humiliated her. And she would do it too – she would do it, if she only knew that they would take her side, not his. They had all known Steve, and his family, much longer than they had known Kendra. If she forced them, whom would they choose?

From outside she could hear someone calling her name in a

high tone of alarm. She pulled her shirt over her head and ran to the back door. Leanne was reaching for the door as Kendra opened it.

"Kendra, Elizabeth fell in the pool!"

Her heart dropping in horror, Kendra raced to the pool and the cluster of adults beside it. Elizabeth was huddled in the midst of them, sobbing and blubbering, with Heidi kneeling beside her. Thank God, she was alive. She was breathing!

Kendra dropped to her knees and gathered her child in her arms, heedless of her dry clothes. "Oh, baby, what happened? Are you all right?"

"I tried to go swimming," Elizabeth sobbed. "And it was too deep – I couldn't breathe – I was scared –"

"Oh, honey, I'm so sorry!" Kendra kissed the wet hair as guilt smote her. "I shouldn't have left you out here alone. But I thought you would be okay with so many people around." She could have lost Elizabeth that quickly. The truth was that she had been so distracted by Steve's appearance that she had forgotten the danger of swimming pools to small children.

"Serena and I had gone to get something to eat, and we didn't see her." Heidi's blue eyes filled with tears. "But Steve saw her in the water, and he pulled her out right away."

Kendra raised startled eyes to Steve, standing a few feet away, his dark hair plastered to his head, watching the scene with a grave expression.

"I think she's more scared than hurt," Serena added. "She couldn't have been in the pool for more than a few seconds."

"She coughed up some water at first, but she seems better now." Randy patted the child's wet curls. "You're okay, aren't you, honey?"

Kendra wrapped a towel around her daughter and lifted her in her arms. She glanced once more at Steve and met his gaze briefly. "Thanks."

As she carried her child across the grass to one of the chairs under the trees, she realized with a sense of irony that it was the first word she had spoken to him in five years.

Several nights later she woke in the middle of the night from another dream. This dream was different from the piano-playing one that had frightened her in the past. She was at a meeting of the Timothy group and Steve was there as well, talking to the other men. She couldn't hear his words, but she could tell by the way that they were all laughing and looking in her direction that they were talking about her. Then Serena laughed in her typical mocking tone, "Yes, Kendra, we've heard how you were all over Steve from the moment he walked in the door." Heidi shook her head with a sorrowful expression and said, "Really, Kendra, you need to learn how to behave better with men." Kendra began to cry and cry uncontrollably, but no one comforted her or displayed any sympathy for her distress.

She awoke in her dark bedroom, her heart racing and sweat chilling her body. What if Steve really told all of her friends what had happened between them? She would be so humiliated – she would never be able to show her face at the group again. It would be almost as terrible as what had actually happened to her five years ago.

In the cold, rational light of day, as she fed Elizabeth and dressed and drove to work, it seemed far less likely that Steve would actually brag about his behavior that night to his Christian friends. Still, he might mention it to someone. If he even told one person, like Dan or Eddie, in a moment of weakness, the story could spread, just like the story about the man at church who beat his wife. She cringed at the thought of everyone whispering and talking about her, about what had happened. She would have no choice but to drop out of the group if something like that happened.

The effect of the dream was so powerful that she almost decided to stay home from the Bible study the next Friday night. Scolding herself for her cowardice, she forced herself to go, but sat on the edge of her chair until it became clear that Steve did not intend to make another appearance. Maybe his visit to the pool party had been a fluke. Heidi had invited him, and he had decided to come and be sociable. But surely he didn't want to be part of a group that included Kendra and Elizabeth any more than she wanted him there. If he ever joined, she would certainly have to drop out. And she didn't want to drop out. Her new friends had become more important to her than anything else in her life, anything except Elizabeth.

      ಬಿ ಚ

As the weeks slipped by and Steve did not show his face again, Kendra allowed herself to relax. No one treated her any differently than before or seemed remotely aware of any connection between her and Steve Dixon. She continued attending the Bible studies and the occasional activities. Early in October, Jean announced that she and Penny were planning a Halloween party for November first, and that Allison had agreed to host it.

Serena spoke up after this announcement. "I don't think we should do that. As Christians we shouldn't be celebrating Halloween. It's a pagan holiday; it glorifies witchcraft."

Vince shrugged. "It's just a kid thing."

"No, I used to know people who were into witchcraft, and they celebrated Halloween. It was their special day."

"I agree with Serena," Heidi said. "I don't think we should do anything that might offend people, whatever you think about Halloween."

Jean glanced around the room, looking for consensus. "I just wanted to have a costume party. We've never done that before, and I thought this might be a good time for it."

"Could we just have a costume party and not call it a Halloween party?" Mark suggested.

Kendra looked up from the pocket calendar where she recorded all her activities. "November first is All Saints Day. Couldn't we call it an All Saints Day party?"

"Because we're all saints," Jesse grinned.

"Maybe we could all dress as famous Christians," Heidi suggested. "I'd be Susanna Wesley."

Allison laughed. "That's perfect for you. But let's not be too particular about costumes. It's hard to come up with ideas for costumes, anyway."

"No witches, ghosts, or goblins – nothing to do with the occult," Randy said, and everyone seemed satisfied.

Kendra had an Indian girl costume for Elizabeth that someone had given her, and decided to create a similar one for herself, so that she and Elizabeth could be mother-and-daughter Indians. On Saturday morning she helped Allison prepare the house for the party. She had long ago discovered that her idea of cleaning before company was quite different from Allison's. "These are my friends. I'm not going to clean the house from top to bottom every time I invite people over," Allison had said the first time Kendra brought out all the cleaning supplies. But Kendra couldn't be comfortable with letting her friends see a dirty house, and insisted on scrubbing her upstairs bathroom in case someone needed to use it, even though Allison told her she was wasting her time.

She changed into her costume and helped Elizabeth on with hers, then braided their hair into two short braids. Elizabeth's dark hair almost looked like an Indian's when it was braided, except for the wisp of curls that kept escaping its confinement. Allison dressed as a fifties girl in a poodle skirt and cardigan sweater, with bobby socks, her blonde hair pulled back in a perky bow. As their friends arrived they admired or laughed over the other costumes as well. Serena, draped in veils, looked like an Arabian princess. Heidi, as promised, wore a seventeenth-century outfit that could pass for Susanna Wesley. Leanne dressed as a Southern belle and announced that she was Scarlett O'Hara or Melanie Wilkes, whichever they all preferred. Dan was a pirate.

"Actually, that suits you, Dan," Kendra remarked as she surveyed his attire, "but this is supposed to be an All Saints Day party, and I don't think there were any Christian pirates."

Dan raised his eyebrows with his sardonic expression. "You don't think so? I would guess, somewhere along the line, some pirate somewhere became a Christian."

"John Newton," Allison suggested. "You know, the guy who wrote 'Amazing Grace.' Actually he was a slave trader, but that isn't very different, is it?"

"I would think pirates and slave traders dressed alike in the eighteenth century," Jean, a Raggedy Ann doll, pointed out. "We'll call Dan John Newton, to make him more respectable."

Allison glanced at Kendra. "Can you help me set out the food and drinks?"

Serena followed them into the kitchen, and as they worked she told the other two about her disagreement with her boss and how completely unreasonable he was. "And he's like that with everyone, not just me. Erica had vacation planned months ahead of time, and he made her cancel it because he gave several others permission to take vacation that same week. It was so ridiculous, we could have covered for Erica, but he was just making life difficult, and now he's doing the same to me –"

Kendra listened with half her attention. Serena always seemed to have some complaint about her boss. In fact, Serena seemed to complain a lot about different people in her life, especially authority figures, and Kendra was never sure how many of her complaints to believe.

She heard the front door opened and someone called out, "Hey, Steve! Great costume, man."

She stiffened and her heart fell. After neither seeing nor hearing anything from Steve Dixon for two months, she had begun to hope he was gone from her life for good – that the first two meetings were simple coincidences. This time could be no coincidence. He certainly knew that she would be at this party: she lived here.

As she listened to Steve greet the others and laugh over some of the costumes, she tried to brace herself for the moment she would see him. She knew it would be impossible to avoid him in such a small, indoor gathering, and all her pleasure in the evening was ruined.

A moment later he appeared in the kitchen. He wore a sheet wrapped around himself like a toga and a crown of leaves on his head.

"Hey, did you see that pirate get-up Dan's wearing? What a hoot. And Randy in that Superman costume! Vince looks like some weird Japanese beetle. Where did he get that idea?" He laughed heartily as he took a brownie from a plate on the table. "You girls look great, too."

Allison cocked her head to one side. "So, which Roman are you supposed to be, Steve? Caesar? Cicero? Caligula?"

He grinned as he took a bite. "Actually, I'm one of the Christians that they threw to the lions in the Coliseum."

Allison shook her head. "I don't think they wore togas, Steve."

"Sure they did. I'll bet some of them did, anyway."

Serena laughed as she set a vegetable tray on the table. "You look more like a frat boy to me, Steve. Like one of those guys in *Animal House*."

He shrugged. "Well, my fraternity used to throw toga parties, and this is the only costume I know how to make."

"I should have known." Allison rolled her eyes. "Just make sure that sheet doesn't fall off you in the middle of the party."

"Don't worry. I can handle my costume. I'd be more worried about Serena. She looks like she's ready to get up and dance for us."

"Oh, don't start." Serena made a dismissive gesture as she set down the ice bucket. "Vince already gave me a hard time about my costume."

"I would think Vince would like your costume. Doesn't he want a girl in a veil?"

Allison laughed. "That's good. Vince and a girl in a veil. I can picture it."

Steve glanced at Kendra as if to speak to her, but she turned away and opened the freezer to fill the bucket with ice. Maybe she couldn't keep him from coming to the party, but she didn't have to look at him or speak to him.

Elizabeth ran into the kitchen and surveyed the spread on the table. Steve stepped back in exaggerated surprise. "Look at you! You look like an Indian princess. Are you Pocahontas?"

Elizabeth glanced down at her costume with a pleased look and nodded.

"Pocahontas was a Christian too," Steve added. "She was baptized before she married John Rolfe."

Dan passed through the kitchen to the back door, his arms full of pumpkins. "Steve, can you give me a hand with these?"

Allison glanced over her shoulder. "Kendra, can you find some newspaper and spread it on the table on the deck?"

Kendra found the paper and spread it on the table while Dan, Steve, and Jesse carried the pumpkins through the house and set them out. "I don't suppose there's anything heathen about carving pumpkins, is there?" Jesse asked.

Dan shrugged. "If there is, I'm sure somebody will tell us about it. Heidi, probably."

Kendra had turned to go back in the house when Steve spoke to her in a hesitant tone. "Kendra, would it be okay if I brought Elizabeth out here and carved a pumpkin with her?"

Kendra bit her lip. But the request seemed harmless enough, and with Dan and Jesse listening, it would sound churlish to refuse. "I guess so."

Dan said, "We need some sharp knives out here too, Kendra."

Kendra fetched the knives and returned to the kitchen, a sense of helpless frustration filling her. A moment later she saw Steve and Elizabeth pass through the kitchen to the back deck, and she positioned herself near a back window so she could watch them as they worked. She hoped Steve would at least have sense enough to keep Elizabeth from touching the knives.

Steve chose a pumpkin, cut out the top with a knife, and began to scoop out the seeds. He talked to Elizabeth as he worked, and although Kendra could not hear the words, she saw the child nod and answer him. Together they turned the pumpkin around, choosing the best side for the face. Elizabeth pointed to show where the features should go. She gave a little jump of excitement as he began to cut.

Seeing them together, side by side for the first time, Kendra found the resemblance startling. She had always known that Elizabeth did not favor her in appearance, but the child's similarity to Steve was eerie. The same hair, the shape of the face, and especially the smile, that beautiful smile that had dazzled Kendra the first night she met him. The shock of it was like a blow. What if someone else noticed the resemblance and guessed the truth?

And then another idea occurred to her. In the last nine months Steve had attended two events of the Timothy group. Both of them were after he had met Kendra, and both were activities where she would be likely to bring a child. Could he possibly be coming here on purpose to see Elizabeth?

The idea, at first, seemed incredible. Could Steve actually have paternal feelings for this daughter he had just discovered? It seemed impossible that any man could love a child conceived under such circumstances. But she could not avoid the evidence right before her eyes.

What if she had given Elizabeth up for adoption, as she had once considered? And what if, four years later, she discovered her daughter living nearby? Would she be able to walk away for the second time – or would she be drawn back, again and again, for one more glimpse of her child?

Could Steve possibly be struggling with those same feelings?

She felt tears sting her eyes and turned away from the window. A moment later the door behind her opened.

"Look, Mommy! Look what we made!"

"It's lovely, honey." Kendra bent down to examine the toothy jack-o-lantern, hiding her face from Steve. "You did a nice job."

"Can I put it in our room?"

Kendra hesitated. Steve said, "Not in your room, Elizabeth. He needs to be kept cold so he doesn't spoil. Let's put him on the front step where everyone will see him."

"Okay!" The two of them carried the pumpkin out the front door. Kendra walked to the sink and wiped her eyes, hoping to gain control of her emotions before she had to join the others.

"Kendra, come here!" Kendra looked up to see Leanne in the kitchen doorway. "We're getting ready to play Bible baseball, and you have to be on our team."

Kendra shook her hair back from her face and tried to compose her features. "Bible baseball? What's that?"

"You've never played it? It's an old game; we used to play it in the youth group when I was a kid."

Kendra followed her back to the living room where the party was dividing into two teams. She and Leanne were on a team with Jesse, Ruth, Dan, and Jean. When Steve returned from the front porch, Leanne recruited him as well. Dan dragged four chairs in from the kitchen and set them up as bases.

The other team was up to bat first, and scored run after run until they finally got three outs.

"These teams aren't fair," Jean objected. "They have Vince, Allison, and Randy."

"Oh, don't worry, we'll be fine." Steve lowered his voice to his teammates. "Three of you go first and ask for singles. Then I'll bat you all home with a home run."

Kendra was glad to ask for a single. She had only been reading the Bible for less than a year and was well aware of her lack of knowledge. She smiled at the question Randy pitched to her. "What queen saved the Jewish people from destruction?"

"Esther!" That was one story she knew well. She moved to first base.

Steve's turn came next. He took the seat on home plate; he glanced around the circle of faces and grinned. "Home run."

Randy read from the list of questions he held. "Name the seven churches of Revelation."

One team hooted while the other team groaned. Kendra hadn't even known there were seven churches in Revelation, let alone their names. Steve frowned and drummed his fingers against the arm of his chair. "Now let me think." He began to count them off on his fingers. "Ephesus...Smyrna...Pergamum...Laodicea..." He paused. "Thyatira..."

A long silence followed. "You forgot the easiest one," Allison whispered loudly.

"Philadelphia!" He gave her a triumphant look.

He was silent again for a long moment. "Time's up!" Serena called.

"Now give me a minute; I had to think of seven names." His face lit up. "Sardis!"

His team cheered for him and Steve made a great show of rounding the bases by moving from chair to chair. He was such a show-off. Kendra rather wished he had missed the question, even if it made her team lose.

Next was Jean's turn, and she got a double. Ruth made the first out.

"Do you know what this game reminds me of?" Leanne lowered her voice to Kendra and Ruth, sitting beside her. "When I was a teenager and had a date, my father would sit me down beforehand and say, 'Remember, Leanne: you're the pitcher. You control the ballgame. You don't want him to get on base.'" She giggled. "So now, whenever I see a baseball game, I remember my father saying that."

Jesse, on the other side of Ruth, glanced at the girls with a grin. "That's great! I'll have to remember that when I have a daughter. A long, long time from now."

"It might not be so long," Leanne teased him.

"Don't say that! Sometimes I'm afraid I'll wake up someday with a wife and three kids and I won't even know how it happened."

Dan glanced at him sideways. "I know just what you mean, man. It's a nightmare I have."

"You guys!" Leanne shook her head. "If we're still around then, we'll be sure to explain to you how it happened."

Steve looked around the group. "Leanne, you're up again."

Leanne took the seat at home plate. Someone from the other team called out, "What's this about Jesse having a wife and three kids?"

"It's Dan," Leanne explained. "He keeps them in his room and only lets them out at night."

Elizabeth wandered into the living room, yawning and looking for her mother. It was past her bedtime already. With a sudden desire to escape the conversation, Kendra took her by the hand and led her upstairs. She helped her into her pajamas and helped her brush her teeth. She knelt by the bed and listened as Elizabeth said her prayers.

"Thank you, God, for this nice day, that I could play, and that I could make a pumpkin..."

Kendra kissed her daughter on the forehead and stared down at her before turning out the light. Already Elizabeth's eyes drooped with sleep; her dark curls framed her face like a halo. She was so beautiful.

Steve Dixon was nothing to Elizabeth, nothing but a sperm donor. He had given her some healthy and beautiful genetic material, but nothing else. He didn't deserve a lovely daughter like Elizabeth. He had never tried to be a real father to her. After four years, it was too late for him to walk back into their lives. And after the way he had treated Kendra, she certainly owed him nothing at all.

❧ *Chapter Nine* ☙

"Do you want to come in for some dessert?" Kendra paused at the front door, her hand on the knob. She had cut her date short to keep down her babysitting costs, and inviting him in seemed like the courteous thing to do.

Sean brightened a bit. "Sure, that would be great."

It was their third date after talking and texting for a few weeks. So far she hadn't allowed more than a kiss on the cheek at the door, and she had the feeling he was getting impatient. Maybe inviting him in hadn't been such a great idea. She liked him, but she wasn't sure how much.

Inside she paid the babysitter, checked on a sleeping Elizabeth, and dropped a kiss on her warm cheek before she returned to the kitchen, where she cut two slices of pie and carried them to the living room. She sat beside Sean on the couch, keeping a careful space between them. Sean smiled wryly as if he could read her mind.

"What are your plans for tomorrow?" she asked hastily, hoping to move the conversation onto some safe, prosaic ground.

He shrugged, closed the magazine he had been reading while he waited, and took the pie from her. "Sleeping in, I hope. In the afternoon I'm going to a friend's house to watch the football game on TV. What about you?"

She crossed her legs and swallowed a bite of pie. "I have church in the morning, and in the evening they're having a pot-luck dinner. We have one every few months, and I wanted to take Elizabeth to this one."

He frowned in thought. "You're pretty involved in your church?"

"I am now." She had wanted to broach the topic with Sean all along, but hadn't found a real opening until now. "I just started going to church about ten months ago. Well, I went when I was a kid, but it didn't mean much to me back then. I never really understood it all. When my father died, my mother stopped taking us, and I didn't go again until January, when a friend invited me." She groped for the right words, to explain the difference it had made in her life. "I've learned so much about God in the last year. I never knew what it meant to have a relationship with God before. I've learned that he really does love me in a personal way, and I really can pray about anything, and he takes care of me just like it says he does in the Bible."

Her words sounded awkward and clumsy to her own ears, and she could tell by the blank expression on Sean's face that they meant nothing to him. She decided to try a different tact. "When I moved in with Allison, she introduced me to all her friends at her church too. They are the best friends, the nicest people I've ever known. I've never known people like them who really love God and want to follow him. The last year has been the most exciting time of my life, learning about God and meeting all these new friends." Yes, it was true, in spite of Steve Dixon's unwelcome reappearance in her life.

"Hey, that's great." She could hear the note of forced enthusiasm in his voice. "My sister's religious, into church and all that kind of thing. I've never really gotten into it."

She made one last try. "Maybe you could come to one of the activities we have sometime and meet my friends. You'd probably like them."

"Sure, maybe I could sometime." He avoided her eyes. "I went to my sister's church once to see her get baptized. Her preacher was a real yeller, and he kept singing the last hymn over and over, trying to get people to come up front. It was pretty wild. I thought we'd never get out of there."

Kendra swallowed. "My pastor doesn't do anything like that."

"Well, that's good. Hey, did I ever tell you about the guy my

Finding Father

sister married? He's kind of obnoxious, always lecturing everybody about religion and politics at family get-togethers. Nobody likes him, but we have to invite him, because he's family. My brother always invites me to his house at the beach, but he never invites our sister, because of her obnoxious husband."

Kendra stared down at her folded hands. "That's too bad. It's a shame when you don't get along with your family. I have a brother I don't feel very close to, but I tolerate him because he's my brother."

When Sean left, she climbed the stairs to her bedroom and dropped down on her bed in the light from the hallway, staring up at the dark ceiling in discouragement. Sean hadn't tried to kiss her this time, so she had the feeling this was their last date. Which wouldn't bother her much if she didn't feel like such a flop. Her effort to explain her faith to Sean had fallen completely flat. Some of the others in the Timothy group talked about sharing with their friends, and often mentioned the positive results they saw. What had she done wrong?

Allison peeked in the bedroom door. "Well, how was the date?"

"Oh, all right." Kendra pushed herself to a sitting position as Allison joined her on the bed, whispering so as not to wake Elizabeth in the next bed. "We had a nice time, but I don't think it's going anywhere. I mean, we're just friends."

Allison nodded; she looked relieved. "Well, it's good you're finding that out now, before you get more involved."

"I wish some of the guys from church would ask me out sometimes," Kendra burst out. "Randy is the only one who ever did. Maybe I should have said yes."

Allison grinned. "I told you to go, didn't I? But I know what you mean, it's really frustrating. We used to have a joke about our college group that applies to the Timothy group too. What's the difference between the girls in this group and the trash? The trash gets taken out once a week."

Kendra laughed. "That's good."

"Most of the guys in this group don't date much. Or they date very casually and just try to be friends with everyone. Dan and Steve and Eddie call themselves 'Bachelors till the Rapture,' and they're always trying to convince the other guys to join their group.

It's a joke, but very annoying. I know Eddie used to like Heidi a lot, but haven't seen him with anyone in a long time, and Dan and Steve never date either."

Kendra didn't ask questions about Steve or mention his name if she could avoid it, but she couldn't help remarking, "Those two don't seem like they would have a hard time finding girlfriends."

"Oh, no. Steve used to date all the time back in his heathen days. Aunt Marilyn used to complain about the sleazy-looking girls he would bring home with him. I don't know about Dan. I think he was engaged once, but I don't know any of the details. But you're right, either of them could go out with anyone he wanted."

Kendra had been bracing herself for her next meeting with Steve, and had almost determined to speak with him whenever that occurred. She had to tell him that this situation was intolerable, that the two of them couldn't belong to the same group, that one of them would have to leave if the other was going to stay. She had almost resolved to speak to him, but not quite. She dreaded the prospect of the conversation, dreaded the awkwardness of it, and dreaded what she guessed Steve's response would be. He would very likely tell her that she was free to stay or leave, but she had no right to tell him what to do. And if he said that, she would have to make a decision. Should she walk away from all these friends who had become so important to her, or should she make up her mind to grit her teeth and tolerate occasional encounters with Steve?

Surely God didn't want her to lose all her new friends, who had become such a positive influence in her life. God had answered her prayers in others areas; perhaps she should pray about this problem as well. So every night before she went to bed, she added in her prayers, "Lord, please let Steve go away so I never have to see him again."

She felt a twinge of unease when she prayed this, although she wasn't sure why. Surely it wasn't an unreasonable request. She didn't want to hurt Steve in any way, retaliate or humiliate him or take vengeance, which she certainly had the right to desire. All she wanted was for him to stay out of her life. Surely God would understand how difficult the situation was for her and would honor her request.

ೞ ೖ

Steve whacked the ball across the net and grinned as Jesse jumped for it, and missed. "Okay, that's the game, and the set," he called. "Are you guys done? Do you want to play another one?"

Dan took his cell phone out of his pocket and checked the time. "I think I'm done. Actually I'm getting hungry, and it's almost dinnertime."

"It's getting cold." Eddie rubbed his hands on his bare arms.

The weather was mild for mid-November, but the sun was setting. "You could put your sweatshirt on," Steve pointed out.

"Naw, I can't play when I'm all bundled up."

The four men collected stray tennis balls and headed for the door of the court. "Do you all have something going on with the Timothy group tonight?" Steve asked.

Dan shook his head. "We had a Bible study last night, so there's nothing tonight, unless we just hang out at someone's house. You could come to my place if you want."

"We could go to Allison's," Jesse suggested. "Do you think she'd mind?"

Dan slid his racket into its cover and zipped it. "Maybe not, but I don't know if she has plans. Why Allison's?"

Jesse grinned a bit self-consciously, glancing from one to the other. "Actually I was thinking about asking Kendra out, but I haven't made up my mind. Have any of you gone out with her yet?"

A moment of silence greeted this news. "I haven't," Eddie said.

Dan frowned. "What about Ruth? I thought you two were an item."

"Oh, no, we went out a few times, but we're really just friends."

"I'm not sure Ruth would agree with that." Dan's mouth curled with irony.

Jesse shrugged the comment off. "I've called Kendra a few times, but nothing more than that yet. She's not as pretty as Heidi, but she's got a great body." Noticing Dan's frown and Steve's sudden involuntary glare, he added, "Oh, come on, don't tell me you've never noticed."

Steve said nothing.

"Anyway, I'd probably ask her out, but being a single mother and all, she might get expectations. She probably doesn't want to just date for fun, and I don't want to get serious too fast."

"I don't know why you'd assume that," Dan shrugged. "She's no more desperate than anyone else in that group. Just ask her out if you like her. But I'm not going to drop over Allison's, since I don't know her plans. I'll grab some dinner and head home, if anyone wants to come with me."

"I might come over later," Eddie said. "I have some stuff to do first."

Eddie and Jesse left. Steve and Dan headed to their cars, parked next to each other.

"I guess I shouldn't have encouraged him to ask her out," Dan remarked as he opened his trunk to put his rackets in. "Poor Kendra doesn't need that complication in her life."

"Jesse? A complication?"

"Oh, maybe you don't know him very well. A different flavor every month. I always feel sorry for the latest one, because I know he's not going to stick around, but I guess he doesn't do any serious damage. Well, do you want to come over?"

Steve hesitated. At first he had wanted to, but now a sense of dejection was settling over him and he didn't want Dan to notice and ask him about it. "Maybe later, like Eddie said. I told my mom I'd be home for dinner, so I'd better be there or she'll get annoyed."

"Okay, see you later then."

He climbed behind the wheel of his car and watched as Dan drove off. For a moment he just sat, staring after his friend, wishing he could open up and spill the whole problem and that somehow talking would help solve it. But it wouldn't, and he couldn't. Dan was his best friend and Steve believed he would understand, but it would be an even worse betrayal of Kendra, adding insult to injury. Slowly he turned the key and shifted into gear.

There was no logical reason he should feel this upset over the conversation that had just passed. The comment Jesse had made about Kendra was no worse than what most of the guys had observed for themselves, if they weren't blind. And Dan was

Finding Father

criticizing Jesse's behavior, not Steve's. He knew his reaction was part of the irrational depression that had settled over him in the last few months, descending on him at the most unexpected moments, when he was having fun with his friends, talking with his family, or especially trying to worship. He felt like a voice was whispering in his ear, *They don't know the truth about you. Who are you trying to kid? You thought you could put your past behind you and start all over, but you were wrong. This is something you can never leave behind.*

He had believed that when he became a Christian, he had been wiped clean, given a fresh slate, a second chance in life. Now he saw that was an illusion. He could repent in sackcloth for the rest of his life, but he could never fix his former reckless, irresponsible, selfish behavior. If God really loved him and forgave him, why would he bring Kendra into his life again? It could only be that God wanted to see him suffer as payback for his sins.

And yet, he couldn't blame God when it was all his own fault. He couldn't blame anyone else, even Kendra, for this mess – except maybe Pete and Ray and the other guys who had set him up and then egged him on. But he wouldn't go there. He had made enough excuses for himself during his life, and that was how he had ended up where he was.

He had attended Heidi's pool party because a part of him couldn't stay away – he had to know if Elizabeth Walton was really his daughter. He had left that day with no clear plan of action, just a conviction that he had to know the truth. Then he'd heard about the costume party and was drawn back again, to see his daughter one more time, to see if he might have a real relationship with her. She was beautiful and adorable and seemed happy carving the pumpkin with him. But he knew Kendra was displeased, even hostile, and he ended up with even less certainty about what to do next.

He had looked at all the old family photos and could easily see that Elizabeth was a cross between himself and his younger sister Joyce when they were the same age. Then he checked the public records and found that Elizabeth's birthday was almost exactly nine months after the party where he remembered meeting Kendra the first time – in August, just before he returned to college for his sophomore year. And he was pretty sure that Kendra had told him the truth when she had said she was a virgin until that night. Maybe those facts all together didn't absolutely prove his paternity – it was possible that Kendra had a high school boyfriend she hadn't mentioned, and the physical resemblance might be coincidental – but short of a DNA test they were pretty conclusive.

He was almost sure that Elizabeth was his – but what could he do, and what should he do? He prayed for guidance, but the more he turned the situation over in his mind, the more convinced he felt that either God or the Devil was mocking him. If he just walked away – as Kendra had told him to do – he would be haunted by the fact that he had abandoned not one, but two children, and had completely shirked his responsibilities. Besides, it was Kendra's desire for him to leave, not Elizabeth's. Shouldn't her needs be considered too? With all his faults, surely he would be a better father than none at all. Wouldn't he?

But how could he possibly be a father to Elizabeth with Kendra so hostile to him? He could go to court and ask for a paternity test, and then demand his parental rights. But it seemed cruel to take Kendra to court when he had already hurt her and made her life so difficult. Surely that would be the worst action of all. And if he won, he would be a constant reminder to her of a terrible experience that she surely longed to put behind her and forget as much as possible. He had observed enough of Kendra's reaction to him on the few occasions when they had met to know that she would never voluntarily allow him to be involved with her daughter.

Since he had no good options, it seemed like such a horrible joke that God would bring this child into his life under these awful circumstances. Whenever he tried to pray, he would be weighed down by an oppression that left him mute. When he saw Kendra, or heard her name, or even thought about her, he felt an overwhelming sense of shame and despair. He had no one to talk to about any of this. Dan, Eddie, Randy – they were all Kendra's friends. His mother would be devastated, and he had already hurt her enough. He couldn't imagine telling his father – they got along well enough, but hadn't been close since his parents' divorce. He just couldn't respect his father's moral judgments anymore.

He opened the front door to smell dinner cooking and could hear his mother moving around in the kitchen. The phone rang and he heard her answer it. She said, "Steve, is that you? The phone is for you."

He went to the kitchen and took the receiver. "Hello."

"Steve? Hey, it's Jay Grady, from church." Jay was one of the leaders of the worship team. "I was wondering if you're planning to be home on Thanksgiving weekend."

"I think so," Steve said. "I wasn't planning to go anywhere."

"We're planning to visit some relatives in Ohio, and I was wondering if you could fill in for me and lead worship that Sunday."

Steve's heart sank. He had done it before, back in the spring a few times after Jay had discovered he had a reasonably good voice. In his present frame of mind the prospect was depressing, but what excuse did he have? "I guess so," he muttered.

"Great, thanks, buddy. I'll get you a list of songs to choose from, and send you the sermon topic when Pastor Mike sends it to me. With Thanksgiving that week it might be difficult to practice, so you can talk to Keith on guitar and Lindsay on piano and decide how you're going to work it. Thanks a lot, man."

"You're welcome," Steve said with a heavy sense of irony, and hung up.

His mother looked up from the stove. "Steve, could you set the table for me?"

"Sure." He pulled the plates out of the cupboard. Only three – Joyce was off at college.

"What did Jay want? Was it about the worship team?"

"Yeah." Steve slapped the three plates around the table. "He asked me to fill in for him Thanksgiving weekend."

"Great!" She looked so happy. "I think it's wonderful that you've been helping out with that. Such a great fit for your talents."

"Yeah, I guess." He had made his mother's life miserable during the years directly after his parents' split, and he knew that her pride and happiness over his spiritual growth were in direct proportion to her former despair. Six months ago he had shared her enthusiasm, but now nothing could shake the blanket of oppression that seemed to be smothering him.

☯ ☪

"I'm glad Gregg was able to make it today," Bonnie remarked as she sipped her coffee and nibbled on a slice of pumpkin pie at the kitchen table after their Thanksgiving turkey. She and Gordon had returned from Hong Kong during the summer and were now settled in Gordon's house in Chicago, where Kendra had visited them once. They had come to Pennsylvania to spend Thanksgiving with the two young people. "I don't know if I told you this yet, but Gordon and I have agreed that we're going to alternate families for holidays. Last year we spent Christmas with you and Elizabeth, and this year Gordon wants to spend it with his daughter in Minneapolis. She has a new baby, and we haven't seen him yet."

Kendra's heart fell. For some reason she had assumed that she would always have her mother for holidays, anyway. She should have known better; she shouldn't be surprised. "So I guess Elizabeth and I will be alone for Christmas this year." She tried not to sound as dejected as she felt.

"I'm sorry, honey." Bonnie patted her daughter's hand with an anxious frown. "Don't you have any friends you could spend Christmas with? What about all your new friends at church?"

Kendra shrugged. "They all have family around." If anything was worse than spending Christmas alone, it was intruding on a strange family and their celebration.

"Well, maybe you could join one of them. Maybe you could go with Allison to her family."

Kendra shook her head, trying to look unconcerned. "No, I don't want to do that. Elizabeth and I can do something together. We'll be okay."

When she mentioned her disappointment to Allison, her friend was full of sympathy.

"It's hard, when people get married and have to divide their time," Allison acknowledged. "Meredith is going to Scott's family this year, so she won't be with us. It will be strange without her and the boys."

But Allison still had her parents and another sister. Kendra had no one except her daughter. It was hard not to feel alone and abandoned.

"Why don't you and Elizabeth come with me to my mother's?" Allison suggested.

Kendra shook her head. "We'll be okay. We'll find something fun to do together. I just wish I could see my mother, that's all."

"That would be strange," Allison agreed. "People expect their kids to get married and leave home, but not their parents."

She had a whole month before Christmas to get used to the idea and try to come up with a positive plan. She enjoyed shopping for her daughter, and Elizabeth, at four, was just at the age to get excited about the holiday. Allison left the house decorating up to Kendra, and Kendra found a small tree that she set up in the corner of the living room and decorated with a mixture of the ornaments they each owned. She mailed gifts to Chicago and received a large box full of presents from her mother in return, which she set out under the tree.

Elizabeth was beside herself with excitement. She had recently learned to write her own name and examined all the tags on the gifts to determine which were hers. Kendra could barely keep her from opening them before Christmas.

"Next year I'll keep them all hidden until Christmas morning," she sighed to Allison as she taped up a present that had been partially ripped. "I don't remember her being this impatient last year."

"I remember when I was a kid, sneaking into my mother's walk-in closet to try to find my Christmas gifts," Allison laughed.

Kendra shook her head with a grin. "I was such a perfect child. That idea never even occurred to me."

Chapter Ten

On Christmas morning Kendra was awakened by the pattering of little feet running out of the bedroom and down the stairs. Kendra buried her head under the covers and tried to doze off again. Ten minutes later the same feet came running back up and into the bedroom. "Mommy, wake up! It's Christmas! We have to open our presents!"

Kendra moaned and rolled over. "In a little bit, Elizabeth. We won't open the presents until Aunt Allie wakes up."

Elizabeth ran out of the room and down the hall. Kendra heard her jumping on Allison's bed. "Aunt Allie, wake up! It's Christmas!"

Sighing, she rolled out of bed and pulled on her jeans and a pretty Christmas sweater. Stumbling down the stairs, she went to the kitchen, turned on the coffee pot and began to scramble eggs. Allison appeared as she was setting the table, using the poinsettia dishes that Allison kept on the shelf above the refrigerator.

"So much for sleeping in," Allison grinned. "Well, isn't this nice, a real breakfast and everything. I never make eggs for myself."

"Are you eating with us?" Kendra set forks around three places. "I made enough eggs for you."

"Yes, I'm not going to my mother's till about noon. I told her I wanted to watch Elizabeth open her presents."

Kendra felt a rush of gratitude. At least Allison would be with them in the morning. It would be almost as nice as having her mother with them.

They forced Elizabeth to wait until they had eaten before they gathered round the tree. The child was bouncing with excitement. "Now, we take turns," Kendra explained. "You open two gifts, then I'll open one, and then we have to give one to Aunt Allie."

Allison gave Elizabeth a music box and a necklace bearing her initial. From her mother and grandmother she received books, a new movie, a game of Chutes and Ladders, a pretty frilly dress, and a box of artwork supplies. Kendra received clothes from her mother and a music CD from Allison. She gave Allison a pair of dangly earrings.

"Now, Elizabeth, here is one last gift for you." Allison handed the child a long rectangular box. Elizabeth ripped off the paper and opened the lid to reveal a large doll in a Victorian dress.

"It's an American Girl doll!" Allison picked up the box to examine it more closely. "My little cousins, the twins, each got one last year. They have a Mexican girl, a Civil War girl – this one is the Victorian girl. This is a really expensive doll. Elizabeth is probably too young to appreciate it."

Kendra had seen the box under the tree and had assumed the gift came from Allison, but her friend seemed as surprised by it as anyone. She found the tag on the discarded paper. It bore Elizabeth's name in large block letters, but nothing more. "Did you give her this, Allison?"

"Me? I love Elizabeth, but not that much," Allison laughed. "No, I came home from work one day and found it by the front door. I assumed your mother had sent it."

Kendra shook her head, frowning over the tag. "My mother would have put her name on it, and she would have told me if she bought Elizabeth something like this."

"Your brother, maybe?"

Kendra shrugged. "Maybe." Gregg had never given Elizabeth an expensive gift or one that required much thought, but anything was possible. "Maybe he was in a generous mood this year."

"Well, Elizabeth, this is your lucky day. Take good care of that dolly and she'll last a lifetime." Allison began to gather up the discarded wrapping paper, crumpling it into a ball. "I guess I need a shower before I go to my mother's. Why don't you come with me, Kendra? I hate to think of you and Elizabeth eating here alone."

Kendra hesitated. The idea of a solitary dinner was less than appealing to her as well. She had baked a pumpkin pie the night before, but there was no point in roasting a turkey for two people. Elizabeth began to jump up and down and clap her hands. "Oh, please, Mommy? Let's go with Aunt Allie! Please?"

"I guess she always has fun at your mother's house," Kendra smiled. "Do you think your mother would mind?"

"I'll call, but I don't see why she would. We always have plenty of food. I told her I'd be there by noon and help her get set up."

Kendra found her spirits rising at the unexpected change in plans. Maybe it would be better than staying home alone, after all. "I'll bring the pumpkin pie that I made last night."

The mouth-watering scent of a roasting turkey, mixed with apple pie and a myriad of other odors, greeted their noses as soon as they stepped into the Andrews' home. As they entered the kitchen Kendra set her pie on the table, which already bore candied sweet potatoes, cranberry sauce, and creamed onions. Judy Andrews was setting stacks of plates and glasses on the counter.

"Do you want us to help set the table, Mom?" Allison began piling silverware from a drawer onto a tray. She handed Kendra a stack of napkins.

"That would be great. We set up a table in the living room and another in the playroom downstairs for the children."

Kendra glanced from the mountains of dishes on the counter to the stack of napkins in her hand, a sudden strange feeling in her gut. "How many people did your parents invite?"

"There are twenty-eight this year," Judy told her. "No, thirty, with you and Elizabeth. Everyone will be here except Meredith and Scott."

"Thirty!" Kendra stared at Allison in sudden horror.

"It's the Kirk family," Allison explained helpfully. "My mother's family. We always get together on Christmas."

Kendra felt her heart sink down to her feet. "I thought – I thought it was just your parents and sister!"

"Oh, no!" Allison shook her head as she led the way to the dining room and started to lay out the knives. "Only four of us! What kind of Christmas would that be!"

It was exactly the kind of Christmas Kendra had spent every year of her life. What a fool she had been! She should have thought to ask if Allison would be spending Christmas with her extended family. All her aunts, uncles, and cousins – including Steve Dixon.

She felt almost sick at the thought of Steve's reaction when he realized that Kendra and Elizabeth had intruded on his family's holiday. She knew she would be furious if the situation were reversed. He might not be angry, but he would certainly be uncomfortable, perhaps annoyed, that she had showed up here with his daughter that none of his family knew about. This time she couldn't blame the encounter on him. It was totally her own fault. But what could she do about it now? Could she feign sudden illness and ask Allison to take her home? But that would seem very strange. Moreover, Elizabeth had wanted to come and would cry at the sudden change of plans.

Automatically she began setting the napkins around the table while her mind wrestled with her dilemma. No brilliant solution occurred to her. She and Allison were finishing the table in the living room when the doorbell rang. In a near panic she retreated to the kitchen, her mouth suddenly dry.

"It's Uncle Dave and Aunt Lisa," Allison sang out.

The house suddenly vibrated with the noisiness of children and the laughing banter of teenage boys. Lisa Kirk appeared in the kitchen with a large casserole dish in her hands. Kendra was introduced to Lisa and her daughters, identical blonde girls of nine or ten.

Perhaps, with so many people in the house, Steve wouldn't even notice Kendra or Elizabeth. Perhaps she could just hide here in the kitchen all day. No, that didn't seem very likely or practical.

The door opened again and Allison's grandparents arrived. Kendra wondered how long it would take to fake a sudden illness. Allison had disappeared now. Kendra tried to make herself invisible in a corner of the kitchen.

She heard one of the boys say, "The Dixons are here!" and her heart sank. It was too late now to make her escape. Oh, this would be so unbelievably awkward and uncomfortable! Why hadn't she just stayed home?

Hiding in the kitchen, she heard the front door open and a female voice call out, "Merry Christmas!" Amid the chorus of responses from the family, she heard Steve's voice saying, "We have songbooks in the car," and, a moment later, in a tone of surprise, "Well, hello! What are you doing here?"

Elizabeth skipped into the kitchen with Steve close behind her. He met Kendra's eyes as he set a covered dish on the kitchen table. She needed to explain, and she might as well do it quickly.

"Allison invited us." She could feel the heat rising up in her neck to her face as she pushed out the explanation. "I thought it would only be her parents and sister; I didn't know the whole family would be here."

"Oh, we always have a big crowd for Christmas." He glanced back at Elizabeth with a smile. "Tell me about your Christmas. Did you get any nice gifts?"

As Elizabeth began to recite her litany of presents, Kendra suddenly thought of the mysterious doll that had appeared at the front door. A gift his young cousins had received the year before. But she could never work up the courage to ask, and she doubted he would ever tell. She pushed the question from her mind.

"Wow, you sure got a lot of nice things." Steve nodded as the child described her new toys and games. "You know, I have a little cousin who's just the same age as you. Have you met Abby?"

Elizabeth shook her head. Steve glanced around the kitchen and spotted one of the twins across the room. "Sarah! Becca! Sarah!"

The girl turned around. "I'm Sarah!"

"Sorry. Do you know where Abby is?"

His cousin came toward them. "I think she and Becca are downstairs in the playroom."

Steve laid his head on Elizabeth's curls. "This is Elizabeth. She's visiting today. Could you take her downstairs and show her Aunt Judy's toys?"

Sarah took Elizabeth by the hand and led her off. Steve smiled at Kendra. "Sarah will take care of her and show her around."

Of course, Steve didn't know that his own aunt – Elizabeth's great-aunt – had often babysat for his daughter. Kendra felt a rush of embarrassed relief. At least he didn't seem too annoyed to see them here. Maybe the day wouldn't be so bad after all.

Betsy Reese spotted Kendra as she entered the kitchen and greeted her warmly. "Oh, Kendra, I am so glad that things are working out with you and Allison. You know, I had such a feeling about giving you her number, a conviction almost. I'm so glad it's working out well."

"I'm glad too," Kendra smiled. "I really like living there."

Betsy pointed out to Kendra her four adult children, two young women and two attractive young men, and her baby granddaughter who was being passed from arm to arm. "I just love being a grandmother. It's just as nice as I always heard tell. I'm sure your mother must miss having her granddaughter nearby."

Kendra heard someone call, "Aunt Marilyn," and she picked out Steve's mother from the bustling crowd of women in the kitchen, a slim, petite, proper lady in a white blouse and green sweater. She identified his sister Joyce as well, a pretty, dark-haired young woman who resembled her brother. She could easily imagine Joyce as an adult version of Elizabeth.

How strange to think that Elizabeth was actually related to this whole family! These were all her aunts, uncles, and cousins, even her grandmother, but none of them knew it. What would they say if they did know, if they ever found out? Kendra felt a chill of apprehension at the idea. No scandal had ever touched this family before. They would be shocked and embarrassed at best, horrified at worst. Well, they would never know. She and Steve were the only ones who had any idea, and neither of them would ever tell. This was a secret she would carry to her grave.

A small girl about Elizabeth's age came crying into the kitchen and Kendra heard her mention Elizabeth's name to her mother. "What's wrong?" she asked Allison with sudden anxiety.

Allison grinned. "Abby is upset because Sarah and Rebecca both want to play with Elizabeth instead of her. Elizabeth is the novelty, and Abby feels left out."

Judy Andrews opened the oven and took out a huge platter of sliced turkey. "Now Abby, run downstairs and tell those girls it's time to eat. Tell them Aunt Judy said to come up right away."

The whole family crowded into the kitchen and dining room,

and Mr. Kirk, Allison's grandfather, asked one of his grandsons to pray. After the prayer, everyone stood in line and filled their plates from the array of dishes on the kitchen table. Kendra waited until she saw Steve head downstairs to the table in the basement with one of his male cousins, and she found a seat with Allison upstairs. Elizabeth scampered off with her new friends with no concern for her mother at all.

There was more food than they could all eat, even with thirty at the tables. Kendra listened to all the talking and laughter around the dinner table and tried to remember the names of the girls near her, Allison's cousins. Betsy's daughters were Kate and Anne, Allison's sister was Heather, and of course there was Joyce Dixon, the easiest to recognize.

"You look so much like your brother," she remarked to the girl when Joyce glanced in her direction.

Heather laughed. "Poor Joyce! Imagine looking like Steve all your life!"

Anne swallowed a bite of sweet potatoes. "Yeah, you never could deny knowing him, no matter how much he embarrassed you."

"Oh, I've heard that all my life! It's the Dixon genes. They're too powerful. We both look like our father, and I think that annoys our mother."

"They're divorced," Allison informed Kendra in a lower tone. "Don't worry, Joyce, you're a Kirk at heart, even if you look like a Dixon."

So Steve's parents were divorced. Kendra hadn't realized that. She felt a twinge of surprise at the news.

When they finished eating she helped Allison and Heather clear the table, fold it up, and put it away. "We always sing in the living room, and we need the space," Allison explained. "Just leave the chairs in here. We need them too."

The whole family began to gather in the living room, and Lisa Kirk went to the piano and opened it. Kendra found a seat on the end of the sofa and someone handed her a hymnal. "What do you want to start with?" Lisa asked.

"'O Come All Ye Faithful,'" someone called out.

They sang carol after carol, all the old familiar ones like "Joy to the World" and "Silent Night," and some that Kendra was less familiar with: "O Come, O Come Emmanuel," "Once in Royal David's City," and "Break Forth, O Beauteous Heavenly Light." Kendra had to follow most of the words in the hymnal, but she was surprised that many in the family knew all the words by heart, even the third or fourth verses. They sang parts as well, alto, tenor and bass. The men sang "Good Christian Men Rejoice," and Betsy's red-haired daughter Kate sang a solo of the Amy Grant song, "Breath of Heaven" in a poignant, lovely soprano. Kendra could not help glancing at Steve from time to time, and was oddly surprised to see him singing with everyone else. Once she thought she could hear him doing a tenor part.

In between some of the songs, Mr. Kirk called on his grandchildren to read scripture passages aloud that he had assigned for them.

Anne Reese read, "For to us a child is born, to us a son is given..."

One of the teenage boys read, "A shoot will come up from the stump of Jesse; from his roots a Branch will bear fruit."

Steve read, "The people walking in darkness have seen a great light..."

The singing went on for almost an hour. Halfway through, Elizabeth came to climb onto her mother's lap and sucked her thumb, listening to the music around her.

"Number 92," Steve called out at the end of one song. Pages flipped in the hymnals.

"That's not a Christmas carol," someone objected.

Steve grinned. "But it's my favorite hymn."

"Oh, we can sing this for Steve," his mother said.

So Lisa began to play and the family joined in. Kendra had never heard the hymn before, but everyone else was clearly familiar with it, and she followed the words as they sang.

Long my imprisoned spirit lay,
Fast bound by sin and nature's night;
Thine eye diffused a quickening ray,

I woke, the dungeon flamed with light.
My chains fell off, my heart was free,
I rose, went forth, and followed Thee.
Amazing love! How can it be
That Thou, my God, shouldst die for me?

"Now the twins would like to recite a passage that they've memorized," Lisa announced. "It's the second chapter of Luke, verses one through sixteen."

The nine-year-old twins stood up in the middle of the room and began to recite. One of them giggled and faltered as she quoted, while the other one plowed with determination.

"Today in the town of David a Savior has been born to you: he is Christ the Lord..."

Everyone clapped when they finished. Then each girl had to take a turn at the piano and play a piece she had memorized.

"Does anyone else want to sing or play anything now?" Mr. Kirk asked, glancing around the crowded room, at his children and grandchildren on chairs and sofas and sprawled on the floor.

Allison turned to Kendra. "Kendra, why don't you play something on the piano?"

Kendra shook her head, nearly panic-stricken at the idea. She often played Allison's piano at home, but never played in front of people. "I don't have any music with me." Thank goodness she had that excuse!

"You have something memorized, don't you? What about 'O Holy Night'? I hear you playing that all the time."

Kendra frowned at Allison, hoping her friend would take the hint and drop the suggestion. It had been years since she had performed, and somehow playing for Steve and his family seemed worse than anything. But Betsy Reese chimed in, "Come on, Kendra, I've never heard you play the piano," and even Mr. Kirk added his urging to the others. To continue to refuse would seem ungracious.

Reluctantly she rose, her hands shaking, and made her way to the piano. For just a second she had a flashback to her awful nightmare. But once her fingers touched the keys her memory took over and she played the whole piece without a mistake. When she finished, she had to play it twice more so the family could sing along.

"Truly he taught us to love one another, His law is love, and his gospel is peace..."

It was all so different from the quiet, uneventful holidays that she usually spent with her mother and Elizabeth. For a moment, as the song ended, she felt a sad yearning for...what? For her daughter to actually be accepted and acknowledged by this family, to be included in all their family events? But unfortunately the family also included Steve, and that made it impossible. She didn't want anyone to know that Steve was Elizabeth's father; if they knew, no one would understand why she didn't want Steve involved in her daughter's life.

"We always watch a movie on Christmas night," Allison told her as everyone rose and stretched and some of them wandered toward the kitchen for drinks and dessert. "We bring our Christmas movies, and every year we pick one."

"*It's a Wonderful Life!*" Kate called out, glancing over her shoulder as she poured herself a glass of tea.

"We watched that last year," one of the men objected.

"Did we? I don't remember that."

"Let's have a comedy this year. Did anyone bring *While You Were Sleeping*?"

A dozen of them gathered in the family room, and someone inserted the disk into the player. It had been several years since Kendra had seen the story of orphaned Lucy, adopted for Christmas by a family who mistakenly believes she is engaged to their son. She laughed along with the rest of the family at the twists and turns of the plot and avoided looking at Steve, who sat in a big rocker across from her.

Elizabeth had disappeared after the singing with the other little girls, and Kendra heard giggling and girlish voices from the playroom in the basement. About halfway through the movie the child wandered into the family room, yawning and looking for her mother.

"Elizabeth!" Steve called, patting the large chair he was sitting in. "Come sit with me!"

Finding Father

Elizabeth looked at him, then willingly climbed up beside him. Kendra looked away and focused her attention on the movie. The son had just awoken from his coma and didn't recognize the girl he was supposed to be engaged to. But his family refused to let him off the hook and told him he had amnesia.

"Look at Steve," Allison whispered to Kendra a few minutes later.

She glanced at him. Elizabeth had fallen asleep against him and her head had fallen forward to rest on his chest, while Steve sat with his arm around her. His cousins all glanced at him and grinned at the picture the two made.

"Isn't that cute?" Allison laughed.

"You look very avuncular, Steve," Kate remarked.

Kate's husband said, "I was going to say he looks very paternal."

"He's practicing for the future," Joyce added.

Kendra said nothing and turned back to the movie.

☙ Chapter Eleven ☜

One January morning at work, Kendra got called into her boss's office. Her trepidation eased a bit when she saw the smile on Diane's face.

"I just wanted to talk to you about your future here." The woman gestured for Kendra to take a seat across from her desk. "You've been a very good employee; you're very dependable and a hard worker. Now I realize you don't have a college degree; if you did you might qualify for a management position. But there are some promotions that you might be able to get even without a degree."

"I hope to get a degree someday." Kendra spoke in a tone of regret.

"Yes, I understand the situation you're in with your daughter. But if you could take a few evening courses, that might qualify you for a better position than you have now. I'd like to recommend you for one, and it would help if you were working toward your education. There are some courses beginning in early February at the community college. You might want to sign up for one."

When she got home that evening, Kendra found the course selection list online and, after considering her options, decided to enroll in a Tuesday evening accounting course. She had always done well in math and wasn't worried about the work itself; she was more concerned with fitting the class in her busy schedule. In particular, she would need to find a babysitter for Elizabeth on Tuesday nights; she couldn't take the child to a college class. If only her mother weren't so far away! She could ask Allison occasionally, but she tried to avoid imposing too often. That was the hardest part of being a single parent: feeling that she was so alone, that she had no one else to assume part of the responsibility.

༄ ༅

Kendra stepped up to the counter at the bowling alley, hearing the clatter and swish of rolling balls and falling pins in the lanes behind her. "I need size eight, and a child's size ten," she said, and the man behind the counter set two pairs of bowling shoes in front of her.

She was opening her purse to pay when she saw Steve a few feet away, joking with Jesse and Ben, although she couldn't hear his words over the noise in the alley. The now-familiar tension and irritation rose in her as she paid and then turned away to put on her bowling shoes. Steve again! At least he was always polite to her and friendly to Elizabeth, but she still didn't like to see him.

Elizabeth had already spotted the snack bar. "Mommy, can we get something to eat? I'm hungry."

"Elizabeth, don't start begging for food right away!" Her tone was sharper than she had intended as she jerked on her shoe laces. "I just spent all my money on the bowling! We're not buying anything to eat. Here – I have a few cookies in my purse."

She was helping Elizabeth on with her shoes when Randy called out, "Kendra, are you ready? We need a fourth in our group. Bring Elizabeth too."

She joined the group that included Penny and Jean, relieved to be separated from Steve for the evening. She felt irritated and moody, and her spirits were not improved by her performance at bowling. She felt so clumsy and uncoordinated, and to her embarrassment kept throwing gutter balls. She was hardly playing any better than Elizabeth.

At the end of the first game Steve came over to her lane. She ignored him until he walked up and spoke to her directly.

"Kendra, would it be all right if I took Elizabeth to get something at the snack bar?" He always spoke to her in a hesitant tone that differed from his normal jocular, confident demeanor; he looked as if he were afraid she might bite him.

The speech she had memorized, that she had planned to give him at their next encounter, came to her mind. Now was her opportunity. She could take him aside and let him know how unwelcome his presence in this group was to her. But somehow she couldn't bring herself to make that speech.

"Sure," she shrugged, and turned away.

Steve took Elizabeth by the hand and the two of them headed for the snack bar. A few minutes later she saw them eating French fries together and laughing. At least Elizabeth was happy; she had her snack. Kendra picked up her bowling ball, swung her arm back, and threw it directly into the gutter. She groaned and shook her head.

Penny gestured toward the two at the snack bar. "Wow, that's really nice of Steve."

Kendra glanced at them, then away. "Yeah." She knew her tone lacked the enthusiasm that Penny expected and noticed the girl's puzzled expression.

After bowling, the whole group went to a restaurant for ice cream. Kendra would have gone directly home, but she had saved gas by riding with Allison and knew that Allison wanted to stay. She chose a seat at the far end of a long table across from Leanne, and put Elizabeth in a high chair on the end. To her dismay, Steve, Emma, and Jean sat next to them.

Kendra ordered the smallest caramel sundae on the menu to share with Elizabeth. The conversation swirled around her as she took a bite of ice cream with sprinkles, then fed one to her daughter. The others seemed engaged in a theological discussion about something called Tulip, a topic completely unfamiliar to Kendra.

"The idea that Jesus only died for certain people – I have a real problem with that one," Leanne argued. "The Bible says in lots of places that Jesus died for the sins of the whole world."

"It depends on how you interpret that," Emma said. She was an intense, intellectual young woman with a pointed chin, dark hair and glasses, who often expressed strong opinions in the Bible studies. "It could mean every person in the world, or it could mean people from every tribe, language, nation, etc. I've heard different explanations of that."

"Oh, that just sounds wrong to me. And it seems to me that people resist the grace of God all the time, so I can't believe that one."

Steve said, "I guess people do resist sometimes, but when God called me, I knew I didn't have a choice."

Leanne waved her spoon as she spoke. "So you really believe that you couldn't have resisted?"

"No, because if I could have, I would have. Believe me, I tried. The last thing I wanted to become was a boring Christian." He grinned around at the circle of girls.

Jean, on Steve's left, leaned forward. "So why didn't you just say no?"

Steve frowned for a minute as if he were wrestling with the question in his mind. "It's the love of God," he said finally. "When you know that God loves you that much, how can you possibly resist?"

Jean shook her head as she scraped out her ice cream bowl. "Well, I still think you could have resisted if you wanted to. I think you're making yourself out to be badder than you really were."

"Badder!" Steve threw back his head and laughed. "Girl, you get a D in English. But maybe I'm influenced by my own experience. I know for other people it's different."

"Well, John would be proud of you, Steve."

Kendra knew of no John in the Timothy group. Maybe he went to their church. "Who's John?"

The four of them turned to stare at her, then broke into laughter. "John Calvin," Leanne giggled. "He was a reformer; he was the one who came up with Tulip."

Blushing at her error, Kendra lapsed back into silence. The waitress brought the check and everyone began to dig into wallets.

"Steve!" Allison called out from the other end of the table. Steve looked up. "Are you going home right away?"

He shrugged. "I guess so. Why?"

"I need to go over to Serena's for a while, but I know Kendra wants to get Elizabeth home. Could you give them a ride?"

Kendra felt herself go cold with horror. Steve threw her a

Finding Father

startled glanced, but he only said, "Sure."

Why had Allison done that? Why hadn't she let Kendra find her own ride? Of course, she was trying to be helpful, so she had asked her cousin. For just a second Kendra remembered all the crime movies she had seen on TV. She pictured herself and Elizabeth killed, dumped in the woods somewhere. But that was silly, wasn't it? Steve had no reason to hurt them. He seemed fond of Elizabeth. Surely he wouldn't hurt either of them as long as Elizabeth was present. It would just be so terribly awkward.

The group was dispersing, people putting on coats and saying goodbye. Kendra sat frozen to her chair as Steve talked to Leanne. He glanced at Kendra once. "Let me know when you're ready."

The table was almost empty. Slowly Kendra rose and put on her coat. She lifted Elizabeth down from the high chair. Kendra picked up the car seat that Allison had left by the front door, and the three of them walked out into the biting cold.

Steve glanced at her as they crossed the parking lot. "That Emma is funny. She likes to debate theology. Sometimes I play the devil's advocate just to make it interesting."

Kendra had no answer. He led them toward a small silver Toyota and unlocked the doors. Kendra fastened her daughter into the car seat in the backseat and climbed into the front. She found herself clinging to the armrest as Steve pulled out of the parking lot.

He glanced at her. "Where do you work, Kendra?"

She swallowed. "At – at a bank."

"Oh. Do you like it?"

"I guess so."

Pause. "Where does Elizabeth go when you work?"

Why was he asking her all these questions? "She – a woman I know keeps her in her home."

"Oh." Steve glanced at her again, then fell silent. After a moment he pushed the button on his stereo and music filled the car. The station was playing a love song, one that Kendra usually liked, but tonight it made her writhe in discomfort.

Come into my arms, let me love you tonight...

Steve pushed another button on his stereo. "I found this old CD around the house," he remarked.

The first song was unfamiliar to Kendra. It sounded like a Christian song; it used the word testify, testify, over and over, and Steve sang under his breath along with the music. Then the song ended and another began. To Kendra's horror she recognized "Butterfly Kisses," the sentimental story of a father watching his little girl grow up.

Steve stopped singing and bit his lip. She saw him glance once into the backseat. The song seemed to go on forever, until the father was crying over his daughter in her wedding gown and Kendra was clutching the armrest with white knuckles. Finally it ended, and Steve began to sing with the music again.

He pulled up in front of Allison's house. He glanced back at Elizabeth. "She's asleep."

"I knew she would be." Kendra climbed out, opened the back door, and lifted Elizabeth onto her shoulder. Her slumbering daughter was a dead weight in her arms.

Steve came around to her side and unhooked the car seat. "Do you need help? Should I carry this for you?"

"No, no." She shook her head as she spoke. "Just leave it here; I'll take care of it. Thanks for the ride." She hurried up the walk. A moment later she heard Steve drive away.

‍ ‍

☙ ❧

She slept poorly that night, and woke at five o'clock from a disturbing dream of driving around in a car and not knowing where she was going. After lying awake for an hour, tossing and turning and reliving the evening before, she knew that her rest was over for the night and got out of bed. She ate breakfast and woke Elizabeth to get her ready for church.

Todd was teaching a series on Jesus' parables, and that morning the topic was the parable of the ungrateful servant. If Kendra had read the story before, she had forgotten it. The king forgives the servant of a huge debt, and then the servant turns around and refuses to forgive his fellow servant of a much smaller debt. The theme, of course, was forgiveness, and Kendra listened in resentful silence as the class discussed reasons for a lack of forgiveness, and how the underlying cause of it all was lack of gratitude toward God. If we really recognize what God has done for us, the class agreed, we will be much more willing to forgive those who have sinned against us in some way.

Kendra hated hearing lessons about forgiveness. People who talked about forgiveness all the time were probably the ones who didn't have anything significant to forgive. This conviction was confirmed as one of the women shared about a relative who had borrowed money and failed to pay it back, and her effort to forgive him. Borrowing money and not repaying – how silly was that. Anybody should be able to forgive a little offense like that.

She knew she hadn't forgiven Steve. He had asked her to, and she had stopped short of any active retaliation, but she knew that in her heart she was still hanging onto resentment. How was a person supposed to erase those memories from her mind? God must expect the impossible if he wanted her to do that.

Wrapped in these thoughts, she found tears in her eyes as the class began to rise and disperse. Slowly she gathered her Bible and purse, allowing the room to empty so she didn't have to talk to anyone.

"Kendra." She raised her eyes to see Todd watching her with concern. "Are you all right?"

She dropped back into her seat and waited for the last stragglers to leave the room. Todd came and sat in the seat across from her.

"It's not that easy, you know." Her voice was thick with tears; she struggled to keep them from spilling down her face.

Todd hesitated a minute. "I didn't mean to imply that forgiveness is easy. It sounds that way until we have a real offense that we need to forgive. And, of course, some of us have more difficult issues than others."

"How are you supposed to forget?" she burst out. "Forgive and forget, that's what everyone says. I just don't know how."

"Maybe that's the problem." He leaned his chin in his hand, frowning and thinking. "As humans, we can't forget. Our minds don't work that way. God is capable of choosing to forget, but we can't really do that. So if you're waiting for memories to magically disappear, that's not going to happen."

Kendra stared down at her hands in her lap. "So what do I do?"

"I think when we choose to forgive, we're making several decisions. First of all, we won't bring up the past offense in order to hurt the person, to remind them of what they've done. Secondly, we won't tell others about the offense in order to hurt the person or retaliate. And thirdly, we won't let the offense stand in the way of having a relationship with the offender. Of course, in some cases that last point depends on the other person's attitude and whether he or she has expressed any remorse."

Kendra sat in silence, meditating on his words. The first two she could manage with Steve. She didn't want to bring up the past, and she hadn't told anyone else about it. The third was the hard one.

"I'm sure you're thinking of something specific," Todd ventured. "Do you want to talk about it? Without mentioning any names, I mean."

It would be a relief to talk to someone besides her mother, who was almost hysterical on the subject – to tell a Christian man she respected and to hear his opinion. And Todd, unlike her other friends, didn't know Steve. At least, she didn't believe he knew him. She was often surprised at all the connections within the Christian community.

"I guess I'll tell you, if you want to hear it." She swallowed and took a deep breath, clasping her hands together. "About five years ago, I was raped at a party. Then six months ago I met the guy again."

Todd's eyes widened and she saw him gulp. "Oh, my goodness." He was silent a moment. "Wow. That's a tough one, I agree."

"We have a lot of mutual friends," Kendra explained, "and I see him sometimes whether I want to or not. And I just don't know how to act around him."

"I can see that." Todd was silent another minute. "Has he expressed any remorse?"

"Yes – yes, he wrote me a letter."

"Well, that's something." He shook his head slowly. "Did he seem sincere, or did you think he was being manipulative?"

"I think – I think he meant it."

Finding Father

"Oh." Another pause. "Well, the first thing I'd say, Kendra, is not to do anything to put yourself in danger. Take care of yourself. That's the most important thing."

"You mean, don't go anywhere with him –"

"I mean, use good judgment. Don't let forgiveness be a rationale for foolishness. You need to protect yourself."

Kendra thought of the car ride the night before. The truth was that she really didn't believe she was in any danger from Steve anymore. She knew he had been drinking and using drugs the night of the party, and he didn't do those things anymore. She believed he was genuinely sorry and ashamed of everything that had happened that night. Furthermore, she guessed he was torn between a desire to avoid Kendra forever and curiosity to know his daughter. Strangely enough, she could almost sympathize with the difficulty of his situation.

"What do you think God is telling you to do?" Todd asked.

Kendra stared down at her folded hands and swallowed. "I think he wants me to forgive him. I'm just not sure I want to, or that I can."

"Then maybe you should just tell God that, Kendra. Ask him for the ability to forgive this guy. Ask him for wisdom on how to deal with it. I have to admit this is outside my realm of experience. But my father was killed by a drunk driver many years ago and I know how I struggled to forgive that man. It was hard, but I believe I can say that I have. Maybe there's someone – a woman in the church who's had a similar experience, who would be more help than I've been."

"I think you've helped," Kendra said. "Thank you."

Elizabeth's Sunday school teacher stuck her head inside the classroom door. "Oh, there's your mommy, Elizabeth. I'm sorry to interrupt, but I didn't know where you were."

"I'm sorry." Kendra rose, wiped her eyes with the back of her hand, and gathered her belongings together. "Come here, honey. Sorry I didn't get you."

She threw Todd one last look and he gave her an encouraging smile. "I'll be praying for you, Kendra."

She felt much lightened by this conversation with Todd,

reassured by his response. It was good to know that he didn't condemn her for her struggle. He admitted to struggling with the same issue himself; he had overcome it, so maybe there was hope for her.

Somehow she sensed she was at a crossroads. She could choose to forgive Steve, or choose to harbor resentment and become a bitter woman for the rest of her life. She didn't want to be bitter. She wanted to put this experience in the past and move on with her life. Would God really help her do this? Was it possible?

When she reached home she fed Elizabeth lunch, settled her with her dolls, and went to her bedroom. She sat on the edge of her bed and prayed.

God, I do want to forgive Steve. Or rather, I'm not sure I want to, but I know that it's the right thing to do. I know you want me to do this. It's not easy for me. Please help me with this. Help me to have the right attitude and to let go of any bitterness I still have.

She felt a sense of peace after she had prayed. Maybe now that she was trying to forgive Steve, God wouldn't keep putting him in her path. Maybe that was his whole purpose in this situation. It would be such a relief to not have to see him again.

Chapter Twelve

That Sunday evening Allison received a phone call from Serena. Kendra listened to one side of the conversation as she cooked dinner and was setting the spaghetti on the table when Allison hung up.

"Are you and Serena making plans together?" Kendra asked as she tied a bib around Elizabeth's neck.

"Yeah, we're going to the March for Life on Thursday with Randy. He's trying to get a group together, and Serena doesn't have school that day. I was wondering if we could take Elizabeth with us too?"

Kendra glanced at Elizabeth, who had perked up at her own name. She had heard of the huge pro-life rally in Washington, D.C., although she had never attended. "Why would you want to take her?"

"A lot of people take their children to the march. I could push her in her stroller so she doesn't get too tired. I wanted to take her because – well, I thought it would be symbolic."

Kendra turned back to the refrigerator to retrieve the salad she had made. She knew that Allison didn't want to spell it out in front of the child. Allison knew that many children conceived by sixteen-year-old mothers with no father around would have been aborted. That was why she thought it would be symbolic to take Elizabeth to the rally.

"Maybe I should go with you," she suggested. "Not that I don't trust you – I just feel nervous about Elizabeth running around in that huge crowd of people."

"Hey, that would be great if you could. Randy always tries to get a group together, but most people have to work. We always stop on the way home and eat dinner somewhere."

"I'll have to ask my boss for the day off," Kendra said.

Her boss agreed to give her a vacation day, and Kendra found herself looking forward to the excursion to Washington with Allison and Serena and Randy. The weather had been bitter all month, but the Thursday forecast showed a slight break in the frigid temperatures. She dressed Elizabeth and herself in layers, with hats and scarves and warm gloves. When they arrived at the church parking lot, Randy and Penny were waiting for them, and Serena pulled up a minute later.

"I hope everybody dressed warm," Randy greeted them with a grin. "Oh, we have a little marcher this year! We might take turns carrying her."

"I have her stroller in the car," Kendra told him.

Serena clasped her arms around herself, shivering. "Are we ready to leave yet?"

Randy glanced at his watch. "Just a few more minutes. Someone else is supposed to come." He glanced up as a silver Toyota pulled into the parking lot. "Oh, I think this is Steve now."

The car pulled into a parking space and Steve bounded out of the front seat. He was halfway to the group when he stopped in his tracks at the sight of Kendra and Elizabeth, then joined them at a slower pace.

"Sorry I'm late. Are we ready to go? I can drive if you want."

"I borrowed my mother's van, and I think we can all fit in that." Randy glanced around the group. "Yes, there are seven of us. We can all ride together."

Kendra turned back to Allison's car to fetch the stroller, her heart sinking. So much for her enjoyable vacation day with her friends. What a waste. Once again Steve had to show up and ruin everything. He had seemed equally surprised to see her there. Well, it appeared as though God wasn't going to make it easy for her after all. She had told him she would forgive Steve, and now she had to prove it by her actions. But all her pleasure in the day was ruined.

She put the stroller in the back of the van and went to the side door. Randy and Penny were sitting in the two front seats, Steve and Serena on the bench seat in the back. Allison had one of the middle seats. Kendra dropped onto the seat next to Allison.

"Elizabeth can sit in the back; she's the littlest," Allison said.

Steve patted the seat between himself and Serena. "Here, Elizabeth, you sit here."

The doors were closed and they pulled off. Kendra turned to stare out of the window, ignoring the conversation of the others. Randy and Penny in front seemed completely engrossed in each other. Could they be dating? They seemed to be hanging around each other a lot lately.

From behind her she heard Steve speaking to Elizabeth. "Look at all those horses out there!"

Elizabeth followed the direction of his finger. "Those aren't horses, they're cows!"

"Are you sure? They look like horses to me."

"No, they're cows!"

"What do you do with cows?"

"They make milk."

"Can't you ride them?"

Elizabeth laughed. "No, silly, you ride horses!"

"You know, you're very smart."

"I know."

"You're also very modest."

"I know."

Steve grinned. "Where did you get your pretty blue eyes?"

Elizabeth fixed her blue eyes on his face. "I was born with them."

"Good answer, Elizabeth." Allison glanced at Kendra with a chuckle. "Isn't it silly, the questions people ask little kids?"

"Can I have them?" Steve gestured as if to pluck out her eyes.

"No!" She squeezed them shut.

"Why not?"

"I need them to see!"

Serena laughed. "Just ignore him, Elizabeth, that's what the rest of us do."

"Elizabeth," Steve said. "That's a pretty name. Do you know

what your name means?" Elizabeth shook her head. "It means 'consecrated to God.'" He glanced up at Serena. "Literally, 'God my oath.'"

Elizabeth, who knew the meaning of neither "consecrated" nor "oath," regarded him solemnly.

Allison twisted around to look at her cousin. "Steve, do you remember those cross-stitch pictures that Grandma made for us with our names and their meanings?"

"I still have mine," Steve said. "Stephen – a crown."

"My name means 'of noble kin.' Actually, I do have noble kin, so I like that."

Steve grinned at Serena. "We won't talk about what Serena's name means. Can you say 'irony'?"

Serena scowled at him. Allison said, "Oh, Serena, tell Steve about what happened with your patient last week."

Kendra turned back to the window. The passing landscape flashed by in a monotonous sheet of trees, occasionally broken by a house or farm. The brilliant blue of the sky almost hurt her eyes.

At least Steve was nice to Elizabeth and always seemed happy to see her. That was something. It was more than she had expected from him, anyway.

From the backseat Serena's voice drifted up to her. "And then at the end of the session, this creepy-looking boy comes up to me and says, 'I want you to know that I'm really attracted to you.' And I'm all alone with this boy and I think, how am I supposed to respond to this? This kid is only sixteen! So I say, 'Well, I'm flattered, but you do understand that nothing can happen between us, don't you?' Then later when I played back the videotape, all I could see were his feet walking toward me, and me looking up, like something in a horror movie." She laughed. "It was so creepy!"

Steve laughed with her. Allison had partly turned in her seat to listen. "Has anything like that ever happened with your students, Steve?"

Steve hesitated. "Actually, one time, but what she said was a lot worse."

Allison's eyes widened. "I can imagine! So what did you do?"

"I got mad at her. I said, 'Do you want me to get fired? Do you want to send me to jail? Because that's what would happen.' Then she tried to turn it into a joke, and I said, 'Don't ever say anything like that to me again.'"

Kendra's attention was caught in spite of herself. She knew that Serena was studying psychology and had a position as an intern, but she had never heard about Steve's job. She turned to glance back at him. "What do you do?"

"I'm a teacher," he said. "I teach English at Fairview High School.

Kendra was surprised, although perhaps she shouldn't have been. She remembered that the night she first met him, he had been considering the teaching profession.

"When I was in high school, one of the teachers was dating one of the students," Serena recalled. "Rosemary and Mr. Larson. I'll never forget."

Steve's eyes widened in horror. "How did he get away with that?"

"I don't know. It was a secret, but everybody knew. You know, 'Mr. Larson is giving Rosemary private French lessons – he-he.' I guess her parents liked him and didn't object."

"So he wasn't married," Allison said.

"No, in fact, Rosemary and Mr. Larson got married sometime after graduation. She was one of those mature types who never dated the high school boys."

Steve shook his head. "I can't believe he wasn't fired. Nobody in my school would get away with that. And some of those girls are really bold; they don't care if you're a teacher, either. You wouldn't believe the way they act."

Serena nodded. "And if anything happened, who would get blamed? Not the girl, that's for sure. You'd better be careful, Steve."

"Poor Steve, fighting those young girls off with a stick," Allison laughed. "Hey, maybe you should invite them all to your Bible study."

"I did that once, and the girl actually came. I guess that was the best thing that could have happened."

For the next hour the three of them exchanged stories about their jobs, their students and co-workers, while Kendra alternately listened and ignored them. Finally the van left the rural scenery behind and approached the suburbs of Washington with its congested streets and crowded buildings.

"We're almost there." Steve pulled something from his coat pocket. "Look, I brought foot warmers. I used them when I went skiing last week, and they worked great." He handed a packet to Elizabeth, tossed one to Serena, Allison, and finally Kendra. "I don't have enough for everybody."

Allison lowered her voice. "We won't tell Randy and Penny. I don't think they'll care, anyway."

Indeed, there was no mistaking the expression on Penny's face as she and Randy lingered together throughout the rally and the beginning of the march from the Washington Monument to the Capitol Building. Glancing at them from time to time, Kendra remembered the occasion last spring when she had turned Randy down for a date. Maybe that had been stupid. He was really one of the nicest guys she knew. Not handsome, but his looks improved with familiarity. Well, her loss was Penny's gain. It was obvious that the two were interested in each other.

The crowd slowly began to move along the wide boulevard that had been cleared of traffic for the event. From her stroller, Elizabeth stared in awe at the huge classical government buildings with their pillars and columns. Some of the marchers were praying; others were singing. Kendra heard the Rosary recited for the first time in years.

"Let's sing something," Steve suggested as a chanting group nearby finally fell silent. "I need one of you women to help me with this one."

He began a worship song, and Allison and Serena echoed each line until they reached the chorus, when they joined together. Kendra wished that she knew the song, although she was a mediocre singer.

They had reached the part of the city where the street began to ascend Capitol Hill. Kendra stopped pushing Elizabeth for a minute to rest her arms and catch her breath.

"Are you tired?" Steve asked. "Elizabeth, do you want to ride up on my shoulders? You can look over everybody's heads."

Finding Father

Elizabeth nodded and climbed out of the stroller. Steve crouched so that the child could climb up on his shoulders. She clutched the hood of his jacket while he held her ankles. He and Kendra quickened their pace to catch up with their group.

Finally they reached the summit of Capitol Hill. The huge dome of the Capitol loomed over them to the right. Surprised to discover that she was actually warm from the exercise, Kendra pulled off her knit cap and smoothed back her hair. Steve paused, and they turned to look down the hill they had just climbed. For two miles, almost as far as the eye could see, the street was packed with row after row of marchers.

"Look at all those people." Steve ran his fingers through his wind-blown hair. "About fifty thousand, I've heard."

She wasn't sure if he were addressing her or Elizabeth, but felt that she should make some response. "Have you been here before?"

"Yes," he said. "This is my second time. I want to come every year if I can."

༺ ༻

They stopped at a Mexican restaurant on the way home. Everyone was tired and hungry from the cold and exercise, and they quickly made their selections from the menu. Kendra ordered two glasses of water and chicken fajitas for herself and Elizabeth to share. The child was so hungry that she gobbled up chips from the basket instead of wanting to play.

"Guess who I ran into last week," Randy remarked as the waitress delivered their food. "Remember Candy Davis? I was standing in line at Kmart, and she was in the same line ahead of me. I think she recognized me, but she didn't speak, and by the time I got through the line, she was gone."

"I haven't seen her in ages." Allison shook her head with an expression of regret. "I wonder what she's up to?"

Kendra tried to remember what she had heard about Candy Davis. Candy had been Allison's roommate for a month or two, the one who liked to party and who stayed out all night.

Steve grinned. "Candy Davis. That girl was pretty wild."

Penny swallowed her bite of enchilada. "Steve, what was that story about you finding her out on the road one night?"

"Oh, that." Steve shook his head. "Yeah, that happened last March. I was over Dan's house one night, and left for home around ten o'clock. Well, I saw this person standing by the side of the road. It was dark and I couldn't see her face at all, but for some reason I thought, Candy –that's Candy. I wasn't sure what to do, but I turned around to go back and see if it was really Candy. I felt a little stupid, but I drove real slow and there was Candy, looking in the window back at me.

"She said, 'Steve Dixon! What are you doing here?' Well, I told her to get in the car and I would take her home. She was so wasted, she couldn't even remember where she lived. We drove around and I would say, 'Does this church look familiar? Do you live near this store?' And she kept saying, 'I don't know, I don't know.'

"I really didn't know what to do with her. I couldn't just leave her by the side of the road, and I could just picture my mom's expression if I showed up at home with Candy in her state." He laughed. "She was so drunk she kept trying to jump out of the car, and when I locked the door, she couldn't figure out how to unlock it. It was pathetic."

"So what did you do?" Randy asked.

"Finally I took her back to Dan's. We called Pastor Mike, who fortunately wasn't asleep yet. Eventually we found out that she was living with the Gardiners, so I got directions and drove her home."

"I think she was embarrassed by the whole thing afterward," Penny recalled.

"Well, she didn't have to be embarrassed on my account. I've sure done plenty of stupid things like that myself. But it's just not safe to wander the streets drunk – especially for a woman. She never seems to get it."

"Oh, she had the biggest crush on Steve," Allison giggled. "When she was living with me, she kept asking me to invite him over. And I wanted to say, 'Candy, if you are my friend at all, please stay away from Steve.'"

Steve frowned. "Give me a break. I have better sense than that."

"Well, I'm glad to know your taste has improved in the last few years." Allison laughed and looked across the table at Kendra. "You know, when Aunt Betsy first told me about Kendra, I was afraid she was someone like Candy. But I quickly found out Kendra's nothing like Candy."

Kendra felt her face grow warm and she turned to give Elizabeth more chicken from her plate. Randy said, "Oh, Kendra's Mother Teresa compared to Candy."

"Mother Kendra," Penny chimed in.

"She's more of a prude than I am," Allison added.

Steve gave her a puzzled look. "So what does that prove? You're not a prude at all!"

Serena laughed. "I told Allison something last week that I read in school: Men hit their sexual peak at age eighteen, and after thirty it's all downhill. I thought she was going to cry."

A round of laughter circled the table. "Well, it does seem unfair," Allison defended herself. "I've waited all these years, and by the time I get married, it will be too late!"

Steve said, "I'm sure he'll force himself once or twice for your sake."

"Oh, there's an easy solution to that!" Serena told her. "We just wait till we're thirty, and then marry guys who are eighteen."

Allison, Serena, and Penny doubled over in laughter; Steve and Randy watched with wry expressions.

"I wouldn't advise that." Steve's tone was exasperated. "Eighteen-year-old guys don't have a clue about sex. They're very selfish and that's what you'd get."

"I think we need to lift this conversation to a higher plane," Randy remarked when the women had subdued their laughter. "Penny, why don't you ask everyone that question we were talking about on the ride down?"

Penny nodded as she set down her glass. "Randy and I were talking about the morning-after pill. I asked Randy if he thinks that morally it's the same as a regular abortion. What do you all think?"

"Of course it is." Serena never expressed any doubt with her opinions.

"Well, it produces the same result." Allison sounded a bit more hesitant. "It keeps the baby from implanting. But I guess it isn't as violent as a regular abortion."

"I'm not sure it's the same," Penny ventured. "And it might not really work that way either."

Serena shrugged. "If fertilization has already taken place, that's the only way it could work. But it's a moot point anyway. None of us should ever need the morning-after pill, should we?"

"But if someone is raped, and goes to the hospital, they give her that pill," Penny argued. "If you were raped, would you take it?"

Kendra bit her lip and stared at Elizabeth, who was playing with the sugar and cream packets on the table. At sixteen she had never thought of the morning-after pill. How would her life be different if she had?

"No," Serena said.

"I don't know." Allison picked at the remains of her taco salad. "It's easy to say now that I wouldn't, or shouldn't, but in a situation like that – it would be hard."

"What do you think, Steve?" Penny persisted.

Steve managed an uncomfortable shrug as he stirred his coffee. "Well, as a man, I guess I'll never have to make a decision like that."

Allison said, "That's a cop-out."

"No – no, it isn't –"

Serena leaned forward and spoke loudly, as she always did when she wanted to make a point. "If your *wife* was raped, and she came home from the hospital and said, 'Steve, they gave me these pills, should I take them or not?' What would you say?"

Steve was silent a moment. Kendra stared down at the bright flowers on her Mexican plate, her face hot, praying that no one looked in her direction.

"I guess I'd have to say no," he said finally. "I'm not trying to make light – I'm sure that would be – would be really – but it all comes down to who you believe is in control. If you really believe that God gives life, you can't say that he gives it in some situations and in others it's just a terrible mistake."

Penny glanced at Kendra as if to solicit her opinion next, but at that moment the waitress brought their check. Rattled by the conversation, relieved by the distraction, Kendra opened her purse and counted out the bills to pay for her dinner. She wiped

Elizabeth's face and hands and lifted her down from her chair.

The van was quiet as they started again for home. Randy put a CD into the stereo. The music wafted over them as they rode for a while in silence.

"What does healing rain symbolize, anyway?" Steve spoke into the darkness.

Randy glanced in the rear view mirror. "Spoken like a true English teacher!"

"Well, it means something, and I've never been sure."

"I thought it was talking about the Holy Spirit," Allison said, "but I guess we'd have to ask Michael W. Smith if we want to know for sure."

Steve grinned. "Sure. I'll call Michael tomorrow and find out."

Silence reigned again as the song continued. Steve sang under his breath with the music. When Kendra glanced into the backseat, she saw that Elizabeth had fallen asleep against his shoulder.

Chapter Thirteen

"I've missed our weekly breakfasts together." Mike Holland, the pastor of Bethel Bible Church, leaned back in the swivel chair behind his desk in the office, showing the dimple that matched his cleft chin. "I'm glad we have this chance to catch up, instead of just passing in the church lobby. How's your job?"

"It's all right," Steve replied. "It's easier than last year, because I'm teaching some of the same classes and so I know what I'm doing. I've started a prayer group that meets twice a month right after school, and have about ten students coming pretty regularly. So I guess I'm doing some good."

"Sounds great. And I've seen you singing with the worship team a few times lately. Are you going to stick with that?"

"They need a drummer when Will moves away, and I said I could do it. I played the drums back in a little band in college."

"You told me." Mike nodded. "I know your mom is really happy you're doing so well. She's so proud of you."

Steve swallowed hard. He knew Mike was right. Maybe his mother's days of feeling happy and proud were numbered.

"But I'm assuming you had a specific reason to want to meet with me," Mike went on, "so why don't we just cut to the chase? What's up?"

"Okay." Now that the moment to explain all this had finally come, Steve wondered how to begin. He ran his hand through his hair. "Well, I've talked to you before about my sexual history, so some of this won't surprise you too much. About five years ago I met a girl at a party, and I didn't see her again for a long time. But just recently I met her again because –" He hesitated, wondering how many details he should reveal about Kendra, "well, she's a friend of my cousin. Allison brought her to church and that's how I saw her again. And it turns out that she has a child – a daughter – and I'm pretty sure I'm the father." Steve listed his reasons for believing so, beginning with his correspondence with Kendra over the summer and ending with Elizabeth's resemblance to his own family photos. "So I just don't know what to do. The mother never told me about her and clearly doesn't want me to be involved, but how can I just walk away? I told you about the abortion, and I couldn't live with myself if I did something like that again. Do you see why?"

Mike listened intently as Steve spoke. "Yes, I can see that. But are you sure the mother feels that way? If this – well, this relationship – was just a one-night stand, she might have felt more comfortable not involving you. Now that you've met again, she might be willing to reconsider. Has she actually told you to stay away?"

"She said in her e-mail that we should go our separate ways, and that's the sense I get whenever we're together. I've seen her in social situations about a half dozen times, and she ignores or avoids me every time. I've tried to spend time talking to the little girl, but I get a definite hostile feeling from the mother. I don't want to make things worse, but it seems wrong to just stay out of her life. If her mother were married and she had a stepfather, I'd probably feel differently – I wouldn't want to disrupt an intact family. But even her grandfather is dead, so she doesn't have anybody but me."

Mike nodded. "You said you wrote to her and apologized? How did she respond?"

Steve hesitated. "Not very well. She's still angry. I don't blame her for that, but I can't fix it now."

"Okay." Mike nodded, his brows knit. "So she's angry, and maybe you need to figure out why. Did she ever try to contact you when she was pregnant, maybe to ask for help? Or was she drunk at the party, and thought you took advantage of her? What's the real reason she's not forgiving you?"

Steve bit his lip. He had known it would come to this, and this was what he had dreaded most. But he knew there was no point in asking for advice unless he was willing to come clean about everything. He stared down at the brown and yellow triangular pattern on the rug and took a deep breath. "I know why she's angry. It's because – well, she says – she says that I raped her."

"Oh." Mike was silent for such a long time that Steve was afraid to look up. Mike knew all his worst secrets, and this was the worst of them all. He had no pride left. "Did you?"

"I didn't – well, I didn't mean to." In his effort to justify himself, was he even lying to himself? What had he really been thinking at that awful moment? But no, he was sure he had never intended that. "I was drunk and high on cocaine, and the other guys said – they said she was hot for me – looking back I know that was ridiculous – but it didn't seem that way at the time."

He stopped for breath and managed to look up at his mentor. Mike was sitting with his elbows leaning on his desk, his hands together with his fingers in a tent. His expression was grave.

Finally he spoke again. "Steve, they say that confession is good for the soul, so I think you ought to start from the beginning and tell me the whole story. I would say to spare me the graphic details, but I'll probably need to hear a few of them. Otherwise I won't know how to advise you. Just tell me how it happened."

Steve sighed, trying to go back through his memory and sort it all out. "I met her at a party that her brother had at their house. At the time she told me she was eighteen, but now I think she must have been only sixteen. She probably lied about that. I thought she was cute, and hot, and – well, we started making out on the couch, so I didn't think she was all that innocent. I was drinking vodka or something – I fixed her a drink, but I don't know if she drank much of it. She wasn't acting drunk at that point, but I thought she liked me and that I'd get lucky before the night was over." He gave Mike a sheepish, apologetic look. "And some of the guys brought cocaine to the party, and at one point we got up and went in the kitchen to use some. She disappeared at that point, which I thought was odd – looking back, maybe she was freaked out by the drugs. She told me in her e-mail that she had never used drugs."

He took a deep breath. "Well, I couldn't find her for a while and so I kept drinking and talking to some of the other girls and hanging out. I remember I was in the hallway and I heard someone call my name from the living room. So I went in there and there were a bunch of guys – maybe about four – and K – this girl was on the couch. And Pete said to me, 'Hey, Steve, you're going to get lucky – this girl's hot for you.' And they were all laughing and cheering me on, and she was just lying there, looking around at the guys and not saying anything."

"She didn't tell you to stop?"

"No – I don't think so – I don't remember that. I think I would have remembered. All she said was 'don't hurt me.'" He gulped. "She looked scared. But I didn't think about that then."

Mike was shaking his head. Steve couldn't bear to look at him. "So it all happened right there, with the other guys in the room?"

"Yeah." Steve stared down at the floor. "I guess that was pretty awful."

"I guess so." Mike expelled his breath audibly. "Was that everything?"

"Well – afterward, she started crying. And that's when I really knew I'd made a big mistake. And one of the other guys said, 'Now it's my turn,' and she looked really scared and looked at me like – like she wanted me to protect her. So I told the guys to leave her alone because she was upset and didn't want any more. I guess that cocaine made me feel like I could fight all four of them. They must have known I would try, so they left her alone after that."

"Why do you think they set you up that way?"

"I don't know – I've wondered the same thing. I think they all got excited by the idea but were a little afraid, and remembered that I had been with her earlier, and so picked me to go first. That's what I think."

"But you should have known better."

"I know."

As awful as he felt, there was a certain relief in finally telling someone this story after so many years. Pastor Mike was one of the few people he trusted enough to confide in. Maybe he would be kicked out of the church – or arrested – but at the moment he still felt relief.

"So that was the last time you saw her, until she showed up at church? Did she ever press charges against anybody?"

"No, thank God. I heard a rumor from one of those guys that she was pregnant, but when she didn't contact me, I assumed it wasn't true, or maybe there was a different guy. But I think now that she just didn't want me to know or be involved."

"Well, I can't blame her for that," Mike said, and Steve felt his heart contract. "When you wrote to her, you apologized for all this?"

"Yes, not in a lot of detail – I just told her I was sorry that I hurt her. I didn't want to – well, confess to anything in writing."

"And that's when she still seemed angry."

"Yes."

Mike sighed. "Well, you've certainly created a big mess here, Steve, but I don't need to tell you that. It's not surprising that she doesn't trust you or want her daughter to be around you. But I don't feel comfortable telling you to just walk away. It's so critical for children to know that their parents care about them and want to be part of their lives, even if the parents don't like each other or get along. With divorced parents, I'm sure you know that too."

"Yes, that's what I thought. I want Eli – I want the little girl to know that I care about her, even if her mom hates me."

"But you don't want to hurt the mother more than you have already, I'm sure. I'm going to give this a lot of thought, but my first advice to you is that you're going to have to be really patient. Take baby steps. Try to find opportunities to see the child without making the mother feel threatened. Show your good intentions, and give her time to start trusting you. That might take a long time or it might never happen, but at least give it some time. And you're going to have to eat a lot of humble pie. Just be prepared for that. If you haven't learned humility yet, you'll learn it now."

"I've thought about asking for a paternity test," Steve said, "but I don't know if that's the right move or not."

Mike pondered a moment. "It might not be a bad idea to ask. It might show your sincerity. If the test turns up negative, then you'd feel comfortable staying out of the situation. But if the mother shows a lot of resistance, don't force the issue. I think that going to court and trying to fight for your rights would be the wrong move right now. You want her to see that you're not the enemy."

Steve nodded. "And if I tried to force it legally, she might very well tell everybody what really happened to try to get rid of me. That's my biggest fear. I know I'm lucky she hasn't done it before now."

℘ ☙

At the Bible study at Randy's house that Friday night, Kendra found herself annoyed and resigned, rather than panic-stricken, when Steve showed up at the door. He had never come to a Bible study before, at least since she had been involved, and the rest of the group greeted him with enthusiasm. He appeared in cheerful high spirits as he seated himself between Leanne and Jesse and joked with them. When the singing began, Steve called out, "Let's sing 'Days of Elijah.'!"

"We haven't done that song since the last time Steve was here," Heidi recalled, "over a year ago."

Steve nudged Leanne. "And Leanne has to help me with the motions."

The rest of the room looked blank, but Leanne laughed.

"Once Steve and I taught that song to a Bible school group, and Steve made up hand motions to the chorus to keep the kids' attention. They loved it."

So they sang the song, which was unfamiliar to Kendra, and Steve did the motions while the rest of the group laughed at him. Kendra had to admit that at least he wasn't afraid to make a fool of himself in front of everyone.

After the Bible study was over, Kendra chatted with the girls in the kitchen, conscious of Steve near the front door with some of the guys. She wondered why he had suddenly decided to show up at a Bible study. Lots of people attended the activities, but usually only the core members of the group came to the Bible studies. It seemed as if she had been seeing him more and more, ever since Christmas, and the realization made her uneasy.

Finding Father

When she wanted to leave she had to walk directly past him to reach the front door. She was prepared to simply nod to him in acknowledgment, but he stepped close to her and spoke in an undertone.

"Are you leaving now? I need to talk to you. Can I walk out with you?"

She nodded, her uneasiness growing, and waited for him to fetch his coat. They walked outside together into the nippy February night with only the streetlights illuminating the street. Kendra hoped that no one in the group had seen them leave together, although she doubted it. People always noticed things like that.

"Are you cold?" he asked. "Do you want to sit in the car?"

"I'm fine." She didn't want to prolong this conversation if she could help it. She leaned against her car door, folded her arms, and looked up at Steve.

"Okay." He took a deep breath, his eyes fixed on the pavement at his feet. "I wanted to talk to you because I've been thinking about getting involved in the Timothy group again. I want to find out how you feel about that."

She was not completely surprised, but her heart fell. Of course she didn't want Steve coming to the group! Now was another opening for her little speech, but somehow she couldn't bring herself to make it. It would sound so – rude, when he was trying to be considerate.

She avoided his eyes, kicking a tiny pebble with the toe of her shoe. "Well, you don't need my permission, Steve. You can do what you want, I guess."

"I know, but I don't want you to drop out if I start coming all the time. I would feel bad if that happened. That's why I'm asking."

Kendra bit her lip. She had decided, months ago, that if Steve began to come regularly she would stop. But she had never expected him to put her on the spot this way. How could she possibly respond?

"You know," he began in a hesitant tone, "we're brother and sister now, and I'd like us to have that relationship. But if you can't handle it, I understand."

Something in his words pricked her pride. It clearly didn't

bother him to see her; he just felt sorry for her. She shrugged. "I can handle it if you can."

He smiled with genuine relief, running a hand through his hair. "Well, good. I'm glad to hear that."

What on earth had she agreed to? With a feeling of disgust at the whole situation, at her own weakness, she turned and reached for the door handle.

"Wait," he said. "There's something else I wanted to ask you."

She turned back. He was staring down at the ground again, biting his lip and looking even more uncomfortable in the dim glow of the streetlights. He took a deep breath.

"I want to get a paternity test for Elizabeth."

For a moment she just stared at him. She had never expected this. When she opened her mouth to speak, only one word came out. "Why?"

"Well, wouldn't you want to know, if you had a child out there?"

The words flew out of her mouth before she could stop to think. "You could have found out five years ago, but you didn't give a damn."

He had the grace to look ashamed. "Look, I was a jerk back then. I admit it. I'm trying to do the right thing now, but – but I need your help."

Kendra shrugged. Something in her rebelled at the thought of taking Elizabeth for a paternity test just to satisfy Steve's idle curiosity. Besides, she knew there would be legal ramifications that she wasn't at all sure she wanted to deal with. She knew full well what her mother's advice would be. Yet Steve could probably demand a test if he wanted it badly enough.

"I don't know why you need a paternity test. It doesn't take a rocket scientist to figure it out. That party was on August twenty-second and Elizabeth was born on May twentieth. You do the math."

"Yes, but–" He looked more uncomfortable than ever, avoiding her gaze, but finally pushed the words out. "Was there anyone else?"

Kendra glared at him. She loaded all the contempt she could muster into one word. "No."

She turned and opened the car door. Not for anything would

Finding Father

she continue this humiliating conversation for another second. She glanced back once at Steve. He was watching her gravely.

"Thanks for telling me," he said.

She slammed the car door and started the ignition. Her hands were shaking and she felt tears spill onto her cheeks, blurring the headlights from approaching cars as she pulled onto the highway. Five miles of road passed before her heart rate slowed to its normal pace.

What was happening in her life? Less than a month ago she had told God that she would try to forgive Steve, and this was the way God responded. Why hadn't she just told Steve that she didn't want him around when he gave her the opportunity? Would that have been wrong? She had never expected him to ask; she had been so totally taken by surprise.

And then his request for a paternity test! That had surprised her more than anything. Her mind wrestled with the dilemma as she sped along the dark road. She had never put Steve Dixon's name on Elizabeth's birth certificate, but a paternity test would establish him as the legal father. He would have to pay child support, as he surely knew himself. He would also have the right to visitation. Perhaps he would be able to take Elizabeth for weekends, even for a whole summer. And her mother had feared that he might even try to get primary custody. Could he possibly win a custody battle? It seemed unlikely, but if he eventually married, he might be considered the more stable parent. She cringed at the idea.

If Steve requested court-ordered visitation, she could think of no reason that a judge would refuse him. He certainly had no criminal record or he wouldn't be teaching in a public school. She didn't believe he abused drugs or alcohol anymore. And if she brought up a rape that had occurred five years ago and had never been reported, who would believe her? Everyone would think she was making up the story to win her case. Once the courts became involved, Kendra would lose control of her daughter. Even the money he might have to pay would not be worth that.

And everyone would know the truth. That seemed the worst of all.

The more she considered both questions, the more convinced

she became that, in spite of her surprise and lack of forethought, she had given him the wisest answers she could. If Steve wanted to spend time with Elizabeth, he could see her in the context of the Timothy group, with other people around. No one would need to know the truth except the two of them. Elizabeth's life would not be turned upside down by the sudden appearance of her father. Kendra was not exactly happy with the compromise, but she could live with it – at least for now.

❧ Chapter Fourteen ☙

True to his word, Steve began showing up regularly at all the events of the Timothy group. Kendra ignored him as much as possible, and within a month became so hardened to his presence that she was able to carry on normal conversations with her friends with only a minimum of self-consciousness. Perhaps in time, she would be able to forget about him completely. She certainly hoped so.

He always seemed happy to see Elizabeth and made a point to spend time with her at each activity. Kendra always nervously wondered if their mutual friends would find this interest odd or suspicious, but so far no one seemed struck by it. Leanne mentioned the subject when the two of them were having lunch together, as they tried to do about once a month.

"Steve's very nice to Elizabeth, isn't he? I think it's sweet the way he talks to her and spends time with her. She seems to like him, too."

"Umm." Kendra knew that Leanne expected more enthusiasm from her, and felt the color rise in her cheeks as she sipped the remains of her soda from her glass. The liquid made a slurping sound through the straw.

"I guess he does that because she doesn't have a father. You know, I do think the men in the church should take an interest in children who don't have fathers – to try to fill that lack. But a lot of guys are probably afraid to get too involved."

"Randy's always been nice to her too." Kendra nibbled on a

French fry, avoiding Leanne's gaze.

"Yes, I guess he has." Leanne fell silent a moment, toying with her salad. "I guess Randy and Penny are a real couple now, aren't they? I keep seeing them together."

Kendra remembered that Leanne had once dated Randy. "I think they are." She studied her friend's expression. "Does it still bother you?"

Leanne shrugged. "I guess I'm over it. For a while I liked to hope that we'd get back together, but I know that's not going to happen now."

"Probably not." If only Leanne could meet someone else. And Kendra would like to meet someone eventually herself. "Is there anyone else you're interested in? Have you dated anyone?"

Leanne shook her head. "No, I haven't gone out in a long time. I've always been a little interested in Steve, but I know he never thought about me, except as a friend."

Steve! Well, it wasn't surprising that Leanne liked him. He was good-looking, bright, friendly – he had all the traits that would attract women, and Leanne didn't know about his history. Should Kendra warn her? She would feel terrible if they started dating and something happened – but somehow she sensed that if Steve dated Leanne, Heidi, Jean, or any of the girls in the group, he would behave like a perfect gentleman. He respected them all too much.

"What about you?" Leanne asked. "How's your love life?"

Kendra laughed. "What love life? I haven't had a date since the guy I met at the bank last November. Jesse was hanging around for a while, calling some, but he never asked me out."

"Jesse!" Leanne rolled her eyes. "Ruth's having an awful time with him!"

"Jesse and Ruth? I didn't know."

"They've been going out off and on for about six months, but Jesse won't commit to anything. They go out for about a month, hang out together, talk on the phone all the time. Then he suddenly disappears and she doesn't know why. Usually he starts showing an interest in someone else; in November it was you, in January another girl from our church. Just when Ruth gets real disgusted and decides to forget him, he starts calling again. It's driving her crazy to

Finding Father

be treated like such a yo-yo."

"Why doesn't she just ask him what's going on?"

"She doesn't want to put pressure on him. She's hoping that if she gives him enough time, he'll settle down. I think she's afraid to get the wrong answer."

Kendra shook her head. "She must really like him."

"She's crazy over him. When he's calling, she's so happy and excited, and then when he stops she gets so depressed. I feel bad for her."

Kendra smiled ruefully. "Well, at least she has a prospect. Which is worse: to be unhappy in love, or to have nobody calling at all?"

Leanne grinned. "Good question. I can never make up my mind about that one."

ಲಾ ಯ

The first Tuesday in April, Kendra arrived home after work to find a message on her answering machine from the babysitter who watched Elizabeth during her accounting class. The girl had decided to join the prom committee and would no longer be able to watch Elizabeth on Tuesdays. Allison had already gone out for the evening, and a half dozen frantic phone calls yielded no alternative. In the end Kendra had to miss her class.

As she cleaned up dinner and folded laundry, she seethed with frustration at her situation. Of course, it wasn't Steve Dixon's fault that her babysitter had canceled, but it wasn't fair that he already had a college degree and a stable teaching career – the very sort of position Kendra had hoped for in the past. He never had to worry about missing school or work because his child was sick or he couldn't find a babysitter. He could go out every night of the week with his friends if he chose. And he thought giving Elizabeth his DNA made him a father? He had no clue what real fatherhood meant – he had no idea of the real responsibilities of being a parent. Of course, she owed him nothing.

He showed up that Friday at the Bible study as usual. Mark was teaching a study on prayer. Kendra listened in silence as Mark went through the Lord's Prayer and used it to give examples of what prayer should involve.

She wasn't especially happy with the subject of prayer these days. She didn't understand God. He had answered some of her prayers in what had seemed a remarkable way, and others he had totally ignored. It made no sense.

As the lesson ended, several in the group gave examples of prayer techniques they had found helpful.

"I like to include songs in my prayer time," Leanne told them. "I've always struggled with worship; I feel that I'm not good at it, that I'm bored and God is probably bored by it too. But I've found when I sing worship songs, it helps."

"It helps if you know how to sing," Jesse grinned, "otherwise, God just has his hands over his ears."

"Make a joyful noise," Heidi pointed out.

The group laughed.

"One thing that's helped me is praying Scripture," Steve said. "There's a passage in Colossians that I use a lot." He flipped to the page and read it aloud. "So, if I wanted to pray for –" he glanced around the room, "– Dan, for example, I would say, 'God, I pray that you will fill Dan with the knowledge of your will through all spiritual wisdom and understanding. And I pray that Dan will live a life worthy of the Lord and will please you in every way and grow in the knowledge of you.' That's the idea. If I'm not sure how to pray for someone, I know that praying scripture will be right."

For just a second, as he finished speaking, he met Kendra's eyes. Suddenly she remembered the e-mail she had sent him last summer, with her ironic statement: "Maybe you could pray for me about that." Somehow she knew that he had been praying for her ever since, and the knowledge made her squirm.

She had never once prayed for Steve, except to pray that he would disappear from her life. It had never occurred to her that she should.

When the Bible study ended she collected her jacket to leave before anyone else. To her surprise Steve followed her out the front door.

"Do you want something?" She realized as soon as she spoke

how ungracious the words sounded, but was in no mood to soften them.

Steve shifted uncomfortably, playing with his jacket zipper. "Not exactly. I was just wondering how Elizabeth is. I haven't seen her in a few weeks."

Kendra shrugged. "She's fine. She had a little cold, so I didn't take her out last weekend, but she seems better now."

"So you might bring her to the game night tomorrow?"

She had planned to come to the game night and bring Elizabeth, but found herself reluctant to promise. "Maybe. If I'm not too tired. It's been a busy week."

She saw by Steve's expression that he knew she was dodging him. His face darkened.

"Look, Kendra, I know you don't like me, but that doesn't change the fact that I'm Elizabeth's father. It just seems like we should try –"

"You're not her father!" The words flew out of her mouth before she could stop to weigh them. "You're not her father, you're her – her sperm donor! You've never done one thing that a father would do for her – never, since the day she was born!"

If she expected to shame him into silence, she was mistaken.

"That's because you wouldn't let me!" he flared back. "You didn't even tell me about her till she was four years old, and now whenever I ask what I can do for her, you say, 'Nothing, nothing, nothing.' What do you want me to do?"

Kendra stared down at the toe of her shoe. "Nothing."

"No, no, no, don't say that! You just accused me of not doing anything. I want you to tell me one thing that I can do for her."

Trapped by her own accusation, Kendra fell silent. What did she want from Steve, anyway? She could ask for money, and knew she had the right to it, but something in her recoiled at the idea. Asking for money would open a legal can of worms that she didn't want to touch. Besides, her mother still helped her out with daycare costs, and if her mother heard that Steve was giving her money, that would surely stop. She didn't really need money, she needed someone to help, to be available, to share the responsibility the way her mother once had.

"I have a class Tuesday night, and last week my babysitter canceled on me, so now I have no one to watch Elizabeth –" She broke off. What was she saying?

Steve nodded eagerly. "You want me to babysit for her?"

"I guess..." Was that what she wanted?

"Tuesday night. I can do that. What time do you need me?"

"I guess – six-thirty..."

He nodded again. "Okay. Six-thirty. I'll be there. See you then." With a much friendlier smile, he turned to go back into the house.

Kendra turned slowly and walked to her car. What had she just agreed to? She didn't want Steve coming to the house, taking care of Elizabeth. On the other hand, was it so terrible for him to share some of the responsibility for his daughter? It would at least spare her from hunting down another babysitter.

She didn't even need to ask her mother's opinion. She knew Bonnie Walton would faint at the thought of Steve Dixon spending time alone with her granddaughter. But this was partly her mother's fault. Her mother had left Kendra to struggle on alone while she enjoyed life with her new husband. This time, Kendra wouldn't bother to ask her.

She agonized over the question all weekend. Was she making a terrible mistake? And yet, if Steve insisted, he could go to court and get visitation rights, which would likely include even longer stretches of time alone with Elizabeth. What should she do?

When Steve pulled into the driveway at six-twenty-five on Tuesday evening, she stepped outside to meet him before he could even knock on the door.

"I don't know if this is going to work." She twisted her hands together nervously as she spoke. "I told Allison that you were babysitting for Elizabeth, and she thought that was strange. How can I explain it to everyone?"

His face, which had darkened as she spoke, now cleared. "Oh, that's no problem. I'll just tell her I'm trying to help you out. That's no big deal."

He moved toward the door, but Kendra remained fixed in her position blocking it.

"There's something else. Steve, I don't mind you seeing

Finding Father

Elizabeth, spending time with her, but I don't want her to know anything. She's too young, she wouldn't understand. And she would tell everybody."

He nodded slowly. "Okay. Okay. I won't tell her anything unless you agree."

She led him into the house and nervously explained Elizabeth's evening routine. She left the two of them sitting side by side on the couch, with Steve reading a story aloud.

She barely heard any of the lecture that evening, her mind completely engrossed by the situation back at the house, and the question of whether she had made a wise or foolish decision. When she arrived home, the house was quiet. Steve was sitting at the kitchen table with papers spread out around him. He looked up at Kendra with a smile.

"Grading papers. The bane of a teacher's existence!"

Kendra bit her lip, glancing around the room. "How'd it go?"

"Fine. We had fun. I gave her some ice cream before bed. I hope that's okay."

Kendra nodded. "I'll take her to the bathroom again. Sometimes she still wets the bed."

He began gathering the papers together and putting them in his briefcase. "Okay, I'll probably see you this weekend, right? And next Tuesday at six-thirty."

That week, as her agony of indecision continued unabated, she decided to consult his cousin. Allison usually showed good judgment and had known Steve all his life. As they sat watching television together one evening, after Elizabeth was put to bed, Kendra asked, with some trepidation, "Allison, do you think it's safe for Steve to be babysitting for Elizabeth?"

Allison looked up from the word puzzle she was working on. "You don't think Steve can watch a child? He is a teacher, after all."

"No, I didn't mean it that way." She felt so awkward explaining her concern to Allison. "You know, I never let teenage boys babysit, because – well, I don't want to take any chances."

"Oh, I see." Allison pursed her lips and frowned. "I can't imagine Steve having a problem like that."

But how much did Allison know about Steve's past? What

should she tell her? "I know he used to be pretty wild in college," Kendra began, feeling more awkward than ever.

"Oh, he was always girl-crazy, if that's what you mean. He was a big partier, and he always had girlfriends, and I'm sure he wasn't all that innocent. But there's a big difference between a rowdy frat boy and – and a pedophile. I just can't picture that."

"I can't picture it either, but I know it happens more than you'd like to think."

"Well, I always thought of pedophiles as nerdy losers who don't have much confidence with women. Not like Steve at all. But Kendra, she's your daughter. You have to do what you feel comfortable with."

Kendra thought in silence a moment. "If she were your daughter, would you let him stay with her?"

"Yes, I would. And I think it's good for Elizabeth to have a man around, showing an interest in her. She doesn't have a father or grandfather or brother or anything. Why don't you talk to Elizabeth about it, if you're really concerned?"

Of course, Allison didn't know the real reason Steve was showing such an interest in Elizabeth. If she knew the truth, what would she say? Knowing Allison's opinions in general, Kendra felt sure she would be even more adamant that Steve should be a part of his daughter's life.

She did talk to Elizabeth, and learned nothing more alarming than that Steve took off his shoes in the house and yelled at the TV when his baseball team was losing. "He says Rodriquez couldn't hit a ball if it was three feet wide," Elizabeth informed her helpfully.

She talked to Elizabeth about good and bad touches, and her daughter nodded with unconcern and returned to her dolls. Maybe Allison was right and she was worrying needlessly. Kendra knew what her mother would say, but her mother didn't know Steve at all, and Allison did.

From that night on Steve showed up faithfully every week at six-thirty. Sometimes when Kendra returned from her class, he was watching a television show and stayed until it was over. His favorite appeared to be *Law and Order*; he seemed fascinated by the intricacies of the legal system. On some nights he and Allison watched a show together, and if Kendra had nothing more important to do, she would sit down and finish it with them. Other nights she would come home to find Steve and Allison deep in a discussion about theology or politics or some book they had both read, or one that Steve was recommending to Allison.

One Tuesday night she walked into the kitchen and found the two of them at the table, engaged in a discussion on whether C. S. Lewis or J. R. R. Tolkien were the greater writer.

"They're so different, it's really hard to compare," Allison was saying.

"I still have to vote for C. S. Lewis," Steve said. "Tolkien was brilliant at what he did, but his scope was narrower than Lewis's. C. S. Lewis was brilliant at everything he did."

Allison sipped her iced tea as she reflected. "I've only read *The Chronicles of Narnia* and *The Screwtape Letters*, and a few parts of *Mere Christianity* in college."

"*Till We Have Faces*." Steve lifted his glass in a dramatic gesture. "That was his best."

"I've never read that. Was it similar to *Screwtape Letters*?"

"Well, *Screwtape* was funny. *Till We Have Faces* wasn't funny at all, it was pretty dark. But it was so brilliant. Do you know my favorite line? 'The Divine Nature can change the past. Nothing is yet in its true form.' Isn't that great? I've read that book three times."

Allison smiled at Kendra, who had set down her purse and was pouring herself a drink from the refrigerator. "Kendra's favorite book is *Gone With the Wind*. She's read that five times."

Kendra frowned at Allison. It was true, but not the sort of thing she would tell Steve Dixon. He would laugh at that.

"I've seen the movie, but I've never read the book," Steve remarked. "Are they the same?"

Kendra shrugged. "Well, the book is longer and has a lot more detail."

"Yeah, that's always true, but are the characters the same?"

Allison laughed. "He's an English teacher, Kendra. Next he'll be asking you to write an essay about it."

Kendra considered as she pulled out a chair at the table. "I thought Rhett was nicer in the movie than in the book. I think they cleaned him up for the movie."

Steve nodded. "Like how?"

Kendra hesitated. The movie had tactfully deleted the scenes when Rhett tried to seduce Scarlett, but she didn't want to mention those. "For example, in the movie he tells Scarlett that he really loves her and wants their marriage to succeed. In the book he doesn't say that; he never would. He was too –"

"Proud," Steve supplied.

"Yes, they were both too proud. That was part of the problem."

Steve nodded. "Well, pride was the original sin."

"Was it?" Kendra asked. She didn't remember that from confirmation classes in the Catholic Church.

"Well, yes. Adam and Eve wanted to be like God; that was the beginning of their downfall."

"I want to know if Rhett and Scarlett ever got back together in the end," Allison broke in. "I was so disgusted when I got to the end of that movie and it left me hanging."

"The movie makes you think they did, but the book makes you think they didn't," Kendra said.

Steve looked at her and laughed. "And you liked the book? Enough to read it five times? I don't know, I don't know. Maybe if their daughter had lived, they would have worked it out. Then again, maybe not." He stood up and carried his glass to the sink. "Well, I'd better get going. I still have to get organized for school tomorrow. And for next week, you'll each read the first three chapters of *Till We Have Faces* and be ready to answer the questions. Okay?"

Allison laughed and shook her head as Steve departed.

Chapter Fifteen

"Three whole days with no responsibilities at all!" Kendra exclaimed to Leanne as they unloaded their belongings from Leanne's car. "I can't remember the last time I had three whole days to myself. Not since before Elizabeth was born."

Penny joined them, lugging her suitcase from Randy's car parked next to theirs. "So where is Elizabeth this weekend?"

"She flew out to Chicago to spend a week with my mother." Kendra grabbed her duffel bag with one hand and her pillow with the other. "She turned five this month, so she's finally able to fly alone. My mother has been wanting her to come for a long visit, so I thought this would be a good time."

"I guess it wouldn't work well for her to come on the retreat," Leanne agreed, "and it's nice that you have a break."

The retreat, which had unfortunately been canceled the summer before, had been scheduled this year for Memorial Day weekend. Kendra surveyed a rustic campground with four cabins, a dining hall, a chapel, and recreation hall. Between the buildings she could see a swimming pool, a volleyball court, and a hilly wooded area that might contain hiking trails. Her spirits buoyant, Kendra deposited her pillow and bag in a bunk next to Leanne, and the two of them set off to explore the grounds. Even Steve's presence here wasn't going to spoil this weekend. She was getting very good at forgetting about him.

After dinner was eaten and cleaned up, the group of thirty-some young people gathered in the recreation hall for the evening entertainment. Serena and Allison had planned games. The first icebreaker required each person to provide answers to a list of questions, and then the group had to guess which person matched each list.

The first few questions were easy for Kendra. Eyes – brown. Favorite movie – *Gone with the Wind*. Best talent – playing the piano. That one would give it away, she guessed. She hesitated when she came to Best Physical Feature. Many people had told her that she had nice legs, but she wasn't going to list that with all these men present. Instead she wrote "straight teeth." The last question said, "Describe your worst date." She knew what her worst date was, if it could be called a date, but she certainly wasn't going to mention that. Instead she wrote, "The time my boyfriend and I broke up."

The game provided much merriment when Serena read the answers aloud. Eddie listed his best feature as his biceps. Jesse described his worst date as "the time I rode my bike five miles to a girl's house, and when I got there she wouldn't let me in and wouldn't give me a drink of water." Allison listed her personal theme song as "You Can't Hurry Love." Steve said that his song was "Who Says You Can't Go Home?" and his favorite movie was *The Princess Bride*.

"It's a great movie," he insisted as everyone laughed at his taste. "Haven't you all seen it? 'My name is Iñigo Montoya. You killed my father – prepare to die.'"

Allison rolled her eyes. "Don't get him started. My cousins love that movie. Steve and Joe have half of it memorized."

When Kendra's list was read aloud, the whole group called out "Kendra!" almost in unison.

"Straight teeth?" Jesse turned to stare at Kendra's teeth. "Are you sure that's your best feature? What about your pretty brown eyes?"

"I never thought they were pretty," Kendra confessed. "And I can't see well."

Eddie chuckled. "Her pretty blind brown eyes."

When the girls retired to their cabin for the night, a discussion arose about the men in the group. The eight women in Kendra's cabin included a new girl, a cute redhead named Monica. Monica asked about Mark, and was informed by the other women that he was totally devoted to his long-distance girlfriend. Nearly everyone agreed that he was the handsomest guy in the group, but they were divided in their admiration of Dan and Steve.

"Steve has that gorgeous smile and those pretty blue eyes," Leanne pointed out from her bunk. "Dan's good-looking, but he never smiles."

Serena laughed. "Maybe that's why I like his looks. Steve's too much of a pretty boy for me."

Allison giggled as she propped herself up with her hands under her chin. "I have to tell you this story about Steve. When he was a baby, he was really pretty and had lots of curly hair, and everybody thought he was a girl. One day a woman came up to him in a store and said, 'Oh, you're so pretty – you're so pretty, you're going to break some boy's heart someday.' So when we were kids, that became our favorite line to annoy Steve."

All the girls laughed. "Steve would shoot you if he knew you told us that," Leanne said.

"I've always thought Jesse was cute," Ruth interjected.

"I think Jesse's cute too," Kendra agreed. "He has such a friendly personality. To me, that makes him cuter."

Someone asked, "What about that new guy, Adam? He seems pretty nice."

Serena shook her head. "He's Heidi's property."

The next morning when breakfast was over, everyone gathered in the chapel for the first teaching session. Randy announced that the topic for the weekend was the Sovereignty of God.

They discussed the life of Job, and why God had allowed so many tragedies to test him. During the discussion Kendra noticed that Heidi was indeed sitting next to Adam, and that they frequently smiled or whispered to each other. At lunch she happened to sit at their table and noticed the way Heidi giggled at everything he said. They must be dating, as Serena had suggested.

She left the dining hall by the back door, and was surprised to see Leanne sitting on the steps outside, tears in her eyes.

"What's wrong?" Kendra regarded her friend in astonishment.

"That Heidi!" Leanne almost spat the word. "Sometimes I can't stand her!"

"Leanne!" Kendra didn't know whether to be shocked or amused. No one ever talked that way about Heidi; everyone loved her. "What did Heidi do?"

Leanne wiped her eyes as Kendra dropped onto the step beside her. "She was going out with that new guy, Adam. And then Adam started calling me. Well, I asked him what was going on with Heidi, because I didn't want to get in the middle. And he said that Heidi had told him she only liked him as a friend. So we went out three or four times, and I thought it was going great. I thought, wow, maybe something will really happen here. But then –" Leanne gave a great sniff, "– he came on this retreat, and now Heidi's hanging all over him, flirting with him, giggling at everything he says."

"Yeah, I noticed that," Kendra agreed.

"Why did she tell him she just wanted to be friends? And then she wants him back when he starts dating me? She's such a man-hog. She has so many boyfriends."

Kendra sighed. "I know. How does she do it?"

The door behind them opened and they both turned to see Steve. He seemed startled at the sight of Leanne's tears. "Hey, what's wrong?"

"I don't want to tell you," Leanne sniffed.

He looked hurt. "Why not?"

"Because I know what you'll say."

"No, you don't. Try me and see."

"Oh, okay." She wiped her eyes and began her sad narrative as Steve dropped down on her other side. "And now you're going to say that I shouldn't be coming to the Timothy group to meet men, anyway."

"No, I wasn't. I know that's not the only reason you come." He thought for a minute. "Do you really like this guy?"

"Well, I was starting to. Before Heidi got her meaty claws into him."

Steve laughed. "Wow, you girls are really catty when you're fighting over a man. Heidi and Leanne, two of the nicest people I know." He pondered a moment. "I don't know this Adam very well, but he seems pretty stuffy to me. No sense of humor. I told him that great joke about the presidents and the Wizard of Oz, and he barely cracked a smile. No, he might be right for Heidi, but not for you, Leanne."

Leanne brightened a moment, then sighed. "I'll never meet the right one."

Steve grinned and ran his hand through his hair. "How old are you? Twenty-five?" She nodded. "Listen: if neither of us is married by time we're thirty, we can get married. Okay?"

Leanne managed a smile. "Like in the movie. But he married someone else, and you will too, Steve." She fell silent a moment. "Two years ago on this retreat, Randy asked me out for the first time. I keep remembering it."

Steve gave her a look of sympathy. "Randy's engaged."

"Randy? To Penny?"

He nodded. "They're going to announce it this weekend. I thought I should give you a heads-up."

"Thanks." Leanne sighed heavily. She kicked a stone with her shoe. "Another one bites the dust."

Steve laughed and put his arm around her shoulder. "Oh, your turn will come. Listen, we're getting ready to start a game of Emperor. Come play with us, both of you. We won't let Heidi play."

They were joined by several others, including the new girl named Monica. They gathered around a table in the dining room and someone produced a deck of cards. Kendra had never played the game before, and as she learned the rules and played the first few hands, she noticed how Monica gazed at Steve and simpered and blushed whenever he looked in her direction.

Suddenly she was back at Gregg's party almost six years ago, seeing in Monica's reaction a perfect reflection of herself as she had been at sixteen. What a fool she had been! No wonder all the guys at that party had seen her as such an easy mark. She felt her face burn with a sudden powerful shame.

And then another thought struck her. Was that the reason that it was so hard for her to be friendly to guys? Why she could never let a guy know when she was attracted to him? It was true that she hadn't dated in the group, but she also didn't encourage any of the men who might be interested. The thought of appearing too bold, too flirtatious, too easy, terrified her.

Steve joked to Monica about the cards they had just exchanged, and Monica made a giggling rejoinder, batting her lashes at him. He glanced up, happened to meet Kendra's gaze, and ducked his head in embarrassment.

Did he remember too? But it was different for men. He hadn't been humiliated that night, as she had been.

She suffered through the game in silence and made her escape afterward to the female sanctuary of her cabin. She stretched out on her bunk, her cheek against her pillow, as all the old questions she had suppressed for so long resurfaced, making an endless circle in her mind. What had Steve been thinking that night? Why had he chosen her, of all the girls at the party? Did he blame her, as Gregg did? Since his apology by letter nine months ago, they had never discussed it, and she didn't know if she would ever have the courage or opportunity to ask him these questions. Maybe she would rather not know the answers.

The next teaching session began at three o'clock in the chapel. Mark taught on the life of Joseph.

"So how do we reconcile the evil choices made by Joseph's brothers with the sovereignty of God?" Mark asked as he concluded his lesson. "This is a difficult topic; it's hard for humans, with our limited perspective, to understand how God can be sovereign when he allows evil to exist and flourish. I'm sure it was hard for Joseph, in the pit, as a slave in Potiphar's household, and then in prison, to understand how God could be sovereign. This certainly wasn't the plan Joseph had for his own life, or what he imagined when he dreamed of the moon and stars and sun bowing to him. But this story is a wonderful illustration of how God took the evil that men could devise in their jealousy and greed and spite, and used it to bring Joseph to the exact place where he could fulfill God's purposes, instead of his own."

Allison chimed in. "Yeah, it's easy to see in this story. We can see how it all works out in the end. In our own lives, or people that we know, we don't understand what God is trying to do, and that's hard."

"That's where we need faith," Randy agreed.

Finding Father

Emma added, "I think it's easy, too, to make light of what Joseph actually suffered. Sure, he became the ruler of Egypt, but he still spent thirteen years in slavery and prison. And that's not a piece of cake. Even if he had known – which he didn't at the time – how it was all going to end, it still wouldn't have been easy."

Kendra pondered the discussion as she went back to the cabin to leave her Bible there before joining the crew to cook dinner. She found Leanne and Ruth sitting side by side on the one of the bunks, and this time Ruth was in tears.

"What's wrong?" Kendra glanced between the two friends with a question in her eyes.

Leanne sighed. "It's Jesse again. He doesn't know what he wants."

"Everything has been going so well for the last month or two." Ruth wiped her eyes with the back of her hand. "Now, this weekend, he's hanging all over that new girl, Monica, and barely talking to me. At the last session, he walked right past me where I had saved a seat for him, and went over and sat next to her!"

"He's acting like a jerk." Leanne put her arm around Ruth and squeezed her.

Monica – the same girl who had been trying to flirt with Steve. Ruth was in love with Jesse, and Jesse was chasing Monica, who clearly liked Steve. Kendra didn't know whether to laugh or cry in sympathy with Ruth. Did any two people ever feel the same way about each other? Sometimes love seemed hopeless.

"I've decided this weekend that I'm going to become a nun," Kendra announced. "Which of you two wants to join me?"

Ruth laughed and wiped her eyes. Leanne sighed and shook her head. "You know, after this weekend, I think I'm ready too. Men! They're more trouble than they're worth!"

❀ ❁

That evening the group gathered again in the chapel. Mark brought out his guitar.

"We're not going to have any teaching tonight," Randy announced. "Instead, I've asked several people if they would share their testimonies with the group. After that I'd like to have a time of singing and sharing and prayer." He glanced at Penny, who was sitting next to him. "Penny, do you want to go first?"

Penny smiled nervously, swallowed, and opened a piece of paper in her lap. "Well, I hope you don't mind, but I wrote this down, so I don't forget anything." She began to read. "I always tried to live a good life and attended church since I was a child. I got married when I was twenty-one, and at that time thought my life was almost perfect. But it wasn't until I was twenty-four that a friend shared with me that being a Christian was more than just going to church and trying to be good. It involved a relationship with Jesus and following wherever he led.

"I told Jesus that I was willing to follow him no matter what. Well, he really tested me on this, because two months later my husband told me that he had met someone else and wanted a divorce. I was devastated. If the person I loved and trusted more than anyone in the world could reject and betray me this way, who could I possibly trust? I prayed and prayed that this divorce would not occur, and when I received the final notice, I was crushed. I didn't understand why God did not answer my prayers."

She paused, glanced around the room, and then back at her paper. She took a deep breath and blinked several times.

"But even in my pain and confusion I clung to God and his word. He promised that he would not let me be tempted beyond what I was able to bear. He said he wanted me to be at peace. So finally I stopped fighting him and told him I would trust him even in these new circumstances. If he wanted me to be single for the rest of my life, I would serve him anyway. I prayed that he would bring me a group of Christian friends who would be a support for me. God quickly answered this prayer through my friend Jean, who introduced me to the Timothy group.

"I don't know why God allowed my divorce to occur. I know that he hates divorce, but I also know he is sovereign and that I can trust him with my life. A verse that has meant a lot to me is Romans 8:28: "And we know that all things work together for good to those that love God, to those that are called according to his purpose."

She looked up at Randy, and he gave her an encouraging smile.

For just second Kendra felt a flash of envy. Penny and Randy were one of those rare lucky couples who felt the same way about each other. And yet, Penny had gone through a hard trial too.

After they sang two songs with the guitar, Randy glanced around the circle of faces. "Steve?"

Steve smiled a wry, uncomfortable smile, and Kendra thought he looked unusually somber, unlike his usual lighthearted self. "Well, I didn't write anything down," he began. "I was raised in this church and attended every Sunday when I was a child. My grandparents, the Kirks, were – still are – really godly people. I knew the Bible inside and out. When I was twelve, I probably understood the gospel as well as anyone in this room. But it hadn't changed my heart.

"When I was about thirteen, my parents started having problems. At least, that's when I became aware of them. They split up when I was fourteen, and at that point I became very angry and rebellious and spiritually hard. I'm sure I was angry at my parents, and probably angry at God too because my parents' faith hadn't been enough to save their marriage. So I rejected the whole thing. I started getting in trouble – drinking, cutting school, staying out late. All the usual stuff.

"When I was eighteen I went away to college. Of course I had more freedom there, and I took advantage of it to 'experiment.' I joined the rowdiest fraternity I could find and indulged in the whole lifestyle. I won't go into detail about all that. At the same time I tried to tell myself that I really wasn't a bad person and that Christians are all hypocrites anyway. But I wasn't happy. I looked happy and acted happy, but as time went on I felt less and less satisfied. There's a passage in *The Screwtape Letters* that talks about Satan taking more and more, and giving less and less satisfaction in return. That's the way I felt."

He paused and took a deep breath, looking down at the floor. "When I was in my final year of college, I had an experience that made me realize how far I had fallen from my upbringing. I became very depressed afterward. I was getting ready to graduate and should have been on the top of the world, but I couldn't shake this sense of really despising myself and feeling that I had already messed up my life. I would remember different things I had done during my college years and I just wanted to hide inside my closet. My parents – all four of them – came to my graduation and I remember my mom saying, 'Oh, Steve, we're so proud of you.' And I thought, you wouldn't be proud if you knew everything.

"I went home after graduation and moved in with my mother. She had remarried and she and her husband were walking with the Lord. And it seemed that spring and summer I couldn't get away from Christians wherever I went. Before I graduated I knew a Christian girl at college, and even though she didn't say much about God, I felt uncomfortable whenever I was with her. Then I got a summer job and one of my coworkers was a Christian. We went to lunch one day and in his car he played a CD of old hymns. One line said over and over, 'Come home, come home, ye who are weary, come home.' I thought it was a stupid song at the time, but those words wouldn't get out of my head. I was so weary and wanted to go home, but I was fighting it too because I was proud.

"One Sunday I decided to go to church with my family. I don't even remember what the sermon was about, but I was shaking inside at the end. I knew I had to do something; I couldn't live with myself and my misery anymore. I went up to Pastor Mike and we talked for two hours, right on the spot. At the end he said to me, 'Steve, I don't need to tell you what to do. You know what you need to do. You know how to get right with the Lord.'

Steve was silent a moment. "I would like to say my life became perfect after that. I know I'm a new creature and I'm in the process of being 'transformed by the renewing of my mind,' like the Bible says. But I still have to deal with a lot of issues from the past. I made a lot of mistakes, and I'm still paying and other people are paying. Last fall I went through a time of real discouragement, of Satan attacking me and making me feel worthless. It got so bad that I would sit in church and hear a voice in my mind saying over and over, 'You are such a useless Christian...you are worthless...you have already ruined your life...how could God ever use you?' I couldn't pray or sing or do anything, I was so depressed.

"One week Jay asked me to fill in for him on the worship team. I didn't really want to, but I agreed because I didn't have a good excuse. As I was standing up on the platform, I looked out over the congregation and saw everyone singing, praising God. And I thought, wow, I am leading the church in worship – what an awesome privilege! And at that moment the cloud of depression lifted and it never came back."

He paused a moment, biting his lip. He swallowed.

"Soon after that I read this passage in the Bible that has been really meaningful to me. It's in Luke seven." He opened his Bible and read a short passage aloud. "'Therefore I tell you, her many sins have been forgiven – for she loved much. But he who has been forgiven little loves little.'

"Of course, this is talking about a sinful woman, but I can relate to that woman. I believe God was telling me that because he has forgiven me of many things, I'll have a greater love for him all my life, and that's something I can be thankful for."

He stopped and looked to Randy.

"Thanks, Steve," Randy said. "And of course, the point of that passage is that all of us have been forgiven of many sins, but some of us recognize it and some of us don't."

Chapter Sixteen

The retreat ended Monday afternoon, and Elizabeth's flight was scheduled to arrive late Tuesday afternoon. Kendra left work an hour early and hurried to the airport to meet her flight. On the ride home she listened to the child bubble over about her adventures with her grandmother and her airplane ride.

When they pulled up in front of the house, Kendra was surprised to see Steve's silver Toyota parked in front. Inside she found him talking to Allison about the retreat. He explained that he had a book he needed to return, but Kendra couldn't help suspecting that he was actually looking for an excuse to see Elizabeth. He greeted the child with enthusiasm.

"Grandma gave me a movie for my birthday." Elizabeth opened her suitcase and pulled it out, showing the three adults. It was *The Parent Trap*. "Can we watch it now?"

"Sometime, honey. First let's get unpacked."

Elizabeth ran upstairs to her room. Kendra started to follow, but stopped at Allison's question. "Did either of you hear about the blowup Serena had with Vince?"

Kendra shook her head. Steve said, "I missed that."

"Well, on Sunday afternoon, Vince pulled Serena aside to talk to her. He said, in essence, 'You're causing me to lust.' He told her things she did that were causing that. And Serena said to him, 'Well, Vince, if you can't keep your mind out of the gutter, that's your problem, not mine.'"

Steve's eyes widened in horror. "You're kidding."

"No, I'm serious. Isn't that awful?"

"Yeah." Steve shook his head. "I don't think she should have said that."

Allison was silent a moment. "What should she have said?"

"I don't know, but not that. I know Vince can be obnoxious at times, but she could have just said, 'Okay, Vince, I'll try to be more careful.' She could have shown a little humility."

Allison sighed. "I guess she was annoyed because of Vince's attitude. He's always putting down women, acting like they're a lower species or something. You know how he is."

"I know how he is," Steve agreed. "I also know how Serena is."

"What do you mean?"

"Oh, I shouldn't have said that. Now you're going to tell Serena I don't like her, and I'll be on her bad list too."

"No, I won't say anything. Do you have a problem with Serena?" Steve was silent. "Does she cause you to lust too?" Allison giggled.

"No!" Steve rolled his eyes in annoyance. "I just see that whenever there's a problem, it's always the other person's fault. Her issues with her boss. And her father. To hear her talk, her ex-husband was totally insane, and I don't believe it. She's never willing to say, 'Okay, I could be part of the problem here.' This whole conflict with Vince is just one more example."

Kendra, listening in silence, had to agree with Steve's analysis. She had noticed that same trait in Serena herself. "She has a problem with men," Kendra said.

Steve glanced at her and nodded. "Especially male authority figures."

Allison sighed. "And Vince has a problem with women. So the two of them are just doomed to clash. What a mess."

"Yeah, Vince has a strange attitude toward women. I don't get it. Whenever he talks about what he wants in a wife, he always mentions submissiveness. When I think about what I want in a wife, that hardly crosses the radar screen. I want someone with common interests, who I enjoy talking to, who would be a good mother – that sort of thing. I don't understand Vince at all."

Finding Father

The weekend had been fun, Kendra reflected, but three whole days together had certainly brought conflicts in the group to the surface: Leanne and Heidi, Ruth and Jesse, and now Serena and Vince. Secretly she found herself relieved that her interactions with Steve appeared so smooth on the surface. No one but the two of them seemed to realize any problem existed at all. She could just imagine how shocked everyone would be if they found out.

That Saturday her mother called as she did most weekends. As Kendra told her about the events of the retreat, trying to avoid mentioning Steve's name, her mother interrupted her. "Kendra, who is this Steve who's been babysitting for Elizabeth?"

Kendra's heart dropped and she gulped. She had hoped that Elizabeth wouldn't mention Steve's weekly visits to her mother. For just a minute she was tempted to lie, but rejected the temptation.

"It's Steve Dixon," she mumbled. She knew exactly the reaction she would get.

"I can't believe it." Her mother's voice was tense with anger. "I can't believe you would let your daughter within ten feet of that creep. Kendra, what are you thinking?"

Kendra swallowed. How could she explain this decision in any way that would make sense to her mother? "He's her father, and he wants to spend time with her –"

"Kendra, do you know how many girls have been molested by their fathers?"

Kendra knew her mother was right, and fell silent for a moment. "But – but I don't have any reason to think Steve would do anything like that –"

"Kendra!" Her mother practically screamed into the phone. "Look what he did to you!"

Kendra bit her lip. "That was different."

"Different! How was it different?"

"I wasn't four years old – and besides, he's changed."

"Changed!" Kendra thought her mother would break a blood vessel. "Kendra, I don't know what's wrong with you that you can rationalize like that. When you think of everything you've been through – I don't know if you have some kind of psychological need to have this guy in your life –"

"I don't have any psychological need!" For almost the first time in her life, Kendra found herself yelling at her mother. "But I'm trying to raise this child all alone and it's really hard! Steve is her father and he wants to help, so I'm letting him. I certainly can't depend on you anymore."

A long moment of silence echoed across the phone lines. When her mother spoke again, her voice trembled. "Kendra, I'm sorry if you feel I've let you down. Maybe I made a mistake in moving so far away. I just don't want you to live with the regret that I've had all these years, that I didn't do enough to protect my daughter."

"Oh, Mother, it wasn't your fault." She took a deep breath and tried to control her own frustration, to lower the tension in the conversation. "Don't you think I've thought of all these things before? I've talked to Elizabeth about it, and – and I'll talk to Steve too." She gulped. "But don't you see? If Steve wanted to, he could go to court and demand visitation rights. That's what I'm trying to avoid. That's why I'm trying to compromise with him."

"I wish that guy would just drop dead! I wish he would get run over by a truck and be out of your life forever!"

Startled, Kendra realized that she didn't share her mother's venom toward Steve. She wasn't happy about his reappearance in her life and still felt uncomfortable around him at times, but she had to admit that he was doing his best with an exceedingly difficult and awkward situation. He was always kind and respectful toward Kendra and seemed genuinely attached to Elizabeth. In her heart of hearts, she had to admit that she would have respected him less if he had been willing to walk away from his daughter forever, even if it made her own life easier.

༄ ༅

"Okay, here's the score." Tom held the golf scorecard to Steve in the front seat. "I beat you by three strokes."

"Oh, you dog." Steve grinned as he glanced at the card. "I was playing pretty well up till this one hole, when I lost my ball."

Scott glanced over from behind the wheel. "Neither of you played as badly as I did. Golf just isn't my sport."

Finding Father

"It's hard to play football on vacation."

Steve rolled down the car window and let the breeze cool his face. He could smell the salt in the air as they approached the beach town on the Jersey shore where the family was spending their annual vacation. It was one of the highlights of the year for all of them. His grandfather rented several houses in town and the whole family piled in together for a week. Some mornings they rode bikes on the boardwalk, often buying homemade donuts at their favorite shop. Afternoons were spent on the beach, or playing tennis or golf. In the evening they all walked on the boardwalk and looked in the shops, sometimes stopping in the video arcades or the amusement rides. Afterward they tended to stay up late, playing games or watching movies. This year the weather had been almost perfect – only one partly rainy day. It didn't get any better than this.

Elizabeth would love this vacation. She would love the miniature golf and the rides on the boardwalk. Would he ever be able to bring her to spend the week with the rest of the family? What would his mother, his sister, his cousins have to say? And would Kendra ever agree?

They reached the large beach house with its striped awnings and wide front porch. His sister Joyce sat on the porch, reading a book. Steve opened the front door and was surprised to see Elizabeth sitting there on the floor, playing with his cousin Abby. Allison had mentioned that she had invited Kendra for a day, but he had doubted that she would actually come.

"Lisbet!"

She looked up, then scrambled to her feet. "Steve!"

He picked her up and grinned as her little arms squeezed around his neck. "Did your mom bring you? Where is she?"

"She's in the shower. We went to the beach and made a sand castle and played in the water. And a wave knocked me down and I got water up my nose."

He touched her fair pink skin. "Looks like you got a little sunburn." Her hair was wet and she smelled like shampoo.

She ran back to Abby and a moment later Kendra came down the stairs. Even with wet hair and no makeup, she still looked pretty. She smiled when she saw him. "Allison told me you were playing golf. So who won?"

He found himself oddly pleased by her friendliness. For her to be smiling at him and speaking voluntarily showed how far he had come in her good graces. And she wouldn't have come today if she still wanted to avoid him. He grinned and shook his head. "Tom beat me by three strokes."

"Too bad. At least you had nice weather for it."

"Yeah, it was great. The whole week has been nice. Are you two staying for dinner?"

"I think so. Your grandmother invited us." She crossed the room to the playing children. "Here, Elizabeth, I need to comb out your hair before it dries." Kneeling behind her, she carefully began combing the child's hair. Elizabeth tried to pull her head away. "Now hold still or it's going to hurt more." She touched the child's shoulders. "Oh, baby, you're sunburned! After all the sunscreen I put on you! I need to get the aloe for you." She glanced at Steve. "Her skin is so fair – she burns more easily than I do."

Kendra was really a very gentle, nurturing sort of person. "I was wondering if I could take Elizabeth up on the boardwalk for a game of miniature golf before dinner," Steve said.

Elizabeth clapped her hands. Abby jumped up from the floor and ran to her cousin. "Oh, can I come too, Steve?"

Rebecca called out from the dining room. "We want to play miniature golf too!"

Steve frowned, annoyed. "Well, I didn't want to take four kids all by myself."

In the end Allison, Kendra, and Joyce joined the golf excursion. The sun was lowering in the sky and the shadows from the buildings lengthening as they walked along the boardwalk. Shops, food stands, and arcades lined the right side of the boardwalk; to the left, across the expanse of beach, the Atlantic Ocean stretched out to the horizon, white-capped waves breaking at regular intervals. The crowd on the beach was thinning out as people headed home for dinner. Steve sniffed caramel popcorn and cotton candy and the omnipresent scent of the ocean. A gang of seagulls pecked at an abandoned hot dog on the boards. It was a lovely day.

Kendra and Allison formed a team with the twins while Steve

Finding Father

and Joyce took the two little girls. Elizabeth had never played before and Steve showed her how to hold her club and aim. Even so, she was erratic with her shots, but laughed as she chased her ball around the green. In the end Allison was declared the winner of both groups and they headed back down the boardwalk toward their beach house.

Steve and Elizabeth lingered a bit behind the rest of the group, allowing the others to outstrip them as they watched seagulls on the boardwalk attack some spilled French fries. Kendra glanced back at them once, and then waited for them to catch up with her.

"Listen honey, could you run and catch up with Aunt Allie? I want to talk to Steve a minute."

Elizabeth ran ahead with the others. Steve gave Kendra a questioning look. "What's up?"

She waited till her daughter was out of earshot. "Elizabeth told my mother that you've been babysitting for her, and my mother freaked out. She thinks you're a child molester."

Outraged, he turned to stare at her. "That's not true! I've never, never done anything – why would your mother –?" He stopped and bit his lip. "Look, I admit I've done some wrong things with women, but I've never, never been interested in children that way – that's disgusting!"

"I was sixteen," Kendra reminded him.

"Yeah, and I was nineteen. I wasn't exactly an old man. I could have been your boyfriend."

Kendra looked away. Of course, he hadn't been her boyfriend – that was part of the whole problem. For a moment they walked in silence as Steve tried to grasp the enormity of this new suspicion – one that hadn't seriously occurred to him until now. It would be the easiest thing in the world for Kendra to make an accusation like this, and then manipulate Elizabeth into backing her up. It would effectively keep him out of her life, and Elizabeth's life, forever. It would be the perfect revenge – would humiliate him in the eyes of his family and friends – cost him his job and his career – even if he managed to stay out of prison. The dreadful possibilities took his breath away.

"Are you serious about this?" he asked finally.

"My mother is."

"Well, that puts me in a pretty impossible position, trying to prove I wouldn't do something." He brightened. "Why don't you ask Elizabeth?"

"I did ask her," Kendra said.

"Well, then, she would tell you – I mean, she wouldn't – she didn't –" He found himself stammering. Had Elizabeth actually accused him of something horrible? But she always seemed so fond of him – so happy to see him!

He had the feeling from Kendra's expression that she was enjoying watching him sweat, but after a minute she said, "No, she didn't say anything like that."

Relief flooded him. He took a deep breath and expelled it audibly. "Look, Kendra, I want to help you out and I want to spend time with Elizabeth, but I don't want to be accused of something I never did, that I would never dream of doing. If someone accused me of that, even if it wasn't true, I would lose my job. It could ruin my career. Do you understand?"

"Yes," she said.

"I know this is hard for you, but you need to decide if you can give me the benefit of the doubt and trust me a little. If you can't, maybe you should tell me so right now."

Kendra was silent a moment and then spoke carefully, her eyes on the boards at her feet. "I want to trust you, Steve, but I want you to know this. I didn't report that – that other incident, but if anything ever happened to Elizabeth, I would. That man would rot in prison forever. I just want you to know."

He nodded. "I know. I understand. But you don't have to protect her from me, because I would never hurt her. I mean it."

Elizabeth turned and ran back to her mother's side. "Look, Mommy!" She pointed to the amusement park rides, where the merry-go-round had just begun to spin. "Rides! Can I go on one? Please?"

Kendra smiled and patted her back. "Not now, honey. We need to get back to the house for dinner."

Elizabeth's face fell. Steve said, "Maybe after dinner, Elizabeth. We'll come up here as soon as we eat and go on a few rides before you have to leave. Okay?"

Elizabeth smiled with delight and made a little skip. She reached out and took Steve's hand and swung his arm as they walked along.

Chapter Seventeen

One hot Saturday afternoon Kendra and Allison were cleaning the house together when Allison's cell phone rang. Kendra, mopping the kitchen floor and listening to her friend's tense, hushed questions, knew that something drastic had occurred. When she hung up and joined Kendra in the kitchen, she had tears in her eyes.

"It's my grandmother," she explained. "That was my mother, and she told me that my grandmother just had a stroke. My grandfather found her unconscious on the couch; he called 911, but when they got to the hospital, she was already dead."

"Oh, I'm so sorry." Kendra had only met Mrs. Kirk twice, at Christmas dinner and again at the beach, but she had heard both Allison and Steve speak of her with great love and respect. "This was a big shock, wasn't it?"

Allison nodded. "We thought she was in good health. I just went shopping with her last week for quilt material. She made a quilt for each of the other girls when they got married, and she told me this would be mine. I can't believe she's gone."

Kendra remembered her father's long and painful battle with cancer. "It's terrible, but at least she didn't suffer much. There are worse ways to go, I think."

"I know. She kept active up till the end, and that's the way she would have wanted it. It's just such a shock. I thought she would live forever."

The next day when Kendra arrived home after church, Allison

told her what she knew of the funeral arrangements. "Some of my cousins are going to sing a hymn at the funeral, and they're coming over here tonight to practice it. I was wondering, Kendra, if you could play it on the piano for us?"

Kendra nodded. "Sure. Just give me the music."

They arrived around seven, Tom Reese and his wife Renee, his sister Kate, and Steve and Joyce Dixon. Renee brought her baby, who could walk now and toddled around the basement as they practiced. Elizabeth seemed fascinated by the baby, so Kendra told her to keep her entertained while they practiced.

Kendra played through the hymn several times. When she had most of the notes right, the cousins sang with her, dividing into four-part harmony. Kate sang most of the second verse as a solo, and after considerable debate, Steve was given a two-line solo as well.

"Kendra, could you bang the tenor out for me? I don't quite have it down," he said, and Kendra obliged.

"Who is playing for the funeral?" Tom looked around the circle. "We'll have to practice with the pianist sometime."

Kendra glanced over her shoulder. "The funeral is Wednesday? If you need me, I could probably take off work to come play for you."

"Aunt Lisa will probably do it," Joyce said.

The next evening Allison's mother called. Kendra heard her own name mentioned, and Allison set down the phone. "Kendra, do you think you could really get off work for the funeral? Aunt Lisa sprained her wrist, and the regular church pianist can't be there. We're having a hard time finding someone else."

Kendra looked up from the laundry she was folding. "I guess so. I'll ask my boss tomorrow. I'll just need the music ahead of time, so I can practice it."

Kendra's accounting course had ended in late May, but Steve continued dropping by the house on most Tuesday evenings. Kendra knew that he wanted to spend that time with Elizabeth, and the arrangement worked for her, as it gave her a free evening to go shopping or run errands. Since their conversation in February he had not pressed for a paternity test or any official agreement, and

Kendra was relieved to be able to leave the situation alone. She didn't try to determine if they could continue in this pattern forever.

Elizabeth also seemed happy to spend one evening a week with Steve. He gave her lots of attention, brought her new books and movies, and exuded more energy and enthusiasm than her tired, overworked mother. Maybe Allison was right when she said that it was good for Elizabeth to have a man in her life who cared about her. Of course, Kendra's fondest hope was that she would marry eventually and provide a good stepfather for her child, and Steve Dixon would become superfluous. What would happen then was another question she did not stop to examine too closely. Maybe by then Steve would have a girlfriend himself and be ready to move on.

She went to work early on Wednesday and took off at ten o'clock to get to church for the funeral, leaving Elizabeth at her daycare. Elizabeth had never been to a funeral before and Kendra feared it would be upsetting for her. The family had given Kendra three hymns that they planned to use, in addition to the one the cousins were singing. Kendra took her place at the piano as the Kirk, Andrews, Reese, and Dixon families filed into the pews and the pastor of Bethel Bible Church took his place at the pulpit.

She expected the funeral to be sad, but it was surprisingly comforting and even joyful as many friends and family members shared about the life of Mrs. Kirk. The faith of the family was so strong and clear in their choice of hymns, the scriptures that were read, and finally in the meditation shared by the pastor, obviously a close friend of the family. It was more personal than any funeral Kendra had ever attended before, and as she played the last hymn tears welled up in her own eyes, although the woman had been mostly a stranger to her.

Why had she agreed to come today? To help the family, of course, but they would have understood if she had used work as an excuse. Was there perhaps a small part of her that felt that she had a right, an obligation to be here? If not for her own sake, then for Elizabeth's – as an unacknowledged part of the family, to mourn for the great-grandmother that her daughter would never know?

As the mourners filed out of the church, Allison approached her. "Can you come to the cemetery with us, or do you need to get back to work?"

Kendra shook her head. "I told my boss I wouldn't be back at all today. I wasn't sure how long it would last."

"Then come with us. There will be a lunch afterward back at the church. You should get something to eat."

Kendra rode in one of the cars with Allison, her sister, and a cousin. The six grandsons were pallbearers; Kendra watched as Steve, in a black suit, took his place by the coffin with the others. After the solemn graveside service, they rode back to the church for the meal. Kendra stood in line at the buffet table and filled a plate of food.

"Do you recognize that man over there?" Allison gestured across the room to an elderly man who was talking to her father.

Heather peered in the direction she indicated. "That's Uncle Horace, isn't it?"

Allison giggled. "I know, I haven't seen him in ages." She lowered her voice as she spoke to Kendra. "He's my grandfather's brother. He spent a long time in jail, so we never saw him much as we were growing up."

"Well, funerals have a way of bringing the family skeletons out of the closet," Steve remarked. "My dad even showed up at the service. Did you see him?"

Allison nodded. Kendra asked, "Were you surprised?"

"Well, my grandparents weren't too happy with him when he left my mother. But at least everybody was polite to him today."

Kendra waited until the others had moved a few feet away and were talking to each other. She leaned close and spoke in a low tone to Steve. "I guess I'm the skeleton in your closet. Don't worry, I'm doing my best to stay there."

Steve threw her a startled look. He opened his mouth to reply, but stopped as his mother approached them.

"Oh, Kendra, I so appreciate you helping us out today with the piano. I'm sure you had to take time off work. That was really sweet of you."

"I didn't mind," Kendra smiled. "I'm glad I could help."

"Well, I just thought the service was really lovely, didn't you? Just the way my mother would have wanted it. And the kids did a nice job with their song too. By the way, have you met my brother?" She paused as a man of about fifty, with glasses and salt-and-pepper hair, joined them. "Jack, this is Kendra, Steve and Allie's friend."

It sounded so strange to hear herself referred to as Steve's friend, but as Kendra reflected on the statement during the rest of the day, she realized that it was true. In a rather odd sort of way, she and Steve had become friends. Certainly they weren't enemies anymore. When the lunch ended, Kendra picked Elizabeth up from her daycare and drove her to Steve's mother's house, where all the females of the family had gathered to watch a movie. Someone had chosen *Phantom of the Opera*, and as they watched, Steve wandered in and out of the living room, singing along with the movie when the songs became especially dramatic.

"Shut up, Steve, you're ruining it," Joyce said.

"You think that guy sings better than I do?"

His cousins laughed.

"I still can't figure out if the Phantom is the hero or the villain," Kendra remarked.

Steve grinned. "Well, Raoul is a tenor. The hero of an opera is always a tenor, you know."

Elizabeth jumped up from the couch and ran to his side, "Steve, can you read to me? This movie is scary."

"Sure, Lisbet. Don't let that old Phantom bother you." He took her hand and led her off to the next room.

⊱ ⊰

At one Bible study toward the end of August, Ben Stafford asked Kendra to go to a church event with him on Sunday night. After some hesitation, she agreed. She had never been particularly interested in Ben, but after complaining with Allison about their dateless situation for the last year, it seemed wrong to refuse. Ben was a nice, quiet sort of boy, and it couldn't hurt to get to know him better.

The date was a disappointment, and she was doubly annoyed when Allison mentioned it to Steve on Tuesday night. Allison had many good traits, but the tendency to keep information private was not one of them.

"Kendra had a date with Ben on Sunday night." The two of them were sitting in the living room, talking, when Kendra joined them. "She came in my bedroom when she got home and said, 'Tonight was the final straw! I'm going to become a nun!'"

Instead of laughing, Steve glanced at Kendra with a quizzical expression. "What's wrong with Ben?"

"There's nothing wrong with Ben," Kendra began in annoyance, "He's a nice guy, he's just so –" She stopped and bit her lip.

Allison leaned toward Steve and spoke in a stage whisper. "Boring!"

Steve began to laugh. "Oh!"

"He doesn't talk," Kendra burst out in frustration. "We drove all the way to his church, and he hardly spoke the whole way. I got sick of trying to think of things to say. I wished I had brought Elizabeth along, just for the entertainment value. And then when we got to this church dinner, we were the only people there under the age of fifty."

Steve was still laughing. "No one will ever accuse Ben of being a great conversationalist. Or the life of the party, either."

Allison folded her arms and leaned forward with an exasperated expression. "What's wrong with all the guys in this group, Steve? We have Ben, who has the social skills of a houseplant, and Jesse, who's been stringing poor Ruth along for a year and can't make a commitment, and Vince, who annoys all the girls and embarrasses Leanne by staring at her chest when he talks to her. Then there are you and Dan and Eddie, who act like girls have cooties..."

Steve scowled. "No, we don't."

"Well, none of you ever date, anyway."

"We do. Sometimes. I went out with Heidi a few times –"

"Heidi!" Allison almost spat the name.

"What's wrong with Heidi?"

"Everybody goes out with Heidi. Why don't you ask some girl who doesn't have a million boyfriends already?"

"Well, so sorry I picked the wrong girl!" Steve glared at her.

To Kendra's horror, Allison actually jerked her thumb at her. "Look at Kendra. She says that guys at work ask her out all the time, but guys at church never do."

"Well, of course the guys at work ask her out –" Steve bit off the words.

Kendra threw Allison a warning glare, but her friend chose to ignore her. "Well, why don't the Christian guys ask her?" Steve was silent. "Do you think the guys at work are just looking for sex?"

"I didn't say that." He ducked his head, running his hand through his hair.

"Then what's the difference?"

Steve hesitated, and Kendra felt her face burn. She knew perfectly well what Steve was thinking, although he was too polite to say it. The guys at church were looking for a nice Christian girl to marry, and they didn't want Kendra. Only someone like Ben, who knew nothing about women, would be interested in her. She stared down at the carpet, wanting to vanish through the floor.

"Some of us have made big mistakes in the past." He sounded hesitant, as if he were choosing his words with care. "We're just trying to be careful, to not make the same mistakes again. I guess that's why some of us don't date very much. I don't think you should criticize us for that."

Kendra rose silently from her chair and climbed the stairs to her bedroom. Elizabeth was already sound asleep in one of the twin beds. Kendra fell across her own bed and buried her face in the coolness of her pillow as her tears soaked into it.

Steve had never referred so directly to their past experience in front of others before. She knew he hadn't intended to hurt her, but the humiliation of that night rushed over her like a tidal wave. She felt so used and dirty, like such a piece of leftover refuse. Who was she kidding, to think that a nice guy, a Christian man, would actually want to marry her? Who would ever want her if he knew everything? Kyle certainly hadn't, even without knowing the whole truth. Maybe she was just kidding herself to hope that there was someone out there who would really love her and accept her completely, with all her baggage.

She heard Allison's footsteps ascend the stairs, and as she tried to dry her eyes, she broke into a fresh spate a weeping. It had been years since she had allowed this feeling of hopelessness to overwhelm her this way, and suddenly she couldn't control it.

She heard the door open.

"Kendra, are you all right? Look I didn't mean to embarrass you down there. I just wanted Steve to explain these guys to me, and I was using you as an example."

Kendra rolled over and sat up in bed. "I hate my life!" She hit her fist against the bedspread. "I hate myself! I hate Steve!" In the other bed Elizabeth stirred at the sound of her mother's voice.

"Steve? What did he do?" Allison looked bewildered. "What are you talking about? Why are you so upset?"

"You heard what he said!" Tears were dripping down her face. "No guy is ever going to want me! My life is ruined!"

"Kendra!" Allison looked at her as if she had lost her mind. "Steve never said that! He didn't say anything like that. He was just trying to explain why the guys don't date much, that's all."

Kendra rolled over again and buried her face. For the first time she had an overpowering urge to spill the whole story into Allison's ear, to tell her everything. But once she told, she could never take it back. Reticence and the habit of secrecy won out, and she said nothing, but wept.

"Those guys have hang-ups about women, but their problems have nothing to do with you, or any other girl in this group. Don't take it so personally." Allison paused a moment, as Kendra continued to hide in her pillow. "Sometimes I've thought Steve might ask you out, if you just gave him a little encouragement."

Kendra had never been so astounded in her life. She rolled over again and sat up. "Whatever gave you that idea?"

"Well, you know how he's always hanging around here, being nice to Elizabeth. But Kendra, you don't encourage him at all. You ignore him most of the time. You need to smile at him more, flirt a little. You're friendly to the other girls, but so cool to the guys."

Of course, Allison didn't know the real reason Steve was so nice to Elizabeth. From her point of view it was logical to think that Steve might be interested in Kendra. "Steve Dixon is not interested in me!" She almost shouted the words, and Elizabeth stirred again.

She lowered her voice. "I am not interested in him! That will never, never happen!"

"Well, all right, if you say so." Allison turned away, looking a bit miffed at her tone. "You don't have to go out with him. But he's a good catch – cute and smart, and has a good job – I think you could do worse." She opened the door as Kendra fought the urge to throw something in frustration. "By the way, I'm cooking dinner for Serena's birthday Friday night. I invited Heidi and Adam, and I invited Steve too, so that Adam won't be the only man."

Kendra stared down sulkily at the flowers on her bedspread. "Maybe I won't be home that night."

"Oh, Kendra, don't be that way. I'm counting on you. I was hoping you would make that apple dish you do sometimes. Heidi's bringing a salad." Allison sighed at her unresponsive friend and headed down the hall to her own room.

Kendra changed into her nightgown, turned out the light, and crawled between the covers. Her tears had expended themselves and instead she felt consumed by a hollow, empty, hopeless feeling. It really didn't matter what Steve Dixon thought of her, she told herself as she struggled to fall asleep. The real question was – would the rest of the world agree?

ಲ Chapter Eighteen ೞ

"Happy birthday!" The chorus greeted Serena as she came through the front door. Adam added, "Which one is this? Or are we allowed to ask?"

Serena groaned. "It's the big one. Three-oh. That's why Allison invited me over tonight, to cheer me up."

The doorbell rang. Allison was heading into the kitchen to set the food out, so Kendra opened the door. "Hi!" Steve said.

"Hi." She really didn't want to talk to him at all and turned away. She had reluctantly agreed to attend the party, and as the days passed had lost her urge to confide in anyone. What good would it do? No one could change the past, not even Steve Dixon, no matter how sorry he might feel. Besides, what if she told Allison her worst fears, and her friend agreed with her? Then she would have no hope at all. There was nothing to do but to go on pretending that she was the same as all the other girls and hoping that maybe someday she would meet someone who could love her in spite of the past.

She let him into the house and immediately went to the kitchen to help Allison set out the food. Steve followed her and found Elizabeth already eating at the kitchen table. Kendra had decided to feed her early, since the table only held six comfortably.

"Hey, how's my princess?" He leaned down and kissed the top of the child's head.

He always said things like that to Elizabeth.

Elizabeth jumped up and Kendra carried her plate to the sink.

She started a movie for her daughter in the living room and then the six adults gathered around the kitchen table. Steve asked the blessing on the food, and they began to fill their plates with Allison's chicken and rice casserole, Kendra's baked apples, and Heidi's salad.

"Yummy." Steve piled his plate high. "Did you make all this, Allie?"

"We all contributed," Allison told him, "all except Serena. She's the guest of honor."

Serena laughed. "Well, you wouldn't want to eat my cooking!"

"I just brought the drinks," Steve said. "I figured I couldn't mess that up."

"I guess you don't need to cook much," Serena observed. "When is your mom going to kick you out of her house? Aren't you getting tired of living at home?"

Steve swallowed the bite in his mouth. "Actually I'm saving up to buy a place. I'm putting all the money I would spend on rent aside for a down payment."

"That's what I did," Allison nodded. "How much have you saved?"

Steve drew his brows together. "I think it's over ten thousand now. I'd have to check."

Ten thousand dollars! Kendra could hardly imagine having that much money sitting in a bank account. She had her own slim savings account that, on a good day, barely topped a thousand dollars. It was hard to save with rent and Elizabeth's expenses, even with her mother's help.

If Steve had to pay child support, he probably wouldn't be able to save so much for a house – and her own account would be healthier. But that was her own fault for never asking him for money. If she did, he would no doubt ask for a paternity test, which she had to admit was a reasonable trade-off. She would feel a bit better about it now than she had six months ago, but she still wasn't ready to upset the status quo.

The talk during dinner moved on to the Timothy group and plans for the next month. Heidi said she was hosting another pool party on Labor Day, and Kendra couldn't help but remember the one the year before, when Steve had shown up and pulled Elizabeth out of the pool. It was just a year ago that she had met Steve again for the second time. It was hard to believe that only a year had passed.

She didn't know Heidi's boyfriend Adam well, but she remembered Steve's remark that he seemed stuffy. Certainly he was extremely attentive to Heidi, refilling her glass, then offering his jacket to keep her warm when he saw the air conditioning blow on her. Once he actually leaned over and cut her meat. Kendra caught Steve and Serena exchanging a glance before Steve looked away to hide a smirk. Serena's expression was a bit less subtle.

Well, she wouldn't listen to Steve's opinion. If he made fun of Adam, he probably made similar unflattering remarks about her.

"You won't believe who Adam and I ran into the other day," Heidi remarked toward the end of the meal. "Candy Davis! Adam was taking me to a doctor's appointment, and she was walking out as I walked in."

"That girl shows up in the strangest places," Steve remarked with a head shake.

"So what's new with her?" Allison asked.

Heidi hesitated and lowered her voice, as if someone in the next room might hear her. "She's pregnant."

Allison's eyes widened. Serena said, "Well, that's a shocker."

"I wouldn't have told you, but she didn't act like it was a secret."

"That's very, very unfortunate." Steve set his glass of tea down with a grave expression. "I just hope she doesn't decide to raise the baby herself. I hope she finds a family to adopt it."

Kendra felt her throat tighten; she swallowed.

"Oh, I think she's planning to keep it," Heidi told them.

"That poor baby." He shook his head. "Candy can barely take care of herself, let alone someone else. Can you imagine?"

Serena scraped the last pieces of baked apple from her plate. "Well, Steve, this might be what she needs to make her get her act together."

"But what if she doesn't? Who suffers then? I think it's a big mistake."

"And knowing Candy, the father probably isn't in the picture, and she doesn't have family around to help," Allison added.

Heidi sighed. "I told her she should come back to church. That would be the best thing for her, but I don't think she will."

Serena gestured in Kendra's direction. "Look at Kendra. She's managed okay."

Kendra felt her face grow hot; she said nothing.

"You can't compare Kendra and Candy," Steve said in exasperation. "Kendra's always been a stable person, and Candy never has. She's stoned half the time, and living with a different guy every week. What kind of life is that for a child?"

"I think we really need to pray for her," Heidi said gently.

Steve shrugged. "Well, that's for sure."

Elizabeth wandered back into the kitchen and climbed onto Steve's lap. He bounced her on his knee and she giggled.

"Remember that other girl who came for a while? Kim. I wonder what happened to her," Heidi remarked.

Serena glanced in Steve's direction with a grin, and Steve rolled his eyes. "Oh, don't go there! I don't know how that whole situation ended up being my fault."

"She liked you," Allison said.

"I know, but I wasn't trying to encourage her. Look, I was proud of myself. That was the first relationship I ever had where I wasn't trying to score."

Serena leaned toward him and spoke in a tone she might use with a less-than-bright child. "But *she* was trying to score. That's what you didn't understand."

Allison laughed and began to gather the empty plates together. "Steve, you can't be a Christian brother to a girl who thinks you're good-looking. Now Heidi and Kendra, they think you're ugly, so you can be a Christian brother to them."

Everyone laughed except for Steve and Kendra. Heidi leaned across and patted his arm. "Don't listen to them, Steve."

Steve gave her a pathetic look. "You're the only friend I have, Heidi."

"Oh, please!" Allison turned and carried the dishes to the sink. "Listen, I rented a movie. Should we watch it now? Serena wanted to see *Much Ado About Nothing*."

Finding Father

Kendra took Elizabeth up and tucked her into bed. When she came down, they gathered around the TV and Allison started the movie. It was based on the Shakespearean comedy, and Kendra had to listen closely to follow it. Heidi and Adam seemed completely bewildered by the sixteenth-century language, but Kendra was surprised to see that Steve thoroughly enjoyed it, until she realized that as an English teacher he was certainly familiar with Shakespeare. Every few minutes he turned to give a modern commentary to Heidi and Adam. "She's saying she'll never meet a man she wants to marry....Benedick is making fun of Claudio for being in love....That's Don John, the Prince's brother. He's the villain."

"How can he be the villain when he's so gorgeous?" Serena remarked.

"I think Claudio is cuter," Kendra said.

"Benedick is my favorite," Allison added. "He has such a quirky personality. I love it."

Steve studied the three of them for a moment and grinned. "That's what I would have pictured. Serena with Don John, Kendra with Claudio, and Allie with Benedick."

The story centered around a beautiful girl named Hero who was accused of losing her virginity before her marriage. Her jealous fiancé, Claudio, believes the lie against her and publicly humiliates her. In the end he recognizes his mistake, begs for forgiveness, and they all live happily ever after.

"Now that's the difference between a comedy and a tragedy," Steve remarked when the movie had ended and Adam and Heidi had departed for the evening. "In *Othello* the girl gets killed; in *Much Ado About Nothing* she marries the idiot after all."

Serena tossed her hair. "I think that Hero was a little too forgiving. I wouldn't marry that jerk, not after the way he was throwing the furniture around."

"He definitely had a temper," Steve agreed, "and a jealous streak."

Allison was putting the movie back in its case. "Well, I'm glad you two liked it, because I could tell that Heidi was completely lost."

Steve laughed. "Poor Heidi, she'll never be a Shakespeare

scholar." He glanced at Kendra. "You understood it, didn't you?"

She nodded. "Most of it. I didn't get every line, but I followed the story."

She returned to the kitchen and began to load the dishes into the dishwasher and wipe down the counters. In the living room she heard voices saying good-night, then Allison climbing the stairs. She looked up and was startled to see Steve standing in the doorway of the kitchen, watching her.

"I thought you had left," she said.

"Well, I wanted to talk to you a minute." He wandered into the room and leaned against the counter. "I felt bad about that conversation Tuesday night. I know you were embarrassed when Allie started talking about your dating life, and I didn't intend that."

For a minute Kendra was speechless. Did he really think she was upset about her dating life? That had been the least of the problem!

"Allie's frustrated because she doesn't have a boyfriend," he went on when she didn't reply. "I know she wants to date more, but I was trying to explain why the guys are cautious about getting involved. You know, in my former life I dated a lot and didn't worry about any of the consequences; now I'm – we're all trying to be more responsible. I don't think she should blame us for that."

"No, she shouldn't," Kendra said after a moment's thought. Was it possible that Steve's remark hadn't been meant as a reflection on her at all?

He looked relieved. "I thought you knew what I meant. You understand these things better than Allie. And that whole situation they mentioned with Kim was just one more example of why I felt I needed to be careful."

Kendra couldn't help but be curious. "What happened with her, anyway?"

Steve sighed. "Let's go sit down and I'll tell you." He led the way back into the living room and they settled themselves on the sofa. "This girl Kim started coming to the Timothy group – oh, about two years ago. She had a lot of personal problems, and sometimes she would talk about them to me after the meetings. I could relate to some of it. Well, one night after the Bible study, we were talking and I invited her to an ice cream place to finish our conversation. We ended up staying about two hours – I guess that was a mistake. And afterward I called her a few times and told her I was praying for her. I was just trying to be encouraging."

He frowned, running his hand through his hair. "Well, after a few weeks Eddie asked me what was going on with Kim. Of course I told him nothing was, and he said that Kim was telling people that we were an item. I guess I should have talked to her then, straightened things out, but instead I sort of backed off. Maybe that was the cowardly way, but I felt awkward and I didn't know what to do. And then one week during the Bible study Kim suddenly burst into tears, and all the girls glared at me, like I'd done something awful."

He looked at Kendra with an anxious pucker between his brows. "I really didn't mean to lead her on, and that made me feel like I'd better be doubly careful with girls from then on."

Kendra recalled the night of the party and their kissing session on the couch. "Did you kiss her?"

"Who? Kim?" Steve looked horrified. "Of course not! It wasn't anything like that – it wasn't like what happened with you. I didn't even think about her that way!"

Kendra felt her face grow hot and she looked away. She could think of no reply.

"And the ironic thing is," Steve continued, "after that experience I was just getting to the point where I thought I could start dating again, when I met you and Elizabeth. And I thought, how could I possibly explain this to some Christian girl? Leanne or Heidi or Jean – what would they say? My life is complicated enough now without adding a woman to it. And Allie doesn't understand that."

Kendra tried to speak lightly. "So I guess I've complicated your life."

He looked at her with a sober expression. "Yeah. Just like I complicated yours six years ago."

It was one of the few times he had actually brought up the subject to her. For a moment Kendra sat in silence, debating within herself, and then she took a deep breath. All the questions that had circled in her mind for years – if she didn't ask now, she might never have another opportunity.

"Steve," she began, biting her lip, "can I ask you about that? The night of the party?"

He looked at her with an odd expression, one that held both dread and resignation, as if he knew he wouldn't want to answer her questions and yet knew he didn't have a choice. "What do you want to know?"

"I guess – I just want to understand what you were thinking that night."

He clasped his hands together and stared down at the floor. "I'll try to tell you, if I remember."

She tried to frame her question in a delicate way, and failed. "When you came to the party that night – were you just looking for sex?"

He turned his hands over, examining the nails. "Kendra, I don't remember exactly, but that was usually what I was looking for back in those days."

"So why me?" It was the question that had haunted her for six years.

He was still staring down at his hands. "I thought you were cute – and I thought you liked me."

She swallowed hard. "Because of the way I acted with you."

"Well, yeah. I did think so."

She was silent for a moment as she felt tears sting her eyes. "So I guess it really was my fault."

"I didn't say that." He looked up at her with a pained expression. "It was my fault, Kendra. I shouldn't have been drinking, I shouldn't have been snorting cocaine, I shouldn't have been trying to get in bed with a total stranger – I shouldn't have been at that party in the first place, actually. I didn't intend to hurt you, but all those things were my fault and that's why it happened."

A long moment of silence stretched between them. "You really thought I wanted to have sex?"

He hesitated. "I hoped you did. I assumed you did. That's where I was wrong."

Her words spilled out in anger. "How could you think I wanted to have sex with anyone with four guys watching? How could you possibly think that?"

For a moment he was silent as tears began to spill down her cheeks, and he gazed at her with misery in his face. Finally he spoke in a tight voice.

"Kendra, when I look back on that whole situation, I'm just as horrified by it now as you are. I have no excuse to offer. When I was high on cocaine, I thought every woman in the world wanted me. It was like a massive ego trip. Afterward I realized I'd made a huge mistake, but it was too late."

She bit her lip, trying to control her tears, but they continued to flow. Steve lifted his hand as if to comfort her, then dropped it.

"I know it sounds so inadequate to say how sorry I am. I could say it over and over till the day I die, and it wouldn't be enough. I don't know what else to say or do. If I had stolen something, I could pay it back, but there's no way for me to undo what I did."

"I guess there isn't really." With an effort she took a deep breath and wiped her eyes with the back of her hand. "No one can change the past."

"No." He hesitated, watching her face. "I'd like to think that something good came out of all this – and that's Elizabeth. Like Joseph said to his brothers in the Bible, 'You intended it for evil, but God intended it for good.' I don't know if that makes sense to you, but I hope it does. I want to believe that he has a plan for all of us in spite of how I messed up so badly six years ago. At least, that's how I try to look at it."

"I hope so." Elizabeth *was* a great blessing. She wished she could have waited ten years before she had Elizabeth, but in that case Elizabeth would be a totally different child. So maybe there really was some sense to what Steve was saying.

"There's one thing you did for me that night," she recalled, staring down at her hands in her lap. "You kept all the other guys away from me. Who knows what would have happened if you hadn't done that –" She broke off, feeling her face flush at the memory.

"I forgot about that. Those guys were crazy. Well, at least I did one thing right."

Anxious to change the subject, she recalled another question she wanted to ask. "Do you remember the Saturday night on the retreat, when you shared your testimony?"

He nodded.

"You mentioned something that happened in your senior year, before you graduated. I know you weren't talking about me because you weren't a senior then, were you?"

"No, that was something else." He raised his head to look her in the eye, and took a deep breath. "That's something I've never told anyone, except Pastor Mike. My family doesn't know; my friends don't know. Allie doesn't know."

Kendra nodded.

"When I was a senior, I got another girl pregnant. She had an abortion, and I went with her and paid for it and everything."

To her amazement she saw that he had tears in his eyes. She wasn't at all surprised by the abortion – it fit everything she had guessed about his lifestyle in those years. She was more surprised that he seemed so upset about it.

"That was the experience that bothered you so much? I didn't think most guys would care about that."

"I don't know. Maybe most guys wouldn't. Maybe it was just the way I was raised. I felt like a total failure as a father – as a man. I felt like I didn't deserve to get married and have a real family someday. You know, I told myself that what happened with you was just a mistake, a misunderstanding, and it would never happen again. And it didn't. I was really careful to be clear with girls after that. But I couldn't say the same thing about the abortion. I knew I had done it deliberately and I had no one else to blame."

"But you went to the March for Life in January," Kendra recalled.

He nodded. "I've gone the last couple of years. I go to remember that child. And then this year I was totally shocked when you and Elizabeth showed up. All day long I kept looking at Elizabeth and I felt that God was saying to me, 'Okay, Steve, I'm giving you another chance to get it right – I'm giving you another chance to do the right thing.'"

He bit his lip and wiped his eyes with the back of his hand. "Of course, I knew you didn't want me around, and that made it hard. Do you understand why I couldn't just walk away from her? I would never have been able to live with myself if I knew I had a child out there somewhere and I hadn't done anything to take care of her. I knew you wanted me to just disappear, but I couldn't."

"That's why you joined the Timothy group?"

"That was one reason. I hoped if I hung around long enough, you would decide to let me spend time with her. And, of course, I prayed continually."

Kendra managed a short laugh. "I guess it worked, didn't it? Your plan or your prayers, one or the other."

"Yes." He hesitated, studying her face. "I know you've been kinder to me than I deserved. You've treated me better than I expected, and I want you to know –" he stopped, fumbling for words, and his voice trembled, "I really, really appreciate that – and I really, really respect that."

Kendra thought of the anger she had harbored for the last year. She wondered if his praise was deserved. "I haven't always felt kind."

"I know. I saw some of the dirty looks you gave me too. But I could tell you were trying. I knew you weren't happy to see me again, and if it hadn't been for Elizabeth, I would have stayed away and not bothered you. But I couldn't."

Kendra groped for the right words. "I know you love Elizabeth. I didn't expect you to."

"I know." He paused again. "I don't know how to say this – I don't want you to take it the wrong way – but I've often thought I'm really lucky that you're Elizabeth's mother. I mean, when I think of some of the girls it could have been..."

Kendra felt her face grow warm and she forced another laugh to cover her embarrassment. "You don't think I'm pretty messed up?"

"Of course not." He frowned, looking puzzled by the question. "You're a very stable person, a good, honest, decent person, a loving mother and a good friend. You're a great mother to Elizabeth and I'm really thankful for that – you can't begin to imagine."

Steve was actually grateful for her? Such a possibility had never occurred to Kendra. It was a very strange idea, and for a moment she considered it in astonishment.

"I actually heard a rumor that you were pregnant," Steve told her, "but then you never contacted me, so I assumed it was false, or that maybe there was another guy. That's why I wasn't sure what to think when I first found out about Elizabeth. I thought, you know, if she were mine, you wouldn't have kept her. I didn't think you would want a baby – under those circumstances. But I didn't know what to believe because the dates seemed to fit. That's why I finally asked you that time, six months ago."

Kendra told him then about her pregnancy, how she had at first considered giving Elizabeth up for adoption, only gradually changing her mind. "I didn't tell you because I didn't want you to be involved. I really didn't think you would want to be, anyway."

"Well, that was probably a wise decision." He stared down at his hands in his lap with a sigh. "I'm not sure how I would have reacted in those days, but it probably wouldn't have done me any credit, and would only have been more hurtful to you."

"That's what I thought," Kendra said.

"You seem so mature compared to myself and my friends when we were your age," he sighed. "When I think that you were only sixteen at the time – I'm amazed at how you've handled all this."

She could hardly believe Steve Dixon was sitting here, saying all these nice things about her. He had always been polite, but had seemed to avoid making any personal comments at all, either negative or positive. Whenever she allowed herself to consider the subject, she had always assumed he held a low opinion of her. Unless he was lying now – and he had no reason to – she must have been wrong in that assumption. She found the realization gratifying in a strange way.

He asked her questions then about Elizabeth's younger years, sounding almost hungry for information, and she traveled back through her memories, trying to impart as much as she could. Both of them lost track of time as they talked, and when Kendra finally checked her watch, she was startled to realize that it was already two o'clock in the morning.

"I really should be going," Steve remarked with an expression of chagrin. He started to rise, then stopped and looked at her intently. He put out his hand as if to take hers, but stopped. "Kendra – can you tell me now – have you really forgiven me?"

She was silent a moment. "Yes," she said. "Yes, I have."

ஐ *Chapter Nineteen* ൽ

Her conversation with Steve played itself over many times in Kendra's mind during the next week. His openness astonished her; she certainly would not have expected him to confide his most private experiences to her the way he had. That he would tell her about the abortion when he hadn't shared it with his own family or his closest male friends, like Dan or Eddie or Randy, surprised her even more as she thought about it. Even more puzzling and gratifying to her were some of the compliments he had paid her – telling her that she was a good mother, and that she had treated him better than he deserved. Where Steve was concerned she had a habit of cynicism, but she could think of no ulterior motive for him to say these things. She could only conclude that, strange as it seemed, he really meant them – that he liked and respected her as a person and felt a genuine appreciation for her efforts to forgive, as weak and reluctant as they sometimes seemed in her own eyes.

For the first time she was able to see the whole experience through Steve's eyes, to recognize the self-reproach that he lived with and would continue to carry, perhaps forever. She could not and did not attempt to absolve Steve of his share of blame in the incident, but as the days passed and she examined her own reactions, she realized that, during their late-night conversation, her chronic anger and resentment had finally disappeared. She had made a decision to forgive Steve last January, but had continued to struggle with her emotions during the ensuing months while she tried to behave the way she believed God wanted. Now, for the first time in six years, she felt completely free, able to put the whole experience in the past and move forward without bitterness. She felt as if a gigantic weight had finally been lifted from her heart.

When her mother called the next time, Kendra mentioned the conversation in passing, but didn't bother to relate the details. She knew her mother's cynicism ran much deeper than her own, and didn't want her mother's response to blight her new-found sense of freedom and release. Her mother didn't know Steve and would never know him, and so there was no point in trying to convince her that Steve had any redeeming qualities at all. Her mother clearly didn't understand that her friendship with Steve, his kindness and respect, was actually a healing experience for her. It didn't matter, really. Her relationship with Steve would have to remain one of those subjects on which they simply disagreed and chose not to discuss.

On Labor Day she made her usual bowl of pasta salad, gathered bathing suits and towels, and drove to Heidi's for the pool party. This year she was determined to watch Elizabeth like a hawk so that that no possible accident could occur. When she arrived at the house Leanne hugged her in greeting and, after a quick dip in the pool, Kendra filled a plate of food for herself and one for Elizabeth. She and Leanne found lawn chairs together and spread a towel on the grass for Elizabeth to eat on.

"I guess Steve won't be here today," she remarked, swallowing her bite of hamburger. "He told me that he's going to his father's for a picnic."

Leanne leaned close to her. "Didn't you go out with Ben that one time? He's over there staring at you."

Kendra glanced casually to the left to where Ben was watching her, then back to the right as if she had seen nothing unusual. "Leanne, you have to protect me today. I'm scared he's going to ask me out again, and I really don't want to go."

Leanne giggled. "Was it that bad?"

"It was worse than bad. The worst date I've ever had."

Leanne leaned down to pick up her soda from the grass. "Well, you just have to tell him no."

"I know, but I'm so cowardly. I hate turning guys down. I'd

rather he just not ask."

"Well, I'll try to stay close, but you'd better have an answer ready in case."

Kendra brightened. "Hey, maybe I could suggest that he ask you."

Leanne frowned. "No, thanks, he's not my type. Don't try to pawn him off on me."

Kendra glanced toward the gaggle of young men surrounding the grill. Next to Randy and Vince she spotted a new one, someone she had never met. Tall and slender, with a light complexion, deep-set eyes, and a sensitive mouth. He wore tropical yellow swim trunks and a navy tee shirt.

"Who's the guy next to Randy?" she asked.

Leanne followed the direction of her gaze. "Oh, that's Jason Hostetler. He goes to our church, but he's never come to the Timothy group before."

"I wonder what made him come today. Maybe he likes to swim."

"Maybe so." Leanne leaned toward Kendra to speak confidentially. "Actually, he was dating Melody Graham up until a few weeks ago, but I heard they broke up. Maybe he's here looking for a new girlfriend." She laughed. "You know how some guys come here when they're hunting, and then we don't see them again until they break up with the next one."

"Yeah, I know. Well, he's come to the right place, anyway. There are plenty of available women in this group."

Leanne laughed again. "Why don't you just say it? Plenty of desperate women!"

Kendra grinned. "Speak for yourself. But he's kind of cute. He'll probably find somebody, if he's looking."

She and Leanne finished their plates of food and returned to the pool. Kendra took Elizabeth in for a few minutes, and then let her play in the shallow end with an inner tube while she and Leanne sat on the edge and dangled their feet in the water and talked. A short while later a group of the men joined them and several jumped into the deep end, creating a splash that rained down on the two women. Kendra noticed that Jason was one of the group.

"Who wants to play Marco Polo?" Randy called out. "Leanne, Kendra, come on. We need you to play."

The two exchanged a glance, slid back into the pool, and the game began with Kendra keeping a close eye on Elizabeth. Jason Hostetler seemed like a quiet sort of guy, Kendra noted, but not unfriendly. Was it her imagination, or was he looking at her often, making eye contact during the game? She didn't want to be conceited and imagine admiration where none existed. But once when she was caught and had to be "it," he seemed to be lingering near her, teasing her by talking and then ducking out of her way before she could touch him.

When the game ended and she returned to the drink table to fill her glass, he poured one for himself and lingered near her.

"They said your name is Kendra?" he asked, smiling. "Do you go to our church? I've never seen you there before."

She shook her head as she gulped down her drink. "Actually I go to Grace Fellowship, but I've visited your church a few times. I'm Allison Andrews' roommate. Well, we share a house, actually, not a room." She gestured toward Elizabeth, who was chasing a butterfly around in the grass. "And that's my daughter." Better get that out in the open right away.

Jason glanced her way. "She's cute. How old is she? About three or four?"

"Actually she's five. She'll be starting kindergarten tomorrow. That will be a new experience for her. Hard for me to believe."

"I guess so." He paused as if looking for a new topic of conversation. "So, do you work? What do you do?"

"I work in a bank. It's okay, not my dream job, but it pays the bills. What about you?"

"I work in a music store," he told her, "and in the evenings and on Saturdays I give music lessons. Piano and violin are my instruments."

Kendra looked up at him with new respect. "You play the piano *and* the violin? I play the piano – well, not as well as I used to – and that was hard enough to learn. You must be very talented."

He accepted the compliment with a modest smile. "I was homeschooled, so my mother spent a lot of time on my music. I spent a lot of time practicing as a child, believe me. In college my primary instrument was the violin, but I know the piano well enough to give lessons at the lower levels." He had a soft, but deep-pitched voice that she had to listen carefully to hear.

Kendra asked him questions about his college career and then confided her own previous dream of being a concert pianist or, as an alternative, music teacher. They found chairs together under the trees, and Kendra watched Elizabeth play while they talked about music and college and teaching, until their conversation was interrupted by Allison urging them to join a volleyball game.

The memory of Jason Hostetler lingered in her mind for the next week, as she put Elizabeth on the school bus in the mornings and daydreamed over her job at the bank. When Saturday night came she had an idea.

"I think I'll visit your church again tomorrow," she remarked casually to Allison. "I haven't been there for a while, and I won't have to wake up as early."

Allison nodded in agreement, betraying no consciousness of her true motive, and the next morning the three of them rode to church together. As they entered the sanctuary and found seats near the front, a quick glance around confirmed Jason's presence not far away, although she tried not to look at him too directly. The worship team moved to the front to lead the singing, and Kendra noticed Steve playing the drums. He caught her eye and smiled, and she gave him a quick wave in return.

Afterward she lingered as long as she could in the lobby, chatting with Serena and Heidi. Steve joined them a moment later.

"Kendra! Hey, it's good to see you here! What inspired you to pay us a visit?"

Kendra laughed. "Oh, laziness really. I just wanted to sleep for an extra hour." Where was Jason, anyway? She didn't want to be too obvious in looking for him.

"Kendra!" She turned at the sound of his soft, low-pitched voice.

"Hi, Jason!" She tried to sound very surprised, as if she hadn't even expected to see him there. "I decided to visit here this week for something different. I really like this church a lot; I've even wondered if I should switch, but I haven't decided yet."

He nodded and smiled, clearly pleased to see her again. They exchanged pleasantries about the service and the weather and their jobs, and Kendra found herself in high spirits as she and Allison drove home together and made lunch. Surely, surely, it wasn't just her imagination. She didn't want to chase Jason, but surely it wouldn't hurt to attend his church again the next week. Would that be wrong?

Wednesday evening the phone rang. Kendra jumped up from the book she was reading to Elizabeth and lifted the receiver. "Hello?"

"Kendra? This is Jason. From Bethel Bible. I met you at the pool party." As if she didn't remember. "How's it going?"

Kendra swallowed. "Fine. How about you?"

"Okay. Listen, I was wondering if you happen to be free Saturday night? A friend of mine is playing in a concert, and I got tickets for it. I thought, since you like music, you might be interested."

Kendra tried not to sound too eager. "That sounds really nice. Saturday night. I'll check my calendar, but I think I'm free then."

"Great. And listen, if you need to bring your daughter just let me know. I think kids are free. That wouldn't be a problem."

"That's really nice, Jason." She was genuinely impressed. "Thanks a lot. I'll let you know."

☼ ☙

Steve slowly turned the pages of the family photo album, studying the pictures of himself and Joyce during their preschool years. He was so used to Elizabeth's appearance by now that he sometimes had doubts about the resemblance, but looking at these photos again reassured him. Really, in some ways she resembled Joyce more than him, and that couldn't be a coincidence.

His mother walked into the kitchen and glanced over his shoulder. "Oh, you got the old photos albums out. What inspired that?"

"Just remembering." Suddenly nervous, he flipped ahead to the later pages showing his teen years. "Look, here's Joyce's birthday party. How old was she then?"

"Twelve," Marilyn said. "That's the year I had a big party for her. Right after your dad and I split up. I guess I was trying to cheer her up, if such a thing was possible."

"Yeah, that was a tough time for everybody."

"The worst time of my life." His mother pulled out a chair and dropped into it, studying the pictures. "I don't know if it was worse for me or for you kids. I just felt like such a failure. And you went through that awful stage afterward, and I knew it was all my fault. I knew you were acting out because of the divorce, and I should have prevented that somehow."

Steve studied his mother with compassion. "But you didn't want Dad to leave. I blamed you, but I can see now that you were the least to blame."

"Thanks." She squeezed his arm. "I'm sure we all made mistakes. That experience was very humbling for me. I had always tried to be so perfect, and then my marriage fell apart and my son went crazy – at least it seemed that way to me. But God taught me so much about his mercy through that. He brought Howard into my life, and he brought you back in the end. It was totally his grace, nothing that I had done to deserve any of it. And now I look at you, and you're everything that I ever wanted you to be when you were young. I'm so thankful that he answered that prayer."

Steve gulped. She wasn't making it easy to bring up the subject he wanted to discuss, but he had made up his mind. "Did Howard go out already?" he asked.

"Yes, he had a missions meeting at church."

"Oh. Well, I need to talk to you sometime. Would this be a good time?"

"Sure, hon. Let me just pour myself a cup of coffee." She rose and picked up the coffee pot on the counter. "Do you want some?"

"Uh – no thanks."

She carried her coffee to the kitchen table and sat across from Steve. He ran his fingers through his hair and bit his lip as he glanced around the kitchen.

"What is it?" she prompted. "Is there a problem?"

Steve managed a shaky laugh. "I guess that depends on how you look at it." He took a deep breath and met her gaze. "What I need to tell you is – I have a child."

For a moment she just stared at him as if his words made no sense to her. "What?"

"She's five years old," he continued, looking down at the table top, "but I didn't find out about her until a year ago."

"Steve – Steve, how could you have a child for – for four years and not know about her? How could that happen?"

He shifted uncomfortably in his chair and scratched at an imaginary speck of dirt on the table. "Well – I met her mother at a party one summer during college. And – and then I didn't see her again for five years. And when I met her again, she had this child, and she told me it was mine."

"Oh, Steve." Marilyn closed her eyes. "This is awful. I knew – I knew you had a lot of girlfriends in college, but this –"

Probably a one-night stand was worse than anything she had imagined. Even during his wild days, she had tried to be optimistic.

"Steve – if you never saw this girl again after only one night, how do you know it's really your child? She could have been with anyone!"

Steve hesitated again. "She told me it's mine, and I believe her. I can't explain why, but I do." He couldn't, with his mother, go into all the details that he had told Pastor Mike.

"So, do you see this child very often?"

"During the last six months I've seen her pretty often. But Mom, I'm tired of keeping the whole thing a secret. That's why I'm telling you now. I'd like to be able to bring her over to the house, have her meet her grandmother and aunt and – and everybody. I'd like her to be part of the family."

"Oh, Steve." Marilyn visibly cringed, and Steve felt a stab of compunction. After the divorce and all the problems during that time, he had to embarrass her again. "Oh, I don't know. Granddad – Aunt Judy – I can't imagine what they'll say. I'll have to think about this."

"I know. I know it's a shock; I know you need time to get used to the idea. But her mother doesn't have any family in the area and

I'd like her to be a part of my family. Just think what a positive influence everyone would be."

She was shaking her head; and to his slight relief she laughed a short, ironic laugh. "I'd like to be a grandmother, Steve, but not this way. I've been hoping you'd meet a girl and get married and all. And what happens when you do? Do you think your wife is going to want this other child hanging around?"

"I know. I've thought of that too. But I have to do what I believe is right and worry about that when the time comes. After all, if I were divorced, you wouldn't tell me to ignore my children because my new wife doesn't want them around, would you?"

"No, I guess not." She sounded very sad. "I wouldn't want you to neglect your child, but I can't believe you're living the life of a divorced father when you've never even been married. You're only twenty-five. And what about the mother? What's your relationship with her like?"

Steve paused a moment in thought, biting his lip. "It's good," he said finally. "It was hard at first – she had a lot of anger against me because of the way I'd treated her before. But I think now she really believes I've changed."

"The way you treated her before – what do you mean?"

Steve squirmed in his seat, avoiding his mother's eyes. "Well, that wasn't exactly my finest hour, if you get the picture."

To his relief his mother dropped that line of questioning. She sighed. "I guess she probably isn't a Christian."

Steve managed an embarrassed laugh. "That's the strangest thing about this whole situation. Neither of us were Christians back then, and now we both are."

"Well – I hate to state the obvious – but is there any chance that you would marry the mother and provide a proper home for this child?"

Steve hesitated. "I don't know. I've thought of that, but even if I wanted to, I don't think she would agree."

His mother shook her head. "So she'll sleep with a total stranger but wouldn't even consider marrying him? I'll never understand this generation of girls! If she wants a father for her daughter, she should!"

"I know, Mom, but it's more complicated than that. There's a lot of – of water under the bridge, or whatever the saying is. A lot of bad feelings from the past. I'm just glad we've gotten to the point of being friends."

Marilyn was silent for a moment, clearly turning this unbelievable development over in her mind.

"I think you should get a paternity test," she said finally. "I know you're taking this girl's word for it, but I'd hate to have you take on this responsibility and find out, ten years down the road, that it isn't your child after all."

Steve shifted impatiently. "If I ask for a paternity test, K – the mother is going to think I don't believe her. I don't want to insult her. Besides," he added with a sheepish look, "she – the child – she looks like me."

"Well, blame it on me, then. Tell this girl that your mother wants you to get one. If you get that test, and it turns out that this is your child, I'm willing to be involved however you want me to be. But I want to be sure first."

Steve nodded slowly. "Maybe that would be a good idea. Make it all official, so there's no doubt in anyone's mind. I think she would understand that."

"I certainly hope so." Marilyn shook her head. "You've really knocked the wind out of me this time, Steve. I never in a million years would have guessed."

"I'm sorry, Mom." He tried to look as contrite as he felt. "I know this is a huge shock for you. It was for me, too. I'm just trying to do the right thing. You understand, don't you?"

"Yes." She sighed. "And I'm glad you're trying to do the right thing. But it's still hard."

༄ Chapter Twenty ༅

When Kendra arrived at the Bible study that Friday night, she was rather disappointed to note Jason's absence. He hadn't told her for sure if he would be there; she had just assumed that he would be coming to the activities of the Timothy group now that they had gone out several times. She squeezed onto the sofa between Heidi and Ruth and turned to respond to Jesse's greeting. Ben was sitting on the floor a few feet away; he turned to stare at her in a way that made her squirm. Steve took a chair across from her; he smiled at her.

"Randy couldn't be here, and he asked me to lead the Bible study tonight," Steve told them after they had finished praying and singing. "Some of you know that I teach high school English. Of course, we're not allowed to teach religion in a public school, but sometimes we're allowed to teach the Bible as literature. Last year I managed to sneak the book of Ruth into my curriculum." He grinned around the circle. "So I thought tonight I'd do a quick overview of my lesson on Ruth – more from a literary perspective, but we'll also be able to draw some spiritual lessons from it." He glanced around. "Who wants to read the first chapter?"

Kendra had read the book of Ruth once but had never studied it. They went through the story chapter by chapter, analyzing the plot structure, character development and repetition of themes. A burst of merriment circled the room when Eddie read the scene of

Ruth visiting Boaz on the threshing floor.

"Of course, this seems a bit shocking to our modern understanding," Steve conceded with a smile, "but you have to understand the customs of the day. Ruth was actually initiating a levirate marriage, a brother-in-law marriage, which was her right in that society. A childless widow had the right to marry her late husband's nearest relative in order to have a child. In Genesis we have another example of a levirate marriage – the story of Judah and Tamar. Tamar went to even greater lengths to have a child by Judah."

Leanne asked, "Was she the one who dressed up like a prostitute and seduced her father-in-law?"

Steve grinned as several of the guys snickered. "Yeah, and nine months later he found out that he was the happy father of twin boys. Ruth actually looks downright tame in comparison."

"I never understood this," Allison broke in. "Why didn't Boaz just propose to Ruth instead of waiting for her to do this?"

"Well, that's a good question, and Boaz gives us a clue why he didn't. He comments that she 'didn't run after the younger men.' This implies that Boaz was a good bit older than Ruth. I think Boaz didn't propose because he didn't believe that Ruth would be willing to marry him. Maybe he even felt that he would put her in an awkward position with Naomi if he asked her and she refused."

Emma raised her hand. Steve pointed. "Little girl in the green sweater."

Emma laughed. "I heard somewhere that Boaz may have been married already. That Ruth was actually his second or third wife."

Steve's eyes widened. "Well, I've never heard that. But we know they practiced polygamy back then, so I guess it's possible. Or he may have been a widower. We don't know for sure; the Bible doesn't say. But we do know that he was willing to fulfill his obligation to Ruth, and as a result they became the great-grandparents of King David."

"And ancestors of Jesus," Leanne added.

The story was engrossing to Kendra, and she couldn't help but be impressed with Steve's insight and teaching ability. Clearly he had chosen the right vocation. When the study ended and everyone began to rise from their seats, she heard Heidi say, "That was really interesting, Steve. I never understood all that about Ruth before."

Steve grinned. "Next week I'll do *Macbeth*." He held out his hand in a dramatic gesture. "'Can all great Neptune's ocean wash this blood clean from my hand?'"

Serena called out, "I think that next someone should teach on Song of Solomon."

Steve laughed. "Well, don't look at me for that!"

Kendra went to the kitchen to find the snacks, and a moment later found Steve beside her. "Listen, I'm ready to leave, but I need to talk to you first. Can you walk outside with me?"

Surprised, she nodded. Probably he wanted to talk to her about Elizabeth. And that might be complicated, now that she was seeing Jason. With a sudden uneasiness she followed him out to his car.

"What is it?" she asked.

He leaned against the door of his silver Toyota. "I had a talk with my mother this week. I told her the truth about Elizabeth."

Kendra's mouth fell open in shock. This was the last thing she had expected.

"I didn't tell her who it was," he added hastily, at the expression on her face. "I – I just said that I have a child, and explained some of the circumstances."

Kendra could only imagine how Marilyn Marsh would respond to that news. Certainly not with joy. "What did she say?"

"Well, she was shocked, that was for sure. She never suspected. And –" he shifted to one foot a bit uncomfortably, "– she told me she thinks I should get a paternity test. And you know, Kendra, I think that might be a good idea. Make everything official, so that there's no question in anyone's mind. I'm especially thinking of my family. I understand how my mother must feel."

Kendra felt as if the wind had been knocked out of her lungs. For a moment she stood in silence, trying to grasp the ramifications of what Steve was suggesting. She no longer distrusted Steve, but the idea was still staggering.

"But Steve, if you tell your whole family, you know that everyone else will find out too. We won't be able to keep it a secret from anyone."

"I know, but I'm getting tired of keeping this secret. I feel like a hypocrite; I feel like I'm living a lie. I'd rather come out with it and get it over with, once and for all."

"But – but Steve," she found herself groping for words, "if we tell people, then – then everyone will find out about – about that party."

"I know." He looked at her anxiously. "We don't have to tell them everything – all the details. Couldn't we just say – say that we were both drunk, that we didn't know what we were doing?"

Kendra tried to imagine saying that to Allison, Leanne, Randy – and Jason. She shuddered. "I don't know."

"I don't understand." His expression displayed confusion and frustration; he bit his lip. "Look, Kendra, everyone assumes you had sex with someone. Why can't you just tell them it was me?"

She blurted out the first words that came into her mind. "There's a big difference between having sex with *someone* and having sex with *you.*"

He didn't speak, but she saw an odd expression cross his face – not anger or hurt, but a blank mask, as if he were carefully hiding his real thoughts. He just stood and looked at her.

"Listen, Steve," she rushed on, feeling her face grow hot. "there's something else I need to tell you. I've been going out with Jason Hostetler for the last few weeks. I really, really don't want him to know about this right now. It would ruin everything." She knew that to Jason there would be a world of difference between Elizabeth's father being a stranger from Kendra's past, and a man he had grown up with and saw every Sunday in church.

His expression did not change. He said in toneless voice, "Jason Hostetler. I guess that's why you've been coming to our church the last few weeks."

"I guess so." She swallowed. "Look, I know I'll have to tell him eventually – if we ever get serious – but I don't want to tell him now. It would really freak him out. Do you understand?"

"Yes," Steve said. He looked away, across the road, and was silent for a moment. "What about Tuesday nights? Do you still want me to come over then?"

Kendra frowned, staring down at the pavement at her feet. That would also be difficult to explain to Jason. "Well – I'm not taking a class this semester. Maybe we should skip that now."

"Okay." With an abrupt movement he turned to his car and pulled open the door.

"Steve –"

He turned back to look at her. "What?"

"Oh – nothing..."

He climbed behind the wheel, started the car, and pulled into the street without looking back at her.

Kendra stared after him, discomfort gnawing at her. She knew she had hurt Steve and she didn't know why, and was annoyed that she felt guilty about it. After all, none of this had been her idea. She hadn't asked Steve to get involved in Elizabeth's life; she hadn't suggested that he tell his mother the truth. It wasn't fair that he should come along and wreck the one promising relationship she'd had in two and a half years by his sudden impulse of candor. Was it?

I could never hurt him as much as he hurt me, she told herself as she turned back toward the house, her steps lagging. Steve was disappointed that she hadn't fallen in with his plan, but he would get over it quickly enough. In a few months he would probably even be relieved that she had squelched this idea. Someday he would thank her.

She thought of Jason then and her spirits lifted. Jason called her almost every night now, even when they didn't see each other. Somehow it seemed very fitting that now, when she had finally resolved her issues with Steve, she might actually meet her future husband. She couldn't take the chance of ruining this. Someday, as she had told Steve, she would tell Jason everything, but not now. Not yet.

ಬ ಜ

Steve drove carefully until he had rounded the corner and was well out of Kendra's sight. He pulled onto the main highway, then pressed the gas pedal all the way to the floor, finding satisfaction for a fleeting second in the angry gunning of the engine. It was a silly, childish gesture, he knew, and it didn't help anything.

He had never felt like such a colossal idiot in his entire life. Going to Kendra with his wonderful idea, his grand gesture, only to see the look of horror on her face when he proposed it. Her words would echo forever in his mind: "There's a big difference between having sex with someone and having sex with you." He would never forget the look on her face, the tone of her voice when she said those words.

What a fool he had been, that night at her house, when he had stayed till two in the morning, baring his soul, telling her all his most intimate secrets! How could he have been so dumb?

He wanted to be angry with Kendra, but knew it was really his own fault. Kendra had never pretended to care about him, after all. It was his own stupidity for spilling his guts to a girl who really didn't give a d – a rip about him anyway. He had let himself become too open, too vulnerable – too emotionally involved. He cringed inside as he remembered some of the things he had told her – secrets he had never shared with even his closest friends. He couldn't believe he had done that.

And now she was dating Jason Hostetler, of all people. Jason Hostetler. Steve had known Jason all his life; they had grown up together in Sunday school. In youth group, Jason had been the "good," nerdy kid while Steve was the popular trouble-maker. Jason didn't have a messy past, as Steve did. He would be a good husband for Kendra, a good father for Elizabeth.

And that meant that he, Steve, was free. He didn't have to worry about Kendra or Elizabeth anymore. He could start dating, get married, start a family of his own. There was Leanne...Monica...that cute new math teacher at school...

And every Sunday he would have to see Jason, Kendra, and Elizabeth – the three of them together, sitting in church like a family.

The raindrops plopping on his windshield blurred together with the tears that stung his eyes as his car roared down the highway.

ಬ ಛ

"I didn't expect that you'd be able to come over tonight,"

Kendra remarked as she set a plate of cookies on the table for Jason. "Don't you normally have students on Wednesday nights?"

Jason sighed as he picked a vanilla wafer and inspected it carefully before taking a bite. "Well, I was supposed to have four students tonight. Rachel at six o'clock, Cody at six-thirty, and the Butler girls at seven. But first Mrs. Butler calls and says that one of her girls came home from school with a bad cold and so she decided to keep both the girls home because the other one is tired and has a lot of homework. Well, that was annoying; I mean, if they're well enough to go to school, you'd think they'd be well enough to come to a piano lesson. And then at six-thirty Cody's mother calls and says that she's stuck because her car is in the shop and her husband hasn't gotten home with his car and so she doesn't have a way to get Cody to his lesson. So there I was with three cancellations in one night. That's when I decided I might as well come over and see you, since I didn't have anything else going on. But the whole situation was very frustrating."

"I'm sure that must be annoying," Kendra agreed sympathetically, "but things like that do happen and I guess the parents can't do much about sickness and cars breaking down. It's bound to happen sometimes."

"I should think they'd find a way around it." He frowned, studying a second cookie. "Her husband should make sure he gets home on time if he knows she needs the car. That's one of the things I hate about my job."

Kendra tried to think of something encouraging to say. After all, he had the job that she had always hoped for. "What about the student you did have? Rachel? How did that go?"

"Oh, Rachel." He shrugged. "Well, I'm coming to the conclusion that she's only taking lessons because her mother is making her. She shows so little interest, and she doesn't practice nearly enough. I told her tonight that at her level she should be practicing an hour every day if she ever expects to be any good. I don't think she was very happy to hear that."

Kendra took a sip from her glass of lemonade and frowned into the depths. "Well, it's hard to know how to handle that. I mean, some kids aren't very motivated, but it's still good for them to know the basics of music, even if they never reach a professional level. Just like some kids aren't that good at math and still have to learn their multiplication tables. Maybe that's why some parents make their children take lessons."

"Rachel could do well, if she cared. She has the ability, she just doesn't have the discipline. And of course, I can't make her practice the way she should. Her mother needs to do that, and she won't."

Kendra smiled and shrugged to make light of the issue. "You don't know what else Rachel has going on in her life. Or what else is happening in the family. Maybe her mother thinks she is progressing fast enough. I didn't always practice for an hour a day, and after Elizabeth was born I hardly ever did."

"I almost always did," Jason insisted. "Sometimes more."

"Well, I guess that's why you're so much better than the rest of us," Kendra laughed, hoping to flatter him into a better humor.

Elizabeth skipped into the kitchen and Kendra handed her a cookie. The child stuffed it in her mouth before running back to her toys in the living room.

"What about Elizabeth?" Jason asked. "Are you planning to start her on lessons soon?"

"Oh –" Kendra spread her hands to indicate she hadn't really considered the idea. "Not yet. She's only five."

"Five isn't too young. I have a student who's five."

"Well, she just started kindergarten. I don't want to push too much at her all at once. I thought when she's seven or eight, when she's had few years of school."

"I started when I was four and a half. If you ever want her to play really well, you should start her early."

Kendra laughed, trying to keep the note of impatience from her voice. "I'm not expecting her to be Mozart." Steve and Allison had both remarked that Kendra was a demanding mother, but compared to Jason, she felt she was positively easy-going. She wondered how he would be with his own children, or whether parenthood would give him a more realistic perspective. She groped for a change of topic, for something they might agree on. "What are you doing Friday night? Do you want to go to the Bible study?"

"I hadn't actually thought about it." He stirred his coffee as a wrinkle formed on his brow. "Actually, I don't know why you still want to go to that Timothy group all the time."

Kendra glanced up, startled. "What do you mean? Why wouldn't I want to go?"

"Well –" he hesitated a moment, "it almost makes me feel like you're still looking at guys, even though you're going out with me."

"Jason!" Such an idea had never entered Kendra's mind. "Of course not! Why would you think that?"

"Well, that's why people go to singles groups, to meet someone."

Kendra remembered Leanne's remark, that Jason had probably come to the group to find a new girlfriend. Leanne was certainly right, for now that he was dating Kendra, Jason showed little interest in attending.

"These are all my friends," Kendra tried to explain. "I didn't go there to find a boyfriend; I went to find friends, and I don't want to drop them all just because I'm going out with you now."

Jason's face cleared; he looked relieved. "Okay, I was just wondering. I guess I've never been into big groups of people. I'd rather just spend time alone with you. But if you want to go to the Bible study Friday, I guess we can. Maybe on Saturday we can stay home and rent a movie. I'll pick up Chinese food."

That was definitely a difference in their personalities, Kendra reflected that night after Jason had left and she was getting ready for bed. She was much more sociable than Jason, and she wondered if it would be a problem if they ever married. It seemed like such a little problem; it shouldn't bother her as much as it did. In fact, all the problems she had found with Jason were very small, and it was hard to decide if they were significant or if she were making mountains out of molehills.

Was she falling in love with Jason, or did she just care about him as a friend? Remembering her ecstatic happiness when she first began dating Kyle, she couldn't help but feel that something was missing. Jason was often negative and moody, and she grew weary of trying to coax him into better spirits. After a long day of working and caring for Elizabeth, she wanted someone who would lift her own spirits, not depress them further.

Still, she didn't want to stop seeing him. He was the first Christian boyfriend she'd ever had, the first quality man who'd shown a serious interest in her. Who could tell if or when she would meet someone else of his caliber? And he did have so very many good qualities. He was gentle and sensitive, honest and sincere, and he never pressured her sexually. They had quite a bit in common with their mutual interest in music. And he was always nice to Elizabeth. Not as doting as Steve, perhaps, but she really couldn't expect that. She sensed that he had little experience with children and wasn't sure how to act with her, but he never objected to Elizabeth's presence on their dates and was very kind to her, if a bit awkward.

Well, she would certainly give this relationship more time. She really did like Jason quite a bit. Sometimes it took a long time to know if someone was right. Not everyone fell in love at first sight.

They went to the Bible study together on Friday, although Jason wanted to leave as soon as it was over instead of staying to socialize as Kendra always did. On Saturday, just before Jason was supposed to arrive with the Chinese food, Allison's cell phone rang.

"Randy's having a bunch of people over his house tonight, just to hang out and maybe play some games. That was Leanne, calling to tell us. Why don't you and Jason come too?"

"I'll ask Jason if he wants to come." But Kendra already knew what the answer would be. After all, he had gone along with her plans on Friday, so she needed to give in to him on Saturday.

They ate the Chinese food and watched the movie, which had a confusing plot, and Jason fell asleep on the couch before it was over. For a moment Kendra thought of her friends at Randy's, who were probably having much more fun than she was. Maybe she could sneak out and leave Jason sleeping on the couch and Elizabeth sleeping in her room, and neither of them would even miss her. But she knew that she couldn't do that, so she woke Jason and sent him home before going to bed herself.

The next day Allison chattered on about how much fun they'd had at Randy's.

"You know that woods behind Randy's parents' house? Well, maybe you've never been there. Anyway, we went out and played

Capture the Flag with flashlights in the woods. The guys played paintball a few weeks ago, and that gave them the idea. Of course, this was much tamer than paintball, but it was still dangerous, because we were bumping into bushes and tripping over things in the dark. Dan got trapped in a briar patch." Allison laughed aloud at the memory.

"Who was there?" Kendra asked.

"Let's see – Randy and Penny, Serena, Leanne, Ruth and Jesse – I think those two are back together again – Steve and Dan, and a new guy, a friend of Randy's named Paul Valentine. Actually I knew Paul in high school, but I hadn't seen him since." She giggled. "I had a big crush on him back then, but he wouldn't give me the time of day. Last night he seemed pretty friendly."

Kendra sighed as she poured milk onto Elizabeth's cereal. "I wish I had been there. Jason isn't a big-group type of person. He isn't very – sociable."

Allison glanced over her shoulder as she spooned yogurt for her breakfast into a bowl. "How's it going with you two?"

"Okay, I guess. Jason's a nice guy, and we don't have any real problems..."

Allison frowned. "You don't sound thrilled about it."

"I know." She wrinkled her forehead and paused, her cereal spoon midway to her mouth. "He's nice, he's just so quiet and serious."

"Well, you're quiet and serious too."

"I know I am, and maybe that's why I've always liked guys who were different from me. Guys who can help me relax and lighten up and have fun."

"You mean someone like Jesse? Or Steve?" Allison threw her a grin. "I told you, you should have gone out with Steve when you had the chance."

Kendra frowned and bit back her tart reply, that her opportunity to date Steve had never existed except in Allison's fertile imagination. It wasn't so much that she could never be attracted to him again – she recognized that the man she knew now was a very different person from the college boy she had met six years ago. And he was handsome, bright, fun-loving, and affectionate with Elizabeth – all qualities she found particularly appealing. It was just that she and Steve had such a messy, painful history. Even if Kendra at times might feel lonely and desperate enough to give it a try, she knew the same would never be true of Steve. He could have his choice of any of the girls, and the last one he would pursue would be Kendra. She wouldn't let herself toy with such a preposterous idea even for a second, Allison's opinion notwithstanding.

Allison's voice broke into her thoughts, punctuated again with laughter. "Well, I probably shouldn't tell you this, but Serena and Steve were making fun of Jason last night. Serena thinks guys who play the violin are nerdy. She kept comparing him to somebody she knew back in high school, who wore polyester pants every day. Steve was laughing at the way Jason always buttons his shirts all the way to the top, even when he isn't wearing a tie. They both kept saying, 'Why is Kendra dating him? What does she see in him, anyway?'"

Kendra looked up from her bowl, her brows drawn together in a scowl. "Jason is a very talented musician," she began in an indignant tone.

"Oh, I know he is. And I stood up for you, Kendra. I told them all that I think you and Jason make a really nice couple." At Kendra's persistent glower she added, "I'm sure they were just having fun. Don't take it seriously."

Kendra dropped the subject, but it stuck in her mind along with a nagging sense of hurt. Why would her friends make fun of Jason? Serena didn't surprise her much; she knew that a gentle, sensitive guy like Jason was unlikely to escape Serena's caustic wit. But why would Steve? She had thought she and Steve were actually friends now. He should be happy that a nice Christian guy was actually pursuing her, instead of making a joke about it.

She had learned over the last year that the best way to deal with any issues with Steve was the direct approach, to diffuse resentment as soon as possible, so at the next group activity, which happened to be a volleyball night, she waited until the two of them were relatively alone on the sidelines of the gym. She said in a cool, crisp tone, "I hear you were making fun of my boyfriend last

Saturday night."

Steve glanced at her with a startled look, and then his face turned a dark red. "Did Allie tell you –? She shouldn't have told you that. We – we didn't mean anything – we were just joking around."

Kendra turned back to the game, where Eddie was spiking the ball across the net. She spoke in the same cool tone. "I'll have you know, the violin is a very difficult instrument to learn to play well. Much harder than the drums, I'm sure."

"I know. I know. Serena said that – she doesn't know anything about music. She got the idea from her high school days that the good musicians were social misfits."

"And you don't like the way he buttons his shirts," Kendra continued.

Steve laughed uncomfortably. "Well, that looks a little goofy, but it's no big deal. It was just a joke. Really, Kendra, I think Jason is a nice guy and – and – I hope things work out for you. I mean it."

Chapter Twenty-one

Steve opened his briefcase and took out the papers that he needed to grade. He wanted to get the personal experience essays handed back to his sophomore class tomorrow. He picked up the first one and scanned it as his mother wiped the table off from dinner.

"Grading papers?" she asked.

"Yeah. They're supposed to be writing about a disappointing experience and what they learned from it. This one is about a time that a girl fell off a horse and broke her arm. Listen to this: 'I was really disappointed that I fell off the horse, but I learned that horses are big and can hurt you if you're not careful.' How do I grade this?"

His mother was silent a moment as she rinsed out the dishcloth. "By the way, Steve, whatever happened with that situation you told me about a couple weeks ago?"

Steve clouded up at the memory and set down the paper he was grading. "Well, I talked to the mother about getting a paternity test like you suggested, but she didn't want to. She has a new boyfriend now and doesn't want me around, messing things up. She told me, in a very nice way, to get lost."

Glancing at his mother's face, he could tell that her main emotion was relief, not disappointment, and he felt annoyed. "Maybe that's really for the best, Steve. After all, it's hard on children, being bounced back and forth between two homes. It was hard enough for you, and you were fifteen."

He shrugged and picked up the essay again. "Yeah, whatever."

"Of course, I'm sure you're concerned about her. What do you know about the boyfriend? Is he all right?"

Steve shrugged again. "He's a nice guy." He knew he sounded resentful, and really wished he could say the opposite. If Jason were a total jerk, he would have justification to try to interfere.

"Well, that's good. The important thing is for this child to have a good home."

Steve said nothing, staring down at the table. He bit his lip.

"I know you feel bad about it," she added in a more sympathetic tone.

He swallowed, and his voice sounded suspiciously tight, tinged with bitterness. "I don't have anybody to blame but myself. I really messed up big this time, didn't I?"

"Well, Steve, maybe now you understand why we tried to tell you to wait when you were younger. This is the sort of thing that happens."

Steve glared at her. This wasn't a moment when he needed or wanted a sermon. Her expression softened. "I'm sorry, honey. I really am. There's just no good solution to a situation like this one. I wish I could fix it for you, but I can't."

"It's stupid," he said in a rough voice, "but I got really attached. I shouldn't have let myself, but I did. It was stupid." He had fallen in love, first with Elizabeth, and then with Kendra. He had let himself be taken in by Kendra's openness with him, and now he was paying for his own stupidity.

Marilyn sighed. "Not stupid. It was natural. And you were trying to do the right thing. I think –" she paused, groping for words, "I think you really need to pray for God's best solution for this child. Whether that includes you or not. That God will give her the family, the parents, he wants her to have."

"I do pray that," Steve said in a low tone. "I do. Every day." He turned and walked out of the kitchen.

ಲ ಚ

The next Sunday Marilyn lingered in the lobby after the

service, waiting for Howard to finish his conversation with the chairman of the missions committee. She suspected that he was being asked to host one of the visiting missionaries for dinner, and she did a swift mental review of her recipes and dishes and silverware as she wondered how many guests would be involved.

Steve stood across the lobby, studying a notice on the bulletin board. He glanced down as a little girl with wavy dark hair ran to him and hugged him around the legs. Steve smiled with pleasure and leaned down to stroke her hair and speak to her.

Marilyn's attention started to move on, and then stopped. She stared at the two.

Steve had said that his daughter was five years old. This child looked about the same age. Could it be...?

No, that was impossible. Marilyn recognized this child. It was the little girl who lived with Allie – Kendra's daughter. Kendra had brought her to the house the evening after the funeral.

And yet...the child bore a remarkable resemblance to Steve and Joyce when they were the same age. The hair, the shape of the face...but especially the smile as she looked into Steve's face and laughed. Could it be a coincidence?

Hadn't Steve said that his daughter looked like him?

She racked her brain, trying to remember everything Steve had told her. He had found out about his daughter a year ago – just around the time Kendra had moved in with Allie. He said that the mother had no family in the area. Did that explain why Kendra had spent last Christmas with the Kirk family? And hadn't Steve mentioned spending time at Allie's house last summer?

She found that she was almost shaking from the shock of this sudden discovery. Of course, she couldn't be sure. Was her imagination running away with her? Maybe these were all simple coincidences. Or could that little girl really be her very own granddaughter?

ಶಿ ೮3

Kendra looked up from the new music she was practicing to Elizabeth, who had followed her mother downstairs to be near her as she played and was chasing a ball around the basement floor. "Elizabeth, come here!" she called. "I want to show you something."

Elizabeth came and Kendra moved over, gesturing for her to climb onto the bench. "How would you like to take some piano lessons?"

"Okay." Elizabeth leaned forward and played several keys.

"All right, but you need to pay attention to Mommy and do what I do. First we're going to learn the names of the keys. All of these white keys have names: A, B, C, D, E, F, G." Kendra played the notes as she said their names.

"Like the alphabet!" Elizabeth knew the alphabet well and was starting to read a little.

"Yes, like the alphabet, but they only go up to the letter G, and then they start over. Now, I'm going to show them to you again, and I want you to see how well you remember."

Kendra went over the names of the notes with Elizabeth several times, and then quizzed her. Elizabeth's attention span was not very long, but she appeared interested in the lesson and learned the notes with no difficulty. She wasn't Mozart, but Kendra imagined that she had some actual talent. Surely, with Steve's genes and her own, Elizabeth must have inherited some musical ability.

༄ ༅

The first weekend in November, Jason asked Kendra to attend his grandparents' golden wedding anniversary with him, which would be held in a nice restaurant. There were no children in the family, so Kendra knew that it would be impossible to take Elizabeth. Besides, she had never met Jason's extended family before and wanted to make a good impression.

She called all her regular babysitters, with no success. Everyone was busy that evening. Finally in desperation she dialed Steve's cell phone.

"Steve? This is Kendra."

"Hi!" He sounded pleased and surprised to hear from her, and she took heart.

"Listen I have a really big favor to ask of you. Would you be able to watch Elizabeth on Saturday night?" A long moment of silence greeted this request. "You don't have to if you don't want to."

"No, I can do it." Another long pause. "I guess you and Jason are going somewhere?"

"Yeah, he has a family thing, and I can't take Elizabeth."

"Okay, I'll watch her." Another pause. "Listen, I have some errands to run that night. Would it be okay if I took her along?"

Well, beggars couldn't be choosers. "Sure, just make sure she's strapped into her car seat properly."

"Okay." Why did he sound so odd, either businesslike or resentful, when at first he had seemed pleased to hear from her? Probably he felt resentful that she only called on him for help when she had no one else. He felt used. Kendra sensed a twinge of guilt.

It would be awkward, as well, trying to explain to Jason why Steve was babysitting for her daughter. She tried to sound very matter-of-fact when she mentioned it to him the next evening, as if there were nothing odd in the arrangement at all. Steve showed up at the required hour and was waiting in the living room when Jason came to pick her up for the dinner. The two men shook hands, although Steve looked a bit cool, unlike his usual high-spirited self.

"We really appreciate you doing this, man," Jason said.

"Sure, anytime." Steve shrugged without smiling. Kendra fetched her coat from the closet and Jason helped her on with it. "Have fun."

Was it her imagination, her guilty conscience, or did she hear a note of irony in his voice? She tried to shrug it off. She hadn't done anything to Steve Dixon, after all. He had no reason to resent her.

The dinner was very nice, although a much quieter affair than the Kirk family events that Kendra had attended. Kendra was introduced to the grandparents, an aunt and uncle, and a pair of cousins in their teens. "I think we've met her before," his uncle said, "at the picnic last Fourth of July."

Kendra glanced at Jason, who looked a bit embarrassed. "No, Uncle Frank, that was Melody Graham. My old girlfriend."

"Oh, so this is a new one." He seemed friendly enough anyway, in spite of the faux pas. "So Melody's out the window, is she?"

Jason quickly changed the subject, but the awkward moment stuck in Kendra's mind. She had known about Melody, of course, but they had never discussed the relationship in detail. As Jason was driving her home after the dinner, she said, "You know, I saw Melody Graham in church last week. Leanne pointed her out to me."

"Melody was at our church?" He glanced swiftly at Kendra, and in the dim light from the headlights she saw a new expression cross his face, sad, even slightly wistful.

"Well, she was there last week." Kendra paused, wondering how Jason felt about Melody and the whole break-up. "Weren't you the one who ended it?"

"I guess you could say that." He sighed. "By the time it ended, it was pretty mutual. We had been dating for two years, and Melody started talking about getting married. And I just wasn't ready for that kind of commitment. And we went back and forth, her asking what the problem was, and me saying that I just wasn't ready. And finally we decided that we weren't at the same place in life, and we should take a break and start seeing other people."

Kendra digested this in silence. Maybe Melody was just wrong for Jason, and that was why he had so much difficulty committing to marriage. On the other hand, how would she feel herself if she dated a guy for two or three years and he couldn't make a commitment? If she were a career woman, maybe she wouldn't mind, but with a child, she didn't want to date endlessly. She wanted a stable home and a father for her daughter.

Almost as if he read her mind, Jason said, "There's something I've always wondered about, Kendra. Elizabeth – does she ever see her father?"

With a guilty pang, she thought of Steve Dixon, babysitting that very evening. How could she possibly answer such a question truthfully, without telling the whole truth? She picked her way carefully through the land mines of truth and falsehood. "She sees him sometimes, but she doesn't know that he's her father. She thinks he's just a – a friend of mine. And I want to keep it that way. I don't want to confuse her."

Jason glanced at her profile in the semi-dark. "So – the two of you are friends?"

"I – I guess so." What was the correct answer to that? "Well, we're not enemies, anyway."

"Oh." A pause pervaded the car. "But – there's nothing between you anymore?"

"Oh, no!" That was easy to answer truthfully. "Actually, there never was anything between us."

She realized as soon as the words were out of her mouth how odd they must sound to Jason. "It was a long time ago," she added hastily. "We met at a party where everyone was drinking, and it was really stupid. But it's been over for a long time, really."

"Oh." Jason glanced at her again, as if he were deciding whether or not to ask another question. Kendra wiped her damp palms on her skirt and groped about for another topic of conversation. "So – you just have that one aunt and uncle? Your family is small like mine. Allison has so many relatives, I can't keep track of them all."

"Yeah, the Kirk family is pretty big. We go way back. My mom went to school with Steve's mother, years ago."

The house was quiet when they arrived at home. Steve was sitting on the couch, reading a book with a picture of what appeared to be a king and queen on the cover. Kendra glanced at the title: *Nicholas and Alexandra.*

She ran upstairs to check on Elizabeth and found her daughter sleeping peacefully, her hair spread around her on the pillow. A bag from a local department store adorned the floor. Glancing inside, Kendra found a variety of clothes in Elizabeth's size. A denim jumper with a matching white blouse with embroidery around the collar, a pair of pants covered with strawberries, and a red shirt with a large strawberry on the pocket.

She had mentioned to Steve once that most of Elizabeth's clothes came from yard sales and resale shops. Steve had seemed a bit shocked by this evidence of her poverty. He must have taken Elizabeth shopping that night and bought her some new clothes.

She was glad he had left the bag in the bedroom, instead of downstairs where Jason might possibly see it.

Two weeks later she and Jason and Allison were sitting and chatting around the kitchen table when the doorbell rang. When Kendra opened the door, she found Steve on the doorstep.

"I need to talk to Allie about the weekend, and I was in the area so I thought I'd just drop by." He almost sounded as if he'd memorized the words.

Kendra hesitated and spoke in an undertone. "Jason's here."

"Well, I'm not going to bother Jason. I just want to see Allie a minute."

Reluctantly she stood back and let him enter. Elizabeth immediately jumped up from her toys and ran to him. He picked her up and kissed her forehead. "I've missed you, Lisbet."

"Can you read me a book, Steve?"

"Sure, honey."

"Elizabeth, it's almost your bedtime." Kendra's voice was sharper than she intended.

The two of them turned matching expressions toward her, Elizabeth's one of disappointment, while Steve's was tinged with hurt.

"Well, maybe just one book, okay?"

Elizabeth found a book and they settled themselves on the couch. Kendra returned to Jason in the kitchen, although Steve's voice floated out to her: "'The kitten was sad and began to cry.' Here, Elizabeth, can you read this word?"

When the book was finished, Kendra took Elizabeth upstairs and tucked her into bed. Returning to the kitchen, she found Steve ensconced in one of the kitchen chairs while he and Jason discussed the football game the previous Sunday. Jason was a Steelers' fan, she discovered, while Steve liked the Eagles. The conversation moved to the election the previous week and from there to politics in general. Steve had read a magazine article about the campaigns behind the scenes and made the others laugh by sharing several anecdotes he had read about.

"That woman always looked drunk to me," Jason remarked when someone mentioned one of the candidates' wives.

Steve's eyes lit up with amusement. "You know, I read that

during the campaign she was drinking a lot and the campaign staff was worried about her. So that explains why she always seemed drunk. It's true!" he insisted.

Allison was shaking her head with laughter. "Can you imagine her as First Lady? It would be awful."

"Yeah, pretty pathetic. She'd be a national embarrassment."

Jason said, "Well, I heard that the other guy used to use cocaine."

"Yeah, I heard that too," Steve shrugged. "That was years ago, back during his college days."

Allison laughed. "At least not on the campaign trail. Can you imagine?"

Steve sighed. "I've always figured I could never be a politician. Too many skeletons in my closet. But I'm sure Jason and Allie would be fine."

"Not me." Jason shook his head. "I'd hate it."

"I think Steve would make a good politician." Allison grinned. "I can picture him out there shaking hands and kissing babies, charming all the women. Just as long as no one investigates your college years."

"And they would," Steve added drily. "They always try to dig up any dirt they can on anybody in office."

It was such a strange feeling, sitting here with Jason and Steve chatting together like old friends. Of course, Steve knew about her relationship with Jason, but Jason still knew nothing about her history with Steve. How would he react, if he did know? Would he be angry? Jealous? Or would they still be sitting here, chatting as friends? She still hadn't gotten up the courage to test his reaction, and she felt a stab of nervous guilt.

Suppressing these thoughts, she turned to Allison. "Tell me about the planning meeting last night. Did Leanne come?"

"No, she wasn't there, but Ruth came and Serena and Heidi. We planned an international dinner and a Christmas party for December, but Penny and Randy are getting married on New Year's Eve, so we had to keep that night open. Oh, and we got into quite a lively discussion afterward. Ruth told us that she finally gave Jesse an ultimatum. She told him to jump or go home, and so far he hasn't jumped. So now she's depressed and wondering if she made the right decision. Serena told her emphatically that if God wants her and Jesse to be together, she doesn't have to worry about making a mistake. In the end it will work out."

Steve frowned, turning around the glass in his hand. "I don't know if I agree with that or not."

Kendra glanced at him. "You don't? I thought you believed in the sovereignty of God." She was learning something about theology, she thought proudly.

Steve hesitated. "I do, but I also believe in human responsibility. Especially in the area of relationships." He glanced around the uncertain expressions at the table. "You can't say that you can mess up a relationship and God will just fix it for you. People mess up relationships all the time, and God doesn't usually step in and work a miracle."

Allison said, "Well, Serena is absolutely convinced that if God wants two people together, he'll make it happen. And if God doesn't want them together, one of them will break a leg or something before the wedding day. I'm not sure I agree, but Serena believes that."

"So where does that leave my parents?" Steve argued. "Either they were wrong to get married, or they were wrong to get divorced. Why didn't God make one of them break a leg before their wedding? Or make my dad have a stroke as he was filing for divorce? I'm saying that obedience is part of the equation, and if we're not obedient, God won't always intervene."

Kendra glanced at Jason and remembered what he had told her about his relationship with Melody. "So you think it was wrong of Ruth to give Jesse an ultimatum?"

"Oh, I'm not saying that. Maybe she's being impatient, but if Jesse doesn't intend to ever marry her, it's probably better for her to find out now. And if Jesse isn't open to marriage, God may not miraculously change his mind. Jesse might lose Ruth, and that's part of the price he'll have to pay."

Allison heaved a great sigh. "Well, that's a depressing thought. Here I've been telling myself for years that I'll meet the right guy when God brings him along. What you're saying is that I might have met the right guy in the past, and maybe one of us messed it up."

Steve gave her a sympathetic look. "Well, human responsibility is one principle, but the sovereignty of God is another. God does work in our lives, in spite of our mistakes. Do you remember that sermon we heard last summer from that visiting missionary? Or maybe it was two summers ago, but the sermon really stayed with me. He was preaching on the resurrection of Lazarus, and how Martha said to Jesus, 'Even now I know God will give you whatever you ask for.' And the whole theme of the sermon was that even now it's not too late for God to accomplish his purpose. It's never too late for God, even when Lazarus is dead and buried and everything seems hopeless." He grinned at his cousin. "So cheer up, Allie! I'm sure it's not too late for God to bring along a husband for you, even at your age."

Allison gave him a sardonic look. "Thanks, Steve. That's really reassuring."

And how did that apply to her? Kendra wondered as she recalled the conversation later. Did God have someone planned for her, or was it her own responsibility to find a husband? And how would she know when she did meet the right man? Some married women she knew described having a sense of certainty as soon as they met their husbands. It would be awfully nice if God would give her some kind of sign so she could be sure not to miss the right man, but when she recalled her past relationships, she knew that nothing that dramatic had ever occurred in her life.

Chapter Twenty-two

On the first Friday night in December Kendra attended the international dinner at Ruth and Leanne's house. Jason called Kendra that afternoon to cancel, but promised he would come over the next night. At the dinner Kendra saw a new girl with curly hair and a bubbly personality who sat next to Steve at the table, the two of them laughing and talking, actually flirting, throughout the meal. Kendra sat at the other end and talked to Leanne. She felt Jason's absence keenly. She had never seen Steve show much interest in any girl before – at least since the party six years ago – and the sight gave her a slightly odd feeling. But even if Jason had come, she knew the two of them would appear staid and boring next to Steve and Shirley Temple.

"You'll never believe who asked me out last night," Allison announced the next morning when she appeared for breakfast. Her eyes were laughing in either amusement or disbelief. "Eddie! Do you believe it?"

Kendra turned to stare at her. "Eddie? The guy who never dates? One of the Bachelors till the Rapture?"

"I couldn't believe it either." Allison turned to take her toast from the toaster and began to butter it. "He wants to see that new movie that's coming out next week for Christmas."

"So you said yes?"

"Well, I've been complaining for so long about never dating that I thought God might strike me dead or something if I said no. And I like Eddie as a friend. I know I can go out with him and have a good time. But – well, I can't picture myself ever marrying him."

Kendra considered the possibility as she carried Elizabeth's cereal bowl to the sink. "Well, he's sort of cute, and he has a good sense of humor. He can be a lot of fun."

"I know. He's nice. But he's not very intellectual. It bugs me the way he uses bad grammar sometimes, and he doesn't like to read. I guess I like really smart guys. That's why I can't picture being married to him."

Kendra laughed. "Well, your pickings are rather slim in this group. Who are the smart guys? Randy, who's engaged, and Steve, who's your cousin, and Vince, who's just plain annoying –"

"Pretty sad, isn't it?" Allison sighed and lowered her voice confidentially. "You know who I'd really like to go out with? That new guy, Paul Valentine."

Kendra had met Paul several times. Tall, lean, and freckled, with a receding hairline and a quirky sense of humor. "The one you knew in high school? He seems smart."

"Yeah, and he's pretty friendly to me, but he's never asked me out. I don't know if it's hopeless or not."

"Well, go out with Eddie, have fun, and maybe Paul will be inspired by jealousy."

Allison laughed. "In my dreams!" She stopped suddenly as if a new thought had occurred to her. "Kendra, have you seen Jason lately?"

"Not since last Sunday. He said he wasn't feeling well last night, but he's coming over tonight." Kendra glanced at her friend, searching her face. "Why?"

"Oh, no reason." Allison turned away to tie up the bread bag. "It's good you're seeing him tonight."

An uneasy suspicious feeling swelled in Kendra's chest. "What have you heard?"

"Nothing, Kendra. It's probably nothing. Anyway, Jason can tell you if there's anything to tell."

She could see by the expression on Allison's face that the news she was hiding wasn't good. Allison couldn't keep a secret to save her life. "I want to know now. I know you heard something. Tell me."

"But it might not be true –"

"I still want to know. I'll find out sooner or later if it's true."

Allison sighed, and Kendra knew she had won. "Okay, but like I said, it might be all a misunderstanding. I was talking to Heidi last night, and she asked if you and Jason had broken up. And I said no, as far as I knew you were still together. And she said –" Allison glanced back at Kendra and sighed again, "she said that she saw Melody Graham on Wednesday at the pageant practice, and Melody was all excited and told her that she and Jason were getting back together."

Kendra just stared at her, a bubble of anger and disbelief welling inside her.

"I told Heidi it was probably just a misunderstanding. Maybe – maybe Jason had said something to give Melody the idea that eventually they might get back together, and Melody got her hopes up. But that's why I asked if you had seen Jason."

Kendra stared down at the pattern of squares on the kitchen floor, trying to make sense of what she was hearing. Had Jason given her any hint that he was on the verge of breaking up with her? She sensed that their relationship had flattened out a bit in the last few weeks, but nothing unusual had occurred. It was natural for the initial newness to wear off a bit. But maybe there was another reason for that feeling – Jason wanted to get back with Melody. And what a way for her to find out! He couldn't even tell her himself – Heidi and Allison had found out before she did. Tears of anger and humiliation stung her eyes.

She could hardly wait for him to show up at her door. She just wanted to get the denouement over with as soon as possible – to let him know how shabbily he had treated her. As soon as the bell rang she threw open the door, and knew her expression was anything but welcoming.

"Hi, Kendra." Was it her imagination, or was he avoiding her gaze? "I brought the pizza."

"Thanks." She almost snatched the box from him and carried it into the kitchen. Elizabeth followed behind, and Kendra lifted her into a chair and let her choose a slice. She glanced at Jason. "Are you ready to eat now?" Her words were clipped.

"Sure." He pulled out a chair and said a brief grace, and they began to eat. Kendra did not even try to make polite small talk.

"Is something bothering you?" he asked when they had chewed their pizza for a minute in silence.

"Not at all!" She forced a bright tone and a false smile. "Maybe you can tell me about your meeting with Melody this week."

His mouth fell open and his Adam's apple bobbed over his buttoned-up shirt collar. He stared at her, his face turning scarlet. "How – how did you –"

"Oh, news travels very quickly in this group, Jason." She smiled at him very sweetly. "It would have been nice to hear about it directly from you instead of through the grapevine."

"I'm sorry, Kendra. I'm really sorry. Maybe you should tell me what you heard."

"No, Jason, I think you're the one who should tell me. I'm all ears."

He sighed and stared down at the oil congealing on his pizza. "Let me explain first how it all happened, Kendra. You know I've never really dated anyone much except for Melody, and I just felt like I needed to sow my wild oats before I settled down..."

"Sow your wild oats?" Kendra's voice rose in disbelief. "So I'm the wild oat that you're sowing?"

"I didn't mean it that way. That sounded bad." He shifted miserably in his chair. "I just felt that I needed to date some other girls before I could marry Melody. I wasn't sure she was the right one. And – and, I've really enjoyed spending time with you and getting to know you. You're a really nice girl, and I like you a lot. But I could never completely get Melody out of my head."

He sighed. "Well, last Tuesday evening I ran into her by accident at the mall, and we spent some time shopping and talking and just hanging out for a while. I didn't plan it, really. And then – I told her I had been thinking about her, and I was wondering if she would be interested in getting back together. I should have talked to you first, I know, but I was being spontaneous. I didn't expect the whole church to find out before you."

"You can thank Melody for that," Kendra told him. "I guess she couldn't resist publishing the good tidings of great joy."

"I'm sorry. Really. Like I said, I like you a lot, but I feel that

Melody and I are a better match for the long term. She's more fun-loving and lighthearted. Sometimes I think you and I are too much alike. Both quiet and serious."

Even though Kendra had wondered the same thing, she resented hearing Jason put the idea into words. She said nothing.

"You're very reserved, and that's a good thing in some ways. But sometimes it's hard to get close to you. Melody's an open book with me. I never have to worry that she's keeping secrets from me or that I can't ask her certain questions."

"I'm not keeping secrets –" Kendra began in an indignant tone, and then stopped. She had kept one very important secret from Jason.

"Well, that was the feeling I had. That there were certain topics we weren't allowed to discuss. It made me uncomfortable."

Kendra wiped Elizabeth's hands and waited until she heard the child turn on the TV in the living room. She lowered her voice. "You mean Elizabeth's father? Was that a problem?"

"Well, that was one topic. You seemed secretive about it."

Kendra swallowed hard as tears burned her eyes. "I'm sorry, I didn't mean to be secretive. It's just hard for me to talk about certain issues. I have to know a guy really well before I open up about those things. I haven't even told Allison everything."

"I know. I'm sorry, Kendra. I know you'll be a great wife for the right guy. I don't mean to criticize, but I just feel more comfortable with someone like Melody."

Kendra bit her lip and looked away. There was no point in discussing this anymore. She just wanted Jason to leave.

"Do you remember that night Steve Dixon came over?" Jason asked. "We were talking about relationships, and he said that if we mess up a relationship, God won't necessarily step in and fix it for us. And I wondered if Melody was really the right girl for me and I had messed it up because I was afraid to move forward. I thought it over and decided I should talk to her and try to fix it. I've really been at peace about this ever since Tuesday night – I just haven't looked forward to telling you."

Kendra shrugged. "Don't worry about me. I'm sure I'll meet someone else sooner or later." At this point she wasn't at all sure, but it sounded like the right thing to say.

"I've always wondered," Jason began in a hesitant tone, "was anything going on between you and Steve Dixon?"

"Steve Dixon!" Kendra felt her face flame as she raised her eyes to his. "No, of course not! Whatever gave you that idea?"

"I don't know. I got funny vibes from him when he was around, like maybe he was jealous or something. I thought maybe he had asked you out once and you turned him down."

"No, no, nothing like that!" Kendra realized that she was protesting a bit too vigorously. She tried to lower her tone to one of careless indifference. "If Steve was ever interested in me, he certainly never told me."

"Well, maybe I was wrong about that. I'd be surprised if you didn't like him. The girls were all nuts for him back in high school."

Maybe she had been wrong to not tell Jason the truth about Steve, she reflected sadly that evening as she changed for bed. And yet, she wouldn't want him to know the truth if he were going to break up with her anyway. Had she messed up a promising relationship, or had she exercised prudent caution? Well, it didn't matter now. Jason was gone. She was alone. And she wasn't sure if she felt sadder over Jason or the fact that she had lost her first real prospect in years.

I am such a loser with men, she thought, tears welling up again as she gazed down at her sleeping daughter before climbing into her own bed. *I'll never get it right. At least I'm a good mother. Even Steve says so. But parenthood would be so much better if I could share it with a man.*

Dating Jason had given her confidence that some Christian man might want her in the end. Maybe that confidence had been false. And yet, Jason might have been sincere when he said she would make a great wife for the right guy. As far as Steve being jealous, that was just silly. Maybe he was a bit jealous over Elizabeth spending so much time with some other man, and Jason had picked up on those vibes.

She still felt hurt and embarrassed over the way the whole break-up had occurred, but when she tried to look at the situation objectively, she had to admit that Jason hadn't treated her all that badly. At least he hadn't lied to her and said he loved her when he didn't mean it. He hadn't pressured her about sex. All he had really done was decide he liked Melody better, and then been foolish enough to tell Melody first. Maybe, when her hurt pride had begun to heal a little, she would be able to wish him well.

☻ ☼

Steve was already sitting on the sofa next to Dan when Kendra entered the Bible study. He laughed in response to Dan's remark, but his eyes followed her as she took a seat on the floor in front of Randy and Penny. He watched as she tilted her head back and smiled in return to their greetings.

When the guys talked about the prettiest girls in the group, they usually mentioned Heidi or Serena. It was true that Kendra didn't have Heidi's soft, kitten-like prettiness or Serena's bold, dramatic good looks. Her attractiveness was more subtle and understated, a wholesome look with a fresh complexion and a graceful quiet dignity to her movements.

She glanced in his direction and he quickly looked away. She would not be pleased to see him staring at her. At least Jason wasn't with her tonight. Whenever he saw Jason sitting next to her, holding her hand, whispering in her ear, Steve just wanted to punch the guy in the face. Which he knew was a completely irrational reaction. Jason hadn't done anything wrong – at least, Steve hoped that he hadn't. In reality, if Jason knew the whole truth, he would want to punch Steve in the face, and with good reason.

Jason was still friendly to him, so Steve felt sure Kendra hadn't told him about their history together. Kendra had an almost paranoid fear of anyone finding out the truth – which was another reason he needed to get over this attraction and move on. Probably he was so stuck on Kendra because he knew she was the last girl in the group who would ever agree to date him. She was the biggest challenge of all. He had told himself this numerous times, but it didn't seem to make a difference in his feelings.

When the Bible study ended, the group broke up into smaller groups to socialize. Steve moved to the end of the couch to where

Allison was sitting.

"Hey, cousin, what's happening?"

She paused a moment in thought. "Well, you won't believe this, but I went out with your friend Eddie this week."

"Yeah, he told me. He asked my permission," Steve grinned.

"I should have known." Allison rolled her eyes. "Well, we had a nice time. I'm sure you'll tell him I said that. Oh, by the way, did you hear about Kendra and Jason?"

They were engaged. He knew it. He braced himself to hear the news. "No. What?"

"They broke up."

"Oh!" He tried to hide the relief he felt coursing through him. "Wow, that's a shock. Who did the breaking?"

"He did. He wants to get back with Melody." She lowered her voice. "The worst of it was that he told Melody before he told Kendra, and she heard about it. She was upset."

"Yeah, I guess so. That was pretty rotten." He paused a moment, sampling one of the chips on Allison's plate. "Well, she'll be all right. She can do better, anyway."

"I know you thought so," Allison laughed, "but I thought Jason was pretty nice. Up until now. Maybe you can console her."

He knew that Kendra wouldn't be looking toward him for consolation, but his spirits couldn't help but rise at this unexpected turn of events. A few minutes later he approached her at the refreshments table.

"How's it going?"

"Fine." She smiled up at him as if her life were perfect. No one would guess that she was upset about anything. Kendra would make a great poker player.

"Are you going to my Aunt Betsy's caroling party tomorrow night?" It was the first idea to occur to him.

Kendra looked surprised. She scooped some dip onto her plate. "I didn't know I was invited."

"Everyone's invited," Steve said. "I'm sure Allie's going."

Kendra considered for a moment, then looked up at him with a smile. "I guess you want me to bring Elizabeth, don't you?"

He smiled in return. "Yes, I would like that."

"Well, I could come, if you don't think I'd be crashing the party. I don't have any other plans."

"I'll vouch for you," he returned with a grin. It was a chickenhearted way of asking a girl out, but the best he could manage at the moment. He would never have acted in such a way back in college.

☞ ☜

The Sunday evening before Christmas the children's Christmas pageant was held at the church. Elizabeth was adorable as a sheep in a white woolly costume with black ears and a tail. Kendra brought her camera and snapped pictures of her daughter with some of the other children in the lobby afterward.

She had wondered if she should return to Grace Fellowship now that she and Jason had broken up, but hadn't completely made up her mind. Seeing Jason and Melody together didn't bother her as much as she had expected, but she didn't want Jason to think that she was staying because of any false hopes of a reconciliation. She decided to wait till after Christmas to make a decision.

Steve's mother, elegant as always in a flowered skirt and matching red sweater, approached Kendra as she lingered in the lobby.

"Your daughter is really adorable," she said. "It was a cute pageant."

Kendra smiled. "Yes, it was."

"I wanted to mention to you," the woman went on, "I'm hosting our Christmas get-together this year. If you and your daughter don't have any other plans, you'd be welcome to come."

"Why, thank you!" Kendra hadn't expected that. "Actually we're flying out to Chicago this week to spend Christmas with my mother. But thanks for asking."

"Your mother lives in Chicago?" Marilyn asked.

"Yes, she moved there a few years ago, after she got married."

"Well, I hope you have a nice visit. I'm sure your mother will be happy to see her little granddaughter." Marilyn glanced down again at Elizabeth in her sheep costume. "Is your daughter in school yet?"

"Yes, she goes to kindergarten in the public school near our house."

Marilyn smiled. "Is she learning to read?"

Why all the questions? Perhaps the woman was just trying to be friendly. "She can read some easy words like cat and dog, but mostly she's learning the letter sounds." Kendra added with a deprecating laugh, "Allison says she's bright – I don't know, I don't have anyone to compare her with."

Marilyn nodded thoughtfully. She remarked in a matter-of-fact tone, "Steve was always very bright. He always did well in school, even when he didn't try hard."

Kendra felt the color flood her face and her mouth fell open. Was the comment just a coincidence, or did Steve's mother know the truth? And if so, how? Had Steve told her? He'd said he hadn't mentioned any names during their conversation, but maybe he had finally broken down and told her. Or maybe the woman was simply comparing Kendra's daughter with her own oldest child.

She could think of nothing to say in response, and was relieved when someone interrupted and Marilyn moved away. She saw Steve entering the front door of the church carrying a large brown bag, and when his mother was out of hearing, he approached and handed it to her.

"Merry Christmas." She saw that the bag contained several gifts in bright Christmas wrapping. "I hope you have a nice trip to Chicago."

"Thanks." Should she have bought him a gift? The idea hadn't occurred to her. Maybe next year she could buy something small and say it was from Elizabeth. "Okay, you can tell me the truth now. Was the doll last year from you?"

He shrugged. "Guilty as charged. I gave her some new clothes for it this year, so it's no secret."

"That's nice. I'm sure you'll have a nice time with your family as well. That was fun last year, with everybody singing and the movie and all."

"Yeah, we usually have a good time together. Probably noisier than your family."

"That's for sure," Kendra laughed. She started to tell him about his mother's invitation, but suddenly felt embarrassed. "Anyway, Merry Christmas."

When she examined the gifts in the bag, she saw that one actually had her name on it. That surprised her more than anything. The gift was the size and weight of a book, and she decided to open it before her trip so she could read on the plane. It was a paperback copy of *Pride and Prejudice.* On the inside flap was written:

Kendra – I didn't know if this book was your style or not, but I thought you might enjoy it. Merry Christmas! Steve

She opened to the first chapter and read:

"It is a truth universally acknowledged, that a single man in possession of a large fortune, must be in want of a wife."

Actually it didn't sound like Steve's type of book at all, but if it turned out to be a love story, Kendra thought she would enjoy it.

Chapter Twenty-three

The church was lit by candlelight, soft organ music playing, when Kendra entered on New Year's Eve for Penny and Randy's wedding. The sanctuary was already beginning to fill; Penny had said it would be a large wedding, even though it was her second. Randy had never been married before and he seemed determined to invite every friend, relative, and acquaintance.

Kendra took the arm of the usher, whom she recognized as Randy's brother, as he led her to her seat. She slid into a pew on the bride's side beside Ruth and Leanne. Glancing around, she could see that everyone in the Timothy group had been invited, and most of the rest of the church as well. Allison had come with Eddie and the two them were sitting on the groom's side, closer to the front. A little behind them sat Mark and his girlfriend, visiting for the holidays, and farther back, Jason and Melody.

Quickly she looked in the opposite direction. Two pews ahead of her she saw Steve, Dan, and Jesse. Clearly Jesse had not decided to make a commitment, or he would be sitting next to Ruth instead of with the other men. None of them had brought dates.

Steve glanced back, caught her eye, and smiled in greeting. She returned his smile. She would need to tell him that she had enjoyed the story of Elizabeth Bennet and Mr. Darcy.

She had read it during her Christmas visit to her mother's, and once her mother had picked up the book and seen the inscription. "Who's Steve?" she'd asked in a sharp tone.

Kendra found herself stammering in reply. "Steve Dixon."

"You give each other presents?"

"We don't usually," she hastened to explain, "but he gave Elizabeth some Christmas presents and I guess he thought he should give me something as well."

She had been careful not to mention Steve's name the rest of the visit.

Now the wedding march was beginning and she turned with the rest of the congregation to watch the bridesmaids glide down the aisle. Jean looked especially pretty in the dark rose-colored gown with matching roses in her hair. Each of the bridesmaids carried a lit candle in a glass globe. Finally Penny entered on her father's arm, glowing with happiness, the classic lovely bride.

Kendra had attended few weddings before, and this was the first overtly Christian ceremony she had seen. She found herself moved by the beautiful music and the use of scripture passages throughout the service. Randy and Penny joined hands and repeated their vows and were finally pronounced husband and wife. Glancing at Leanne, Kendra saw a tear in her friend's eye. Was it a tear of happiness or pain? Leanne had once been in love with Randy. Maybe she was wishing this could be her own wedding. Kendra saw Ruth glance at Jesse several times with wistful sadness in her eyes.

We've all been heartbroken at least once, Kendra reflected. Somehow she felt better about Jason and Melody.

After the ceremony the guests moved to the church fellowship hall for the reception, and most of the Timothy group found seats together. The three dateless men had saved seats at a table for the three girls, although Kendra wondered if that were a wise arrangement for Ruth and Jesse. Allison and Eddie joined them, and Paul Valentine squeezed in. Several of the men, including Steve, seemed in high spirits. They kept clanging their glasses to make the bride and groom kiss, until Allison told them they were annoying.

"If we're going to have more weddings in this group, we'll need to come up with a better idea for the bachelor parties," Steve announced. "Randy's bachelor party was pretty lame."

Ruth wrinkled her brow. "How do you have a Christian bachelor party?"

"Well, that was the problem. No one knew what to do, so we just sat around eating pretzels and drinking soda till we all got bored and went home. But I have some ideas for the next bachelor party." His bright blue eyes sparkled with mischief.

"It had better not include any girls jumping out of cakes," Allison scolded.

"No, nothing like that. Don't worry; I'll run it by Pastor Mike. I'll give you a clue: It has something to do with Song of Solomon."

Kendra tried to remember what she knew of Song of Solomon. It was in the Bible, part of the Old Testament, but she had never read it.

"We can draw another picture," Dan remarked with his usual deadpan expression.

Some of the guys laughed, but the girls looked blank.

"Once during a Bible study we read part of Song of Solomon, and I guess we were in a crazy mood, because Dan decided to draw the girl in the story. You know, where it says, 'Your hair is like a flock of goats, descending from Mount Gilead,' Dan drew a girl with a flock of goats running down her back. And, 'Your neck is like the tower of David, built with elegance.' He drew a tower for her neck." Steve laughed, glancing at Dan. "Dan's a pretty good artist, and when he was finished, that girl was – quite lovely."

Laughter circled the table. "You should post that picture on the church bulletin board," Paul suggested.

"Or I could show it to my class at school. I read sections of Song of Solomon in one of my poetry classes as examples of metaphor," Steve told them. "My students loved it."

"You'd better hope the parents don't get upset," Leanne told him.

"Oh, I stopped before it got too steamy."

Kendra decided she would have to go home and read Song of Solomon.

They had finished eating and now Penny and Randy rose from their seats to cut the cake and feed each other. Penny threw the bouquet as her friends gathered round and Ruth caught it. She ignored Jesse as her friends teased her about being the next bride.

"We can't go home yet," Steve objected as the guests began to gather their belongings to leave. "It's only ten o'clock on New Year's Eve. We have to stay up till midnight at least." He glanced from Allison to Kendra with a smile.

"I have to go home," Kendra told him regretfully. "I told my babysitter I would be back around ten. She wants to go to a party."

"You can all come to my house if you want." Allison pulled on her coat. "We can watch a movie. Eddie already rented one."

Steve looked pleased. "I'll bring some snacks. Dan will probably come too."

Allison hesitated and stepped closer to her cousin. "Steve, could you invite Paul Valentine?"

Steve grinned, his eyes picking Paul out of the crowd. "Why don't you ask him?"

Allison hesitated. "Well, I came with Eddie, and I thought it would be a little tacky to invite Paul –"

Steve laughed. "I get it. You came with Eddie, but you'd rather be with Paul. Sure, I'll invite him. I'll tell him my cousin really wants him to come."

"Steve!"

Steve threw a grin over his shoulder as he walked away to talk to Paul. Allison grimaced and turned her back to him.

Kendra drove home, paid the babysitter, and checked on her sleeping daughter. A moment later her friends began arriving.

"I invited Jean, and she'll be here after she goes home to change," Allison announced.

"Paul Valentine said he would come." Steve glanced at his cousin but kept a straight face. "Serena had another party to go to. I invited Randy and Penny, but they're busy. I don't know why; I can't imagine what they have to do that's so important."

His friends laughed at his exaggerated tone. "I hope they're having more fun than we are," Dan added.

Allison shook her head as she collected coats. "Now boys, get your minds out of the gutter."

"Who said anything about the gutter? We just came from a beautiful wedding."

The doorbell rang and Paul entered; Kendra saw Allison's face light up. A moment later Jean arrived.

"Eddie rented *When Harry Met Sally,*" Allison told them. "I've never seen it, and Eddie said it was a good movie for New Year's Eve."

Jean frowned. "I've heard it has a lot of sex in it."

"It doesn't really have a lot of sex, but it has a lot of sex talk," Steve said. "I've seen it before, but I wouldn't mind seeing it again. It isn't a Christian movie of course, and it uses some bad language, but it has some interesting ideas too. The story is good."

"I have some other movies we can choose from," Allison offered.

After some discussion they agreed to watch the movie. With Steve's help Kendra set out the snacks he had brought in baskets. When they returned to the living room, she noticed that Paul and Allison were sitting on the love seat together, talking, while Eddie and Jean occupied the couch. Kendra was glad that Paul was paying attention to Allison tonight. She took the empty space on the couch and Steve dropped into the rocker across from her. Dan sprawled on the floor.

Kendra found the movie entertaining, and Steve looked at her with a significant smile at some of the lines, as if they shared an inside joke, which embarrassed her a tiny bit. A few minutes before midnight they stopped the movie and counted down to the new year, and everyone cheered and hugged each other. Kendra accepted hugs from Eddie and Dan and finally Steve. She noticed that Paul gave Allison a kiss on the cheek, which made her friend blush.

The movie ended with Harry and Sally declaring their love on New Year's Eve, and then describing their wedding three months later. Steve laughed at the line, "It only took three months. Twelve years and three months."

"That was a good movie," Jean remarked when it was over. "Not a very Christian movie, like you said, but it had a good story."

"Well, it definitely had a worldly attitude toward dating and relationships," Allison agreed, "but one thing I liked about it. It made the point that after Harry and Sally went to bed together, they couldn't just go on and pretend that nothing had happened. It changed their relationship. Even though Harry slept around with all those women, he knew it was really supposed to mean something."

"I had a hard time believing that guy would ever marry anyone," Kendra declared.

"No, I can believe it." Paul shook his head. "He had been married before, and he just had to get to the point of being able to trust someone again."

A knock sounded on the front door and everyone exchanged looks. "Who can it be this time of night?" Allison asked. Kendra, who was closer, went to open it. A policeman stood outside.

"I had a complaint about a loud party here." He glanced around at the quiet room, looking puzzled. "Well, it doesn't seem too loud – just keep it down."

The group waited until the door was shut before they broke into laughter. "If this is someone's idea of a wild party, I'd hate to see how they spend New Year's Eve," Dan said.

"I guess we'd better get home," Jean rose from the couch and scanned the room for her purse. "I hope we don't meet any drunks on the road."

"Why don't you all stay here tonight?" Allison asked suddenly. "We can all go out for breakfast together in the morning. Wouldn't that be fun?" Her eyes sparkled.

"Where would we sleep?" Dan asked.

"I get the couch!" Eddie stretched out with a grin.

Steve patted the recliner. "I'm comfortable right here."

"We have extra pillows and blankets." Allison started for the stairs, and laughed suddenly. "When Kendra moved in with me, we agreed we wouldn't have any men spending the night. This is the first time we've broken that rule."

Steve glanced at Jean. "What about Jean? I don't think she wants to sleep in the living room with all the men."

"She can have Elizabeth's bed," Kendra offered. "I'll put Elizabeth on the floor.

She was deep in sleep the next morning when her daughter climbed on her bed. "Mommy, there's a whole lot of men sleeping in the living room."

Kendra blinked and rolled over. "It's all right," she murmured groggily. "They're just the guys from church. Steve and Dan and the others. Let them sleep."

A moment later she heard the music from a children's television program drift upstairs, and she groaned. The others would quickly discover what she had learned long ago. There was no sleeping late with a child in the house.

"So where are we going for breakfast?" Allison asked happily when everyone had reluctantly arisen. "What about the pancake house a few miles from here?"

Steve's hair was mussed, his curls a riot of confusion. "I wish I had a comb. And a toothbrush."

"You look very pretty, Steve," Allison smirked. "Well, you can borrow my comb, but not my toothbrush."

Kendra was glad that she had just stepped out of the shower, although her hair was still damp. Allison and Jean both looked particularly bright-eyed and well-groomed for such an early hour. She knew they each had a man they were interested in.

"Maybe we can all fit in one car," Paul suggested, "like we used to do in high school. If the girls sit on our laps, we can all squeeze in."

Allison clearly liked the notion. "You have a pretty big car, don't you? Can you drive?"

With good-natured laughter the others agreed to the plan. Kendra climbed into the middle of the back seat with Elizabeth on her lap. She was usually scrupulous about putting Elizabeth in her car seat, but she hated to ruin everyone's fun, and the pancake house was only a few miles away. Steve and Dan sat on either side, holding Allison and Jean. Eddie and Paul drove in front. The group in back was packed so tightly they could hardly move.

"Now if we see a cop car, you girls need to duck," Steve warned. He glanced out the window. "Police!"

The girls shrieked and tried to fall on the floor.

"Just kidding," Steve grinned.

"Oh, I feel so decadent," Allison giggled. "Watching a slightly racy movie last night, having the cops called on us, four guys crashing in my living room, and now this. I feel so naughty."

Paul threw a grin to her over the back of his seat. "Was that the Christian version of a wild orgy?"

"Allie's a bad influence on all of us," Steve announced. "Wait till I tell my mother that I finally got arrested because eight of us were squeezed in a car with no proper seat belts. Allie's turning me into a criminal."

"Somebody keeps kicking me," Dan said.

Kendra said, "It's probably Elizabeth."

"No, it's me," Jean apologized. "Sorry."

Steve shifted in his seat. "Allie feels like a ton of bricks. My legs are falling asleep."

Allison glared at him. Paul said, "I never heard a couple guys complain so much about holding girls on their laps. Eddie and I wouldn't complain if we were back there."

"Well, we can switch on the way home," Dan told him.

Kendra thought of Jason and how he would likely react to this situation. Suddenly she was not at all sorry that they had broken up. If she and Jason were still dating, she probably wouldn't be here now, having fun with her friends. Or Jason would be with her, and she'd have to worry about whether he was having a good time and feeling comfortable. There were, after all, worse things in life than not having a boyfriend.

"Hey, I found these old seventies CD's at a yard sale," Paul told them. "Beach Boys, Kenny Rogers, Neil Diamond. Fifty cents apiece!"

"My parents used to listen to Kenny Rogers," Steve recalled with irony, "back when they liked each other. My mother's favorite was 'Love the World Away.'"

Paul slipped a CD into the player and the conversation was drowned under the sentimental introduction to "Lady." "A knight in shining armor," he quipped with a glance over his shoulder. "Is that what you women are looking for?"

"I'll take it," Allison returned.

A minute later they arrived at the pancake house and piled out of the car. "It's empty in here," Jean almost whispered as they entered the restaurant.

"Everyone else is home sleeping off their hangovers," Dan said.

The waitress led them to a table and they all chose seats. "Now, I think we should all share our New Year's resolutions," Steve announced when they had been seated, "and no one's allowed to say exercising or losing weight. Especially the girls."

"You took mine," Kendra laughed.

"Come on, Kendra, you can do better. Be creative –"

"Okay, Steve, you start," Jean told him.

Steve looked around the group solemnly. "Mine is to get married."

The table broke into laughter. "How can that be your resolution?" Jean asked.

"Well, it's a goal, isn't it?"

Allison was shaking her head, still laughing. "I thought you guys were all Bachelors Till the Rapture!"

"Not by choice," Eddie told her.

"Randy and Penny inspired me," Steve insisted with a straight face. "That wedding was so moving last night, I think we should all participate in marital bliss."

"Your wedding song will be the theme from *Mission Impossible*," Eddie grinned.

"That would be mine," Paul added.

Allison shook out her napkin. "Well, I don't buy it for a minute. Steve could get married tomorrow if he wants, and he knows it. In fact, all you guys could. If you're not married, it's because you don't want to be, and that's all there is to it."

"You're hard on us," Paul told her. Allison tossed her head and smiled.

"I'd like to know who all these mysterious women are who want to marry us," Eddie said.

Steve raised his eyebrows. "I'd like to know that too."

Allison shook her head. "Well, I'm not going to swell your egos by naming names. I can think of a couple for each of you, and if you haven't found them, it's because you don't want to. That's all."

Kendra knew that Allison liked Paul and that Jean was interested in Eddie. She had suspected as much before, but it had become more obvious in the last day. As for Dan and Steve, she agreed with Allison that they would have no trouble finding girlfriends and wives as well. She reflected, a little sadly, that Steve would probably make a good husband and father. It was really too bad the way things had started out between them. Under different circumstances, they might have made a nice couple. Now it was too late.

"How soon do you think you could buy your house?" Allison asked Steve. "You'd better do it in the next year, if you want to get married that soon."

Steve grinned. "Good idea. Actually I'd like to start looking in the spring. I hope by then I'll have about fifteen thousand for a down payment."

Dan whistled. "Hear that, girls? If any of you want to get married, Steve's the guy for you."

"Yeah, better him than me," Paul added.

Their breakfast arrived and they ate their meal with more stories and laughter. Kendra had ordered a Belgian waffle for herself, but when Elizabeth begged for chocolate chip pancakes, Steve insisted on ordering them for her. Finally the bill arrived and they all dug into wallets for cash.

When they trooped out to the car, Eddie climbed in the back seat with Jean on his lap. Before Kendra realized what was happening, Allison had climbed into Kendra's place and took Elizabeth on her lap.

"Sorry, Kendra, but I'm not sitting on Steve's lap again. You take him. I don't want to hear how heavy I am again."

Kendra hesitated, but it would seem rude to object to the arrangement. Dan couldn't very well sit on Steve's lap, and everyone else was settled. Rather gingerly she climbed in and perched herself on his knees. He seemed to keep his hands carefully away from her. She wondered if he felt as oddly about the situation as she did.

Paul started the engine and the music flowed through the car. As each of the songs played on the stereo, those who knew the words sang enthusiastically along as they rode through the winter morning.

Chapter Twenty-four

"I have a question I've been wanting to ask you, Kendra," Steve said. It was Sunday just after the service, and he had stopped her in the church lobby. "The worship team is looking for a pianist – the woman who was playing for us just left because she's ready to have a baby. And I thought of you."

Kendra had never thought of playing on the worship team before. "Well, that's nice, Steve, but – why don't you ask Jason? He's a better pianist than I am."

"Oh, no, Jason couldn't play for our worship team!" Steve shook his head with amusement in his face. "We're too much like what it says in the book of Judges: 'Every man did what was right in his own eyes.' We would completely drive Jason crazy."

Laughing, Kendra had to agree. Jason was so very particular about his music. "To be honest, Steve, I haven't completely decided if I'm staying at Bethel or going back to Grace Fellowship."

Steve looked surprised, and not exactly pleased. "Why would you go back there?"

"Well, you know, because of Jason..."

His expression turned sympathetic. "Does it bother you so much to see him?"

"No, not really, it's just that I don't want him to think I'm stalking him or something..."

Steve threw back his head and laughed. "Kendra the stalker! Don't be silly, Kendra. Jason won't think that. You have a lot of friends here. You should go to whatever church makes you comfortable. And we need you on the worship team here."

It felt good to be wanted, and this was an opportunity to use her talent to serve the Lord. Perhaps she should stay after all. She was very happy at Bethel, in spite of Jason.

"Maybe I will. Let me think about it, okay?"

"And there's something else I wanted to ask." He swallowed, looking slightly nervous. "I thought that maybe I could come over on Tuesdays like I did last year, and watch Elizabeth for you. Even if you don't have a class now, it would give you a free night. You could go shopping or whatever."

She blushed slightly as she remembered how she had declined his help in the fall when she was dating Jason. Perhaps that had been wrong. He was the only father that Elizabeth had; he clearly cared about her, and Elizabeth was fond of him. In May her daughter would be six, and Kendra was no closer to being married than she had ever been. Surely some father was better than none at all.

"Well, that would be nice, if you really want to."

He smiled. "Okay. I'll see you this Tuesday at seven."

The next week Kendra began to practice with the worship team and was pleased to be welcomed by the other members. She found enjoyment in playing regularly for such a positive purpose, satisfaction in leading the church in worship. Steve played the drums, and the group included several guitar players and vocalists as well.

On Tuesday nights when Steve came to the house, Kendra sometimes ran errands or shopped for groceries. At other times she stayed home and did chores while Steve played with Elizabeth. Sometimes Steve would find a good movie or show on TV and Kendra would end up watching it with him. If Allison were home, they might all sit around and visit together.

It was strange to think back and remember that only a year ago she had tried to avoid Steve and hated being around him. It was hard to believe that their relationship had changed so much. Now she saw him at least four times a week, on Tuesday when he spent the evening, on Thursday at worship team practice, at the weekend Timothy group activities, and also in church Sunday morning. She felt a bit chagrined when she realized how her mother would react to this friendship, but decided that the simplest solution was to not mention it. God had given her the grace to forgive Steve, and she had gotten to the point of seeing him as a very different person than he had been in the past. She knew her mother would never see him that way, and so it was easiest to simply avoid the confrontation.

℘ ℘

"So I'm curious about something, Kendra." Steve leaned against the kitchen counter, watching Kendra clean up her late dinner. "You took that class last spring, but you haven't taken another one since. Have you given up on it?"

"Oh, that." Kendra opened the refrigerator and put the leftover lasagna inside. "I haven't exactly given up, but I'm still trying to decide what I really want to do. I suppose getting a degree in accounting would help my career. But my dream was always to study music. I know I'll never be a concert pianist at this point, but I might be able to teach music. When I was dating Jason and he talked about his students, I started thinking about it and how I would enjoy teaching – more than Jason seemed to at times. And in the last few months I've been giving Elizabeth piano lessons – nothing very difficult, but she likes it, and I like teaching her. So I'm in this quandary, not sure which direction I should go, and I don't want to waste my money until I'm sure."

Steve nodded. "Did you like accounting?"

"I liked it pretty well, and I got an A in the course, but it isn't my dream job. On the other hand, it's probably more practical. If I could even get an associate's degree in accounting, I could get a better job and make more money." She paused and looked up at Steve. "What do you think I should do?"

"It's a good question." Steve ran his hand through his hair. "You'd need a bachelor's degree to teach music in a school, but with less than that you could start giving private lessons at home, couldn't you?"

"I suppose so, at least at the lower levels. But I don't know if I could support myself very well with private lessons. Jason had a hard time with it, and he had more training than me. If I were married – if it were a second income – then it might be a good plan, but that's not the case."

"But if you got married and had more children, teaching piano at home might be a very handy second income."

"I suppose so, but I can't read the future." At the moment, the possibility of marriage seemed far off. Kendra shrugged. "Well, you see my dilemma."

"Yes, I do. I'd take a little more time and think it over. But overall, I'd say that if music is what you love, you should follow your heart."

She looked up at him and smiled. "Maybe you're right. I'll think about it."

"Speaking of Jason –" Steve grinned as if a new thought had just occurred to him, "Ben was talking about you the other night when the guys were together."

"Ben?" Kendra frowned.

"Yeah, he's hoping now that you and Jason have broken up, he might have another chance." Kendra's eyes widened in horror. "Okay, I take it that means no!"

"He's so weird." Kendra pulled out a kitchen chair and dropped into it. "He stares at me all the time, and it creeps me out. And Leanne says that she saw him taking pictures of me when I wasn't looking. Isn't that creepy?"

Steve laughed. "Poor Ben."

"Poor *Ben*?" Kendra glared at him.

"Well, he obviously likes you, and he obviously isn't getting anywhere."

It was clear that Steve wanted to find her a new boyfriend now that she had lost Jason. For some reason she found the idea insulting – and doubly insulting that he thought Ben was a good match for her. "Do you really think I should date him? We have nothing in common – absolutely nothing!"

"Oh, no, no, I'm not saying that. If you don't like him, don't go out with him. Just tell him you're not interested." Kendra heaved a sigh. "Do you want me to tell him? I'll just say he needs to back off and look elsewhere."

"I don't want to be mean –"

"Look, he's a big boy, he can take it. Guys want honesty. If you say yes just to be nice, it confuses them. They need to know if they're barking up the wrong tree."

Kendra laughed. "Barking up the wrong tree? What's that mean?"

"Oh, you know, it's an old hunting expression. Dogs bark at the bottom of a tree when they think they have a squirrel caught up there."

"Oh, so now I'm a squirrel and Ben's a hunting dog."

"Sure, all guys are hunting dogs. It's our nature."

Elizabeth emerged from the basement stairs and ran to Steve. Steve picked her up and began to roughhouse with her as he often did, making her shriek and giggle. Watching them together, Kendra felt a sudden wistfulness.

He whispered in the child's ear and Elizabeth ran to her mother and spoke in a stage whisper. "You're prettier than any squirrel!"

"Why, thank you, honey." Had Steve told her to say that? Kendra suddenly felt herself blush. "Listen, I have to run out to the grocery store. I'll be back in an hour."

She had noticed a difference in Steve's behavior to her over the last few weeks, since her breakup with Jason to be exact, and was not entirely sure how to interpret it. He didn't flirt with her, he never said or did anything that was remotely suggestive, but he was very...attentive. It was the only word she could think of to describe his attitude. He made a point to speak to her whenever they were in a group together, often offered to help her, looked and smiled at her more than he ever had in the past. Like offering to help her with Ben. It was really very sweet, but disconcerting. If any other guy had behaved the same way, she would have thought he wanted to date her. But she knew that Steve didn't have a romantic interest in her. As she roamed the aisles of the grocery store and ruminated on the matter, she came to the conclusion that he finally felt comfortable enough with her to treat her the same way he treated all the girls.

Still, it made her a bit uneasy. Steve should know better than to pay too much attention to girls he didn't want to date. She thought he had learned that lesson with Kim. Of course, *she* knew that it meant nothing, but other people could get the wrong idea. Some girl who was lonely and hungry for male attention could easily become infatuated by a good-looking guy who was so nice to her. Maybe she should offer him a subtle warning, but the situation was so awkward.

A recent conversation with Serena and Allison about Heidi's relationship flashed through her mind, and she stopped in act of reaching for a can of corn on the grocery shelf. What had Serena said? "You know, whenever a man and woman spend a lot of time together, one of them will usually fall in love with the other." After moment of consideration, Allison had agreed with the comment.

Now Kendra and Steve were spending a lot of time together. She certainly couldn't let herself fall in love with Steve. She felt a chill at the very thought. Such an ending to their unusual friendship would be completely unacceptable, for of course she would be the one to get hurt. She would have to guard her heart carefully, and in the future, when he leaned over to whisper to her, or helped her carry something, she should behave with great dignity to let him know she understood, as he certainly did, the boundaries in their relationship.

※ ※

One Tuesday evening when Steve was visiting, Allison joined them in the living room and dropped onto the sofa. Kendra could tell by her expression that something was weighing on her mind.

"Steve," she began abruptly, "did you know that Paul is divorced?"

Allison and Paul had started dating soon after New Year's Day, and Allison seemed blissful in the new relationship. Kendra was happy for her, just as Allison had been happy for Kendra when she dated Jason. But she couldn't help but feel the loss now that Allison was part of a couple and she was alone again.

Steve looked up. "I did not."

Allison sighed. "I don't think he tells many people. He's embarrassed by it."

"I guess there were no children?"

"No. He says the only smart thing about that marriage was that they didn't have children."

Kendra looked down at the floor.

Steve nodded. "It sounds like it bothers you."

Allison spread her hands. "Well, I've never dated a divorced guy before. I don't know what to think. I really like Paul, but don't want to be blinded by love and make a big mistake."

Steve knit his brow and sat a moment in silence. "Are you concerned because you think it would be wrong to marry him, or because you're afraid of ending up divorced yourself? They're really two different issues."

"Well, I know if you ask twenty Christians, you'll get twenty opinions on this topic. I don't think it would be wrong to marry him, because his ex-wife is remarried and so they can't get back together. I just think it was stupid of him to marry her in the first place."

"So it's more of a character issue." Steve thought a moment. "Was he very young?"

"Yes, they were both twenty when they got married."

Steve shrugged and spread his hands. "I know if I had gotten married when I was twenty, I'd be divorced by now. I was just too self-centered and immature."

"But you were smart enough not to do it."

"Smart – or selfish. I don't know which. Maybe I should have been willing back then. Why did he marry so young?"

Allison sighed. "He said she was having problems with her parents, and wanted to move out but couldn't afford it. She wanted to move in with him, and he said they should get married, thinking he was being the hero. Then after they were married he understood why she had problems with her parents. They fought a lot, and in the end she left him and moved in with another guy."

Steve thought a minute, slowly shaking his head. "Allie, you've lived a sheltered life and not had to deal with some of these tough issues before. That's to your credit, because you haven't made any really big mistakes and messed up your life. I agree you have to look carefully at Paul's character before you marry him. On the other hand, people can learn from mistakes they've made in the past, even a big one like that. You have to decide if you're willing to forgive him and allow him to be fallible."

"Of course I don't expect him to be perfect." She clasped her hands in her lap and studied them. "I just don't want to look back in twenty years and see that I ignored all the warning signs before I married him."

"That's smart. But you have to look at all sides of the situation, including how Paul has changed since he was twenty."

Allison nodded, her expression brighter, and Kendra suspected that Steve had told her what she really wanted to hear. She liked Paul a lot, and wanted to believe that the two of them could live happily ever after.

Chapter Twenty-five

During the first Sunday in February the pastor at Bethel Bible announced that a baptism service would be held later that month. Kendra had seen one baptism service during the fall, and the idea stayed with her during the week.

"Allison," she began one evening after putting Elizabeth to bed, "do you think I should be baptized?"

Allison looked up from the book she was reading. "Have you ever been baptized, Kendra?"

"Only when I was a baby, in the Catholic Church."

Allison laughed. "That wouldn't count in our church – we only baptize adults, or kids who are old enough to choose. I'm sure it would depend on what church you attend, and its theology. But you know, I think there's something positive about a public profession of faith, whether it's in the form of baptism or something else."

Kendra remembered the service she had seen. "I guess I'd have to speak to the church, wouldn't I? That's what makes me nervous."

"Yeah, but it shouldn't be that hard. You can write down what you want to say and read it, so you don't forget anything. Really, if those young kids can do it, I'm sure you can."

But most of those young kids didn't have anything really difficult to share. Knowing how much to say, and how to say it – that was the difficult part.

The next Sunday she decided to take the plunge and told the pastor that she wanted to be baptized. That afternoon she sat down with a pen and paper and struggled to write her testimony. After an hour of writing and rewriting, she showed the result to Allison. "I'm not exactly sure how to end it."

"That's good," her friend nodded when she had finished reading. "Maybe you should add something about how your faith has made a difference in your life. Why is it important to you to be a Christian? Maybe you could end with a Bible verse that's been meaningful to you."

Kendra found her Bible and pored over it, looking up all her favorite passages. Still, the thought of reading the end result to the whole congregation made her a bit nervous. It was never easy for her to share personal experiences with strangers.

On the designated Sunday she gathered with the other baptismal candidates to change out of their Sunday clothes. Each was given a white robe to put on. Three candidates waited in the room with Kendra: a brother and sister of about ten and twelve, and a teenage girl.

"I'll take you in order of age," the pastor told them. "Brittany will be first and Kendra last."

Kendra waited nervously while the other three young people were baptized ahead of her. When the pastor beckoned to her she walked into the baptistry.

"Finally we have Kendra Walton," he said. "Kendra, do you have something to share with us?"

Kendra unfolded the paper she held. She glanced around the church and saw her friends scattered among the many strangers in the congregation. Allison and Paul, Randy and Penny, Leanne, Steve.

She looked down and began to read, her palms damp.

"I was raised in a good home with parents who took me to church every Sunday. I always believed in God and tried to be a good person, but I didn't understand what it meant to have a relationship with him.

"My whole life changed when I was fourteen and my father was diagnosed with a brain tumor. He died a year later, and it seemed that after that my family fell apart. My brother got involved with drugs, and I had a baby when I was sixteen. I still believed in God, but I couldn't see that he cared about me or the problems my family was struggling with."

She swallowed and wiped her hand on her robe.

"When I was twenty, my mother decided to remarry and moved to Chicago with her new husband. This left me alone with my three-year-old daughter. I felt very deserted after my mother left. I felt that I had no one who cared about me and no one to turn to with my problems. I can see now that God was using this to bring me to himself.

"Around that time, a friend invited me to her church. At that church I met people who seemed to know God personally, and I began to read the Bible for the first time. I started to pray about my problems, and I was surprised when God actually answered me. He provided me with a new home and a circle of friends who cared about me. He has provided for all of my needs.

"During the last two years I have been learning what it means to have God as my Heavenly Father. He –"

Suddenly her throat closed up and she had to stop reading to keep from crying in front of everyone. She swallowed hard and took a deep breath to regain control and steady her shaking voice. "He says that he will never leave me or forsake me, that he will be a father to the fatherless, and that when my father and mother forsake me, the Lord will take me up. I want to be baptized today to show that I belong to Jesus."

She read the last sentence in a rush for fear that she would get choked up again.

"Thank you, Kendra." The pastor smiled. He took her hand and helped her into the water. "Are you ready?"

Kendra nodded. The pastor put his hands on her shoulder and back.

"Kendra Elizabeth Walton, I baptize you in the name of the Father, and the Son, and the Holy Spirit."

He lowered her down and she felt the water close over her head.

ಸು ಲ

He had never realized, until he heard Kendra share her

testimony, how abandoned she had felt by everyone important in her life. Her father – who, of course, had no control over his own death – her mother, her brother. And every man she had become involved with – including himself.

Although he had been curious to hear what she had to say, he found himself more moved than he had expected when she finished speaking. And he wanted to be the one to turn her life around, to break the pattern of abandonment she had experienced. He wanted to show her that not everyone would walk away from her. To show her that, however badly he had messed up in the past, he was a different person, someone she could depend on. He wanted to be the hero, Kendra's hero, as corny as it sounded when he tried to put it into words. He saw now that Kendra was his beautiful princess, the one he wanted to rescue and protect and win over for himself.

It all seemed very fine and romantic as long as he kept the idea in his imagination. It was when he actually saw Kendra, when they watched TV together at her house or played together on the worship team or went bowling with the Timothy group, that it somehow became much more complicated. She was friendly to him, but with a calm, dignified, aloof manner that somehow intimidated him more than her coldness a year before. Of course, he reminded himself frequently, they had come very far in the last year. She no longer gave him those frigid stares, and she didn't mind being in the same room with him anymore. Sometimes she even seemed happy to see him.

But whenever he almost was ready to move to the next level, he froze. He couldn't afford to make any more mistakes with Kendra. He only had one more shot – if he even had that – and if he moved too quickly, or in the wrong way, or at the wrong time, it was all over. And so he continued on the safe path of being friends, helping with Elizabeth, spending time with the group, and left unanswered the eternal question of whether he could ever be a hero to Kendra.

☒ ☓

"I heard some cool news this week," Steve announced to Kendra and Allison one Tuesday evening after putting Elizabeth to

Finding Father

bed. He glanced from one woman to the other as if to draw out their anticipation. "Eddie called me last night and asked me to be in his wedding. He and Jean are engaged."

"Eddie and Jean?" Kendra looked up from the laundry she was folding. "But – but they've only been dating two months! I'm sure of it, because he was with Allison on New Year's Eve."

"That's what I said to Eddie. But he and Jean have been friends for a long time, so I guess they know each other pretty well."

Allison smiled. "Now, I take credit for that one. You know I was going out with Eddie in December, but I wasn't really interested in him and I knew that Jean was. So at Penny's wedding, when Jean was walking down the aisle, I leaned over and said to Eddie, 'Wow, Jean really looks pretty, doesn't she?' And Eddie looked at her like he was seeing her for the first time, and said, 'Yeah, she really does!' During the evening I said the same thing to him several times, and I invited them both over here to watch the movie. That's when it all got started."

Steve laughed. "Well, I guess your little matchmaking worked out. They're getting married in October. Eddie sounds really happy."

"I've heard of another engagement," Kendra told them as she folded a pair of her jeans. "Leanne told me that Ruth is engaged."

"Ruth!" Steve stared at her. "To Jesse?"

"No, she's marrying some guy that she dated a few years ago, but he wasn't a Christian at the time and they eventually broke up. Right around Christmas he called her and said, 'Guess what – I just became a Christian and had a dream about you, and God told me to call you.' And now they're engaged."

Steve was chuckling. "I guess that'll teach Jesse a thing or two. He can't keep stringing her along forever."

"That's what Leanne says. She told me this guy is head over heels in love with Ruth and absolutely convinced that they're meant to be together."

Steve shook his head. "All these weddings. Soon we won't have anyone left in the Timothy group."

Allison heaved a loud sigh. "It must be nice." Her tone was gloomy.

Steve raised his eyebrows in a question. "Aren't you and Paul getting along?"

"Oh, we're getting along. We don't fight. But sometimes I wonder if he'll ever want to get married again. He always makes negative, sarcastic comments about marriage. It's so annoying."

"He had a bad experience the first time," Kendra pointed out. "You have to be patient."

"Do you know what he told me the other day? I heard a song on the radio I liked, and said it would be nice for a wedding. And Paul said that if he ever gets married again, the songs he wants for his wedding are 'Send in the Clowns' and 'The Fool on the Hill.'"

Steve laughed. "Hey, that's great."

"No, it isn't! I'm almost twenty-nine; I don't want to waste time with a guy who isn't serious about me."

"I've thought of the song I want for my wedding," Steve went on, mischief in his eyes. "You know the Steven Curtis Chapman song 'Dive'?"

Kendra wasn't familiar with the song, but Allison clearly knew it. "That's awful, Steve."

"No, it's great. I think the words are very apropos, especially the part about the leap of faith." Steve laughed as he quoted the lines.

"I think your wife will have something to say about that." But Allison was clearly preoccupied with her own dilemma. "Do you think I'm wasting my time with Paul?"

"Oh, Allie, Kendra's right. Don't be so impatient. I know you wanted to get married yesterday, but Paul just isn't ready yet."

Allison pursed her lips. "I don't want to be impatient. But I don't want to wait three years and find he wasn't serious after all, and I was just kidding myself."

"Well, I think it'll be obvious before three years are up." When his cousin's expression remained doubtful, he added, "Look, I hang out with Paul and I hear the way he talks. He's a horny guy. If he didn't want to get married, he wouldn't be dating you, of all people."

Kendra shot him a suspicious look. "What's that supposed to mean?"

Steve managed an embarrassed laugh. "Well, you know, she's almost twenty-nine and never – if he doesn't want to get married, he surely knows he's wasting his time. He's a normal guy who's just anxious about making another big mistake."

Allison smiled. "Maybe you're right! I just need to be patient. I can do that." With a happier expression she rose and skipped up the stairs.

Kendra watched her leave. "Well, you cheered Allison up, anyway."

"Yeah, I think Paul's just jerking her chain with all that anti-marriage talk. He knows how it annoys her."

Kendra grinned. "That seems like something he would do."

"Yeah." Steve glanced at her and Kendra guessed that he wanted to say something else. "Did you hear about the other engagement on Sunday? Jason and Melody."

"Oh! No, I didn't." She knew Steve was watching her reaction and kept her expression carefully blank. "Well, I'm not too surprised."

"Whatever happened between you two, anyway?"

"Nothing, really." Kendra shrugged. "He told me he wanted to get back with Melody. And I guess he was telling the truth."

"And that was all?"

"Yes." She shot him a quick glare. "We weren't sleeping together, if that's what you mean."

"Well, I hope not!" Steve looked outraged at the idea. "I'd be really upset if I thought that was going on!"

His reaction struck Kendra as strange. "Upset? Why upset?"

"Well, you know, you shouldn't be doing that, with him –" She gave him an ironic look and he had the grace to look ashamed. "Anyway, I guess I wasn't the only one..."

The statement trailed off with a question in it. Kendra remembered Kyle and sighed, turning her face away from him and picking up another shirt. "No. There was one other guy."

"Only one?"

"Yes." She glared at him again. "Only one!"

"No, I didn't mean – I just meant it was good that there was only one, that's all."

He seemed in an inquisitive mood and next he would be asking why she and Kyle had broken up. She forestalled him, turning the topic back on himself. "I'm sure there was more than one for you."

"Yeah." He sighed. "I don't even remember how many."

She shrugged, not surprised, yet oddly stung. "I should have figured."

"Well, I could probably count them up if I tried –"

He sounded as if he were ready to start listing names, and Kendra hastily intervened. "Don't bother, Steve. I really don't want to hear about it."

She turned back to her laundry pile and folded Elizabeth's little Sunday dress. Steve studied her a moment, frowning. "Does it bother you to talk about it?"

Kendra wondered how anyone so smart could be so dense. "Do you think I like being one of fifty, or whatever the number was? That wouldn't make any girl feel special, no matter what the circumstances."

"It wasn't fifty."

"Okay, whatever."

"Maybe twenty-five –"

"Okay, Steve, whatever!"

She rose and walked into the kitchen, determined to end this bizarre conversation once and for all. She turned on the faucet and rinsed out the bowl from Elizabeth's snack. Steve followed her, leaning against the edge of the counter.

"Don't be mad at me, Kendra." His tone was pleading.

"I'm not mad, I just don't want to talk about it."

"You know you're special to me."

Kendra gave him a look of incredulity. Did he really think he had to lie, after all this time, to make her feel better about something that had happened so long ago? He reached his hand up and stroked her hair away from her face.

"I love you."

Kendra's mouth fell open as the heat flooded her face. "You don't really expect me to believe that!"

Steve dropped his hand as though it had been stung. "Why don't you believe me?"

"I – I don't – why – I just –" She was stammering like an idiot. She searched his face in confusion. "You mean – in a Christian brother way."

Steve bit his lip, glancing around the kitchen. "Well, yeah. Of course. That's what I meant."

"Oh." She felt curiously deflated, but it was silly to think Steve could have meant anything else. "Really, Steve, you shouldn't go around saying that to girls. Someone might get the wrong idea if she doesn't know you as well as I do."

"I guess you're right." He moved to the kitchen table and began to collect the pile of papers he had been grading earlier, gathering them up with hurried movements. "You know, I'd better get on home. It's pretty late, and I still have these papers to finish grading."

He suddenly seemed anxious to leave. "Well, okay. I guess I'll see you Thursday night then."

"Okay, sure." He stuffed the papers in his bag and gave her a crooked smile. "See you then."

She listened to his car pull away from the house, then turned off the downstairs lights and carried the pile of laundry up to her bedroom. She could hear Allison in her room, talking to someone, probably Paul, on the phone. Elizabeth was sleeping but stirred slightly when her mother turned on the light.

So now Jason was getting married. And Eddie and Jean. And Ruth. Steve was right when he said that soon the group would be all married off. Allison and Paul would probably be next, and where would that leave Kendra? She and Elizabeth would have to find a new place to live.

At least she had Elizabeth. She wasn't completely alone. But it would be so nice to have a husband as well.

She stretched out on her bed and stared up at the ceiling. She remembered the way it had felt when Steve stroked her hair. How sweet it sounded to have someone say he loved her. Maybe she *was* special to Steve in being the mother of his daughter. He had told her she was a good mother. That surely meant something to him. But –

Would her turn ever come? Would she ever meet someone who really loved her? Would she ever have first place in anyone's heart? She was not quite twenty-three, and knew she was too young to despair. Allison, after all, was six years older. But Kendra had always felt older than her years. Since her mother's marriage she had felt so alone. God had been good to her and had provided a wonderful group of friends to support her. But sometimes, on nights like tonight, it wasn't quite enough.

Chapter Twenty-six

One Thursday afternoon, as Kendra was deeply engrossed at her teller's window, she was startled by a soft wolf whistle from the next customer in line. When she looked up and saw Steve, she broke into laughter.

"What are you doing here?"

He grinned and stepped up to the counter. "I was just driving by and thought of this check burning a hole in my pocket, and decided to get it cashed."

"You don't usually do business here, do you? I've never seen you here before."

"No, but maybe I should open an account. That would give me a good excuse."

Kendra smiled, examined the check he handed her, and looked up the account to see if there was money to cover it. "Aren't you working today?"

"I had a free period because the seniors are on a field trip, so I decided to run some errands."

"What a life. Our tax dollars at work." She handed him his cash with a grin.

"I don't feel guilty. Personally I think I earn every dollar I make."

"I'm sure you do. I'll see you at practice tonight?"

"Sure. See you there." He turned away with a salute.

Her coworker Lauren, working at the next window, spoke to

Kendra as soon as Steve was out of earshot. "Hey, who was that guy? Do you know him?"

Kendra hesitated just for a second. "That was Elizabeth's father." Why had she said it? She had never told anyone before, and hadn't intended to now. She was surprised at the feeling of satisfaction – almost pride – the words gave her. At least no one at the bank knew Steve or his family, so she was still safe.

Lauren's eyes widened. "Wow, he's really cute. Are you two still – involved?"

"Oh, no." Kendra shook her head, blushing slightly. "We're just friends."

That evening when she picked Elizabeth up from the babysitter's, she noticed that her daughter's cold seemed worse. She was coughing more than she had been in the morning, and seemed tired. Sometimes Kendra took Elizabeth to practice with her Thursday evenings, but she didn't want to do that if the child was sick. And Allison had plans for the evening and couldn't help her.

As the two of them ate dinner, she called Steve.

"I don't know if I can come to practice tonight," she explained when he answered the phone. "Elizabeth isn't feeling all that well. She has a cold and needs to rest."

"Oh, that's too bad. We're practicing the music for Easter tonight. Look, why don't you bring her over here, and she can just lie on the couch and watch TV, or sleep." Before she could reply, she heard him say, "Mom, are you busy tonight? How would you like to babysit?" Pause. "She says okay."

Kendra hesitated. "Are you sure?"

"Sure, I'm sure. Look, you bring Elizabeth over here and then we'll ride to church together."

She told herself that there was nothing so strange about Steve's mother babysitting Elizabeth. After all, Allison's mother had often done the same to help her out. She wouldn't feel so odd if it hadn't been for that conversation with Marilyn Marsh before Christmas.

She packed a few books and Elizabeth's favorite doll and bundled her daughter into the car. When she arrived at Steve's house, he met her at the door, hugged Elizabeth, and carried her to the sofa where he had prepared a pillow and afghan.

Finding Father

"Now just lie here and rest, or watch TV. Maybe my mom can read some stories to you." He glanced up as his mother entered the room. "Do you remember my mother? This is Mrs. –" He paused. "What do you want her to call you?"

Marilyn Marsh raised her eyebrows, and her expression was not lost on Kendra. "I don't know, Steve. What should she call me?"

Steve swallowed and looked away as he hurried to put on his jacket. Kendra kissed her daughter and admonished her to be good, avoiding Marilyn's eyes. She hurried outside and climbed into the front seat beside Steve.

"Did you tell your mother about Elizabeth?" she asked abruptly as he pulled into the highway.

He shook his head. "No, I never mentioned any names. I was careful not to do that. I'm sure I didn't."

Kendra thought of the few contacts she'd had with Steve's mother over the last few months. "She knows, Steve. I'm sure she does."

He was silent a moment, frowning. "I know I didn't tell her. Maybe – maybe she figured it out."

Kendra meditated in silence as they sped along the highway. Whatever Marilyn knew, she must be keeping the knowledge to herself. If the word had trickled down to Allison, Kendra knew her friend would never be able to keep it quiet. But how long could they keep this secret from the world? Elizabeth herself would want to know eventually, or would guess the truth. And once she found out, the news would become public. The child would be far too excited to keep such information to herself.

As if he read her mind, Steve glanced at her sideways from the driver's seat. "Do you know what Elizabeth said to me last week? When I was putting her to bed, she said, 'I wish you could be my daddy.' What was I supposed to say?"

Kendra's eyes widened in horror. "You didn't tell her, did you?"

"No, I promised you I wouldn't, and I didn't. I just said, 'You need to talk to your mommy about that.' But it doesn't seem right to lie to her, either."

Kendra bit her lip and fell silent. Elizabeth hadn't mentioned the subject to her, and she had no idea what she would say if it came up. She had long ago abandoned the idea that Steve could in any way be harmful to her daughter. He was loving and affectionate to her, a sincere and exemplary Christian, and the only real male role model she had in her life. But once Elizabeth knew the truth, he would be part of their lives forever. She couldn't very easily make Elizabeth's father disappear when his presence became inconvenient. That wouldn't be fair to her daughter or to Steve. If they each married other people, they would be in the position of a divorced couple, sharing custody and visitation of their child for the next twelve years. Did she want that complication in her life forever? Would that be best for Elizabeth?

She glanced at Steve's profile beside her in the dusky light, and guessed that, whatever they told Elizabeth, he planned to stick around. The notion gave her a sense of reassurance, a surprising contrast to her feelings on the subject just a year ago.

But, oh, the awkwardness of telling the truth! Kendra had been part of the church long enough to know that it was like a big family, and everyone knew Steve. The shock, the incredulity, the whispers, the speculation about what must have happened. Everyone would look at Kendra and Steve and be able to picture that scene from nearly seven years ago now, even if they didn't know the details. Kendra cringed inside.

"Do you think we could tell everybody that Elizabeth was born from artificial insemination?" she asked.

Steve threw her a glance, frowning. "No one would believe that, Kendra."

"No, I guess not." If she were thirty or forty, the story might be plausible, but no sixteen-year-old would have a baby that way.

"Is that your hang-up about this?" He glanced at her again, a pucker between his brows. "You don't want anyone to know that, seven years ago, in another lifetime, we had sex one time?"

She shrugged and stared down at the carpet on the floor. "Well, it's embarrassing."

"It's embarrassing for me too."

"No – no, it's different for men. You know it is. It would be like – like you carrying my underwear into church with you."

Steve threw back his head and laughed. Kendra frowned. "It's not funny."

"I'm sorry, that was just such a great image." With an effort he wiped the amusement from his face. "Look, if it would make you feel better, I could say I blacked out and don't remember anything."

"Is that true?" What a relief if it were!

"No, but it's a lot more believable than that artificial insemination story."

"I guess you're right. I guess neither of those stories would really work." She sighed and stared out the window at the houses slipping by as a lump rose in her throat.

"You know, other couples have children out of wedlock. There's a teenage couple in our church right now who are expecting. No one is exactly celebrating, but it does happen."

"Yes, but –" How could she explain the difference to him? "I know who you mean, but they're dating. They have a real relationship."

"I see." He drove in silence for a moment. "So it's the way it happened. But no one will know that – unless – unless we tell them."

"But they'll guess part of it, anyway. They'll know we weren't dating or – or you would have been involved from the beginning and not found out five years later."

"You're afraid they'll think badly of you?"

"Well, of course!" That seemed obvious to her. "They'll think I'm a slut, going to bed with some guy at a party who left for college the next day and forgot about me."

Steve sighed as he pulled into the church parking lot. "Oh, Kendra!"

She swallowed hard, determined not to cry. "I know you think I'm being silly about this."

He shifted the car into park and turned to face her. "No, I don't think you're being silly. I guess it's an issue of – of pride for you, and I can understand that." He stopped, and his face contorted for an instant. "Do you want me to explain to everybody what really happened?"

"Oh, no!" That seemed worse than anything.

He looked relieved. "I don't know what the solution is, Kendra.

I just feel that sooner or later we have to tell people, and we have to figure out the best way to do that. I honestly don't know. I just want to do what's right."

She believed him, and felt a twinge of gratitude that he understood and wasn't trying to pressure her. And then another realization struck her. Next Saturday her mother was coming out from Chicago to spend the week before Easter with her and Elizabeth, since Elizabeth had vacation from school. She knew, without asking, what her mother's opinion on the subject would be. She couldn't possibly tell Elizabeth anything before her mother came. She could just imagine her mother's reaction to that.

She felt a sensation of relief at being able to postpone the decision.

ಸಂ ಲ

"I usually have to play with the worship team on Sunday mornings," Kendra said as she and her mother sat visiting on Saturday evening. "But I wasn't sure what we would be doing tomorrow, so I told them I'd have to take this week off. I was wondering if you'd want to visit my church, to see what it's like."

Bonnie stirred the coffee Kendra had made for her, and Kendra wondered if she was trying to think of an excuse. "I suppose so," she said finally. "I'll have a chance to meet your friends and see what you're learning there."

So the next morning her mother put on the one dress she had brought for the week and accompanied Kendra and Elizabeth. Kendra saw her glance around at the modern sanctuary as they entered, no doubt comparing it to the church she had once attended. Kendra greeted several friends and introduced her mother to Leanne. Then the two of them with Elizabeth found seats in the middle, about a third of the way back.

She was glad her mother had agreed to come with her, but she felt unaccountably nervous about it as well. She didn't want her to criticize anything or to find it very strange. The music, the preaching, all of it was different from what her mother must remember from her church days.

Finding Father

The sanctuary began to fill. During the reading Steve came down the center aisle and smiled at Kendra and Elizabeth. Elizabeth smiled in return and spoke in a stage whisper. "Hi, Steve!"

Kendra winced inside. Bonnie had surely heard the name and would put two and two together.

Steve walked up to the platform, joining the rest of the worship team at the microphones. They began a lively hymn that reminded Kendra of a merry-go-round.

Wonderful grace of Jesus, greater than all my sin.
How shall my tongue describe it, where shall its praise begin?

Kendra sang along with the hymn, trying to ignore her mother's reaction. Even if Bonnie didn't like the music or the service, at least she would see that Kendra did.

Wonderful grace of Jesus, reaching the most defiled,
By its transforming power, making him God's dear child.

Bonnie leaned toward Kendra. "Doesn't it bother you to see him?"

For a moment Kendra was confused, unsure who Bonnie was talking about. She followed the direction of her mother's eyes, to Steve on the platform. "No – it used to, but not anymore."

The music ended and the musicians returned to their seats among the congregation. When Elizabeth left to go to the children's class, the pastor rose and began his sermon. His topic, he announced, was "Grace and Mercy." Kendra opened her Bible and followed along with the various passages the pastor read. From the corner of her eye she saw Steve sitting a few pews away, directly in her mother's line of vision, taking notes on a paper.

Finally the service was over and Kendra led her mother back to the lobby. Steve had disappeared in the crowd. Kendra had just turned away from talking to Penny when he reappeared.

"Some of us are going out for lunch today," he said, an easy smile on his face. "Can you come?"

Bonnie looked at Kendra almost indignantly. Kendra felt a

blush rise to her cheeks. Of course, her mother had no idea how friendly she and Steve had become, and would find this situation bizarre. "Well, I guess I can't today. My mother is visiting." She gestured toward Bonnie.

Steve's mouth fell open and he actually turned pale. A second of silence followed this statement as they simply looked at each other. Then Steve said rapidly, "Is Elizabeth still in her class? I'll get her."

He disappeared down the hallway.

Bonnie was silent on the ride home, and Kendra knew she was upset by seeing Steve at church. She couldn't blame her mother for that, remembering her own reaction when she had met him again for the first time. She felt oddly shamed by the whole situation, as if her friendship with Steve were demeaning in some way. Seeing the relationship through her mother's eyes made her realize how much she had changed in the last year. But surely she was right and her mother was wrong. Surely there was nothing wrong with being friends with Steve. Was there?

☞ ☜

Kendra and her mother liked to shop together, and on Monday night the three of them set out for the mall. Kendra found a new pink sweater with embroidery and a summer purse; Elizabeth got an Easter dress and a new pair of shoes. When they arrived home, Kendra and Bonnie both saw a note Allison had left on the kitchen table: "Call Steve."

Kendra swallowed hard and carried her phone to the next room, dialing the number from memory. Steve answered the phone. "Hello?"

"It's me." She spoke softly to avoid being overheard.

"Oh, hi, Kendra. Yeah, I was just wondering what you want to do about Tuesday night."

"I thought so. Maybe we should skip that." She was afraid to say more for fear her mother would pick up her meaning.

"Okay, I see. How long is your mother staying?"

"Saturday."

"Okay. Well, I'll see you this weekend sometime, right?"

"Yeah, sure. Bye."

She hung up the phone. She knew she had sounded very terse with Steve, but also knew he understood the reason. She joined her mother and daughter in the kitchen, avoiding her mother's gaze.

"He was just calling to ask about something," she said with a vague wave of the hand. "Here, Elizabeth, do you want some ice cream? Mommy will get you some."

"Is Steve coming over tomorrow?" Elizabeth asked as she climbed into her seat.

"No." She gave her daughter a warning glare as she clipped off the syllable.

Her mother said nothing until Elizabeth had finished her ice cream and ran off into the living room. "What's going on with you two?" she asked abruptly.

"Who? Steve?" Kendra felt her heart begin to pound guiltily, but she looked up with what she hoped was an innocent look. "Nothing. We're just friends."

Bonnie studied her. "Has he ever indicated he wants to be more than friends?"

Kendra shook her head a bit too quickly, feeling the heat rise to her face. "No. Oh, no. He loves Elizabeth. That's why he hangs around sometimes."

Her mother stirred her cup of tea, frowning as if she didn't believe her daughter. Why wouldn't she believe her? Surely there was nothing so strange about Steve wanting to spend time with his daughter. Kendra swallowed hard and tried to adjust her features to an expression of indifference.

"Elizabeth doesn't know anything, does she?"

"No." Kendra pondered the cracker in her hand. "But I've wondered if I should tell her."

"Why would you do that?" Her mother's tone was sharp.

"Don't you think it would be good for her to know she has a father who cares about her?"

Bonnie pursed her lips. "And what happens when he gets married and starts a family of his own, and doesn't want to be bothered with Elizabeth anymore? Don't you think that will hurt her more?"

Kendra's heart fell. Of course, her mother was right. Steve was very likely to marry in the foreseeable future, and what would happen to Elizabeth then? Would she be welcomed into his new family, treated as a sibling by any other children he had? And how would Kendra feel? Of course Steve wouldn't be coming over to her house then, hanging out and talking. Not if he had a wife. Maybe she would have a husband by then, or maybe she wouldn't. He would probably get married before she did. Desolation filled her heart at the prospect.

She was relieved that her mother changed the subject then, and tried to put it out of her own mind, but later that night as she lay awake in bed, she mentally canvassed the conversation again. Why would her mother, of all people, suspect that she was romantically involved with Steve? Several of her friends had asked her the same question, but of course they didn't know the whole story. She would have assumed that her mother would be so horrified at the possibility that the idea wouldn't even occur to her. It was almost as if her mother had read her most secret thoughts. And if her mother could read them, who else might have such penetration? Would Steve?

Sometimes when Steve hugged Elizabeth or held her on his lap, Kendra felt a terrible envy at the affection he lavished on the child. When they sat together on the couch, talking or watching television, she often longed for him to put his arm around her or touch her. Sometimes she even let herself imagine that they were a family together, sharing a home and a life.

She knew these thoughts were wrong, and felt heartily ashamed of herself even at the moment. It could only be a measure of her own loneliness that the idea would ever enter her mind. After everything she and Steve had been through together, how could he still have the ability to attract her? And that was something she could never, never let him know. He had cruelly rejected her once; if he knew she had these thoughts, he would be embarrassed and uncomfortable. Pitying her, he would wonder how she could be so lonely and desperate that she might imagine anything more than friendship could exist between them.

Finding Father

❦ ☙

There was no other pianist for Good Friday, so they attended the service that evening, and Kendra took her usual place at the keyboard. There were no drums for this service, but Steve was one of the vocalists and stood on the platform with a microphone in his hand. After the pastor began the service, Kendra played the introduction of the first hymn, and the rest of the team joined in.

Alas, and did my Savior bleed, and did my Sovereign die,
Would he devote that sacred head for sinners such as I?

Was it for crimes that I had done he groaned upon the tree?
Amazing pity, grace unknown, and love beyond degree!

At the cross, at the cross, where I first saw the light,
And the burden of my heart rolled away...

She looked down at her mother and Elizabeth, sitting near the front, and saw the emotionless expression on her mother's face. A sudden yearning, almost an urge to weep, swept over her. How could her mother be so indifferent to spiritual issues? Kendra loved her more than anyone else in the world, except Elizabeth, but her mother was so spiritually cold. If only she could understand the peace and comfort Kendra had found in her faith! Perhaps then she would understand how Steve had changed. Perhaps she would even open her heart to the Lord as well. But any effort to discuss these issues with her brought only a reaction of either apathy or actual hostility.

Randy stepped to the pulpit and read the beginning of the passion story, the trial of Jesus. The service consisted of mostly music and scripture reading, with a short meditation and communion at the end. When it was over they all filed in silence back to the church lobby. Elizabeth saw Steve and ran to hug him. Wincing, Kendra glanced at her mother.

"Allie invited me to come with you tomorrow night," Steve

remarked to Kendra. "I think she invited Paul, and wanted another guy to keep him company. We're meeting at your house at six-thirty."

Kendra nodded and called Elizabeth to come. She knew, she was almost sure, that her mother had heard that last comment.

"What's tomorrow night?" Bonnie asked as soon as they were out of hearing.

"Oh, that!" Kendra made a dismissive gesture. "Allison's cousin Josh has the lead role in his school play. It's *Cinderella*, and we thought Elizabeth would like to see it. I guess she invited Steve and Paul too. I didn't know that. But Josh is Steve's cousin too." She unlocked the car doors and opened hers. "What time do you want to get up in the morning? You said your flight leaves at one, didn't you? We probably should leave the house by ten."

                            ஐ ☙

"You'll never believe what's going on with Kendra," Bonnie burst out as she unlocked her suitcase the next evening in her bedroom in Chicago. "Do you know who she's spending time with? Steve Dixon, of all people! Steve Dixon! She says they aren't dating, but, honestly, I don't know what to believe. I could tell, by the way she acted around him, by the way they're both acting – how could she be so foolish?" Bonnie spilled out the story of the week in detail to her husband. But to her dismay, when she finished he showed less sympathy than she had hoped.

"She's an adult, Bonnie," he said as he watched her throw her clothes into dresser drawers. "You have to let her make her own decisions about relationships."

"You don't understand, Gordon." She turned to him and spread her hands in frustration. "This guy ruined her life. He's a creep and a jerk, and now he's worming his way back into her life. Why would she get mixed up with someone like him again?"

Gordon shrugged. "Maybe he's grown up since then. Maybe he's trying to step up to the plate. He's trying to take responsibility for his daughter. Or maybe he's still a jerk and he's going to break her heart again. Either way, it's her decision now. You have to let her decide."

Of course, he wouldn't be saying that if it was his daughter. Overall Bonnie had been happy in this second marriage, but leaving Kendra was the one part that she regretted. If only she had insisted her daughter and granddaughter move here with her – even if Gordon didn't really want them. If only Kendra were safely here by her mother's side, she wouldn't be at the mercy of the likes of Steve Dixon.

Chapter Twenty-seven

To Kendra, it was almost a relief when her mother went home. She loved her and missed her, but they thought so differently on certain topics and Kendra knew that neither of them could change the other's mind. She felt especially relieved that she could enjoy the play Saturday night without her mother's glowering presence in the background when Paul and Steve arrived.

At six-thirty the doorbell rang and Elizabeth ran to open it. Steve and Paul had arrived at the same moment. Steve wore jeans and a blue and white polo shirt, and looked freshly shaved and smelled like soap. He smiled at Kendra.

"Who's driving?" He glanced from Allison to Paul. "Maybe I should drive, since I know the way and Paul doesn't."

Paul grinned and put his arm around Allison. "Sure, you drive, and Allison and I can smooch in the back seat."

Steve shook his head. "Elizabeth, you need to sit between those two. I don't want anything to happen in my car."

Allison laughed as she picked up her purse. "Look who's talking. As if I'd do anything your car hasn't seen."

Kendra climbed into the front seat with Steve and the other three climbed in back. Elizabeth wasn't between them, Kendra noted.

"So this is your cousin in the play tonight?" Paul asked as they took off. "Which cousin? I lose track."

"Josh Kirk, Uncle Dave's son. He's a junior. Matt's in college now."

"Abby's older brothers," Kendra recalled for Elizabeth's benefit.

"I remember reading a book about the Kennedys once, and it talked about their 'cousin groups,'" Allison remarked. "And I realized our family has cousin groups too. Kate, Meredith and I are one, then Tom, Joe, and Steve, then Heather, Joyce, and Anne."

"The boys, Matt, Josh, and Derek," Steve added. "I guess the twins are their own group. And Abby's all alone."

"She plays with my nephews," Allison said.

"And Elizabeth." Steve shot Kendra a sly look. She was glad that the pair in the back seat didn't seem to notice.

Allison chuckled as she leaned closer to Paul. "Aunt Lisa told my mother that Josh has to kiss Cinderella in this play, and he's really nervous about it."

Steve rolled his eyes. "I don't believe Josh is nervous about kissing Cinderella! That's just Aunt Lisa's wishful thinking."

"Well, those Kirk boys aren't as worldly-wise as you were at that age, Steve."

"Maybe not."

Allison laughed. "I'll never forget the year when Steve was about sixteen, he showed up at Thanksgiving dinner with hickeys all over his neck. Aunt Marilyn was mortified, and the rest of us kept laughing about it. Uncle Dave said, 'I think Steve got attacked by a vacuum cleaner.'"

Steve scowled over his shoulder at his cousin. "Thank you for sharing that."

"Which girl was that, Steve?" she teased.

"I really don't remember. And I'd watch out, Allie. I could share some stories about you that Paul might like to hear."

"Me?" She gave him a look of mock innocence. "Everyone knows I'm as pure as the driven snow."

"What about you and that older guy in the church?"

"Oh, Chet. That was nothing. Just my dad being nervous." She glanced at Paul. "When I was sixteen, there was a guy in the church who was about twenty-five, and we used to hang out and talk and flirt, but we didn't date, because of the age difference. He was a new

Christian and had kind of a wild past, but I liked the attention. One night he and Randy and I stayed out till two o'clock, just talking and all, but when I got home my dad was furious and told me to never do that again. I said, 'Daddy, it's just Chet and Randy. You know those guys.' At the time I thought my father had totally lost his mind to be so distrustful. But looking back, I think he was really keeping an eye on Chet."

"Knowing your dad, I'm sure he was," Steve said dryly, "and he was probably right."

Paul laughed and squeezed Allison. "Innocent little Allison didn't have any idea what that guy was really up to. But her daddy knew."

"Oh, he wasn't so bad."

Steve said, "My daughter isn't going to date till she's twenty-five at least."

Allison laughed. "Good luck. I hope you can make that happen."

Kendra looked at Steve's clean, handsome profile beside her in the driver's seat. Her mother's words had been echoing in her mind all week: "And what happens when he gets married and starts a family of his own, and doesn't want to be bothered with Elizabeth anymore?" Whenever she thought of those words, they brought a fresh pang. He loved Elizabeth now, but maybe that was only because he didn't have a family of his own. Maybe her mother had a point. Surely it would be worse for Elizabeth to face such rejection.

Or was she, Kendra, the one who was really afraid of rejection?

It took almost a half hour to drive to the school where the play was held. When the group entered the auditorium, they were met by Lisa and Abby Kirk.

"Oh, I'm so glad you all could come," Lisa greeted them. "I know it will mean a lot to Josh too. Look, Abby, it's Elizabeth Walton. Do you remember her?"

Allison glanced around. "Is the rest of your family here?"

"Yes, even Matt. He came home from college for the weekend."

"How's he doing there?" Steve asked.

"Really well. He had a hard first semester, but this one seems to be better. And he's gotten involved in a very good campus ministry. That was a big concern for me. I prayed a lot when he first left."

"You probably prayed that he wouldn't turn out like me," Steve remarked wryly.

Lisa laughed. "Oh, you turned out okay, Steve. But you did have us worried for a while there. I know you gave your mother a few gray hairs."

The five of them found seats together and a few moments later the play started. Kendra had agreed to come mostly to please Elizabeth, but it had been many years since she had seen the Rodgers and Hammerstein version of *Cinderella,* and she found herself caught up in the magic of it. There was something so timeless about the fairy tale that even an adult could enjoy it, and she found herself singing fragments of the songs in her head even after the curtain came down and the teenage actors came forward to take their bows.

She wasn't alone. As they piled into Steve's car after the play, she found Allison singing one of the songs aloud.

"I like the ugly stepsisters' song," Paul said. "The one that says, why would anyone want a gorgeous girl like her?"

Kendra would never sing aloud if she was in danger of being heard, but she said, "I liked the 'Lovely Night' song."

Allison obligingly broke into the song.

Steve glanced over his shoulder at Elizabeth in the back seat. "Which part of the play did you like?"

Elizabeth bounced on the back seat. "I like the part where the fairy godmother comes and turns her into a princess."

Steve smiled. "Would you like to be a princess, Elizabeth?"

"You know, I read somewhere that we really shouldn't teach our children fairy tales," Kendra remarked. "It gives them an unrealistic view of life. You know, Prince Charming and being rescued and all that. It isn't healthy."

Steve glanced over at her with a thoughtful expression. "I read a book recently that said the opposite. That fairy tales express profound truths about human nature, and that's why they're so powerful and enduring."

Kendra laughed. "And what profound truth does Cinderella express?"

Steve wrinkled his brow. "Let's see. A woman's deepest need is to be loved and pursued in spite of all obstacles. Is there any truth to that?"

Kendra gulped and forced another laugh. "I told you it wasn't realistic, didn't I?"

"Maybe." Steve threw her another quick glance as he drove. "Especially if she'll never let him catch her."

She laughed again, but he didn't, and she sensed that his words had a more serious meaning. What was he trying to tell her? She was glad that Allison changed the subject just then.

"Did I ever tell you about Paul and me back in high school?" Allison was saying. "I liked Paul, but he hardly noticed me, and once he made a disparaging comment about me that a mutual friend very kindly passed on."

"I did not –" Paul broke in.

"You probably don't remember," Allison said, "but I do."

"And she'll never let you forget it," Steve chimed in.

"What did he say?" Kendra asked.

"Oh, something like, 'Who would ever go out with her?' I was devastated, and went home and cried and cried."

Kendra glanced at Paul in the back seat. He looked a bit ashamed. "Okay, I was stupid back then."

"A universal characteristic of high school guys," Steve added dryly. "Most college guys, too. Right, Kendra?"

Kendra glanced sideways at him with a half-smile.

Paul nuzzled his head against Allison's shoulder. "You were just too good for me, honey."

"I know," Allison replied in a tart tone.

Steve looked at the pair in the rear view mirror. "Well, I'm sure you and Paul are both very different people than you were back then. Don't be too hard on him, cousin." He glanced around the car. "Who wants ice cream? We can stop up the road here."

The suggestion was met with approval. Steve pulled into an ice cream place and they were shown to a booth inside. The waitress brought a chair for Elizabeth and placed it at the end of the booth.

"Can I have a strawberry sundae, Mommy?" Elizabeth asked as they studied the menus.

Kendra gave her daughter a warning look. "We'll share

something, honey. How about a banana split? That has strawberries too."

"Oh, let her get her own sundae," Steve said easily. "Paul and I can afford it."

Kendra shook her head but closed her menu with a smile. "You spoil her."

"Well, let me spoil her a little. It's the least I can do."

Kendra dropped the topic, relieved that Allison was talking to Paul and had missed that last comment. If Steve wasn't careful, everyone would guess the truth whether they wanted them to or not. Maybe that's what he wanted. As for the food, she wouldn't have expected either Steve or Paul to pay; that seemed too much like a double date. But if Steve insisted, she could only be gracious and accept. Did he think this was a date? It almost felt like one, but that was surely a coincidence. After all, Allison had arranged it, not Steve.

"So tell us about your house hunt, Steve." Paul closed his menu and handed it to the waitress.

"Well, I found a realtor and went out one evening last week. We looked at three houses, but two of them were all wrong. The other was better, a nice size and in good condition, but it had a really small kitchen. I wouldn't mind a small kitchen myself because I don't really cook, except for using the microwave. But I'm not sure if a woman would think the kitchen is too small."

"You need a woman's eye," Allison laughed. "Maybe you should take a girl with you as your surrogate wife, to help you make the decision."

"Bad idea." Paul shook his head. "You do that, and she might try moving in with you. Just pick the house you like and don't worry about it."

"But Steve has a point. He doesn't want to buy a house that won't work once he has a family. It's a big investment and he'll want it to last a long time."

Paul waved his hand in a dismissive gesture. "Don't let her rush you, Steve. You can always trade up to a bigger house when you need it."

Kendra sat silent during this discussion. She couldn't help

envying Steve's financial situation. It would be so wonderful to be able to buy her own home, but that seemed so far off in her future. And it would be fun to look at houses. She wished Steve would take her to help him, but she would never in a million years suggest it.

"Did you all hear about Penny?" Allison asked. "She told me last night that she's pregnant! The baby's due in November. She seemed really excited about it."

"Well, that didn't take long," Paul said. "They just got married New Year's Eve."

Steve shrugged. "Sometimes it only takes once."

Allison giggled. "Can you imagine a little Randy running around? That will be so funny!"

"It will be sad if he looks like Randy," Paul said. "That big nose, and ears sticking out. Can you picture a little kid like that?"

Kendra shook her head. "You're mean."

"Oh, Randy's a good guy. But he's not going to win any beauty contests."

Kendra laughed. "Well, he won Penny, and I guess she's the only one that matters."

"Little Randy," Steve mused. "I wonder if they'll use that name. I definitely don't want a son named Steve. My dad was Steve, and I was Steve, and it was always confusing. When I was little they called me Stevie, and I hated that. Little Stevie!" He shuddered.

"Oh, I remember!" Allison chimed in. "When you got to high school you finally graduated to Steve."

"The one good thing about my dad moving out," Steve said dryly. "I do like the name Stephanie, though. If I ever have another – if I have a daughter someday, maybe I'll use that name. Stephanie Dixon."

Kendra shot him a look of alarm, but at least Paul and Allison hadn't noticed the slip. "I was named after my father," she remarked aloud.

Steve nodded. "That's right; your dad's name was Ken." At Kendra's puzzled look he added, "You told me that, remember? That first time we met."

Kendra looked up at him, astonished. "I can't believe you remembered all these years."

"Oh, I have a very good memory."

"I guess my daughter could be Pauline," Paul said.

Allison frowned. "I'll have to think about that one."

Paul gave her a look of mock surprise. "You! Why would you have any say about it?"

Allison scowled at him, but Kendra barely noticed the exchange, for her mind was arrested on Steve's words. So he had remembered a casual comment she had made to him all those years ago. And if he was picking names for his children, he must be thinking about having a family someday, even though he didn't seem interested in dating yet. She shouldn't be surprised, of course. He was a normal guy, like Paul, and he surely didn't want to be celibate for the rest of his life.

She wondered if he was interested in any particular girl. She hoped not.

The waitress brought their ice cream and they dug in. Paul said, "Hey, Steve, how was that ballgame you went to last week?"

Steve gulped down a swallow of water. "How'd you hear about that?"

"Oh, I think Eddie told me." He nudged Allison. "Steve had a hot date."

Kendra felt her heart plummet to her stomach. Allison looked at Steve in surprise. "You did? I didn't hear about that!"

"Well, if I told you, the whole world would know." Steve shrugged. "It was nice."

Allison's eyes sparkled; Kendra knew how much she loved romance. "Who'd you go out with?"

Steve hesitated. Paul said, "It was Christy, right? The chatty girl with the long curly hair?"

Kendra remembered Christy, the girl who looked like a grown-up Shirley Temple. She had shown up at a handful of activities of the Timothy group in the last several months. Lively, self-confident, flirtatious – the complete opposite of Kendra in every way. And she never made a secret of the fact that she found Steve attractive as well. Kendra's face felt suddenly stiff as she turned to wipe strawberry syrup off Elizabeth's hands. She hoped none of the others looked her way as she tried to look normal, not at all sure what normal was supposed to look like.

"Yeah, it was Christy." Steve's tone was casual. "Actually, she was the one who asked me. She called me up and said, 'Someone gave me two tickets to a baseball game. Do you want to come?' And I thought, why not? It was fun."

"Did you mind that?" Allison asked. "I always hear that guys don't like girls to take the initiative. They want to be the aggressors."

"Actually it was kind of nice for a change. Back in my heathen days girls used to hit on me all the time. It was nice to know I haven't lost it."

Allison laughed; Kendra tried to smile as well.

"Allison took the initiative with me," Paul told them. "She called me up after our first date and said, 'You are so hot. I want to marry you and have your babies.'"

Steve laughed while Allison swatted at Paul with her napkin. "Oh, you are such a liar!"

"Elizabeth is sticky," Kendra said. She lifted the child down from her chair, took her hand and led her back to the restroom. She scrubbed the child's small hands and her own, then took a deep breath and studied her reflection in the harsh light above the mirror. Her dark eyes stared back at her from the angles of her face.

She would never have the courage to do what Christy had done. She would never have that much self-confidence. And what guy would chose Kendra if he had the choice of Christy instead? A sense of despair swept over her as she pictured the two of them together at the ball field, laughing and sharing hot dogs and cheering for their team. How could she possibly compete?

She felt Elizabeth tugging on her arm. "Why are you crying, Mommy?"

"I'm not!" Tears burned in her eyes, and she yanked some paper towels from the holder, ran them under the water, and laid them on her eyes. The worst thing in the world would be for the other three to suspect she had been crying. She needed to paste a smile on her face and walk back out and pretend that everything was fine, that she couldn't care less what girl Steve took to a ballgame.

Her mother was right. She was such a fool. A big enough fool to fall for Steve Dixon, even after everything they had been through together. And she knew her mother was right when she had said that Kendra was only setting herself up to get hurt again.

Chapter Twenty-eight

"Elizabeth's birthday is this month," Kendra remarked to Steve one Tuesday evening in May after her daughter had gone to bed. "I need to start planning for it, I guess. I haven't bought a single present yet."

Steve reached for his shoes. "Maybe we could take her to an amusement park. Has she ever been to one? I bet she would like that."

"Yeah, she probably would." Steve had said "we," and Kendra found herself secretly pleased that he wanted the three of them to do something together. "Maybe Hershey Park! She'd like seeing the chocolate factory."

Steve nodded as he tied his shoes. "Let's pick a Saturday and plan to do that. Not this Saturday – not next Saturday either; that's my cousin's wedding. That reminds me. Hey, Allie!" He raised his voice so that Allison could hear him in the kitchen, and his cousin stepped into the living room. "Are you bringing Paul to Anne's wedding?"

"I guess so." Allison scowled at the ceiling. "I'm kind of mad at Paul about that. When I invited him he said, 'Inviting a guy to a wedding is like inviting Napoleon to Waterloo.'"

Steve laughed.

"I told him, 'Forget it, I'll go alone,' and he said, 'No, I have to go with you, or your family will think you can't get a date.'"

"Oh, Allie, don't let him bother you. He's just saying that to get a rise out of you."

Steve rose and glanced at Kendra with a grin, which she returned. As he started for the door he gave her a sly beckoning gesture, as if he didn't want Allison to notice. Probably he wanted to talk about Elizabeth in private. She followed him out the front door and closed it.

"What do you want?"

"I was just wondering –" He slid his hand into his pocket and she heard him jiggling some loose change, "if you would want to go to Anne's wedding with me."

"Oh!" For a minute Kendra was so surprised she could think of no other response.

"You know my family," he added with an apologetic smile, "so I thought you might feel comfortable there."

"Oh, well, that would be nice." She tried to think what else she should say. "It's a week from Saturday?"

"Yes, at five o'clock."

She thought aloud. "I guess I'd need a babysitter."

"I guess so. You find the babysitter, and I'll pay for it. And tell Elizabeth we'll take her to Hershey Park the next weekend for her birthday." He grinned.

"Sure, Steve. That sounds nice."

She watched him drive off and slowly went back into the house. Allison was reading a book and drinking tea at the kitchen table, but she looked up at Kendra.

"Steve just asked me to your cousin's wedding." Kendra turned to open a cupboard, hoping her tone sounded more casual than she felt.

"Oh!" Allison's eyes lit up. "Is this a date?"

"Oh, I don't know." Kendra shrugged and closed the cupboard. "He said he invited me because I know all your family. I guess he thinks I'd be comfortable there."

"Oh." Allison was silent a moment, frowning to herself.

"I think he's interested in Christy," Kendra offered.

"Steve? Did he say so?"

"No, but he acts like it. They went to that baseball game."

Allison frowned and shook her head. "I don't know about that. I think Christy's after him, more than the other way. Why don't you ask him?"

Kendra turned to her friend with an expression of horror. "Who? Steve?"

"Why not? You two are friends, aren't you? Ask him if he's interested in Christy, and then you'll know. I bet he'd tell you."

Kendra shook her head. "I couldn't do that. I'd feel too weird about it."

ಲ ಆ

Marilyn looked up from the checkbook she was balancing as Steve entered the kitchen. He opened the refrigerator and took out a pitcher of lemonade.

"I talked to Aunt Betsy today," she told him. "They're trying to get a final head count for Anne's wedding, and she wants to know if you've invited anyone."

Steve poured himself a glass and took a quick gulp. "Yes," he said. "I'm bringing Kendra."

Marilyn turned back to the checkbook and put a check next to one of the items in the register. "Good," she said.

ಲ ಆ

In spite of her effort to downplay the event to Allison, as the week passed Kendra found herself looking forward to the wedding with an eagerness that she hadn't expected. She needed a haircut soon, and decided to schedule it the morning of the wedding. For a few extra dollars her hairdresser would style her hair in a pretty way as well. And as she thought about it, she hadn't bought herself a new summer dress in a while, either. Ruth's wedding was in August and Jean's in October. She needed something dressy for all those occasions.

On Saturday she went shopping with Elizabeth, and in between chasing her daughter through the clothes racks, found a pretty ivory-colored dress in a frothy fabric, covered with tiny pink, purple, and yellow flowers, with a pale pink ribbon around the waist and the edge of the hem. When she studied her reflection in the fitting room mirror, she found the dress flattering to her complexion and figure.

Would Steve think she looked pretty in this dress?

She swung away from the mirror to the hallway where Elizabeth was prancing around in circles. "Honey, how do you like Mommy's dress?"

Elizabeth turned to gaze up at her mother. "You look like a princess, Mommy!"

Of course, Elizabeth was very into princesses these days. Maybe she should buy a princess doll for her birthday. But her daughter's approbation made up Kendra's mind. She paid for the dress and headed back to the car, holding Elizabeth's hand to keep her from running in front of traffic.

"You have a birthday coming up, honey," she remarked as she pulled up to the red light at the entrance to the shopping center. "How would you like to go to an amusement park for something special? We – I thought about taking you to Hershey Park. Wouldn't that be fun?"

"Hershey Park? Do they have chocolate there?"

Kendra laughed as the light turned green. "Oh, they have lots of chocolate! A big chocolate factory, and lots of rides –"

As she crossed the intersection she suddenly realized the car turning right into the lane ahead of her did not intend to yield. Frantically she scanned the street for somewhere to swerve to avoid a collision, but a truck was approaching in the opposite lane as well. She slammed on her brakes and the car spun around in a sickening slow-motion effect as the right side careened into the car ahead of her. She heard squealing tires and shattering glass, her head hit the side window as the air bag exploded, and then everything was still.

For a long moment she could only sit in stunned silence, unable to move, wondering if she was still breathing. Her head hurt and she felt as if she had been punched in the stomach, but when she moved her arms and legs, everything seemed to be working all right. At least she didn't appear to have any broken bones.

She glanced into the back seat to Elizabeth's car seat. Her daughter was lying sideways in her car seat with her eyes closed, not moving. On the opposite side of the car, she had taken the brunt of the collision.

Frantically she reached for the car door and opened it. As she squeezed out from under the airbag, she saw people hurrying toward her from neighboring cars. A heavy-set gray-haired man reached her first. "Lady, are you all right?"

"I – I think so." Kendra found her hands and voice shaking as she clutched the door of the car. "My daughter – my daughter's in the backseat. I need to see if she's okay."

A younger man in cut-off jeans and a blue hoodie joined them. "We'll check on your daughter. Don't move. You might have whiplash or something."

"I don't think I have whiplash." She really didn't know what whiplash would feel like, but as she put her hand up to a damp spot on her face she realized that she was bleeding. Glass from the shattered windshield must have cut her face.

"I've already called 9-1-1," the younger man said. He was trying to open the door next to Elizabeth. "Hey, I don't think this door is going to open. It's all caved in. We'll have to get her out from the other side."

Kendra opened the left back door and crawled across the seat to her daughter. The entire door next to Elizabeth was bashed in and the car seat had been knocked sideways so that the child was lying on her side. Glass from the broken window covered the floor, the car seat, and Elizabeth. "Elizabeth!" Kendra's voice was shaking. "Honey, are you all right? Talk to me, baby!" She put her hand on the child's forehead and then her cheek, feeling for signs of life. At least she seemed to be breathing. Maybe the impact of the crash had knocked her unconscious.

"Is she all right?" one of the men asked her.

Kendra twisted around to look at him. "I don't know. She's breathing, but I think she's unconscious. I don't know what to do." She could feel the panic rising in her as she spoke; her breath came fast and shallow.

"The ambulance should be here soon," he said. "I think we should leave her where she is and let the paramedics get her out. They'll know what to do."

Kendra turned back to her daughter and reached for her small hand. The child moaned and, as Kendra looked down, she realized that her arm was hanging at an odd angle. Her arm was broken.

"Oh, God, please let her be okay!" She spoke aloud without thinking. "Don't let anything be wrong but a broken arm! Why won't she wake up! Oh, God, help!"

Sirens approached, their shrieking growing louder by the second, and a moment later Kendra saw the paramedics at the car door. She climbed out and watched as they began to dislodge her daughter's car seat.

"Ma'am, are you all right?" One of the paramedics was at her elbow. "You were the driver of the car? You have some cuts and bruises, and we'd better check you over, just to be sure."

"Is Elizabeth going to be okay?" It was the only question she could think of.

"We're getting her out, and we'll get her to the hospital right away. Come along with me and let us make sure you're all right. As soon as we get her on a stretcher, you can see her. Is there anyone you need to call?"

Call. Who should she call? Her mother in Chicago? But what could her mother do, as far away as she was? "My – my cell phone is in my purse, in the car."

"We'll bring it to you. First let's get you checked out."

Kendra allowed herself to be led to the ambulance, where the paramedics determined she had no life-threatening injuries. A moment later the stretcher bearing Elizabeth was slid into the back of the ambulance. The driver shifted into gear and the vehicle leaped into action, siren clamoring.

Elizabeth opened her eyes. "Mommy?"

"Yes, honey. We've been in an accident, and we're going to the hospital. You'll be okay, honey."

Elizabeth whimpered. "It hurts."

Kendra wiped tears off her daughter's cheeks and stroked her hair. "I know. I know it hurts. You're being very brave, and we'll be there soon."

She fumbled in her purse and found her cell phone, dialing her mother's number. No answer. Oh, why couldn't her mother answer, today of all days? But even if she got the call, she was too far away to help. The aloneness of her situation overwhelmed her.

☼ ☙

From the cubicle in the emergency room where they wheeled Elizabeth, she tried her mother again, and got the same infuriating message. Leave a message. She didn't want to leave a message, to talk to a machine; she wanted a real person to be with her in the flesh and to share the fear, to talk to her, to help her carry the burden. If only there was someone close by, someone who cared for Elizabeth and would be there for her.

Steve. Of course. He would want to know that Elizabeth had been hurt. She wouldn't bother him with her own problems, but he would want to know about Elizabeth.

She found his number in her phone and dialed. Without even ringing, the phone went to the answering machine. "Hey, it's Steve. Leave a message." That probably meant that the phone battery was dead. Steve had mentioned once that he sometimes forgot to charge up his phone and let the battery run down.

Blinking back tears of frustration, she found his home phone in her call log and dialed. "Hello?" It was Marilyn Marsh. Finally a real human being.

"Mrs. Marsh? Is Steve there?" Her voice sounded shaky and tearful to her own ears.

"No, he's not home right now. Is this Kendra?"

Kendra was able to feel a momentary surprise that Steve's mother had recognized her voice. "Yes, it's Kendra. Listen, I really need to get ahold of Steve. Elizabeth and I were just in an accident, and Elizabeth is hurt."

Kendra heard a gasp on the other end of the line. "Oh, my goodness! Where are you now?"

"We're at the hospital, in the emergency room. Elizabeth has a broken arm, and the doctor said she may need surgery. I tried Steve's cell phone, but it's dead."

"Oh, dear! I think he's out somewhere with Dan. I'll try to track him down and let him know what happened. Are you at St. Mary's?"

"Yes. Thanks so much."

"Okay, Kendra. I'll find him. And we'll be praying."

"Thanks. Please pray. We need that."

She ended the call as a nurse came into the cubicle. "Mrs. Walton?"

Kendra decided to ignore the mistake. "Yes, I'm her mother."

"We're going to prep your daughter for surgery now. The CT scan showed that she has a spleen laceration, and we need to operate to stop the bleeding."

"Oh, God." Kendra twisted her hands together in anguish and leaned over her daughter to kiss her forehead. "How long will it take?"

"It will probably be an hour or more before she's in recovery. You can wait in the surgical waiting room near the ER. We'll let you know as soon as the surgery is over."

Medical personnel seemed to fill the little cubicle. Kendra kissed her daughter again and then watched, her hands to her mouth, as her daughter was wheeled down the long corridor. Slowly she followed the nurse to the surgical waiting room and dropped into a chair. Small clusters of family huddled together in different parts of the room, but Kendra sat alone. All her mental energy centered on that one operating room where the surgeons were trying to save Elizabeth.

"Oh, God, please save her," she prayed in desperation, her face buried in her hands. "Let the doctors find the bleeding right away and make it stop. Oh, God, I feel so alone and helpless, and I need you more than ever before. You're the only one I can turn to now – the only one who can help me, or Elizabeth. I know you love us both, and I know you want what is best for us – but I just want my little girl to be okay."

She lowered her hands to her lap and took a long, jagged breath. Knowing that God was with her was a great comfort – but there were moments when she needed human comfort too.

She looked up as the door to the room opened and Steve walked through. An overwhelming relief and thankfulness swept over Kendra.

He threw a quick glance around the room and came toward her, face taut with alarm. "Are you all right?"

She stood, shaking with relief. "Yes, I'm fine."

"You look like you got beat up."

She had forgotten her own cuts and bruises. "It's not bad, really."

He pulled her toward him and held her tightly for a minute. She felt the tension drain away as if he had taken it off her shoulders with his own hands. It felt so wonderful to be held this way. "Elizabeth? Where is she?"

She pulled away from him, wiping her eyes with the back of her hand. "She's in surgery now. The nurse told me she has a spleen laceration, whatever that is. She said that it's bleeding."

His face darkened. "My mom called Dan's cell phone. I guess mine was dead. She said that Elizabeth was hurt. I came right away."

"Thanks for coming," she said. "It helps so much having you here."

He held both her hands in his, looking down into her face. "Thanks for calling me. Of course I came. I always will come."

They sat side by side in the chairs in the waiting room, and sometimes Steve held her hand and sometimes he put his arm around her, and she knew that his presence was the one thing that she needed for comfort and reassurance.

As the hour wore on more people arrived in the little waiting room. First Marilyn Marsh, who hugged Kendra and then listened somberly to the story of the accident and Elizabeth's surgery. Next Dan appeared, his usual stoic self, but more grave than normal. Finally Allison and Paul appeared. They had been together when Kendra called Allison's cell phone to tell her about the accident, and they hurried to the hospital together as soon as they were free. The presence of so many friends acted as a balm on Kendra's overwrought nerves as she waited to hear about the surgery.

Finally after nearly an hour and a half, a doctor appeared in the waiting room and approached the group. "I'm looking for Elizabeth Walton's parents."

Kendra opened her mouth, but nothing came out.

Steve stood and reached for Kendra's hand. "That's us. We're her parents."

"Your daughter is in recovery now. The surgery went fine, and she should be okay. You'll be able to see her as soon as she wakes up."

"Oh, thank you so much!" Kendra's first sensation was one of pure relief, but as she glanced back at her friends she saw that Allison's mouth had fallen open, and even Dan wore a stunned expression. Only Marilyn Marsh showed no surprise. Well, the cat was out of the bag for sure now. There was no putting it back in.

Chapter Twenty-nine

"So it's true!" Back in their own kitchen, Allison turned an accusatory face on Kendra. "Elizabeth asked me if Steve was her father, and I told her no. I couldn't believe you would keep a secret like that from me. But it's been true all along, and I had no idea!"

They had barely seen each other since the accident, except for Allison's occasional visits to the hospital, where Kendra had spent all her time. Now it was Tuesday evening, Elizabeth had been discharged, and Kendra had leisure for this long-anticipated interrogation by Allison.

She turned her back on her friend and began to load the dinner dishes into the dishwasher. "Well, I didn't want anyone to know. The whole situation was really embarrassing for me."

"And that's why he's been coming around all the time, babysitting for Elizabeth and playing with her," Allison continued in the same tone. Then she laughed. "I just thought he had the hots for you. Well, I guess he did have the hots for you, once."

Kendra glared at her and said nothing, clattering the dishes as she handled them.

"You said you met him years ago at a party. Was that where all this happened?"

"Yes," Kendra said, "and I'm not giving you any details, so don't ask. It was a stupid, stupid thing and we both wish it had never happened."

"I'm not going to ask for details!" Allison sounded offended.

"Hey, I know what Steve was like back then. So he was the jerk you told me about?"

"He was a jerk, but he's changed since then. I'm trying to move forward and not dwell on all that."

"Well, that's smart of you, and I know Steve will be a good father now. And he really loves Elizabeth. Hey, that means Elizabeth's my second cousin, or first cousin once removed, or something." She laughed. "When I told her to call me Aunt Allie, I didn't know how true it was. I suppose you didn't know all this when you moved in here?"

"Of course not! I never would have moved here if I'd known you were related to Steve. The day I found out – that was the biggest shock of my life."

Allison nodded. "I remember that day. You did seem shocked to see him. And I had no idea." She shook her head. "I still can't believe you kept it a secret from me all this time."

Kendra suspected she would be hearing that refrain for quite a while, from Allison and also her other friends. Well, she would have to get used to it. She moved to change the subject. "I told you that my mother is coming tomorrow? She wants to help me with Elizabeth so I don't have to miss too much work."

"That's good. I can see why she'd want to come." Allison was clearly cogitating. "Does she know all this about Steve?"

Kendra sighed. "Yes, and she's the biggest problem. She still can't stand him, and I don't know how it's going to work out when she's here."

ಜ ಛ

Steve pulled up in front of Allison's house and turned off the car, his stomach knotting. He had made up his mind and was determined to go through with this meeting, but it wouldn't be easy. In fact, this would be harder than any other conversation he had initiated in the last three years, and that was saying a lot. His mom, Cassie, Pastor Mike – even talking to Kendra had not been as bad as this.

He rang the doorbell and waited. Kendra's mother opened the

door. An expression of shock and dismay crossed her face when she saw him there.

"Hi, Mrs. Baker." If he gave her a chance she might slam the door in her face, so he needed to show confidence. "I'm Steve. I've come to see Elizabeth."

She stood silent for a moment, but stepped back. Steve walked into the familiar living room.

"Elizabeth is upstairs asleep." Bonnie Baker seemed to have suddenly found her voice. "Kendra is at work and I'm staying with her. Now really isn't a good time for you to visit."

"Oh, I see." He glanced around the empty living room and saw a pillow and blanket on the couch. Someone must be sleeping there at night now that Bonnie was visiting. "Actually I wanted to talk to you for a minute as well."

She hesitated. "Aren't you supposed to be at work?"

"I have a teacher covering for me." He had deliberately chosen a time when he knew Kendra would not be home, and it was fortunate as well that Elizabeth was sleeping. He would rather not have her overhear this conversation.

"Well." Bonnie eyed him for a moment and then headed to the kitchen. "I suppose I should hear what you have to say."

He had not expected a gracious reception, but even so he felt his face flushing. He would have to eat a lot of humble pie, as Pastor Mike had once told him. Even more than Kendra had made him eat, but he could do it.

They sat at the kitchen table, Bonnie on the end, Steve at an angle to her.

"I want to tell you first of all," Bonnie began before Steve could frame his opening statement, "I don't know what's going on with you and Kendra, but I don't like it. I've told her she should stay away from you, but she won't listen to me. For some reason she's allowing you to be part of Elizabeth's life. And I understand that – at least partly – she's raising this child all alone and it's hard for her, and she wants help. If I lived closer I would be able to help her more and she wouldn't need you to be involved. I suppose that legally you could insist on visitation and I couldn't prevent it anyway. But I want to know if you have any – any –" she seemed to be groping for the right word, "– any interest in Kendra beyond that. Any romantic interest, or sexual interest, or anything. That's what I'm really worried about, and what I'm really against. You may have a right to be part of Elizabeth's life, but not Kendra's, and I don't want you ruining her life more than you have already."

In a way it was a relief to have her address the topic so directly, to spare him the necessity of leading into it. Steve took a deep breath. "I'm glad you've brought this up, because that's what I've wanted to talk to you about. I've gathered, from things Kendra has said, that you haven't approved of me being around either of them. And I understand that – really I do. I know I hurt Kendra badly in the past and you probably feel that I ruined her life in some ways. Kendra and I have talked about this several times and I've apologized to her. And I want to take this chance to apologize to you as well."

Bonnie sat in silence for a moment, looking taken aback. "I don't know." She folded her arms across her chest, eying him suspiciously. "I'm not as soft as Kendra is. You can't charm me the way you do her."

Steve wanted to laugh as he thought of the last year and his relationship with Kendra. Charm was the last word he would have used to describe his interactions with her. "Kendra wasn't always so soft. She was plenty hard on me in the beginning, you can believe that." Bonnie looked surprised, and grimly pleased. "It took a long time for us to get to the point of being friends, and I'm really thankful that we've gotten there."

Bonnie shook her head, disgust on her face. "I don't understand it. Honestly, I don't know why she would even want to be friends with you, after everything you put her through. You and – and those other guys at the party – if it were up to me you'd all be sitting in jail right now. If she had told me about it right away, you would be, too. But by the time I knew what happened – well, my attorney told me that it would be too hard to prove in court, and too big of an ordeal to put Kendra through, on top of everything else. He said I should put my energies into collecting child support for Elizabeth, but I didn't want to. I didn't want you to be involved or even to know that you had a daughter. But now – after all that – you've gotten off free and clear, get to see Elizabeth whenever you want, with no obligations at all. Kendra's been way too easy on you, and all I can figure is that you've worked your charm on her and somehow she thinks that you're going to turn into good husband and father material."

It was no more than he had expected, but somehow hearing her opinion of him put into words left him with a sinking sense of dejection. If she had spoken in anger or hatred he might have known how to respond, but the cold, calm, contemptuous tone of her assertions left him helpless. He couldn't deny or refute a single thing she had said.

"You're right." He fell silent, staring down at the light scratches on the tabletop. "You're right, I've gotten off easy, and Kendra has treated me way better than I deserve. But – but – I want you to know that I really love Elizabeth and I really love Kendra, and I want to do right by both of them and try to make it up to them for everything in the past. I'm not trying to get out of my obligations, but I don't want you to oppose my relationship with them, or make Kendra feel that she has to choose between us. I want you to at least give me a chance to show you that I can make Kendra happy. If – if there's anything I can do to show you that I've changed – that I want to take care of them – I would like you to tell me what it is."

He had intended to ask the question when he planned this meeting in his mind, but by the time it came out he felt rather hopeless about the whole conversation. What could he possibly do, after all, that would change Bonnie's mind about him?

"Well," she said, "you've never supported Elizabeth, not from the very beginning. I was the one who covered her medical bills, and I'm still paying for her daycare costs. Do you give Kendra any child support?"

"No, but I'm willing to do that. Kendra's always tried to be so secretive about the whole relationship, so I haven't pressed for anything official. But if that would make a difference, I'm certainly willing."

Bonnie pursed her lips as if a new idea had occurred to her. "Well, Elizabeth's almost six now. So if you're serious about making up to her for all she's lost, you actually owe her six years of back child support. *That* would certainly show me you're serious about this."

"Six years of child support!" The words sprang out of him in spite of himself. "But – but I don't have that much money just sitting around! I can give her money every month, but – not six years' worth!"

Bonnie shrugged, and he imagined he saw a look of triumph cross her face. She actually seemed pleased that she had put such an impossible condition on his rehabilitation. "Well, I guess it might take you awhile."

Steve sat still for a moment, thinking hard. It was true that he didn't have six years' of child support sitting in the bank – he actually wasn't sure how much money that would be. But he did have some money. The money he had saved for a down payment on a house. He could give it all to Kendra if that would show her mother that he was sincere. Maybe that would start to buy her forgiveness.

"I do have some money," he said. "I'll write Kendra a check for the whole amount, if that's what you think I should do. It might not be enough, but it's all I have." He took his checkbook out of his pocket and began to fill out the check. Fifteen thousand, three hundred dollars. He had checked his balance just yesterday. It would leave just a few dollars in the account to start over with.

Bonnie took the check and studied it hard. "I'll give this to Kendra," was all she said, but he saw an expression of dawning respect come into her eyes.

As he drove away from the house, he didn't know whether to laugh or cry. All the money he had saved in the last three years by living at home, the money he had planned to put toward his house, gone – just like that. Now he'd have to keep living with his mother, or maybe give up on the idea of buying and move in with Dan as they had talked about. A sense of loss washed over him.

And yet, he couldn't say that Bonnie was wrong to ask it of him. In a way, Kendra needed the money more than he did. Maybe she would be able to buy a home for herself and Elizabeth. That was really the right thing to happen. At least he had demonstrated his sincerity to her mother in the only way that she had offered him.

&) ⊗

"He did *what?*" Kendra stared down at the huge check in her hand with more horror than delight. "He gave me all his money?"

"I told him he owed it to you, and I was right. Think of all the years when I helped support both of you when he should have been doing it. I don't need the money since I've married Gordon, but you do, and now you have a nest egg."

"But – but – Steve was going to use that as a down payment on a house! He's been talking about it for a year – he even started looking at houses last month."

Bonnie shrugged. "Well, now you can buy the house instead. You have a child – you need it more than he does."

"Oh, Mother!" Kendra couldn't decide whether to cry or shake her mother. "I couldn't afford to make the mortgage payments even if I could buy something! So now neither of us can use it!"

"Well, invest it for Elizabeth's education. By the time she needs it he might be long gone, out of her life, but at least she'll have something from the deadbeat."

Kendra studied the check, Steve's distinctive signature signing all his worldly goods over to her. Maybe her mother was right. Steve really did owe Elizabeth. A year ago she would have been pleased by the boon. But, right or wrong, she didn't want his money this way. She knew he had given it out of guilt, and it was almost impossible that he wouldn't resent her if she kept it. Maybe she was foolish, but she would rather not have his money if it created a barrier between them.

I love him, she thought suddenly. I guess I'm stupid to love him – Mother thinks I am. I should take the money and run. But I can't help it.

She waited until her mother had gone up to the bedroom and took her cell phone down to the basement where she could be alone. At least Allison had gone out for the evening. She stared at her phone for a long moment, then pushed the button for Steve's number.

"Hey, Kendra."

"Hi." She swallowed. She really hadn't planned what she would say. "My mother told me you came by today."

"Oh, yeah." Pause. "Did she give you the check?"

"Yes. Oh, Steve, I didn't mean for that to happen! I don't need your money! Why did you do that?"

"It's the price of your mother's forgiveness." She heard a touch of irony in his voice and couldn't decide if he were joking or not.

"Oh, Steve! Did she say that?"

"Not in those exact words, but that was the essence. And she's right, Kendra. I should have been paying child support for six years and I'm sure it would come to more than fifteen thousand dollars."

"But – but I know you were getting ready to buy a house with that money. If you feel that you owe me something, you can start giving me money every month. There's no reason to empty out all your savings."

"Maybe you should buy a house yourself. Allison will probably get married one of these days, and you and Elizabeth will need somewhere to live."

Kendra was silent for a moment. "Maybe we should split it in half."

"Like Solomon, splitting the baby." She was relieved to hear a smile in his voice. "No, there's no point in that, Kendra. I make more money than you do, and I can save. A house would be nice, but there's no urgency to it. If you don't feel right about spending it, put it aside for Elizabeth. She might need it someday."

Just what her mother had suggested. "I don't feel good about this. You could invest it for Elizabeth just as easily as I could."

He paused a moment. "Tell me this, Kendra. If I give you this, will your mother actually forgive me?"

Kendra thought. "I think so. She did seem impressed, although she didn't admit it. I think – I think she respects you more than she did before."

"Then it's worth it." There was a sad, wry note in his voice. "Really, it's a small price to pay, all things considered. Don't worry about it anymore."

Kendra sighed. "Well, let's just think about it. We don't have to make a decision now. Something might happen to make it all clear."

"Okay."

"Well, I'd better get going. I just called to talk about that." She wanted to ask if he felt differently toward her because of her mother's demand, but couldn't imagine how to frame the question. Better to let the subject drop, as he seemed ready to do.

"Wait a minute. I've been wanting to ask you if you're still going with me on Saturday."

Saturday. The wedding. She had almost forgotten. "I don't know. What do you think I should do?"

"I'd really like you to go with me. But if you feel you can't leave Elizabeth, I understand."

"I guess my mother could stay with her." She bit her lip. "I'll have to ask her. I don't know what she'll say."

"Okay. Let me know."

"I feel a little weird about it." She bit her lip, picturing herself at a family event – with Steve – for the first time since Elizabeth's accident. "All your relatives – do they know? Have you told them about Elizabeth?"

"I haven't talked to anybody but Dan, and I don't think my mother has yet either. She felt she should wait till after the wedding because Aunt Betsy has so much on her mind. She said that she's going to sit down with my aunts afterward and explain everything, but she hasn't done it yet."

Kendra swallowed. "Well, maybe it won't be so bad then. Allison was pretty surprised, but I think she's gotten over it."

"I told you it would be okay, Kendra. A nine-day wonder."

She hung up the phone and went up to the bedroom. Her mother was sitting on the bed, reading a book to Elizabeth. Kendra sat across from them on her own bed. She needed to ask about the wedding and tried to sound very casual as she mentioned it.

"Mother, would you be able to stay with Elizabeth on Saturday night? I had plans I'd really like to keep, and I thought since you were here, I'd be able to."

"I suppose." Her mother looked up from her suitcase and gave her a probing look. "Where are you going?"

"It's Allison's cousin's wedding." She busied herself with Elizabeth's afghan, tucking it under her daughter's feet, avoiding her mother's gaze. "I was planning to go before the accident; I had told them I would go."

Her mother was silent a moment. "Are you going with Steve?"

Kendra's heart fell. "Yes," she said in a short tone. "He asked me to go."

Another long moment of silence stretched between them. "A wedding. With Steve. I've heard everything now."

Elizabeth piped up. "Can I go too, Mommy? I want to go with Steve."

"No, honey, this is for grown-ups." She scowled at her mother. "What's wrong with me going to a wedding?"

"You're going with Steve." Her mother sounded very calm, but exasperated. "Next you'll tell me that you're marrying Steve."

Kendra felt her face grow hot. "I'm not marrying Steve! It's just a family wedding. It doesn't mean anything."

"Oh, well." Bonnie shrugged. "I guess it's a small price to pay for the money he gave you. Just don't think that you have to sleep with him, okay? Or are you doing that already?"

"Mother!" Kendra glanced at her daughter, hoping that Elizabeth didn't understand the comment. "No, I'm not! And I'm not going to! We're just going to a wedding – that's it!"

Chapter Thirty

Kendra stepped into her new dress and fastened the tiny ivory buttons down the front before surveying her reflection in the mirror. The hairdresser had done such a nice job on her hair, creating soft waves over her shoulders. She tossed her head and enjoyed the effect in the mirror. And Elizabeth was right – the new dress did make her look like a princess. Well, not exactly – not quite like the pictures of Princess Kate on her wedding day. Still, she felt pretty – prettier than she had felt for a long time. Her bruises were almost gone and her hair covered the one cut on her forehead. Even if Steve didn't consider the occasion a date, for one evening she was going to indulge in the fantasy. The words from the *Cinderella* musical replayed in her mind as she applied her blush and lipstick. Maybe tonight would be her own "lovely night."

Silly! She shook herself and turned away from the mirror. She wasn't going to a ball, after all, and she wasn't Cinderella. It was just a family wedding, and with a guy who might not even be remotely interested in her. But sometimes a girl had to dream, to believe that she could be beautiful and desirable and catch the eye of a wonderful man.

She heard the doorbell ring and skipped down the stairs. Allison had already left for the church; her cousin had needed her help getting ready. Kendra opened the front door to see Steve.

"Hi, Kendra." His eyes lit up at the sight of her. "Wow, you look really pretty."

She felt a rush of warmth that he had noticed. He didn't usually comment on her appearance. "You look nice too." He actually looked quite gorgeous. He wore a gray suit with a pale blue shirt and a deeper blue tie that matched his eyes. When he stepped into the room beside her he smelled like soap and aftershave.

"Hey, Lisbet, how are you feeling?" He stepped over to the couch to kiss Elizabeth. "You're looking a lot better. Soon you'll be running around like nothing happened."

Kendra looked up at her mother descending the stairs.

"Elizabeth will be fine here with me." Kendra could hear the irony in her mother's voice and hoped that Steve didn't notice it. "Have fun at the wedding."

"Thanks, Mother." Kendra busied herself with her purse. "Bye, honey. Be good for Grandma."

Steve held the door for Kendra. "Thanks, Mrs. Baker. See you later."

The wedding was held in Grace Fellowship – what Kendra would always consider her first church. She and Steve signed the guest book and Kendra took the arm of the usher as he seated them on the bride's side. Across the aisle she saw Todd, her old Sunday school teacher, and waved to him. Looking around, she recognized many of the Kirk family members: Allison's parents, her sister Meredith, Steve's mother, many of the cousins. Allison and Paul slid into the pew behind them. Betsy Reese, the bride's mother, who had introduced Kendra to Allison and her family in the first place, was escorted to her seat in the first pew.

The processional began and the bridesmaids glided down the aisle, each wearing a different color. Kendra recognized Joyce Dixon in yellow, Anne's sister Kate in blue, and then Abby Kirk, the flower girl, in pink. Finally Anne herself, looking like a blonde angel in white.

Someday, Kendra thought. Someday she would have a wedding just as beautiful as this. She would wear an elegant ivory Cinderella-style dress, with a full skirt of yards and yards of tulle. She hadn't quite decided between a traditional veil and flowers in her hair. She would have to see which was more flattering. But the bridesmaids would wear peach, her favorite color, even though it wasn't

Finding Father

fashionable now. Allison would be a bridesmaid, and Leanne, and – if her fiancé had a sister, Kendra would ask her too. (For some reason she pictured that bridesmaid looking a lot like Joyce Dixon.) Elizabeth, of course, would be the flower girl, either dressed in peach or in ivory like her mother. The women would carry peach and white roses and wear the same roses in their hair.

The only part she couldn't decide was who would give her away. She didn't want her brother, and she wasn't close to her uncles or stepfather. Could her mother give her away? But her mother might not agree to that. Maybe she would defy tradition and walk down the aisle alone. After all, no one could quite take the place of her father.

She felt Steve's eyes on her and shook herself out of her daydream. How silly, having her wedding all planned, when she didn't even know who she would marry! She glanced up and met his gaze and he smiled, before they both turned their attention back to the ceremony.

Anne was speaking now, repeating after the minister. "In token and pledge of the vows between us made, with this ring I thee wed, in the name of the Father, and of the Son, and of the Holy Spirit, amen."

ಬಿ ಆ

The reception was held at the local country club. Kendra doubted that she could ever afford something this elegant for her own wedding. Her mother perhaps would be able, but she didn't know if her mother would offer to pay for it.

She and Steve found the little cards that showed them their assigned table. "Oh, good, we're at the same table with Allison and Paul," she said.

He was also studying the cards. "My cousins Tom and Joe are seated there too. Probably the eight of us."

In a few minutes the other three couples joined them. Allison looked particularly happy tonight, and she and Paul were being quite affectionate. Kendra was glad to see that they had made up their spat and that Paul, at least, wasn't ruining the wedding for her by being difficult. Tom Reese and his wife Renee had brought their new baby, and Joe had brought his girlfriend Wendy, whom Kendra had never met. Steve introduced them.

"I remember Kendra," Renee said as she took the seat beside her. "You have a little girl, don't you? She played with my daughter when we came to your house to practice for the funeral."

Kendra nodded. "I remember that too."

"We left our daughter home tonight," Renee gestured to a sleeping baby in an infant seat, "but I had to bring this little guy. He's still too small to leave."

Kendra leaned over the seat and gazed at the child. "He's so tiny! How old?"

"Just six weeks on Monday."

The wedding party was announced, and then the dinner served. As they ate, the four cousins shared funny stories about their growing up years, their holidays and family vacations. Kendra listened eagerly, especially when they told stories about Steve.

"I heard about the lady who said you would break some boy's heart someday," she reminded him.

He laughed, shaking his head. "Oh, that! That was my mother's fault for dressing me in purple booties."

"I think when Steve got to be a teenager, he was determined to prove everybody wrong," Joe added with a grin. "He had more girlfriends than any of us."

"I've heard that," Kendra said in a wry tone. Steve smiled at her and squeezed her arm under the table.

The baby woke and began to fuss. Renee picked him up and tried to hold him in one arm as she ate with the other.

"I can hold him for you till you finish your dinner," Kendra offered.

Renee handed the baby to her. Kendra cradled him in her arms, marveling at his small size, aware of Steve's eyes on her.

She looked up at Steve. "It's hard to believe Elizabeth used to be this small."

He reached out and let the baby grab his finger. "How big was she?"

"Only six and a half pounds. A little peanut."

"This one was almost nine pounds," Renee told her. "He was bigger than my daughter, and believe me, I felt it."

Kendra stared down at the baby's face. "I remember when I was in labor, my mother said, 'You'll forget it – you'll forget the pain tomorrow.' I thought, 'I will never forget this!' But the amazing thing is, you really do forget."

Steve drew his brows together. "Isn't that what the Bible says? Something about how a woman has sorrow when she gives birth, but afterward forgets because of her joy."

Renee laughed. "You have to forget, or you'd never have another one. You forget until you're in the middle of it the second time and you think, 'Oh, I remember this feeling, and it's really bad.'"

Paul leaned over the table to peek at the baby. "I've heard that most newborn babies are really ugly."

"I thought Elizabeth was beautiful," Kendra said softly. "I'll never forget that." She stroked the baby's soft hair. At least she did have one child, but it would be so lovely to have another baby someday.

Allison wiped her fingers on her napkin. "Do you remember when Aunt Lisa was pregnant with Abby? She called my mother and described all the symptoms of pregnancy and said, 'You know, I think I must have a sinus infection.' When my mother suggested it might be something else, Aunt Lisa said, 'Oh, I couldn't possibly be pregnant.'" She laughed and glanced at Kendra. "So the joke in our family is that Abby is Aunt Lisa's little sinus infection."

"I thought I had bulimia," Kendra remembered. "I thought that's why I was throwing up all the time. I guess I was in major denial."

Steve was watching her face. "So when did you actually realize?"

"I felt the baby move, and that's when I knew for sure." Had that terrified girl from those days actually been her? It felt so long ago, and that terrible experience almost seemed as if it had happened to someone else.

Renee reached for her son and Kendra handed him to her. "I brought a bottle for him, but I don't know if he'll take it. He isn't used to bottles. If he won't, I'll have to nurse him or he'll start screaming, and that won't be fun for anyone."

"That's something I miss," Kendra told her. "I nursed my daughter till she was over a year old." Would she ever have another child? Holding a baby again, watching Renee with her tiny son, revived all those maternal longings. Of course Elizabeth was wonderful, but it would be even more wonderful to have a real family – to have a child with the man she loved beside her.

Joe called across the table to Steve. "How's the job going? Do you still like teaching?"

He grinned. "Most days I do. I love my college prep classes, but some of the others can be difficult."

"I heard that you're looking for a house."

Kendra swallowed hard. Steve glanced at her sideways. "I was, but I've decided to put that on hold for a while. What about you?"

"Well, this is a good time for it, with interest rates so low."

Tom spoke up in a dry tone. "Well, I have the feeling we'll be having a lot of weddings in this family in the next year or so."

A moment of dead silence greeted this statement.

Renee burst into laughter. "You should have seen all your faces when Tom said that!"

With a grin Steve rose to his feet and took Kendra's hand. "Let's go say hello to the relatives." He led her over to a neighboring table where his mother sat, along with his aunts and uncles and grandfather. As they greeted him Kendra held back, but Steve put his hand on her back to draw her forward. "Have you all met Kendra? Granddad, Uncle Jack, do you remember Kendra?"

His grandfather smiled a greeting. "Sure, I remember Kendra. She was the girl who played the piano for us."

"She came to Josh's play," Lisa Kirk added.

Kendra smiled at her a bit shyly. "I guess your daughter loves being a flower girl. Allison told Elizabeth that when she gets married, Elizabeth can be in her wedding. I just hope Allison doesn't change her mind when the time comes."

Judy Andrews added, "I just hope Allie gets married before Elizabeth does!"

Marilyn Marsh spoke in her quiet, proper tone. "I'm glad you could come, Kendra. Have you spoken to Betsy? I know she'd like to see you. She was surprised – and happy – when I told her you were coming."

Kendra flushed with pleasure and glanced up at Steve. It was so nice being here as his date, even if only for one evening. In her imagination she could see everyone looking at them together, thinking what an attractive couple they made. She was sure the other single women must be envious of her escort.

Perhaps it wasn't totally her imagination, for when she and Allison went to the ladies room, her friend said as she put on her lipstick, "I don't know what the story is with you and Steve, but you've got my family all excited. He hasn't brought a girl to a family event in years. Everyone keeps asking me if you're dating, and I just say that you never tell me anything."

Kendra opened her mouth to repeat her habitual statement, that she and Steve were just friends. She stopped. Somehow it seemed silly to keep saying that. "Did you tell them all about – about Steve and Elizabeth?"

"Not yet. I figured it's your story to tell, and Steve's, not mine. But they're going to find out soon. Are you two a couple?"

"We haven't talked about it," she began slowly. "I don't know what Steve is thinking, actually."

Allison closed her purse with a snap. "You need to talk to him, Kendra. It's ridiculous for the two of you to go on this way after all these years. He owes you an explanation, certainly."

When they returned to their table the bride and groom were dancing their first dance together. They all watched as Anne danced with her father and the groom with his mother. Then the deejay announced that the bride and groom wanted to dedicate a song to both sets of parents, and wanted all the married couples to join them on the dance floor.

"Tom and Renee, that means you." Allison gestured to her cousins and reached for the baby.

"I guess I couldn't do this at my wedding," Steve remarked in a wry tone. "I don't think my parents would want to dance together."

"You don't think they'd do it once for old time's sake?" Allison laughed at the expression on Steve's face.

"I doubt it very much. And I'm sure my stepparents wouldn't

care for the idea."

"I couldn't dance with my father." Kendra spoke so softly she wondered if anyone would hear, but Steve met her gaze with a sympathetic expression.

After the formal dances the young people got out on the floor for the usual wedding dances. Allison and Kendra danced the Electric Slide and Allison dragged Paul onto the floor for the Chicken Dance. After an instant of hesitation Kendra took Steve by the arm and pulled him up with her. He made no objection and they laughed their way through all the silly motions. Joe and Wendy surprised everyone by waltzing gracefully and then doing the swing together. When they finally returned to their seats to catch their breath, a slow song began to play. Kendra recognized Peter Cetera singing "After All," a romantic song that she had always loved.

Tom took Renee's hand and led her to the floor. Joe and Wendy followed, and Paul and Allison. Steve and Kendra were left at the table alone.

He glanced at her with a hesitant, almost shy expression. "Do you want to dance?"

She ducked her head and nodded. He took her hand and led her to the floor, circling an arm around her waist. The music flowed around them.

She felt sudden tears sting her eyes and prayed that Steve wouldn't notice. Did he also remember that hot summer night, almost seven years ago, when they had first danced together? It felt like a lifetime ago, and she and Steve were such different people than they had been back then. How her life had changed since that night – at first it had seemed only for the worse, but now she could say for the better.

The music ended and Steve smiled down at her. He squeezed her hand as he released it. "Thanks, Kendra."

಄ ಐ

The house was quiet when they returned after the wedding. Elizabeth was asleep on the couch. Kendra could hear the shower running and was grateful that her mother wasn't waiting for them in the living room.

"I really thought Allison and Paul would get home before us." Kendra glanced around the room in puzzlement. "Didn't they leave the reception almost an hour ago?"

Steve shrugged. "Oh, they must have stopped somewhere on the way." He stepped over to the couch and looked down at the sleeping child. "Do you want me to carry her up?"

"If you want. She's getting heavy for me."

Still he didn't move. Kendra stepped over to stand beside him.

"She's so beautiful," he said softly.

Kendra raised her eyebrows with an arch expression. "She looks just like you."

"Does she?" He gave her a sly look. "Do you think she's beautiful too?"

Kendra smiled coyly. "I'm her mother. I have to think so."

He was silent a moment. "You know, we did such a good job the first time, we ought to have another one."

"Steve!" Kendra stepped back from him in indignation.

He laughed as he turned toward her. "Don't you think Elizabeth would like a little brother or sister? I hear her mention that in her prayers."

Kendra sighed. "I guess that was my fault. She told me she wanted a brother or sister, and I told her she'd have to pray about it. I didn't realize she'd take it to heart."

He was still laughing softly. "God might have to work a real miracle, huh?"

"Maybe."

For a moment they just looked at each other in silence.

"Thanks for going with me tonight," he said. "I had a really good time."

"Thanks for taking me," she said. "And for being here for me all this week – after the accident. You don't know how much it means to know that I'm not alone, that I have somebody to depend on."

"You never need to be alone again," he said.

Without thinking, Kendra leaned forward and kissed him on the lips.

Horrified at her own boldness, she drew back immediately, but

Steve caught her in his arms and kissed her again, longer this time.

"I don't know what got into me," she gasped as soon as he released her. "I never do that, never."

Steve was laughing softly. "You don't hear me complaining."

"I don't want you to think – you know – that I go around kissing guys – when it doesn't mean anything –"

"I know you don't." He watched her face, still smiling. "So maybe I should ask you what it meant."

Kendra found herself blushing and stammering like a high school girl with her first crush. "I appreciate you – being there for me – and Elizabeth."

"I hope it's more than that." His tone was slightly aggrieved. "Do you kiss every guy you appreciate?"

Kendra looked away. "You know I don't. Maybe I should ask why you kissed me."

"That shouldn't be any mystery to you. When I said 'I love you,' that should have been a clue that I want to date you."

Kendra looked up at him; her mouth fell open. "But – but you said –"

"Well, you looked so shocked, I figured I'd better backpedal before I ruined things for good." He watched her anxiously. "I need to know if this relationship can work out before I move on with my life. I want you to give me a chance, to give us a chance. I want us to be a family. Do you see?"

"Yes," Kendra said, and suddenly she began to laugh and cry at the same time. "Are you saying you've been thinking about this for a while?"

"To be honest, ever since you and Jason broke up."

"And I had no idea." Kendra put her hand to her face. "I thought I was the last girl in the world you would ever think about."

He laughed then too and started to draw her to him again, when they heard footsteps and voices on the front path. Kendra stepped backwards as the door opened and Paul and Allison appeared.

"We wondered where you were," Steve began, and then Kendra saw Allison's face. She looked happier than Kendra had ever seen her, her face alight with joy. Kendra looked at her left hand she saw

Finding Father

a pear-shaped diamond glittering on her friend's finger.

"Are you engaged?" She ran to her friend and hugged her as Allison laughed aloud.

"Yes! He asked me tonight, after the wedding. I was so surprised!"

"I've had the ring in my pocket for a week," Paul grinned. "I was planning to wait for her birthday, but then I thought, why wait? The time seemed right."

Kendra caught Allison's hand to examine the ring. "Oh, it's gorgeous. I guess you haven't picked a date yet, have you?"

Allison looked up at her fiancé. "We're talking about Valentine's Day."

"Valentine's Day!" Kendra laughed. "Oh, how funny. That would be perfect."

"Congratulations, man." Steve shook Paul's hand. "Welcome to the family. And congratulations to you too, Mrs. Valentine. So he came around in the end. Didn't I tell you to be patient?"

"You were right, Steve."

Steve grinned at Kendra and put an arm around her shoulder. "Kendra and I will come to your wedding and sing 'Send in the Clowns.' Or rather, I'll sing and Kendra will play the piano."

"Oh, you'll be there, but not singing that song. And I promised Elizabeth she could be the flower girl."

As if she heard her name, Elizabeth stirred on the couch in her sleep. Allison giggled and put her hand to her mouth. She and Paul went to the kitchen, where they carried on their conversation in hushed tones, punctuated with laughter.

Steve looked at Kendra and smiled. "Well, Allie got her man. I hope she's really happy. She deserves to be."

"I think she will be. They seem perfect for each other." Kendra lowered her gaze. "Valentine's Day. That gives me nine months to find a new place to live. But the Lord will provide. He did before."

Steve nodded. "I'm sure he will. It will all work out." He gestured toward the stairs. "I guess we should take Elizabeth upstairs before all this excitement wakes her."

Kendra nodded. "I'll go up and turn down the covers."

Steve lifted Elizabeth in his arms and followed her up the stairs to the bedroom. Kendra turned down the covers and Steve laid her on the bed. He covered her up. For a minute they stood side by side, watching their sleeping child. Then Steve put his arm around her and they went down the stairs together.

◈ Author's Note ◈

This is a work of fiction. I debated long and hard about the proper conclusion for Steve and Kendra's story. The last thing I would ever want to do is to make light of Kendra's experience or to offend anyone with a similar experience.

After spending years with these characters, I felt that they should be together, and many of my readers agreed. Some readers may feel that this relationship could never succeed. Either way, I believe the real message of the story is the redemption and healing that they experienced, and this is the message that I want to leave with my readers.